Showdown

Also by Tilly Bagshawe

Adored

TILLY
BAGSHAWE

WARNER BOOKS

NEW YORK   BOSTON

Copyright © 2006 by Tilly Bagshawe

Warner Books, Inc.,
Hachette Book Group, USA
1271 Avenue of the Americas,
New York, NY 10020

Printed in the United States of America

First Edition: June 2006

10 9 8 7 6 5 4 3 2 1

Warner Books and the "W" logo are trademarks of Time Warner Inc. or an affiliated company. Used under license by Hachette Book Group, which is not affiliated with Time Warner, Inc.

Library of Congress Cataloging-in-Publication Data
Bagshawe, Tilly.
Showdown / Tilly Bagshawe.—1st ed.
p.   cm.
ISBN-13: 978-0-446-57689-5
ISBN-10: 0-446-57689-1
1. Horse racing—England—Fiction.   2. Women jockeys—Fiction.   I. Title.
PR6102.A525S56 2006
823'.92—dc22   2006003509

For Sefi,
Queen of my heart

THANKS

Thanks as always to my family: Robin, Sefi, Zac, Mum and Dad, Loo Loo, James, and Big Bad Al. You are the best.

To my friends, who know who they are, and particularly to those I woefully failed to mention when I wrote *Adored*—including Emma French, Will Thomas, Sonia Walger, Sarah Hughes, and many others who I hope will forgive me once again if they're not listed here. Special thanks, again and always, to Fred Metcalf, for being himself and unique and completely irreplaceable in my life; and to Alison Murray, nanny, friend, and general lifesaver. There is no way I could have finished *Showdown* without you.

To my editors, Kate Mills, Jamie Raab, Genevieve Pegg, and Frances Jalet-Miller; also to Susan Lamb, Sharon Krassney, and everyone at Orion and Warner who put up with me. Your help is invaluable, and your support and encouragement has kept me sane in this crazy roller coaster of a year. Thank you.

Tif Loehnis and Luke Janklow: not just fantastic agents, but wonderful people and spookily good-looking too, the pair of you. I always thought agents were supposed to look like a cross between Quasimodo and Scrooge, but I guess you both missed that part of the training. . . . Seriously though, I am immensely grateful for all that you've done and continue to do for me, and that goes for Rebecca Folland, Christelle Chamouton, Claire Dippel, Jack Carieri, and everyone at Janklow and Nesbit. You are the best agency in the world, and that's all there is to it.

I owe a debt of gratitude to Kevin Conley and Kate Fox, whose respective books *Stud* and *The Racing Tribe* were invaluable in researching *Showdown*. The story about confusing horse semen for egg whites was just too good not to steal—sorry!

Showdown is dedicated to my darling daughter, Sefi. But I'd also like to give an official high five to my son, Zac, who was born halfway through the writing of this book and helped enormously by providing many sleepless nights in which I mulled over problems with the plot.

Finally, I would like to thank my husband, Robin. Living with me is not always easy, particularly when I'm nine months pregnant, fatter than a silver-backed gorilla, and have a deadline looming. But someone has to do it. And I'm so glad it's you.

Thank you for marrying me.

T xxx

CHAPTER ONE

Bobby Cameron was in the south of France on the day his father died.

Leaning hard into the filly's left flank—he was breaking in a feisty bay yearling called Mirage for the legendary French racehorse owner Pascal Bremeau—he brought her around for a third time as the dry dust of the training ring billowed and plumed up around him, enveloping both horse and rider once again in a thick, stifling cloud. Fighting back the urge to choke—he didn't want to do anything now that might frighten or unsettle the horse—he leaned back in the saddle, relaxing into the languorous, cowboy-style riding that he was famed for, closing his eyes to help himself tune in to her movements. Soon he could feel every pulse of her taut young muscles between his thighs and the nervous straining of every sinew as she cantered into the turn. It was as if he and the filly had become one being, one fluid organism, circling rhythmically beneath the blazing Cote d'Azur sun.

"*Non! Pas comme ça. Regard,* she is steel favoring the left. You see?"

The voice came from Henri Duval, Bremeau's trainer, who was standing by the side of the schooling ring, scowling, in shorts and a T-shirt, his few remaining strands of straggly dark hair stuck with sweat to his otherwise bald forehead, alternately yelling instructions to Bobby or roaring with Gallic bad temper into his cell phone.

"*Écoute!* She needs more steek, Bobby, uh? Deesmount! Deesmount!"

Keeping his eyes closed, Bobby tried to block out the sound. He wished Henri would go terrorize someone else. He was ruining his concentration, not to mention Mirage's. Was it any wonder the filly was so goddamn flighty, if all she ever heard from her trainer was screaming?

"*Arrête!*" The Frenchman was yelling so loudly now that reluctantly Bobby was forced to open his eyes and bring the horse to a stop.

A fine spray of white foam had formed across Mirage's shoulders, frothing like milk above the gleaming coffee color of her coat, a testament to the intensity of her morning's efforts. She was a terrific little horse, this one, brave and determined. Bobby could quite see why Bremeau had paid three hundred thousand for her, even though on paper she'd been a risky investment. Sired by the great Love's Young Dream, a Belmont winner, but out of the unknown, unplaced mare Miracle— she could go either way. She'd either make a great racehorse or burn herself out before she ever got as far as the track. But that was just the sort of horse he loved: a ball of raw energy and speed, just waiting for a little gentle, Cameron-style direction.

At only twenty-three, Bobby Cameron already had a reputation as one of the most skilled horse breakers and trainers in the world. With his straw-blond hair, endlessly long legs, and soulful hazel eyes, the brilliant but notoriously arrogant son of the famous cowboy Hank Cameron had been born with an incredible gift: a unique rapport with difficult horses. Animals that other, skilled trainers could barely get a bridle on seemed to calm instantly at his touch, soothed into submission by the low murmuring drawl of his voice. It was a talent that owners like Pascal Bremeau were prepared to pay handsomely for.

Even as a small boy Bobby had showed no fear around violent, kicking stallions, animals that could easily have killed him with one carefully placed hoof to the head. Instead, he radiated a quiet, calm authority that even the most stubborn or disturbed horses seemed to respect. By the age of twelve he was breaking in wild mustangs for his father. At sixteen, he was earning pocket money doing the same thing with valuable standardbreds and quarter horses, the classic cowboy's mount, for other wealthy California breeders and owners. And by the time he hit twenty, his reputation had spread beyond the state line. He spent what ought to have been his college years training difficult Thoroughbreds on some of the most prestigious, multimillion-dollar Kentucky farms, eventually getting commissions from owners as far afield as Ireland, Dubai, and, most recently, the south of France.

Born into one of the oldest, most respected ranching families in the

West, Bobby grew up running semiwild at Highwood, the stunning three-thousand-acre Cameron ranch nestled deep in California's Santa Ynez valley. All the local kids envied him his freedom—neither of his parents seemed to mind much that he regularly skipped school to disappear into the hills on his father's horses—but in fact his childhood wasn't the idyll it appeared.

His mother, Diana, a teenage rebel from the Danish tourist-trap town of Solvang, had conceived him during a one-night stand with his aging cowboy father, Hank. A local legend, the reclusive Hank Cameron was a natural with cattle and horses, but children were another matter entirely. Having acknowledged the kid was his and named him as his heir, he considered his paternal duties to be completely fulfilled. Beyond that, Diana was on her own.

She loved her son—that wasn't the problem. But this was California in the early seventies, the era of free love and cheap drugs, and she was still only seventeen. Consequently Bobby spent the first ten years of his life on the road, traveling with his mother from one hippie commune to the next, never staying in one place long enough to put down any roots or make any real friends at school.

Sometimes, overwhelmed by the responsibility of it all, Diana would disappear completely for months at a stretch, usually on the back of some scary-looking guy's bike. Terrified that she had gone for good, Bobby spent her long absences being passed miserably like an unwanted parcel from one distant relative to another. Eventually, of course, she always returned, disillusioned with her biker and full of kisses and promises to get her act together. But by then it was too late. Her son had already learned two important life lessons: that loving people was a risky business; and that the only person he could truly depend on in this world was himself.

Shortly after Bobby's tenth birthday, broke and exhausted, Diana decided to pay Hank Cameron a visit.

Bobby would never forget the drive out to Highwood that day. It was the first time he'd seen the property that would one day be his, and he couldn't believe his eyes. Sitting in the front passenger seat of his mom's dilapidated VW bus as they bumped and spluttered down the long, winding drive, he gazed in awe at hills so green they looked like something out of a cartoon and seemed to stretch as far as the eye could see. All across this emerald canvas were grazing herds of cattle, searching for shade beneath the ancient sycamores that peppered the landscape or making their way down to the river that rushed alongside the driveway like a dancing stream of molten silver. Not even in his imagination, on those many long, lonely nights when he'd lain awake fantasizing about the mythical Highwood, had he ever seen anything quite so beautiful.

Hank, needless to say, was less than thrilled to see the pair of them.

"What the hell are you doing here?" he barked as Diana clambered out of the bus, her dirty, skinny son loitering behind her like a stray dog. It wasn't exactly the welcome that Bobby had hoped for from the father he had long built up in his mind as some sort of cool, romantic hero. But he didn't dwell on it. By this time he was used to being an unwelcome guest, and he was stoic when Diana announced she was leaving him with his father for the summer while she went to try to find work in Santa Barbara.

"Leave him here? With me? You can't be serious," Hank spluttered incredulously. "I don't know what to do with him."

"Yeah?" said Diana, climbing purposefully back up into the driver's seat. "Well, guess what? Neither did I when I was seventeen years old and you sent me packing. But we did okay, right, Bobby? Now it's your turn."

While the two of them fought it out, Bobby stood calmly on the porch steps beside the one pitifully small suitcase that held all his worldly possessions. Most of what they said was a blur, although he could remember his mother's parting words as she sped off down the driveway in a plume of dust: "He's your son, Hank," she yelled out the window. "Deal with it."

Hank had dealt with it—by ignoring his son completely.

"You do your thing, kid," he said, showing Bobby up to what would be his new bedroom, "and I'll do mine."

And for the next thirteen years, that was pretty much the way things had gone between them. Bobby never did go back to live with his mother again, although Diana continued to pay semiregular visits and had him down to Santa Barbara for the occasional birthday or Christmas. But whatever disappointment Bobby may have felt at her abandonment, or Hank's lack of paternal concern, was more than made up for by the sheer magic of being at Highwood. Before that first summer was over, he had become fast friends with the other ranch hands' kids. But much more important, he'd discovered what was to become the one great love of his life: horses.

For the first time in his life, he felt he really belonged somewhere.

This, at last, was home.

Vaulting down lightly from Mirage's back, he took off his hat, an automatic gesture of courtesy that belied the dismissive, irritated scowl on his face as he approached Henri.

"What's the problem?" Handing the filly's reins to a hovering groom, he glowered at the French trainer. Even without the hat, Bobby stood a good six inches taller than Henri in his cowboy boots and jeans and looked an almost menacing figure.

"You're breaking my concentration," he snapped. "I think you should leave."

The already irate Duval now began to turn a worrying shade of purple. Having been let down by adults all his life, Bobby famously had zero respect for authority. It was a trait that had always infuriated his father; and it did him no favors with horse trainers either, themselves a notoriously difficult and arrogant breed.

"You theenk *I* should leave?" Henri couldn't believe his ears. "She is my 'orse, Monsieur Cameron. *Tu comprend?* Mine!"

"Well, now." Bobby smiled maddeningly, revealing a row of perfectly straight white teeth. "She's actually Monsieur Bremeau's horse, isn't she? If we're gonna get technical about it."

His voice was low and rich, like syrup, with a deep Western twang that seemed to soothe horses and excite women in equal measure. Unfortunately, it appeared to be having quite a different effect on the apoplectic Frenchman, who had started hopping from foot to foot with rage, like a lizard on burning sand.

"He hired me to do a job, and you're making that job impossible," Bobby continued. "I'd like you to leave."

"'Ow dare you!"

Henri was livid. Who did this Yankee whippersnapper think he was, waltzing into *his* stables and presuming to tell *him* how to get the best out of the new filly? If Bobby hadn't been six foot four of rock-solid cowboy muscle, he'd have hit him. As it was, the strain of holding himself back looked set to give him an imminent coronary.

"You arrogant leetle sheet," he shouted. "What the fuck do you know about Mirage? Four days you 'ave been 'ere now and what 'ave you achieved with 'er? Fuck all, that's what, *mon ami*. Nosing." Henri was literally spitting with fury. "She needs the steek, I am telling you. What is the English expression? You do not make the omelet without break-ing the eggs, uh?"

Reaching out toward another cowering groom, he grabbed a vicious-looking leather hunting whip—the French variety with split leather strips at the end tipped with steel—and marched over toward the exhausted horse, waving it menacingly in her direction as she cringed and whin-nied in fear.

Silently Bobby stepped forward, shielding Mirage and blocking Henri's path with his huge torso.

"Don't touch her."

His spoke so softly it was almost a whisper, but his tone was menac-ing enough to stop Duval in his tracks. For a few seconds the two men remained stock-still in a pantomime standoff, while Henri's eyes bored into Bobby's. Eventually, when it became clear that the infuriating, ar-rogant American was not going to move and that he needed reinforce-ments, he turned furiously on his heel and stormed off toward the house, hurling his whip down on the ground in frustration as he went.

"Pascal will 'ave somesing to say about theese," he muttered. "Total fucking deesrespect . . ."

Once he was gone and the grooms had scurried away, no doubt eager to spread the gossip about his latest temper tantrum around the estate, Bobby turned back to Mirage.

"It's all right girl," he whispered, stroking her reassuringly between the ears and feeling her relax instantly beneath his practiced fingers. "Don't you worry now. I won't let him hurt you."

Pressing his face into her neck, he breathed in the heady smell of horsehair and sweat that never failed to calm him.

Duval was an asshole. He wished he could take Mirage with him, back to California, and protect her from the guy's brutality forever. But that was the one downside of this job: the minute you became close to a horse, and won its trust, you had to leave.

He'd faced the same dilemma a thousand times before, of course.

But it still hurt. With Mirage more than most.

A few hours later, lying in the bath in his luxurious suite of rooms up at the house, he wondered how he was going to explain himself to Bremeau when he got back from Paris tomorrow morning.

He was hours away from a breakthrough with Mirage, he could feel it. But as of tonight, much as it pained him to admit it, Duval did have a point: She was not yet ready to progress. He dreaded being forced to hand her back to Duval's brutal schooling regime and knew for certain that it would set her back. But the fact remained, she *was* still favoring her left leg on the turn. He should have fixed that by now and he hadn't. It drove him crazy.

Emerging dripping from the hot, lavender-scented water he dried himself off with a towel and, wrapping it Turkish style around his waist, walked over to the window. Unlocking the heavy, white wooden shutters, he gazed outside. Bremeau's estate, in the hills above Ramatouelle, near St.-Tropez, was breathtakingly beautiful. The house itself was an old sixteenth-century château, and the stables had been built around the adjoining former winery. As well as being horse country, this part of the Var was also littered with vineyards. The endless, neat rows of vines lent the rolling landscape a symmetrical, regimented air that reminded him of Napa.

Closing his eyes for a moment, he breathed in the warm, honeysuckle-scented evening air, faintly intermingled with the ubiquitous smell of horses and leather that always made him feel at home wherever he was. In the distance, he could hear the soft whinnying of Bremeau's

Thoroughbreds, fighting to be heard above the deafening background cacophony of the cicadas.

Paradise.

He dreamed of training horses as spirited and magnificent as the prancing Mirage one day, back home in California. He had long ago given up talking about these dreams to his father—their conversations always ended in a screaming row—but silently, whenever he was alone, he continued to nurse his fantasy.

Like most cowboys, Hank looked on horse racing as anathema to Western culture: fine for Arab sheiks and white-collar billionaires with their pristine Kentucky stud farms, all neat white fences, manicured lawns, and state-of-the-art technology. But not for the likes of real working men, men bound to the land and to their cattle herds, proud inheritors of their long-cherished cowboy traditions.

Personally, Bobby had never gotten it. He was as proud of his cowboy roots as the next man. But he also loved horses—all types of horses, from mustangs to quarter horses to exotic Arab Thoroughbreds. His father would rather die than see Highwood used for anything other than raising cattle, he knew that. But, really, what was so wrong about applying traditional cowboy skills and techniques to racehorse training? And where was it written that a great ranch had to be about beef cattle and nothing else?

One day. One day, when Highwood was his . . .

He broke away from his daydreaming with a start at the touch of a cold hand against his back.

"Sorry. Did I scare you?"

It was Chantal, Pascal Bremeau's young and very beautiful wife. He hadn't heard her come in, and the cold of her fingers against his warm skin gave him a shock—albeit a not altogether unpleasant one.

"No." Like his father, Bobby was a man of few words.

"I did knock," she lied, "but I guess you didn't hear me. You looked like you were miles away."

Half French and half Venezuelan, Chantal oozed the dark, heavy-lidded sultriness of South America, although her English was faultless and bore no trace of an accent. Oddly, that clipped British voice coming from such a pneumatically Latin body only seemed to enhance her sexiness.

Bobby bit his lip and tried to think unsexy thoughts: his eighth grade math teacher naked—that usually did the trick—but not today. Nothing seemed to be working.

She's Bremeau's wife, he told himself sternly.

He mustn't.

He absolutely must *not.*

"I thought you might like some company," she said with practiced innocence, before slowly and deliberately starting to twirl her fingers through the still-damp curls of his chest hair.

Inevitably he felt his cock start to harden and wished he had more than a skimpy towel between him and this stunning girl. It didn't help that she was looking even more gorgeous than usual this evening in a crotch-skimming yellow sundress, which did little to restrain her full, braless cappuccino-brown breasts.

"No thanks." He tried to sound firm. He had started to pry away her hand, but somehow ended up with his fingers intertwined with hers and his eyes locked into her brazenly inviting gaze.

Goddamnit. This was going to be difficult.

With his heart rate rising and his dick taking on a life of its own, twitching and jumping like it was being electrocuted, it was all he could do to remember to breathe in and out.

He'd seen this coming, of course. Chantal was a shameless flirt. From the very first morning he arrived at the estate, she'd taken to "dropping by" the schooling ring where he and Mirage were working, often wearing nothing more than a pair of frayed denim hot pants and a bikini top that wouldn't have looked out of place on a Vegas stripper. Not that he blamed her for trying. Her old man was no oil painting, and that was putting it nicely. Truth be told, Pascal Bremeau was one fat, humorless, garlic-munching son of a bitch. Plus, he was old, really old, and seemed to spend 90 percent of his time away on business leaving his bored, beautiful young wife to her own devices. What did the guy expect?

But the fact remained, women and training didn't mix. Bobby resented anything that threatened to distract him when he was working—

and Madame Bremeau certainly fit right into that category. He had tried ignoring her, had even been outright rude to her on a couple of occasions—telling her to leave him alone and stay away from the stables, that he wasn't interested. But his rejection only seemed to make her more determined.

Tonight was the last night that Pascal would be away.

And he wasn't training now.

"Look," he whispered, desperately trying not to focus on her pupils, which were so dilated with lust she looked like she'd had a shot of horse tranquilizer. "This really isn't a great idea, you know. Your husband—"

"Isn't here," she finished for him, backing him toward the bed and slipping her hand expertly up beneath his towel. "But you are. You know, it's funny"—she flashed him a wicked smile, wrapping her fingers around his cock like a vise. "Duval thinks you are too soft with Mirage. But you don't feel at *all* soft to me."

Fuck it.

Groaning, Bobby staggered backward onto the antique lace bedspread, pulling her down on top of him. God knew he shouldn't be doing this—not with Bremeau's wife—but the girl was a force of nature. Trying to resist her was like trying to turn back the tide with your bare hands. It would take a stronger man than he was.

Agonizingly slowly, she started to stroke him, licking her palm for more lubrication, increasing her pace gradually as he instinctively arched his pelvis forward and bucked against her. He closed his eyes, just for a moment, and when he opened them again found that she was kneeling over him, lifting up her lemon-yellow dress to reveal a neatly trimmed, very dark bush and no panties. Just as she was about to lower herself down onto him he grabbed her around the waist, flipping her over onto her back as easily as he would a rag doll.

"What are you doing?" she giggled, gasping as he climbed on top of her, nudging her already spread legs wider.

"I don't like girls on top," he said. And with that he thrust into her like a rocket with so much force that she had to reach back and hold on to the headboard for support.

Bobby enjoyed sex in a simple, matter-of-fact sort of way. But it had never consumed him with passion in the same way that his horses did. Since the age of sixteen he'd attracted women so effortlessly that he'd come to accept whatever sexual opportunities presented themselves as no more than his due, enjoying them in the same way that he might enjoy a good game of golf or a side of home-cooked ribs.

There were women that he loved, naturally—his mother, for all her faults, was still very dear to him, and the McDonald girls, Tara and Summer, the daughters of his father's ranch manager, were like surrogate sisters to him back home. But he had certainly never been *in* love, let alone had a steady, serious girlfriend. The idea had never even occurred to him.

This pointed lack of commitment didn't seem to put women off, however. If anything, his indifferent, take-it-or-leave-it attitude only heightened his desirability to the opposite sex. Unfortunately, experience had failed to turn him into a sensitive lover. With girls falling into his lap like overripe apples, he had never learned to curb his natural selfishness in bed. At twenty-three he still pursued his own pleasure with the same robust single-mindedness as a young stud stallion, quite oblivious of his partner's needs or desires.

Feeling his orgasm building almost immediately now, as Chantal writhed and clenched beneath him, he made no effort to hold it back, exploding into her like a breaking dam, burying his face in her neck to muffle the sound of his own release.

Happily, she seemed amused rather than offended by the "wham, bam, thank you, ma'am" approach and not in the least bit put out that she hadn't come herself.

"My goodness." She laughed, smoothing down her dress and rearranging her hair as he slumped back onto the bed. "Short but sweet, eh? Is that how all the cowboys do it?"

"I have no idea." He grinned up at her like a little boy, happy now that he'd gotten what he wanted. "You'd have to ask them."

Bobby couldn't help but admire Chantal. She was that rarest of creatures: a gorgeous girl with a nice, uncomplicated attitude to sex. It was a welcome change from all the clingy, my-love-can-change-you girls he seemed to wind up in bed with back home.

11

"I know I ought to feel guilty," he drawled, watching her peering into the mirror and rubbing off the telltale makeup smudges with her finger, "but I don't. You're far too beautiful to regret."

Chantal smiled. From anyone else it would have sounded like a line. But Bobby was not given to flattery, and something told her that a compliment from him was probably the real deal. She was just about to turn and thank him, with another offer he couldn't refuse, when an unexpected knock on the door froze both of them to the spot.

"Bobby? Are you een zere?"

Oh fuck. Pascal.

"Just a minute." Struggling to keep the panic out of his voice, he leaped off the bed in an instant. "I'm, er . . . I'm not dressed. Give me a second, okay?

"What the hell is he doing home?" he hissed in a stage whisper to Chantal, scrambling back into his pants while frantically gesturing for her to go and hide in the wardrobe.

"I don't know." She shrugged. She seemed marvelously unconcerned by their current, dangerous predicament. "Why don't you ask him?"

Jeez, French women had balls of steel. What a piece of work! If he hadn't known better, he could have sworn he actually saw her smile as she clambered into the huge, antique armoire.

Briefly he wondered how many errant wives of the French aristocracy had used it as a hiding place before her. Hundreds probably. But this was no time to get historical. Shoving her right to the back, he pulled the walnut doors closed behind her and turned the key. Then with one long, deep breath to steady his nerves, he opened the door to her husband.

Bremeau had obviously only just arrived home from his business trip. Still dressed in his formal three-piece suit, he looked white as a sheet and even more miserable than usual.

Bobby's heart skipped a beat. He couldn't have heard them, could he?

"Bobby." The Frenchman's short, stubby fingers worked nervously as he spoke. "This is very bad, *mon ami.* Very, very bad."

Holy crap. He *had* heard them.

That was it then: the end of his career and quite possibly his life if

Pascal turned out to be the murderously jealous type, which he looked like he very well might be. And all over a stupid girl! How could he have been so reckless? And with his work with Mirage only half finished too . . .

"Eet's your father," Bremeau abruptly interrupted his panicked internal monologue.

For a minute Bobby thought he'd misheard him.

"What? My *father*? I don't understand."

"I'm sorry," the older man mumbled awkwardly. "I—I don't really know 'ow to say these, but . . . 'e 'as died, Bobby. In 'is sleep. About four hours ago."

Bobby stared impassively at the jowly, pale face opposite him.

No. No, there must be some mistake. It wasn't supposed to happen like this. He wasn't ready.

"I 'ave arranged for the chopper to fly you to Nice airport in 'alf an hour. You understand, no?"

Bremeau's look of concern deepened. Perhaps the boy hadn't grasped his broken English? He kept waiting for him to say something, but he looked utterly shell-shocked.

"Bobby? Are you all right?"

Stunned and mute, Bobby eventually managed a nod.

"Yes. Er . . . yes. I'm fine. I understand," he said quietly. "Thank you."

"I'm so sorry."

Reaching up, Bremeau laid a comforting hand on his shoulder. All of a sudden the guilt he'd been unable to feel a few moments ago seemed to punch Bobby full force in the stomach. Hank was dead. His father. Dead. And here was this Frenchman, this total stranger, trying to comfort him, little knowing that not five minutes ago he'd been banging the living daylights out of the poor guy's wife—the same wife who was hiding in the closet right now.

The whole thing was like a sketch from a bad sitcom. Only it no longer seemed funny.

His father was dead.

"I'm sorry too, Pascal," he whispered, almost to himself. "Believe me. Sorrier than you know. For everything."

CHAPTER TWO

Milly Lockwood Groves glared at her reflection in the mirror in despair.

She was in her bedroom at home in Newmarket, dressed in a grotesque, frilly pink ball gown, complete with white gloves and with her great-grandmother's pearl and diamond tiara perched on top of her carefully swept up and intricately pinned chestnut hair.

"Please, Mummy, no," she moaned. "It's awful. I look like a blancmange."

Though she would have been the last person ever to think so, Milly was in fact a strikingly pretty girl, something that even this monstrosity of a dress couldn't hide completely. At five foot two she had the perfect jockey's build: slight and boyish, although in the last year she had to her great annoyance developed a noticeable bust, which seemed to get in the way of everything and jiggled about embarrassingly whenever she ran, even in a bra.

Shifting her attention from the dress to her face, her frown deepened. She despised the smattering of freckles across the bridge of her nose that she'd never grown out of and the full, wide mouth that kept half her father's grooms awake at night but that she privately thought ugly and much too big for her face.

The only thing about herself that Milly did quite like was her hair. On the rare occasions she let it down, it tumbled over her shoulders in a glorious, shining chestnut cascade, like the overbrushed tail of a show pony. But today she didn't even have that going for her, thanks to her mother insisting she wear it pinned up under this ridiculous crown. Honestly, she felt like one of those plastic ballerinas from inside a cheap music box.

"A blancmange? Oh, darling, what nonsense." Linda Lockwood Groves stepped forward and carefully smoothed out the creases at the front of her daughter's skirt. "You look absolutely divine. Doesn't she, Cecil?"

Milly's father, who had ill-advisedly stuck his head around the door on his way down to the stallion barn, took one look at his daughter's pleading, desperate face and his wife's determined smile, and decided to keep well out of it.

"Mmmm," he said noncommittally, glancing pointedly at his watch. "Sorry, girls, I can't hang about. Michael Delaney's bringing his new mare over for a cover with Easy Victory in half an hour. I need to make sure the old boy's up to it."

"Up to it? Easy?" said Milly indignantly. "Of course he's up to it! He's an absolute star. Delaney's stupid mare is lucky to have him. I bet she's a right old plodder anyway."

"Hardly," Cecil chuckled. "It's Bethlehem Star."

Milly's eyes instantly widened. Bethlehem Star was the product of two world-class parents. Her dam had placed third in the Kentucky Derby five years ago, and her sire, Starlight, was a winner at Goodwood. "I didn't know Delaney had bought her. When did that happen? Has Rachel ridden her yet?"

Rachel Delaney was Milly's sworn enemy. Both children of Newmarket racing families—Rachel's father, Sir Michael Delaney, was a wealthy racehorse owner while Cecil Lockwood Groves ran Newells, one of the most respected and successful stud farms in the country— the two girls had been at daggers drawn since kindergarten. For reasons best known to herself Rachel had always delighted in tormenting poor Milly, whose only crime as a little girl had been to be a better rider than she was, despite being a year younger.

Even after Milly had been forced to give up riding at fifteen—Cecil had refused to let her back in the saddle after a neck injury that came within a whisker of killing her—Rachel's persecution had continued. Now, two years later, relations between the two girls were at an all-time low. The mere mention of Rachel's name was enough to send Milly into a tailspin of fury, and the very idea of her riding a horse as famous as Bethlehem Star made her blood boil.

"Darling, do keep still," said Linda. "You're creasing everything up again."

"He picked her up at Keeneland last season for over a mill," said Cecil, answering his daughter's first question but not her last. "Then he never raced her. Beautiful horse, though. She's a maiden, so she might be a bit jumpy with Easy. I want to be on hand if things get nasty."

"I doubt that's very likely," said Milly dismissively. "If she's anything like the rest of the Delaney women, she'll be opening her legs nice as pie before you can say 'spoiled bitch.'"

Cecil laughed, but Linda looked horrified.

"Milly!" she said sternly. If there was one thing she couldn't stand, it was coarse, unladylike language. "There was no need for that. Now let your father get on, please. He's got a lot to do, and so have we."

Taking this as his cue, Cecil disappeared, leaving Milly to her fate.

"Do I really have to wear this one?" she asked plaintively, her upper lip curling in disgust as she reached around and pulled at the bow on her bottom. "It makes my arse look ginormous."

Why did she have to go to this bloody debs' ball anyway? All these preparations were doing her head in. Her mother, Linda, though well-meaning, was a pathological social climber, and Milly's coming-out ball was merely the latest and most irksome of her many schemes to fix her daughter up with a "nice" boyfriend—"nice" in this case having the very specific meaning of titled, Eton educated, and set to inherit three quarters of Scotland: attributes that meant everything to Linda but nothing at all to Milly.

"What about the blue one?" she asked hopefully.

"The one you wore for the Jockey Club party last summer?" Linda looked surprised. "But it's *so* last season, darling. Besides, I thought you said you hated it and it washed you out?"

"I do, and it does," said Milly, wriggling out of the pink dress and pulling on her jodhpurs, despite her mother's protests. "But it's the lesser of two evils, isn't it?"

Though no longer allowed to ride herself, Milly spent as much time as possible helping out at the stud, desperate to be near her beloved horses one way or another, and she'd never gotten out of the habit of wearing her riding gear.

Gesturing toward the pile of pink ruffles on the floor, she grimaced. "Honestly, Mummy," she said with a shudder, "if the whole point of this cattle market is to get one of those chinless boys to fancy me, you can't send me out there in *that*."

"For the last time, darling, it is not a cattle market," said Linda, a note of exasperation creeping into her voice. Having come from decidedly humble beginnings herself—she'd grown up in a nondescript semi on the outskirts of Cambridge, a fact she went out of her way to keep hidden from the other smart Newmarket society wives (all of whom, naturally, had known about it for years)—Linda worked like a slave to ensure that Milly would never want for the sort of social opportunities that she, as a girl, had been denied. A smidgen of enthusiasm, even gratitude for her efforts, would have been nice.

"It's a debutantes' ball," she sighed. "If you gave yourself half a chance you might actually enjoy it. When I was your age, I would have killed to go to an event like this. Killed."

"When you were my age, there'd have been a point to it," said Milly tactlessly. "The queen would have been there, and at least coming-out would have actually meant something. Now we have to curtsey to a bloody cake! I'm going to look like a right lemon."

Scowling, she pulled on her riding boots and a filthy green sweater covered in cat hair from where Luther, the Lockwood Groves ancient tom, had slept on it. Only once she'd pulled it over her head did she realize she was still wearing the tiara.

"Careful!" screeched Linda, watching her tugging at the fragile headdress like a lead rope. "If you break that, Milly, you won't be going near those blasted stables for the next millennium. Let me do it."

Threatening to keep her away from Cecil's horses, Linda had long ago learned, was the one threat her daughter took seriously. As a child, there were times when the only way to cajole Milly into doing her homework or tidying her room was the promise of an evening ride or a weekend trip to a point-to-point with her father. She was seventeen now, but some things hadn't changed.

Ignoring her wails of protest—that child could sulk in the Olympics if she put her mind to it—Linda carefully unpinned the tiara and placed it gently back into the tissue-paper–lined safety of its box.

"Can I go now?" said Milly gracelessly. "Dad might need some help. Anyway, I want to have a look at Bethlehem Star before Easy has his wicked way with her."

"Oh, all right," said Linda. She did wish Milly would make some effort to hide her unashamed interest in the nitty-gritty of the horse-breeding business. Ever since she'd had to give up riding herself, she'd become obsessed with the stud. No one liked to hear their only daughter talking about the quality of stallion ejaculate or the pros and cons of artificial vaginas. It was bad enough when Cecil did it.

"But don't be a nuisance," she called down the stairs after Milly's disappearing back. "And if you must handle the horses, please be extra careful not to bruise yourself anywhere that shows. I don't want you looking like a prop forward at the ball. Milly? Are you listening to me? *Milly!*"

But it was too late. With the lure of the stables beckoning, her daughter was already long gone.

Outside in the yard, a steady drizzle was falling. Connor, the newest and youngest of the stable lads, was sweeping away the wet mud with a stiff broom.

"Morning," said Milly brightly as she passed him. He blushed and mumbled something incoherent that may or may not have been "hello." He was only seventeen himself and fancied his boss's daughter like mad. Not that Milly had ever noticed. A dyed-in-the-wool tomboy, she had yet to show much interest in boys, to her mother's crushing disappointment. With the honorable exceptions of Frankie Dettori and the latest heartthrob jockey on the scene, Robbie Pemberton, both of whose posters hung above her bed, the only males she had ever been interested in were four legged and shared her own penchant for Polo mints and sugar lumps.

"Just in time." Nancy MacIntosh, Newells's chief vet, greeted her warmly as she strolled into the stallion barn. "Oh, by the way, bad news. Rachel's here with her dad."

"You're kidding!" said Milly furiously. "Since when did that cow come to coverings?"

"Dunno." Nancy shrugged. "But she's here now. Waltzing around the breeding shed like the Queen of Sheba apparently."

Hovering behind Nancy were Pablo, Easy's Argentine groom, and Davey Dunlop, who rejoiced in the title of penis washer. Both grinned when they looked up and saw Milly. All the staff at Newells liked the boss's daughter. Unlike her brother, Jasper, she was never rude or arrogant, and she knew enough about her father's horses to make herself actively useful around the yard.

Since the day she had been old enough to toddle over to a mounting block, Milly had been crazy about horses. Growing up on such a prestigious and successful stud farm—clients came to her father from all over the racing world, from Dublin to Dubai and Kentucky to Kempton, to stand their prize stallions at his stud—she had dreamed of one day riding Thoroughbreds to victory herself.

But that was before her accident changed everything.

Milly herself remembered nothing of the fateful day two years ago: her fall, headfirst at the water jump; the six minutes in which the paramedics had frantically tried and failed to get her to regain consciousness; her father, ashen faced in the ambulance, holding her hand. It was as if it had all happened to someone else.

Up until that point, riding had been her life and racing her future. The archetypal daddy's girl, she was Cecil's constant shadow, begging to accompany him to point-to-points or on his many trips around the country, sourcing new stallions. Not that he had needed much persuading. He adored his little daughter and loved nothing more than watching her clamber fearlessly up onto ponies ten times her size or canter hatless around the fields at Newells, whooping with delight and abandon.

From a very early age it was clear that she was an extraordinarily talented rider. After sweeping the board at all the local gymkhanas and

Pony Club events—her room was plastered wall-to-wall with rosettes, almost all of them firsts—she had gone on to compete at regional and even national level, roundly trouncing all the other young Newmarket hopefuls, Rachel Delaney included. Her greatest triumph was being named by the Newmarket Pony Club as the Most Promising Under-Sixteen-Year-Old when she was only fourteen, a title that stuck in Rachel's throat far more than Milly knew.

Ironically, it was Cecil himself who had pushed her to enter the three-day event. Milly hadn't wanted to do it because it meant missing a big race weekend in Newmarket. But he'd convinced her it would be good for her to broaden her skill base. And she, always eager to please him, had gone along with it.

All he could think of at the hospital, as his darling girl's life hung in the balance, was that if she died it would have been his fault. When the doctors told him she was going to be okay, it was as though he'd been given a second chance: a chance to protect her properly, as a father should. And that meant no more riding. Ever.

Milly, of course, had other ideas.

"But the doctor says I'm fine, Daddy," she'd pleaded desperately, when Cecil announced his decision in the car on the way home from the hospital. "All my verteb . . . vraeteb—"

"Vertebrae," corrected Linda absently.

"They're all fine. In six months they'll be exactly like they were before, Dr. Stafford said. I'll be back in the saddle in no time, he said. Please, Daddy. You can't stop me riding. You can't!"

"I don't give a damn what Dr. Stafford said!" Turning around to the backseat, the father she had always worshipped as her champion and protector roared at her like never before. "You could have bloody died, Mill, do you understand me? You're not riding again, not in six months, not ever while you live under my roof. It's for your own good. And I don't want to hear another word about it."

Unfortunately for Cecil, he was to hear plenty more words about it. His own stubbornness was more than matched by his daughter's, and in the two years since their conversation in the car, Milly had never ceased trying to persuade him to change his mind. She was convinced that if she just chipped away at the stone for long enough it would eventually crumble.

But it hadn't. Not yet, anyway. And in the meantime, she'd been forced to watch as not just Rachel but Jasper too—Jasper who had all the horsemanship skills of a paralyzed dung beetle—began their professional careers as jockeys, moving forward with what ought to have been her life.

Having loafed his way through an extortionately expensive private school education, Milly's brother Jasper left school at sixteen with little more than an F in woodworking to his name. His own plan—to sit around and do nothing, indefinitely—was roundly vetoed by Cecil, who presented him with a stark choice: he could either join the army, where with any luck a bit of string-pulling could help him into his grandfather's old regiment; or he could try to ride out his claim as an apprentice and become a professional jockey.

Both options sounded hellish to Jasper, but in the end he'd chosen the latter, on the simple grounds that he hated the sight of blood, especially his own, and was therefore probably marginally more likely to survive his twenties as a jockey than as a soldier. Eight years later, at twenty-four, he found the job actually suited him rather well. Despite his evident lack of flair, trainers would still give him rides out of loyalty to his father. And though the pay wasn't great, the opportunities for pulling girls more than made up for it.

But for poor Milly, watching her brother's career was like pouring sulfuric acid into an open wound. Worse still, now that she was no longer riding competitively, her mother had decided to seize the opportunity and "reclaim" her from Cecil, filling her newly-freed-up time with what she deemed to be more suitable, feminine pursuits, like amateur dramatics and, of course, the never-ending round of dreaded parties and balls.

"It's no good moping around the stables day and night looking like a scarecrow," Linda insisted. "You need to get out more."

"Honestly, Mummy," said Milly indignantly. "You make me sound like a mental patient."

But Linda took no notice. Once she got an idea into her head, she plowed ahead regardless with all the unstoppable determination of a Sherman tank. Milly's fate was well and truly sealed.

The staff at Newells were like a family, and having witnessed Milly's blissfully carefree childhood, it was horrible for them to have to watch her teenage years unfold so unhappily. Not only had the love of her life, her riding, been taken away from her but her parents seemed determined to add insult to injury by turning her into something she wasn't, dragging her off to endless dances and plays and cookery classes, all of which she quite patently loathed.

The hours she spent at the stud with Nancy, Pablo, and the others soon became Milly's lifeline—the one thing that made living at home even slightly bearable.

Sidling up to Easy, she nuzzled affectionately against his shoulder.

"I'd leave him be if I were you," said Pablo. "'E's very overexcited this morning. Aren't you, boy?"

Easy, contrary as usual, decided to prove his groom wrong by standing stock-still at this pronouncement, as if suddenly engaged in a very competitive game of musical statues. But a glance down toward his business end, as the vets called it, quickly gave him away.

"Bloody hell!" Milly laughed, clocking his impressively swollen appendage. "Look at that.

"I know," said Nancy. "And he hasn't even seen the mare yet. She's been locked away with a teaser for the past fifteen minutes."

"Teasers" were cheap, standard bred colts that were used to put mares in the mood before their real "date" showed up. No one wanted Easy rocking up at the breeding shed unwelcomed, especially not with a partner as valuable as Bethlehem Star.

"I hope they don't keep him waiting long," Milly said, looking at her watch. "Look at him—he's ready to rumble."

"Morning, all."

The collective sigh was audible as Jasper swaggered into the barn. Extremely handsome in a classic tall, dark, and handsome sort of way, Milly's older brother was also hideously vain, not to mention lazy and spoiled. Overindulged since babyhood by his doting mother—he had always been Linda's favorite—his natural egotism had been allowed to run rampant to the point where now, in adulthood, it teetered on the brink of megalomania.

"What do you want?" Milly scowled. She'd been looking forward to helping supervise this morning's cover. The last thing she wanted was J. hanging around, making trouble.

"Oh, well, that's charming." He pouted, catching sight of his reflection in the grimy mirror next to the message board and taking a few moments to rearrange his hair and remove a stray strand of spinach from between his teeth. "I thought I'd pop down and lend you all a hand, that's all. No need to throw your toys out of the pram."

"Bollocks," said Milly, accurately voicing the silent sentiments of the others. Jasper had never shown the remotest interest in the stud, or Easy, nor did he ever "lend a hand" unless there was something in it for him. "You're here to see Rachel, aren't you?"

"Rachel? Is she here too?" His feigned innocence was utterly unconvincing. Like the rest of the male population of Newmarket, Jasper thought Rachel Delaney was gorgeous—not as gorgeous as himself, obviously, but gorgeous enough to warrant being flirted with nonetheless.

Milly ground her teeth in frustration. As if that bitch being here weren't bad enough, now she had her idiot brother in Casanova mode to contend with.

"Just keep out of our way, all right?" she hissed. "The mare's a maiden, so things could get tricky."

Maiden mares especially were known for lashing out and kicking their would-be suitors. Milly had seen more than one stud so badly injured by a recalcitrant mare that he had had to be put down. If anything like that were to happen to Easy, she'd never forgive herself.

"Keep your hair on," said Jasper. "Like I said, I'm here to help. I'll be good as gold."

"J.?" Cecil walked in and did a double take to see his son loitering by the mirror, looking as out of place as a lost extra who'd somehow stumbled onto the wrong film set. "What are you doing here?"

"Christ, not you too," said Jasper, tossing back his handsome head and doing his best to look wounded. "You're always on at me to take more of an interest in the stud. And then when I do, you complain about it. I can't win."

Cecil frowned. His son's drama queen antics irritated him beyond belief. If only Linda weren't always so bloody soft on the boy.

"Yes, yes, all right," he said. "Just keep out of the way, okay? This is an important cover. I don't want anyone fucking it up."

Jasper's pout intensified.

"As if I would!"

Turning to her father, Milly changed the subject. "How's the mare?" she asked anxiously.

"She's fine, I think," said Cecil. "A little jumpy, but we've given her a nice big shot of Dormosedan to take the edge off. I don't think she'll give him any trouble."

Jasper's eyes narrowed. It drove him mad the way that everyone at the stud, including his father, treated Milly with respect while he got dismissed like a meddlesome schoolboy. Who the hell did his sister think she was, anyway?

"You know Rachel's over there," said Cecil in an aside to Milly as they made their way over to the breeding shed, with Nancy and Easy leading the way.

"So I hear."

"Be polite, all right?"

"Hmmm," Milly grunted. "I'll try."

"Don't try," said Cecil firmly. "Do it. This is business, Mill. I'm not having you piss off my biggest owner because of some silly, childish vendetta. Are we clear?"

"Yeah, yeah, okay." She nodded grudgingly. "We're clear. I'll keep my mouth shut."

"Don't worry," said Pablo quietly, once her father was out of ear-shot. "Rachel Delaney is a snooty beetch. We all hate her."

Milly grinned. "Thanks. Nice to know I'm not the only one around here who does. J.'s got his tongue hanging out, and even Mummy seems to think the sun shines out of the girl's arse."

"She does?" said Pablo, raising a skeptical eyebrow. "Well"—he dropped his voice even lower—"I tell you what. Her ass is certainly beeg enough to have planets orbit around it, that's for sure."

Even Milly couldn't help but laugh at that.

"Oh, Pablo," she said, flinging her arms around his neck and kissing him on the cheek. "I do love you."

In fact, very annoyingly, and despite Pablo's unflattering pronouncement about her rear end, Rachel was looking even hotter than usual that morning. Standing arm in arm with her doting father in skintight white leggings and half chaps, her black riding jacket tailored to within an inch of its life to emphasize both her slim waist and her supernaturally large breasts, she looked not unlike Jessica Rabbit going hunting.

Though it had always baffled Milly, Rachel's hatred of her was in fact very straightforward. Milly was the bug on her windscreen, the grit in her oyster, the one small, insignificant, and yet utterly infuriating obstacle in her otherwise perfect life. Rachel was already the richest, prettiest, most envied girl in Newmarket. But what she wanted more than anything, what she considered nothing less than her birthright, was to be the best, most admired female rider in the country too. Milly Lockwood Groves had made that impossible.

The fact that Milly had never bothered to think of herself as being in competition with Rachel—that she rode for the sheer love of it and nothing else—only infuriated Rachel more. To her, Milly's obliviousness of her rage was an insult. By the time of Milly's accident, her hatred ran so deep that she could no more let it go than stop breathing. Milly was, and always would be, the enemy.

"Oh look, Daddy, here he comes," she squealed as Easy made his stately entrance into the breeding shed. One of the things that Milly hated most about Rachel was her voice: a contrived, high-pitched, little-girlish squeak that made her sound as if she'd been inhaling helium balloons. Men, needless to say, all seemed to adore it.

"Good heavens, he's no spring chicken, is he? How old is that horse now?"

"He's fifteen, and he's in terrific condition," bridled Milly. Cecil shot her an early warning glance, but she ignored him. "His sperm are all Olympic swimmers too, aren't they, boy?" she couldn't resist adding.

"Oh, hello, Milly," said Rachel in the tone of a duchess acknowledging the presence of a new underhousemaid. "I didn't see you there. Have you come to have a look at my mare? Isn't she a beauty?"

My mare? Give me a fucking break, thought Milly.

"She's a doll," said Jasper, oozing forward to kiss Rachel on both cheeks. "You must be thrilled with her."

"I am. She was a present from Daddy." Rachel beamed.

Of course she was, thought Milly bitterly. Sir Michael Delaney was a lovely man, but he had a complete blind spot when it came to his daughter. Whatever small success Rachel had enjoyed as a junior jockey, she owed almost entirely to the fact that her father had poured millions into getting her not just the very best horses but state-of-the-art training facilities, trailers, and equipment way beyond anything that other riders at her level could afford.

"If you don't mind me asking, Sir Michael," she said, pointedly ignoring Rachel, "how come you never raced her?"

"Do you know, Milly, I can't quite put my finger on it," he said, rubbing his spreading paunch thoughtfully. "She had a bit of lameness right after I bought her in Kentucky. The vets thought they had it under control, but I always felt she wasn't quite right. I suppose I just didn't want to risk her."

Milly wondered again how on earth such a decent, unassuming man could have produced such a monster of a daughter. Not many owners would drop a million on a racehorse and then "not risk" running her. Clearly Rachel's father had a genuine affection for his animals.

"It was always *my* intention to breed her," chipped in Rachel self-importantly. "Wasn't it, Daddy?"

Silly cow. Who did she think she was, John bloody Magnier?

"Right," said Cecil, sensing the rising tension between the two girls. "Let's get on with it, shall we?"

Easy, his nostrils flared and eyes rolling with desire, intoxicated by the mare's smell, was shoved unceremoniously forward by Pablo. Letting out an almighty bellow, he reared up and came down on Bethlehem Star's back. Davey had rushed forward at exactly the right moment and grabbed the base of the stallion's penis, guiding him firmly into her and helping to hold him in place until the deed was done, which it was within about twenty seconds.

Fifty thousand pounds for twenty seconds of action, thought Milly. Nice work if you could get it.

Even she had to admit that the mare had behaved beautifully. No kicking, no bolting, nothing. The Dormosedan seemed to have worked wonders. For a moment she felt another, sudden stab of envy at the thought that this beautiful horse, and soon her foal too, would belong to Rachel. Sometimes it felt as though the girl had been put on this earth to torment her.

"Will we see you at Epsom on the fourth?"

To her horror, Milly saw that Rachel was not only addressing this question to Jasper but gazing up at him coquettishly and flicking back her long blond hair in an unmistakable gesture of flirtation as she did so.

Oh please, please God, no. Don't let him fall for her!

Until recently, Rachel had been on the junior circuit, so her path and Jasper's had rarely crossed. But whereas Milly's brother took six long years to ride out his claim, Rachel's apprenticeship was a "blink-and-you'll-miss-it" affair. Now she'd turned eighteen she'd already started to get entered in some of the same events as him. As far as Milly knew they were nothing more than acquaintances. But now the hideous prospect dawned that perhaps there could be more to their relationship.

"Absolutely." He smiled. "I'm confirmed for the Oaks actually. Wasn't sure if you knew that."

Milly felt her insides churning as she saw her brother's hand slip over Rachel's white, jodhpur-clad bottom and give it a highly visible squeeze.

"I didn't know that." She sounded suitably impressed. "How exciting. You must be thrilled for him," she added vindictively to Milly, knowing full well how miserably envious she must be.

Epsom, in fact, had become a huge sore point in the Lockwood

27

Groves household for more reasons than one. Not only had Jasper, by some miracle, been picked to ride in the Oaks—Marcus O'Reilly, an up-and-coming Irish owner and one of Cecil's clients, had lost his first choice of jockey to injury after a fall in the 1,000 Guineas and had persuaded his reluctant trainer to give Jasper a shot on his gorgeous three-year-old filly, Marigold Kiss—but Milly was being forced to miss the event altogether. June 4th was the night of her dreaded debs' ball and Linda had insisted she spend the whole day in London "preparing."

"Milly won't be there on the day," said Jasper, deliberately rubbing his sister's nose in it. "But it would mean so much to me to know that you were there, Rachel, cheering me on."

"Of course I'll be there!" There was that voice again, like a speeded-up record. Just listening to it made Milly's hands twitch. She found herself wishing she had a pillow at hand. Surely no one could blame her if she smothered the shit-stirring little witch?

"But do tell, Milly. What are you up to on the fourth?" She couldn't have sounded more patronizing if she'd tried. "One of your little plays, is it?"

"No, actually," said Cecil, apparently unaware that Rachel was goading her, "Milly's going to her coming-out ball."

Milly's heart sank. Why, oh why couldn't he have kept his mouth shut? Just for once.

"Are you, Milly?" Rachel giggled. If her voice got any higher, she'd be audible only to bats. "How sweet. You must get your mother to take some lovely pictures. I can't imagine you in a coming-out dress though, can you, Daddy?"

"Hmm? Er, no, I suppose not." Sir Michael's gaze was still glued to his mare and he wasn't really listening.

"She's going to look an absolute knockout." Cecil beamed, wrapping a proud, paternal arm around his scowling daughter.

"I'm sure she is," said Rachel, looking triumphant. "And I'm sure Jasper's going to do us all proud in the Oaks."

Another hand squeeze. Milly thought she might be sick.

Both Cecil and Sir Michael were completely oblivious to the little tableau being played out in front of them. But Nancy, who had seen it all, smiled at Milly in silent sympathy.

Poor kid. As if her life weren't bad enough already.

She was dreading that ball and absolutely gutted about missing the Oaks, even if it was her poisonous brother who got to race there and not her. But Rachel and Jasper getting it together? Now that really would be adding insult to injury.

CHAPTER THREE

"Can I get you something, sir? A drink?"

The oversolicitous French stewardess cocked her head slightly, her long ponytail swishing behind her as she did so, and smiled down at Bobby. She was a pretty girl, but tonight he barely registered her presence, let alone her looks.

"Coffee," he said. He had so much to think about before he got home tomorrow, he needed to stay awake. "Please," he added as an afterthought.

It was only a few hours since Pascal had told him about Hank's death, and it still hadn't really sunk in. He'd barely had time to get rid of Chantal and throw his stuff into a bag before the helicopter had shown up to take him to Nice. All noise and fury, blades whirring, the chopper had frightened the horses. His last image of the farm was of their anxious whinnying and circling in the paddocks below him, their ears flattened in protest. He'd looked around for Mirage, but she had sensibly chosen to stay in the barn. She was a smart horse, that one. He felt bad leaving her with the irascible Henri, but it couldn't be helped.

Now he was on the late flight to London. It was too late to catch a direct flight to California. He'd have to lay over at Heathrow and catch the first plane out to LA in the morning. Normally he hated layovers, but this time he was happy for the delay. He needed more time to get his head together.

His dad's death had not been totally unexpected. Already sixty when his only son was born, he was now in his eighties and his heart had been playing him up for a while. Even so, Hank Cameron was one of those men who you could never quite imagine not being there. One of the last of California's old-school cowboys, he had been as much a part of the landscape in the Santa Ynez valley as the vineyards and the lush, rolling hills. For as long as Bobby had known him, the two of them had clashed like fire and water. But still, his father had always been the walking embodiment of the expression "larger than life." Somehow it was a shock to discover that he hadn't been larger than death as well.

And now he, Bobby, was expected to fill Hank's shoes, a thought that made his already aching head start pounding even harder every time it dawned on him. He was to inherit Highwood in its entirety— "free and clear" as Hank used to say, although in reality the Cameron estate was neither of those things. Although Bobby didn't know all the details, he knew that the ranch had struggled to break even for years and that his father had been forced to borrow a chunk of money against the value of the land. If Hank wasn't broke he must have been pretty close to it.

The irony was that, on paper, he had been a very rich man. The Highwood land was worth a not-so-small fortune, ever since Hank's father, Toby Cameron, had discovered a rich vein of oil on the property back in the twenties.

Developers and mining companies had swarmed to Santa Barbara County back then, offering Toby what was at the time an obscene amount of money to sell. But he hadn't been interested.

"I'm a cowboy. And this here is cowboy land. Always has been. Always will be," he'd told them.

Bobby must have heard that story from his own father more than a thousand times. It was a mantra he'd grown up with as a small boy, and he'd always imagined that one day, he'd say those same words to his own son: "This is cowboy land. Always will be."

Carrying on the family tradition.

Making his father proud.

Unfortunately, holding fast to their principles and preserving the Old West way of life had cost the Camerons dear. With profits from the cattle business falling, they had badly needed to diversify. Many local ranches were turning to tourism to boost their incomes, some very successfully. They charged astronomical sums to take wealthy LA businessmen riding through the valleys, teaching them how to ride like cowboys. Some of these so-called dude ranches were more gimmicky than others, offering lassoing classes, even yodeling. But Hank wouldn't hear of it.

"Turn Highwood into some goddamn Disney theme park? Over my dead body," he would rage at anyone foolish enough to suggest he open to the public. "This life is our heritage, our history. It's what this great nation was built on. And you want me to exploit that?"

It still made Bobby laugh when he met people who assumed he must be mega-rich and living some kind of millionaire lifestyle.

"You're Hank Cameron's son? The guy that owns the Highwood ranch? Jeez, man, you must be rollin' in it. Isn't that, like, the most valuable land in California or somethin'?"

They refused to believe that he had never owned a new car. That as a kid he hadn't gone to a private school or spent his summer vacations in Hawaii. Even as an adult he had never flown anything other than coach (unless, like today, a rich owner like Bremeau was picking up the tab). True, in the last two years he'd started making good money as a horse trainer on the international circuit. But he still poured every last cent of his earnings back into Highwood's beleaguered coffers.

He might be officially rich, now that Highwood was finally his. But the reality was he was also desperately strapped for cash.

Pressing his forehead against the cool plastic of the plane window, he strained to make out any shapes or shadows in the darkness outside, but there wasn't so much as a star to help orient him in the blackness. It would be two in the morning back home. He wondered if Wyatt and Dylan and the rest of the ranch hands would be asleep. Or if they too were lying awake, their minds racing, trying to imagine a world—their world—without Hank Cameron in it.

"Your coffee, sir."

The girl was back. She handed him a cup of what looked and smelled like liquid mud. In first class, he reflected, the mud came in a china cup, but it was still mud. He grimaced as he took a gulp. At least it was strong.

"Thanks," he said, rolling back his broad shoulders to try to release the stiffness in his muscles. He was deathly tired, but it didn't seem right to go to sleep. That would be like letting the sun set on Hank's death. That would make it real.

And he wasn't ready for that. Not yet.

Dylan McDonald gave his pony a perfunctory pat on the neck and tied his lead rope loosely to the stake in front of the house. Making sure the horse could reach the water trough but didn't have enough rope to make it to his mother's petunia bed, he pulled off his hat and began walking up to the porch.

"Oh, Dyl, there you are." His sister Summer, known as "Summer lovin'" to the local boys because she was so good-looking, all long tanned legs and white-blond California hair, was waving at him from across the yard. Dressed in her favorite pair of green Gap shorts and a T-shirt, she had a big pile of books under one arm and a half-eaten bagel in her free hand, obviously off to the library for another day of studying. Summer was the brains of the family. She'd been working like a demon all summer in preparation for her SATs in the fall, and was determined to score high enough to get into Berkeley next year.

"Dad's been looking for you," she said. "I think he wants you to go to the airport later and pick up Bobby."

"Cool," said Dylan. "Where is he?"

"In the kitchen, I think." Clambering up into her ancient pickup, she hurled her books on top of a pile of broken bridles on the passenger seat. "He and Mom have been talking about the funeral all morning. It's depressing."

The McDonald kids—Dylan and his two sisters, Tara and Summer—had all been born at Highwood and had lived on the ranch their whole lives. Their father, Wyatt, was ranch manager and had been Hank Cameron's right-hand man for more than forty years. Wyatt was also the closest thing Hank had ever had to a friend, although the largely silent, symbiotic relationship between the two men was more complicated than simple friendship. Hank had relied on Wyatt and trusted him. Wyatt, in turn, had offered his boss the sort of unswerving, unquestioning loyalty that was part and parcel of the culture at Highwood.

Both were hardworking, honest men. But while Wyatt was devoted to his wife, Maggie, and their children and led a full social life in the local community—sitting on church and school committees, acting as treasurer for the sports fishing club and the like—Hank was taciturn and withdrawn to the point of being reclusive. Truth be told, he had been a difficult man to know and an even harder one to like.

But Wyatt had understood him, and his kids had been used to Hank's taciturn, broody presence at the periphery of their lives since babyhood. Neither Dylan nor Summer could pretend to feel real grief at his passing, but that didn't stop them worrying about their dad. Wyatt had been with the old man yesterday when he died, holding his hand in death just as surely and steadfastly as he always had in life.

Dylan was sure his dad must have been hit hard by the boss's death. But Wyatt was not a great shower of feelings, and so far his response to what had happened had been characteristically practical. Within an hour, he'd been on the phone to the local undertaker in Solvang and sent word to both Bobby and to his mother down in Santa Barbara with the sad news. This morning, instead of riding out with Dylan at dawn as he usually did to move the herd to the lower pastures, he had stayed home with Maggie drawing up a to-do list in preparation for the funeral, which was tentatively scheduled for next Tuesday.

Walking into the kitchen, Dylan found both his parents at the table, surrounded by a sea of Post-it notes and with the phone book open beside them.

"Hey." Maggie McDonald beamed at her only son as he walked over and kissed her. With his strong legs, slightly bowed from so much riding; his mop of dark curls; and his honest, rugged, slightly sunburned face, Dylan wasn't classically handsome like Bobby. At five foot nine he was a little on the short side, with a wide neck and stocky torso that gave him the look of a young bull. But there was such a playfulness and warmth in his eyes that even the faults in his features—his broken nose, his top lip so thin it disappeared into nothing whenever he smiled— somehow seemed to work. Maggie was biased, of course. But no one could deny he was a fine figure of a boy and that he had grown up to be every inch the seasoned rancher, on the outside anyway.

Inside, his mother knew, it was a different story. Dylan had always struggled with the cowboy life. While his sisters were free to go off to college and would eventually marry and move away from the valley, he had no such freedom. His destiny was already mapped out: He was expected to take over from his father one day and to make his life at Highwood. Turning his back on that heritage would break Wyatt's heart. It simply wasn't an option.

For his father, ranching was a true vocation—Wyatt loved every second of it. But Dylan was different. A talented artist, he had produced some brilliant landscape canvases: vast, vibrant explosions of ocher and iris blue, easily good enough for the galleries in Los Olivos. But he kept his talent close to his chest, knowing that the life of a professional painter would forever be closed to him.

Not that he didn't love the ranch. Highwood was his home, with its wonderfully lush pastures, its grand old trees, and its soil so rich and fecund you could almost smell it through the grass; and, like the rest of his family, he was inordinately proud of the place. But Maggie could tell that at times he felt trapped here—if not by the land itself then by the weight of Wyatt's expectations lying heavy and immovable on his shoulders. He never complained about it—never—but she felt for him all the same.

"There's coffee on the stove and bacon and muffins in the warming oven if you're hungry," she said.

"Oh, I'm okay. I ate with the guys a couple hours ago." Pouring himself a cup of coffee into which he shoveled three heaped spoonfuls of sugar, he sat down to join her. "Summer said you were lookin' for me?"

"What? Oh. Yeah." Wyatt glanced up from his paperwork and rubbed his tired, baggy eyes with the back of his hand. Once very handsome, years of hard-riding, outdoor life had taken their toll on his skin, and it was now a permanent leathery brown crisscrossed with a fine latticework of wrinkles, like a dried-out riverbed. Usually his irrepressible energy shone through in his eyes, like two chips of lapis lazuli twinkling in the cracked earth of his face. Not today though. Today he looked beaten and exhausted, like he'd been hit by a truck.

Christ, thought Dylan. He must not have closed his eyes all night.

"Bobby's flight lands this afternoon at three." His voice also sounded tired but focused. There was still a lot to organize. "I figured you might like to go get him?"

"What about the new shipment?" asked Dylan, taking a big slug of his mom's delicious coffee. "We have fifty head of cattle turning up here at twelve, remember?"

Wyatt put his head in his hands and groaned. "Darn it. I totally forgot. That's all I need today, I tell you."

"It'll be okay," said Maggie, reaching across the table and massaging the back of her husband's neck. "I'm sure Willy can manage it."

Wyatt shook his head doubtfully. "Not on his own he can't."

"Well, Little Bob can help him, can't he? And one of the girls can go out for the afternoon roundup if need be. I really think Dylan needs to be there for Bobby. Who knows what state the poor kid'll be in?"

Dylan and Bobby were only a month apart in age and had been inseparable best friends, brothers really, since Bobby had first shown up at Highwood as a scrawny little ten-year-old. Even back then, Dylan had never met anyone quite like him. Brought up to respect his own father almost like a god, he watched in silent awe as Bobby fought his corner with Hank on everything from his bedtime to school attendance to the amount of time he spent riding.

His parents had tried to explain to him that Bobby was troubled, that his bad behavior stemmed from the lawless, hippie existence he'd lived with his mother for so long. But Bobby seemed anything but troubled to Dylan. He seemed fearless and exotic and just wonderful in every way. When Hank would beat him for some misdemeanor or other, he'd show off his bruises to Dylan with all the macho pride of a returning war hero. And when kids at school, envious because they knew he would grow up to inherit Highwood, ostracized him from their little cliques and didn't invite him to their birthday parties, he shrugged it off with a cool indifference that left Dylan speechless with admiration.

For his part, Bobby confided in Dylan and trusted him like no one else. He'd never encountered true loyalty in his short life—other than from horses—and Dylan's steadfast friendship had been a revelation.

It was a testament to Dylan's sweet, devoted nature that it had never occurred to him to feel envious that Bobby was to inherit Highwood, while he was destined to spend his life there as a hired hand. That his best friend would one day be his boss seemed as natural and inevitable to him as the sun rising in the morning. It was just the way it was.

Nor did his devotion waver when, as teenagers, Bobby always ended up with the best-looking girls. While they all thought Dylan was "cute" and "sweet," the truth was he was far too nice to impress them in the same way that Bobby Cameron, Solvang's answer to James Dean, could. Mostly they used him shamelessly to get close to Bobby, then after it all went wrong, returned to him as a shoulder to cry on. But Dylan, ever easygoing, ever the gentleman, didn't seem to mind.

At nineteen, when Bobby had defied Hank once again to take a training job out in Florida, the boys were physically separated for the first time. But as different as their adult lives became, they never outgrew the bond they had forged in childhood. Bobby remained Dylan's hero. And Dylan remained one of the few constants in Bobby's otherwise tumultuous life—an anchor that he relied on more than he liked to admit.

"I guess you're right," said Wyatt, giving his wife a tired smile. "Bobby's the most important thing right now. I'll handle the shipment. Dyl should go to LAX."

"Yes, sir." Dylan nodded respectfully. He was glad to be able to go but also a little nervous. He knew, probably better than anyone, how difficult and complex Bobby and Hank's relationship had been: how, deep down, all Bobby had ever wanted was for his father to recognize his talent as a horse trainer, to tell him that he was proud of him, to pat him on the back.

But it had never happened.

And now it never would.

Bobby had always been the strong one. But now he, Dylan, was supposed to take on that role and support his friend in his grief. Honestly, he had no idea where to begin.

By the time Dylan reached LAX, his bones had started to ache with tiredness.

He'd been up since five, which was his usual routine, but as no one on the ranch had gotten to sleep much before two A.M., he felt like he was running on empty. Plus the drive into LA had been as hellish as ever, with traffic on the 101 crawling to a virtual standstill in the blistering afternoon heat as he got closer and closer to the city. It wouldn't have been so bad if his truck had AC. As it was, the halfhearted stuttering of his ancient fan had done nothing to combat temperatures in the low nineties, and by the time he reached the airport he was literally dripping in sweat, his T-shirt soaked through to the skin.

It was beyond him why anyone would choose to live in LA. He could understand the appeal of city life all right—Paris, London, even San Francisco were all places he dreamed of one day living. In his wilder, more fantastical daydreams he pictured his little artists' studio and the cosmopolitan life he might lead there, if only he weren't shackled to the ranch. But LA? It was like one huge, dry, ugly, soulless parking lot.

It seemed incredible that the rural idyll of Highwood, with its mind-blowing scenery, its work ethic, history, and family values, could exist so close to this smog-ridden, seething hive of materialism and sterility. To Dylan, LA was like suburbia gone mad but without the Brady Bunch suburban families to inject it with some heart, some kind of moral anchor. Every time he came here, he got depressed.

He'd tried to distract himself on the drive down by thinking about what he was going to say to Bobby when he saw him. What do you say to someone whose dad has just died? "Sorry for your loss" sounded way too formal, but his usual "how are you, man?" didn't cut it either, under the circumstances.

Unfortunately, or perhaps fortunately, he had no experience of grief, his own or anyone else's. The closest he'd ever come was when his beloved first pony, Sapphire Blue, broke her leg trying to kick her way out of her stall and had to be euthanized. He was eight at the time, and it took him months and months to get over it.

But even he could see that that hardly counted as adequate preparation for the task ahead of him today.

By the time Bobby finally emerged into arrivals, looking pretty exhausted himself, Dylan had given up on finding the perfect opening line. Marching forward he simply put his arms around his friend and enveloped him in a bear hug that he hoped would say it all.

"It's good to see you," he said, relieving Bobby of his bag when he eventually released him.

"You too," said Bobby. He was smiling, which was a good sign. In typical Bobby style, he seemed to be coping better than everyone expected.

"I didn't think you'd come meet me," he said. "It's not like the boss to give you that much time off on a workday."

"The boss?" Dylan looked puzzled. Hank had always been referred to as the boss. "You mean Dad?"

"Sure," said Bobby. "Who else? Now that Hank's gone, Wyatt's running the place, right?"

"Come on, man." Dylan looked at him affectionately. "He always has run the place, you know that. But that doesn't make him the boss. You're the boss now. The one and only."

Bobby frowned and stared down at his boots.

"Don't say that."

"Why not?" said Dylan. "It's true."

"It may be true." Bobby sighed. "But it just sounds too weird, you know? I'm not ready, Dyl," he admitted. "You don't know what it's like."

It was a rare flash of vulnerability. Not knowing how to respond, Dylan listened in silence.

"All my life I've tried to make him proud. And all my life I've failed. And now he's dead, and I wasn't even there. I couldn't even do *that* right."

"Hey, c'mon," protested Dylan. "That's not true. You couldn't have known—"

But Bobby waved him down.

"Maybe not. But that's not the worst part. You know what the worst part is?" Dylan shook his head. "The only thing I've been thinking about since it happened—the only fucking thing—is how am I supposed to be the boss? I mean, how heartless is that? Hank's dead, and I'm worried about myself. Worried I won't fill his shoes."

"What do you mean?"

"Oh, c'mon," said Bobby. "You know what I mean. I'll never be half the cowboy he was, and everybody knows it."

Dylan's heart went out to him. He had trouble enough dealing with his own father's expectations. How much harder must it be for Bobby, as the son of a bona fide cowboy legend?

"Look," he said firmly, striding out through the sliding double doors into the sweltering air in his bandy-legged gait, while Bobby mooched alongside him. "Forget about filling Hank's shoes, okay? You've always been your own man, haven't you?"

"I guess," said Bobby.

"So? Wear your own shoes."

Bobby gave a rueful smile. If only it were that easy.

He knew how Dylan saw him—how everyone saw him—as Hank's rebel son, the kid who broke the rules, who always did exactly what he wanted. But now that his father was dead, there was no one left to kick against. And where did that leave him?

For the first time in his life he was faced with real responsibility. Highwood was his. Everyone who worked there would now depend on him for their livelihoods. It was time to bury the self-indulgent, rebellious kid he'd been once and for all—time to grow up. Quite frankly, the thought scared the shit out of him.

"Trust me," said Dylan. "You're gonna make a great boss. It's what you've been waiting for all your life, isn't it?"

Yeah, thought Bobby. Yeah, it is.

So why did he feel so terrified?

"Thanks, man," he said. They'd emerged into the parking lot now, and he watched as Dylan hurled his suitcase unceremoniously into the back of the truck like it weighed nothing. For the thousandth time, he thanked whatever god might be up there for Dylan McDonald.

Whatever the future held for him and Highwood, he felt better knowing that Dylan would be in it.

CHAPTER FOUR

Jasper Lockwood Groves was shaking so much in the saddle he thought he might be about to throw up. Perched nervously on top of Marcus O'Reilly's prancing bay filly, Marigold Kiss, he was also very aware that he was sweating profusely and unattractively in the blazing June sun as he made his final walk around the paddock at Epsom Downs.

Around him, race goers of all sexes, ages, and classes milled about between the various enclosures chatting happily. Some were glued to their race cards, darting back and forth between the stands of the ringside bookies. Others, apparently oblivious to either the betting or the racing, were focused purely on enjoying the party atmosphere—drinking, flirting, and generally enjoying themselves.

Almost everyone had dressed up for the occasion. In the cheapest seats up on the Hill, women had taken advantage of the hot weather to put on some of the shortest skirts and lowest-cut tops ever seen outside the King's Cross red-light district. There were plenty of short skirts and stilettos in the Grandstand too but mingled with a good smattering of tweed, "sensible" shoes, and modestly covered, matronly bosoms heaving uncomfortably in the heat beneath their twin sets and pearls; while the most exclusive Queen's Stand was a riot of multicolored hats and feathers.

The men had made an effort as well. Corporate parties, who had arrived this morning in pristine suits, were now in rolled-up shirtsleeves and loosened ties, enjoying their fourth or fifth pints of Guinness and discussing their (usually woeful) performance at the bookies so far. Country gents, flat-capped farmers, even gangs of tattooed barrow boys from the East End out on their mates' stag weekend—they were all there and mingling happily, if somewhat drunkenly, around Epsom Downs.

Sweating his guts out in the paddock, Jasper felt none of their carefree abandon. His primary concern right now was not the race—which he hadn't a snowball's chance in hell of winning anyway—but the thought of how his flushed face must be clashing horribly with the pink and purple silks he was wearing to signify he was riding for Marcus. Why couldn't the bloody Paddy have chosen more flattering colors? Like the dark green and brown that Robbie Pemberton was looking so fucking smug in, chatting with his owner and trainer in a confident, relaxed little huddle on the other side of the paddock?

Rachel had shown up, as promised, looking even more fuckable than she had that day at Newells in a bottom-skimming, neon-pink minidress with huge black buttons down the front, knee-high black Jimmy Choos, and some elaborate, black-feathered headdress, no doubt from Philip Treacy or some other outrageously priced designer. It worked though, in a slutty, I'm-so-foxy-I-can-wear-what-I-like sort of a way. Just picturing her now was giving him the beginnings of an erection he could ill afford before the race. After weeks of anticipation, if he didn't get to shag her tonight he reckoned his bollocks were going to explode.

She'd seemed keen enough when she came over to chat earlier: flicking her hair, giggling, and pressing her breasts together to give him a better view of her cleavage—a definite come-on if ever he saw one. But that was before he'd had to change into these hideous silks. And before that bastard Pemberton had shown up, preening about the paddock like he owned the place.

Every woman in the world seemed to fancy Robbie, and Jasper could only assume that Rachel was no exception. Even his goody-two-shoes little sister, who as far as he could tell had all the sexual awareness of an amoeba, drooled over the guy. Personally he had never understood what the fuss was about. Okay, so Pemberton was by far the most successful of the new generation of flat race jockeys snapping at Frankie Dettori's heels. But that didn't stop him being a swarthy little midget.

Unusually short, even for a jockey, with a tiny, ski-jump nose and floppy black hair, he looked, in Jasper's opinion anyway, like the love child of a leprechaun and some greasy, dago waiter. Hardly Brad Pitt, however you cut it.

Being long on looks and short on talent himself, Jasper was chronically envious of anyone in whom this ratio was reversed. He resented Robbie's success, both at the track and with women, bitterly.

As a little boy, Jasper had dreamed of becoming famous. Unfortunately, it became apparent early on that while he might be a perfectly competent jockey, he lacked the talent necessary to make it to the very top of the sport that his father had frog-marched him into. It was Milly, with her instinctive rapport with horses and kamikaze determination to win at all costs, who was the undeniable equestrian star of the family.

If it hadn't been for her accident, Jasper might well have given up competitive riding in his teens. But with his sister out of the picture, and his doting mother willing to throw not just money but Cecil's first-rate horses and invaluable racing connections behind his career, it seemed churlish not to give it a shot—especially as the alternative was either the army or knuckling down to work at the stud. Unlike Milly, Jasper's interest in breeding was strictly confined to human activity, preferably his own. All that bloodlines nonsense bored him to tears.

His father would have loved him to learn the family business. But Jasper was so lazy, getting him to set foot in the covering shed was like trying to get blood from a stone. It didn't help that Linda, whose devotion bordered on the oedipal, backed her work-shy son to the hilt.

"He's only young, darling," she'd insisted last summer, after an apoplectic Cecil had found out about the three grand Jasper had blown on girls and parties before Sandown. "There's plenty of time for him to learn the business later. We mustn't begrudge him a little fun, or the chance to make the most of his talent now. He worked so hard to ride out his claim."

"Talent? What talent?" Cecil had fumed.

But Linda didn't want to hear it. No amount of hard evidence would ever convince her that her dashing, handsome boy was not the best jockey in England. As the years went by, she steadfastly blamed his lackluster performances on poor horses or inadequate trainers. Being naturally vain, it wasn't long before he began to convince himself that perhaps his mother was right: maybe he *did* have more talent than people gave him credit for? With girls from York to Epsom reinforcing this impression by throwing themselves at him left, right, and center, dazzled by his smooth charm and toothpaste-ad good looks, his ego rapidly inflated to a point of no return.

"Nice horse."

Robbie had suddenly materialized at Jasper's side. With the race effectively in the bag, he could afford to be friendly, and showed none of the nerves of the other jockeys, many of whom viewed the Oaks as the pinnacle of their careers.

"This old nag?" said Jasper waspishly. "You're joking, aren't you? She's practically on crutches."

It was a cardinal sin among jockeys to slag off your own mount, but Jasper did it all the time. He knew it earned him a bad reputation, but the alternative would have been to blame himself for his poor performances, something his fragile self-image would never allow.

"Saw you chatting up the delectable Miss Delaney earlier," said Robbie, changing the subject with what he thought was a matey wink but which Jasper immediately misconstrued as patronizing. "Fancy your chances, do you?"

"And what if I do?" Jasper bridled. "You don't have a monopoly on all the decent-looking girls, you know, mate."

"All right. There's no need to be so touchy," said Robbie, the smile dying on his lips. Cecil Lockwood Groves was a decent bloke, but his son was obviously an arsehole. "I was only making conversation."

"Twat," muttered Jasper as he rode off. Only making conversation indeed. It was obvious he was after Rachel—he just wasn't man enough to admit it. Well, screw him. This was one race the greasy woppo bastard wasn't going to win, not if he could help it.

His heart sank still further as he caught sight of his mother chatting animatedly to the Delaneys. Linda was a crashing snob, and always made an effort to ingratiate herself with anyone titled. Sir Michael Delaney may have been born in Barnsley and earned his knighthood building a textiles empire, but he still qualified, as, by extension, did his daughter. Linda had always considered the so-called feud between Milly and Rachel to be a lot of adolescent nonsense. Certainly, she wasn't about to let it dampen her obsequious enthusiasm for the Delaneys' company.

She gave Jasper an enthusiastic wave, encouraging Lady Delaney to do the same, before heading back toward the Queen's stand. Christ, she looked shocking. Even at this distance, he couldn't miss her in that godawful lime-green suit and matching hat. Sadly, Linda's blind love for her son was not reciprocated. Although Jasper recognized the need to keep her sweet, especially if he wanted to keep his allowance, he had always found her public doting a hideous embarrassment.

What the fuck was she doing here anyway? Wasn't she supposed to be up in London, arranging flowers or something for Milly's stupid ball?

Gritting his teeth, he waved back, praying that she didn't do anything too stupid to fuck things up for him with Rachel.

Thankfully he was soon distracted from this awful prospect by the officious, clipped voice of the steward ringing out around the paddock.

"To the gates, please!"

A frisson of excitement swept visibly across the crowded Lonsdale Enclosure and up to the Hill, where families, local enthusiasts, and truckloads of grinning Irishmen had bought out all but a couple of the cheaper tickets. Feeling his intestines give another ominous rumble, Jasper made his way toward the starting gate with the other nine jockeys. Some of the fillies were wild-eyed with excitement already, frothing at the mouth and flaring their nostrils frenziedly in anticipation of the race to come. Others, like Marigold Kiss, stood calmly, looking as supremely uninterested in the proceedings as the Queen at a royal variety performance.

Fucking Irish plodder, thought Jasper grimly. She'd better pull her finger out once they got going.

Almost before he knew it, the starting stalls had miraculously opened and they were off. He was dimly aware of the roaring of the crowd in his ears, the sound trying to battle its way through the deafening pounding of hooves and beating of equine hearts that surrounded him as Marigold Kiss lurched forward into the fray.

Unfortunately, her initial burst of speed when faced with real, live competition threw him completely.

"Fuck!" he yelled, as his left foot slipped out of the stirrup and he felt himself sliding dangerously around in the saddle. He'd almost come unseated completely before he eventually managed to wrench himself back upright and regain his balance. "Double fuck!"

By the time he'd gotten his breath back the crucial seconds had already been lost. Sensing his loss of focus and control, his horse had already eased back into her usual, more sedate pace. A few seconds later, to his absolute fury, Jasper saw Robbie's distinctive gray careering past him on the far left, moving up to join the early leaders, as he and Marigold slipped ever farther toward the back of the center pack.

"Come on, you bitch!" he bellowed against the din, his whip going almost constantly against the filly's right flank. "Run!"

A more sensitive, more responsive rider might have found a way to squeeze those vital few ounces of reserve energy and speed from the young horse when it mattered most. But Jasper's crazed, indiscriminate whipping and straining seemed to be having the opposite effect. Before he realized it, the first mile of the undulating, U-shaped course was already behind him. By the time he reached the uphill run-in in the final furlong, he had fallen back still farther, trailing the pack to finish a less than heroic ninth.

Winded with wasted effort and disappointment, he brought the horse to a stop directly in front of the grandstand. He was just in time to hear the tannoy announcing that Robbie Pemberton, as predicted, had won by a length and a half.

A wave of envy washed over him as he watched his rival make his way slowly over to the winner's enclosure, answering the shouted press questions with the shy nods and monosyllabic mumbles he was famed for. Robbie was not given to Dettori-like flying dismounts or unseemly displays of emotion. He was an old-school jockey—the strong and silent type—beloved, it appeared, of both women and owners alike.

Even more so now, Jasper supposed, with two of the fillies' triple crown races under his belt. The jammy bastard.

Turning disconsolately back to the paddock, he was soon cornered by a despondent Marcus O'Reilly and Dominic Beale, Marigold's trainer.

"Bad luck," said Marcus, disappointment lacing his broad Dublin accent as he patted Marigold's neck. "You did yer best, son."

A fat, jovial Irishman who owned racehorses for the sheer love of it, and looked on wining races as merely the icing on an already very satisfying cake, Marcus was not in the habit of tearing a strip off his jockeys, no matter how badly they may have performed. Besides, he stabled three of his top stallions with Cecil Lockwood Groves, so he wasn't inclined to look for a falling-out with the breeder's son.

"Luck had nothing to do with it."

Dom Beale, who had watched with his head in his hands as months of his hard work were washed down the drain by this clueless excuse for a jockey, was clearly not in the same stoic, forgiving mood as his boss. Unlike Marcus, he trained racehorses because he liked to win and regularly ate far more experienced riders than Jasper for breakfast if their performance was subpar.

Jasper's performance had been horrific.

"Call yourself a jockey? My blind grandmother could have ridden a better race than that!" he fumed. "You're not in the Pony Club egg and spoon now, my boy. This is fucking Epsom. You were a disgrace. And in case you were wondering, you can forget about the fucking St. Leger." He shook his head in disgust. "Jesus Christ!"

"Oh, now come on, Dom, go easy," said Marcus. "I'm sure the lad was trying."

Jasper had turned bright red, whether from anger, embarrassment, or exertion it was impossible to tell. Over his right shoulder, he was dimly aware of Rachel sashaying over toward him, her fabulous fuck-me boots sinking into the turf with each swing of her hips. Gorgeous as she was, his heart sank. The last thing he needed was for her to see him like this, being given a dressing-down from Dom Beale like a naughty child.

Thankfully she was waylaid by a stray reporter, no doubt wanting to hear her opinion on the result and Pemberton's performance. Though she hadn't ridden today, Rachel was already making something of a name for herself as an up-and-coming competitor and was frequently quoted by the racing press, all of whom adored her, partly because she was Sir Michael Delaney's daughter and partly because she was such a beauty.

Good girl jockeys were rare enough. Pretty ones were like gold dust.

While she was otherwise engaged, Linda, looking like a human Starburst candy in her lime-green suit, began fighting her way through the paddock to Jasper's side.

"Darling," she said, her face a picture of sympathy and concern. "What bad luck."

For once he was actually pleased to see her. Even Beale would have to ease up now that a lady was present.

"You must be absolutely exhausted."

"Hello, Mother," he said, dismounting and pointedly turning away from the trainer in midrant to kiss her. "I didn't expect to see you here. Shouldn't you be up in London sorting things out for tonight?"

"I should really." She gazed up at him from under her fringe with the same adoring, Princess Di gaze that she always reserved for her son. Still attractive in an expensive, put-together, older-woman sort of a way, she had always been whip thin and blessed with naturally youthful skin. Sadly, she had a tendency to take the edge off this gift by wearing too much heavy makeup and mistakenly believing that an expensive designer label could excuse outfits as loud and vulgar as the green Jean Muir monstrosity she was wearing today.

"But I couldn't have missed your first Classic ride, now could I?" she simpered. "Daddy got stuck at the farm with some ghastly client, but the Delaneys kindly took me under their wing. Oh, hullo, Marcus darling."

Turning to O'Reilly, Linda deftly, though quite inadvertently, succeeded in edging the still-fuming Dominic completely out of their little huddle. Eventually he stalked off, unable to bear the air kissing and pleasantries any longer. Jasper breathed a sigh of relief.

Moments later Rachel bounded over. Her interview finished, she flung her arms around Jasper like a long-lost puppy returning to its master. Evidently he needn't have worried: his unflattering silks and disastrous performance didn't seem to have put her off in the slightest.

"Are you all right?" she said, slipping her hand into his and giving it a very deliberate squeeze. "You must be terribly disappointed."

"I was," he said, squeezing back and dropping his voice to a whisper so Marcus couldn't hear him. "Bloody horse had her hand brake on right from the gate, unfortunately. Nothing I could do."

If Rachel disagreed with this assessment of his options, she didn't show it.

Pulling her closer, Jasper grinned lasciviously. "I'm starting to feel better now though. Much better, in fact."

Rubbing the ball of his thumb against the inside of her wrist, he was gratified to hear her breathing quicken with desire. This would be like taking candy from a baby.

"D'you want to get out of here?" he whispered in her ear, surreptitiously slipping one warm, rough hand inside her dress. His mother was still deep in conversation with O'Reilly, so they might as well make a break for it while the going was good.

"Absolutely." She giggled. "I was beginning to think you'd never ask."

Half an hour later, Jasper was lying on his back on the floor of Marigold's horse trailer with a naked Rachel straddled magnificently above him, tossing her head back and moaning in a reassuringly convincing display of sexual ecstasy.

"Ooo, yes!" she gasped, her muscles spasming tightly around his cock as her orgasm took hold. "Oh God, yes!"

"Say my name," he breathed. "Say I'm the best you've ever had."

"Oh, Jasper," she rasped dutifully. "Don't stop! You're the best! You're the best ever!"

He came then in three short, hard thrusts, grabbing hold of her taut, round bottom to pull himself even deeper into her and letting out a small, involuntary sound that was part sigh and part whoop of triumph.

He'd done it. He'd officially scored the fittest bird in racing.

Robbie Pemberton might be the bookies' favorite, but he still played second fiddle to Jasper Lockwood Groves when it came to the ladies. Rachel could have had any man she wanted on the racing circuit—but he was the one she'd chosen.

Not Robbie. Him.

Easing herself slowly up off his rapidly softening dick, Rachel reached down for a handful of straw to wipe herself with. The sex had been fine. Not fabulous, but perfectly adequate, and at least his dick had been a reasonable size.

More important, though, it was mission accomplished: she'd successfully seduced Milly's brother—and for this she couldn't help but allow herself a small smile.

As Jasper's girlfriend she'd have unlimited opportunities to get under Milly's skin. She could hang around the stables all the time, riding the Newells horses that were forbidden to her rival. And what could be simpler than ingratiating herself with Milly and Jasper's ghastly, common, social-climbing mother?

After the way Milly had lorded it over her when they were kids, beating her so effortlessly at every gymkhana, not to mention stealing what should have been *her* place in the junior eventing team, this would be nothing more than just deserts.

Delightful, delicious karma.

The whole thing had been so easy too. She couldn't imagine why she hadn't thought of it years ago. She'd even managed to convince the vain, self-obsessed Jasper that it had all been his idea. Evidently he fancied himself as a major Don Juan. Still, if he wanted to delude himself that she was some wide-eyed innocent, powerless in the face of his animal magnetism, that was fine by her. All that mattered was putting one over on Milly. And this time, by God, she'd well and truly done it.

Sitting in the back of a black cab later that evening beside her mother, Milly was just about ready to shoot someone—quite possibly herself.

By the time Linda had arrived back at the Pimlico flat, bursting with garrulous excitement about Robbie Pemberton's triumph and armed with her usual array of excuses for Jasper's latest shitty performance—it was beyond Milly how on earth a serious owner like Marcus had picked a meathead like her brother to ride in such a prestigious race in the first place—she was already at the end of her tether. As if missing the Oaks and having to go to some stupid bloody ball wasn't bad enough, she'd been forced to spend the whole afternoon having pedicures and blow-dries and waxes until she felt like an overplucked chicken.

What possessed the women who *chose* to put themselves through this sort of torture every week? she wondered bitterly, as the sweet but moronic girl Linda had paid a small fortune to come to the flat and do her hair before the ball launched into yet another lecture about the state of her split ends.

"Have you heard of conditioner at all?" she'd asked, valiantly trying to run a comb through Milly's tangled thatch of hair. "You really ought to think about cutting it more often, you know. And getting regular hot oil treatments."

I'd rather boil myself alive in hot oil than go through all this again, thought Milly, but she tried to be polite and keep her temper. The only time she slipped all day was when Karen, the officious, dumpy lady from *Color Me Beautiful,* tried to convince her that all her life's troubles stemmed from the fact that she didn't wear enough purple.

"If you blend the purple wiv the pink on your upper lids, like *so*," she'd bleated mindlessly, "I fink you'll agree you get a lovely, subtle effect."

"Subtle? Are you blind?" Unable to contain herself a moment longer, Milly's frayed temper had finally snapped. "I already look like Barbara Cartland in the blasted dress. And now you want to turn me into Dame Edna?"

In fact, despite the frown she wore now in the back of the cab, she didn't look half as bad as she thought. Having won the battle with her mother and opted for the blue dress, a long, figure-hugging taffeta affair, rather than the froufrou pink monstrosity, she actually looked quite sophisticated, at least when she sat down. (Though they were beautiful, she could barely stand, let alone walk, in her diamante Manolo

Blahnik shoes.) The fake tan that she'd objected to so vociferously this afternoon had in fact worked wonders with her skin tone, so the icy blue of the dress no longer washed her out. And with her hair, worn loose for once, tumbling down her back, newly washed and gleaming, a smidgen of smoky eye makeup, and bronzer on her usually bare cheeks, she seemed older, more elegant and, though she herself would never have thought so, really quite sexy.

"I knew he'd bottle it." She was still harking back to Jasper's failure to trouble the judges at Epsom earlier. "Horses can tell when a jockey hasn't got a clue what he's doing."

"Don't talk nonsense, Milly," said Linda tersely. "That filly had been overtrained. Any fool could see that."

"Bullshit," said Milly succinctly. "I bet you I could have gotten more out of her. She did well enough in Ireland earlier this year. It's Jasper that's the problem."

"Darling, I know that your brother riding professionally has been difficult for you," chided Linda, "but there's really no point in your constantly putting him down."

"Did you say 'professional'?" Milly spluttered. "Jasper? That's a joke! O'Reilly only picked him because he wants to keep sweet with Dad. Besides, I'm not putting him down. I'm just telling it like it is."

"You weren't even there, darling," Linda pointed out reasonably.

"Which was incredibly unfair," said Milly, jumping onto her hobby horse for the umpteenth time that evening. "Rachel bloody Delaney gets to race all over the country, but I can't even go and *watch* while my own brother makes a tit of himself at one of the most important meetings of the year."

Linda sighed. She was tired of having this pointless, circular conversation. Beyond tired.

"Let's not go over this again, darling," she said wearily. "Not tonight. You know why we don't let you ride, and what Rachel does or doesn't do is neither here nor there. As a matter of fact I was sitting with her and her parents in the Queen's Stand today, and I must say I found her to be perfectly charming."

Milly rolled her eyes to heaven. How could her mother be so blind?

"She was terribly complimentary about Jasper too," Linda went on. "Do you think perhaps this silly feud you keep talking about might have run its course? Because I certainly didn't see much sign of it from Rachel's side. She even asked after you. Wanted to hear all about your dress . . ."

But Milly wasn't listening. Rachel being "complimentary" about Jasper could mean only one thing.

"Oh, so she was sniffing around J. again, was she?" she said, shaking her head in disbelief. "What a surprise. He's so vain, I bet he fell for it hook, line, and sinker, didn't he?"

"I have no idea what you're talking about, Milly," said Linda stiffly. "But your brother is not vain."

"Ha! Not much!" Milly's voice was dripping with sarcasm. "Am I the only person that can see the way she's using him?"

"Using him?" Linda looked puzzled.

"To get at me," said Milly, exasperated. "Honestly, Mummy. She's even got *you* convinced she's on the level. My own mother!"

"Now you're just being ridiculous." Dropping her powder compact back into her handbag, Linda clicked the clasp firmly shut, an indication that the conversation was closed. "Let's try to focus on this evening, shall we? And do try to smile once we get there, darling. No one's going to want to dance with you if you keep sulking like a three-year-old."

Milly gazed sullenly out of the window. When would her parents ever understand? If only her father would get over his fears and give her another chance at racing, everything could be different. But no. Her mother already had her grand plan—a racing career and a fat inheritance for Jasper, and marriage and immolation on some ghastly estate for her—and Cecil was going to sit back and let it happen.

And now, to cap it all, Rachel Delaney seemed determined on turning her own family against her. Wasn't taking her place as the top girl rider in Newmarket enough?

Apparently not.

"Look, darling," said Linda, sensing her darkening mood. "I know you were disappointed not to be there today. But won't you try, just try, to enjoy yourself tonight? It's your coming-out ball, for heaven's sake.

There's a whole world out there beyond racing, you know. I don't understand why you're so hell-bent on limiting yourself."

No, thought Milly gloomily, gazing out at the silvery reflection of the moonlight in the still, murky water of the Thames. They were approaching Westminster along the embankment, and she could see the familiar white face of Big Ben lit up by floodlights from below. You don't understand, do you? But that's because you never listen, you or Dad.

No one ever listens to me.

Her mother was obsessed with punctuality and was usually always the first to turn up at parties, so Milly was relieved when, for once, they arrived at the Grosvenor House hotel at a sensible time. Paying the cabbie, they made their way into the ballroom, Linda striding gracefully, Milly teetering behind her in her Manolos like a baby giraffe on stilts.

A group of awkward-looking boys, none of them older than twenty-one, were already huddled in a corner close to the bar, laughing too loudly at one another's jokes. Most of them looked like they had dressed up for the night in Daddy's tux, although one or two had tried to stand out from the crowd and proclaim themselves as one of the "lads" by wearing a novelty waistcoat, covered either with red lipstick marks or luridly colored cartoon characters.

Milly's heart sank. What a bunch of prepubescent, hooray tossers. What on earth was she doing here?

"Look, darling, there's Harry Lyon," said Linda enthusiastically, pointing out one of the shortest and spottiest of the crowd, who was sporting a tartan waistcoat, presumably an allusion to his aristocratic Scottish ancestry. "You know Harry. He was Algernon in the Amateur Dramatic Club's *The Importance of Being Earnest* last Christmas. Remember?"

Milly shook her head. She had made a concentrated mental effort to forget the posse of nerds and losers from the Newmarket theater group that she'd been forced to spend endless weekends with, missing out on all the excitement at the racetrack that Jasper got to enjoy.

But Linda was on a roll and ignored her head shake and accompanying look of tedium. "Harry was at Eton until last year," she gushed, her smile seeming to indicate that this was considered a selling point. "I think he must be at Sandhurst now, going into the guards like his father. Yoo-hoo! Harry!"

She waved gaily across at the hapless boy, who was instantly ribbed by his little gaggle of friends. Moments later she was dragging a mortified Milly across the room toward him.

"You remember Milly," she said brightly, thrusting her daughter forward, like a ritual sacrifice. "She doesn't know very many people here. I wonder if you'd be kind and take care of her for me until more of the girls arrive?"

Oh God, please, let me die, thought Milly, managing a weak, hopeless smile at Harry and his leering friends. He smiled back, looking every bit as miserably awkward as she did. Clearly, he didn't remember her from the ADC either. For a moment they both stood, shuffling shyly from foot to foot while Linda disappeared to join Harry's mother on the other side of the dance floor. The other boys, completely thrown by the presence of a real, live, attractive girl among them, had also mooched off, leaving their friend to his fate.

"Would, er, would you like to dance?" he mumbled eventually, trying to maintain eye contact without letting his gaze wander down to Milly's newly bronzed cleavage as it strained for escape from its blue taffeta prison.

Poor thing. He looked utterly terrified.

"Not really," she said. "I could murder a drink though."

"All they're serving at the minute is that awful nonalcoholic punch." He pointed to a huge silver bowl behind them, with some Chernobyl-green liquid and half the EU fruit mountain swilling around in it. "I think some of the mothers were worried about all the blokes getting shit faced before the coming-out ceremony. Apparently, last year Milo Saunders got really drunk and tried to stick his hand down Rachel Delaney's dress just as she was about to be presented."

"Hmmm," sniffed Milly. "He must have been drunk to go for that old slapper."

Harry grinned. He'd also been on the receiving end of Rachel's vanity and bitchiness in the past, and was not a fan.

"I gather there should be beer later, but not for a couple of hours at least."

Milly's face fell. Never in her short life had she felt more in need of a stiff drink than she did this evening.

"I've got a couple of spliffs though," he said tentatively, sounding her out. He hoped she wasn't one of those bonkers "Just Say No" crusaders who'd go shrieking to her mother and accuse him of being a drug dealer in front of the entire room. But he was soon relieved to see her smiling naughtily back at him.

Pulling a silver cigarette case out of his inside jacket pocket he gave her a surreptitious flash of three immaculately rolled joints.

"Here's some Harry made earlier," she said with a giggle in her best schoolma'am voice.

"Using double-sided sticky tape for speed!" He finished the catchphrase for her and they both roared with laughter. Suddenly Milly didn't seem quite so hard to talk to after all. "You smoke, then?"

"Well, I do tonight." She rolled her eyes in the direction of the other debutantes chattering overexcitedly and pointing at the boys as though they'd never set eyes on the male of the species before. "What a fucking nightmare."

"I know," said Harry with feeling. "My mother forced me to come."

"Mine too," sighed Milly. "I think she's trying to sell me off to the highest bidder. Come on." She grabbed Harry's hand and pulled him toward the fire escape. Perhaps he wasn't such a chinless wonder after all. "Bring those spliffs and let's get the hell out of here."

Two hours later, she was sprawled out on a flat roof at the back of the hotel, wrapped up warmly in Harry's tuxedo, staring up at the stars. The pair of them were helplessly, hopelessly stoned.

"D'you think anyone's missed us yet?" asked Harry, taking a big bite of the crunchy bar he'd purloined from the gift shop downstairs before offering it to Milly. His munchies were kicking in big-time now.

"Dunno," she said, nibbling gratefully at the chocolate. "Probably. Oh!" she gasped suddenly, as though she'd just remembered something desperately important. "Do you think we've missed the curtseying to the cake? My mother'll go spare if we have."

Harry dissolved into yet more giggles. "Curtseying to a cake!" he said, repeating the words over and over until they sounded so ridiculous that they were both doubled over with laughter.

"Did I mention," said Milly, once she'd finally gotten her breath back, "how much I hate Rachel Delaney? Hate her, hate her, HATE her!"

"You did." Harry nodded slowly. "Twice, in fact. Or was it three times? And you told me that she's after your brother—"

"Who I also hate."

"Who you also hate. And that she's a crap rider, and that the sole purpose of her existence is to make yours hell."

Milly beamed at him. "So you have been listening, then?"

"Of course." Harry smiled. "How could I not listen to a girl as beautiful as you?"

Milly blushed. Suddenly she felt uncomfortably out of her depth. Harry was adorable, but she definitely didn't fancy him and she was too inexperienced to know how to take a compliment without making a hash of it. In fairness, she hadn't had a lot of practice: Most boys were scared off by her tomboy stroppiness long before they got the chance to say anything nice about her.

"Maybe we should go back in?" she mumbled awkwardly. "I've no idea how long we've been out here, have you?"

Harry shook his head. He longed to lean over and kiss her, but he didn't have the nerve. Besides, it had been such a lovely, relaxed evening—Milly really was an amazing girl. He'd hate to ruin it all now for the sake of one misjudged lunge.

"I don't know," he said. "But you're right. We ought to be getting back." Standing up a little unsteadily and brushing the dust from his evening trousers, he chivalrously offered her his hand and pulled her up to her feet. Soon the awkwardness was past and they were giggling again like a couple of infants as they tottered and swayed across the rooftop. At one point Milly was so beside herself with laughter that she slipped and fell on the fire escape ladder, twisting her ankle painfully in the process.

"Blast!" she said as she felt an ominous snapping beneath her feet. "I think the heel's come off one of my Manolos. They cost Mummy a fortune."

"Never mind that," said Harry, concerned. "Are *you* all right?"

"Oh, yes, I'm fine," she said blithely. Having spent her formative years being thrown from galloping horses, she had a high pain threshold. "I'm not sure if I can walk though. You might have to help me back inside."

Staggering into the ballroom a few minutes later, they were horrified to find that a good half of the debs and their partners seemed to have left and the party was evidently winding down. The beautiful white-iced, four-tiered cake, the focal point of the evening and the coming-out ceremony, had already, Milly noticed with a rising sense of dread, been butchered into hundreds of tiny slices, some of which were still being greedily consumed by the few remaining mothers or folded into paper napkins and stuffed into their handbags to be kept, presumably, for posterity.

Oh fuck. Her mother was going to hit the roof.

"Milly!" Right on cue, Linda appeared, her eyes narrowed and lips puckered in fury. She was accompanied by a thunderous-looking Mrs. Lyon, Harry's mother. "Where the *hell* have you been? We were looking everywhere for you. If I hadn't known you were with Harry I'd have called the police."

"It's my fault, Mrs. Lockwood Groves," said Harry nobly. He might be a soldier in the British army, but Milly doubted he'd ever been faced with two quite so fearsome opponents as their respective mothers, and she was very grateful for his support. "We were out on the roof talking. We must have lost track of time."

"Lost track of time? You missed the entire thing! After all my hard work, Milly. How could you?"

There were tears stinging the backs of her eyes, and Milly could see that beneath the anger her mother was genuinely hurt. For the first time that day, she felt a twinge of guilt about her own behavior. Okay, so she'd had to miss the Oaks for a stupid, pretentious ball, and she had every right to be pissed off about that. But deep down she knew that her mother, however misguidedly, did have her best interests at heart. She also knew that she'd sweated blood organizing everything tonight.

"I'm sorry," she said and meant it. Sadly, the impact of her apology was rather undermined when she stumbled again on her broken shoe and slithered down to the floor, dragging poor Harry with her. Tangled up in one another's limbs, they were both overcome yet again with tears of mirth. She knew it wasn't funny. But she was so wasted, she couldn't help it.

"Go downstairs and get in the car," snapped Linda. Milly laughing at her, after everything that had happened, was the absolute last straw. "Look at you!" She was shaking with anger. "Do you ever, *ever* think about anyone but yourself?"

Milly didn't dare look up at her. She caught Harry's eye for a moment and thought she saw him give her a fleeting, rueful smile as she hobbled to her feet again. But there was no point looking to him or anyone for support. Nothing he could do or say would save her now.

"Your father will be hearing about this, young lady, the moment we get home," Linda hissed. And then she delivered her coup de grâce: "And you can forget about helping out at the stud for the rest of the summer. Until you can learn how to behave properly you're not going near a horse and that's final."

Milly's eyes widened in horror. The rest of the summer? She couldn't be serious, could she?

"I mean it, Milly," said Linda in a tone that made her blood run cold. "As far as you're concerned those stables are closed as of tomorrow."

CHAPTER FIVE

Hank Cameron's funeral was the biggest event anyone had seen in Solvang in over forty years.

Cowboys from all across the state came to pay their respects and honor the passing of a California legend. It was strange, in a way, how the old man's reputation had grown throughout his lifetime. Despite, or perhaps because of, his reclusiveness and the jealously guarded privacy at Highwood, the image of Hank Cameron as the last of the true cowboys seemed to have taken deep root in people's consciousnesses.

Bobby's mom had told him once, in a rare moment of wisdom, that people idolized Hank because they needed something to believe in. Some sort of hero to cling to as they felt their way of life, their traditional Western culture, slipping inexorably away. Nowadays, when folks thought of cowboys they thought of the Hollywood version—Clint Eastwood, John Wayne—the Marlboro Man. Possibly they drove upstate in their station wagons and SUVs, with their overweight kids glued to Game Boys in the backseat, and spent a weekend on a dude ranch, where Western heritage was served up on a plate with a complimentary ten-gallon hat and a side order of ribs. But the real cowboy traditions, the old life of cattle ranching that had once been the beating heart of the Santa Ynez valley, that was all but dead now. Hank Cameron, his Highwood ranch, and all it had stood for—for many people they were the last bastions of that much-loved but disappearing world.

Looking stiff and formal in his black suit and tie, Bobby couldn't remember the last time he'd felt so uncomfortable. As if the heat and the itchy, constraining fabric of his pants weren't bad enough, he had the unsettling feeling that all eyes were on him, watching and waiting for some sort of outpouring of emotion.

What did they want from him, for Christ's sake? Everyone knew that he and his father hadn't gotten along. Still, he couldn't help but feel kind of heartless, seeing perfect strangers dabbing at their eyes all around him while he couldn't muster a single tear.

It wasn't that he didn't have feelings. It was just that the feelings he had were so confused—a torrent of grief and relief, anger and regret, pounding through his head until it throbbed with noise. Besides, he was his father's son and had never been one for wearing his heart on his sleeve.

"Don't you be too hard on yourself," said Maggie McDonald, taking his arm as they walked back toward the ranch once the last of the mourners had finally gone. "Everyone deals with things in different ways. There's more to grief than tears, you know."

Bobby smiled at her gratefully. Maggie had long ago become like a surrogate mother to him. He still loved Diana—both rebellious, restless spirits, the two of them had become close again in recent years—but it was a relief to have a second mom who provided all the stability and wisdom that his first one lacked.

"Running the ranch is gonna be challenge enough without worrying about what other folks are saying about you," she insisted. "Besides, people do understand, Bobby. More than you might think."

"I guess," he said doubtfully. Having been an outsider and a loner for so much of his life, he didn't share Maggie's faith in human nature. Still, he thought, opening the gate for her as they turned in to the long drive, she was right about one thing: Highwood was gonna be one hell of a challenge. What with all the funeral preparations, he'd barely had time to glance at the books yet, let alone figure out a strategy for turning the failing ranch around.

But now there could be no more procrastinating. He'd have to come up with something. And he'd have to do it soon.

The next afternoon, he and Wyatt saddled up for a long ride out around the property. Bobby listened, mostly in silence, while the older man pointed out some of the worst of the problem areas and gave him a rundown of Highwood's woeful finances.

"Things are bad," Wyatt opened matter-of-factly, as they rode up to the high meadows on the far side of the creek that wound its way through the valley, below the old adobe houses and stable yard. "Real bad. But I'm guessin' you already knew that, right?"

"I knew the big picture," said Bobby, dismounting quickly to break off a rotten piece of fencing that had come loose and was jutting out dangerously. A sharp spike like that could have injured one of his cattle. "But you knew Dad. He never did like to talk numbers. Not with me anyway."

Wyatt chuckled. "Don't take it personal, son. I worked with your father for most of my life, and never once could I sit him down to look at the accounts without an almighty fight on my hands. Out here—" he waved a hand at the softly undulating pastures that surrounded them as Bobby hopped lithely back up onto his pony. "Out here, Hank was a genius, I can't deny it. But down there"—he pointed to the ranch office, now a tiny red-roofed speck far down in the valley below them—"your father was about as much use as a water pistol in a forest fire."

They rode on for a while while Wyatt explained the main issues that the ranch, as a business, was facing. The price of beef had almost halved in the last three years, so all the local ranches were suffering. But Hank's insistence on rearing the traditional breeds, rather than the more common and more profitable standard British beef cattle, meant that Highwood had suffered more than most. His absolute refusal to diversify out of farming had also harmed the ranch financially.

"Truthfully," said Wyatt, once he'd run through the whole sorry litany of their business problems, "if it hadn't been for your earnings from horse training these past two years, I really don't know if we'd have made our interest payments at all. I really don't."

"Jesus," said Bobby, shaking his head in frustration more than in anger. He had always respected Dylan's father immensely and always would. But how could Wyatt have allowed Hank to let things get quite this bad?

"Why didn't you tell me any of this sooner? Maybe I could have done something to help."

Wyatt fixed him with a gimlet stare.

"Now, Bobby Cameron," he said gently. "You know the answer to that question. It wasn't my place to do that. Your father was the boss."

He was right, of course. Hank wouldn't have dreamed of sharing his financial problems with anyone, least of all his wayward son. It would have been more than his pride could bear.

"I'm telling you now," said Wyatt, "because you're the boss now."

So they keep telling me, thought Bobby.

How ironic, to think that it had been his earnings from horse training that had been propping Highwood up all this time. His old man had never approved of his career, particularly once it started taking him out of California. "That fancy-pants Kentucky crowd" was how he'd always referred to Bobby's clients, with a disdain that encompassed everyone from small-time local breeders with a runner or two in the San Rafael Stakes, to Sheikh Mohammed himself. Had anyone asked him, he would probably have described the Queen of England as "one o' them fancy-pants, Kentucky owners."

Leaning back down in the saddle, Bobby loosened up his reins. They had almost reached the highest point of the property now. It was past five, but the late summer sun still had a kick to it, and he surveyed his little piece of paradise through a shimmering heat haze. In the far distance, beyond the borders of the ranch, the land looked dry and dusty, a testament to four long months without so much as a drop of rain. But Highwood, with her carefully tended, irrigated fields full of cattle, glowed green below him, like the Emerald City of Oz.

Looking down, he felt quite choked with love for the place. For a moment he thought that the tears he'd been unable to shed for his father might finally be about to flow.

"I'm not gonna lose this place, Wyatt," he whispered. "I'm not gonna let us go under."

"I'm glad to hear it," said Wyatt, pulling his pony up to a stop beside him. "Never crossed my mind that you would, son."

Wyatt loved Bobby almost like one of his own. Though he'd always disapproved of his rebelliousness, he understood the reasons behind it.

Hank hadn't been much of a father, and Diana was still a child herself when Bobby was born. It was little wonder the kid had learned to live by his own rules.

But for all that he kicked against authority, especially his father's, underneath it all Bobby clearly had a deep sense of duty not only to Highwood but to the cowboy traditions that the Cameron family had upheld, unbroken, for seven generations. Hank had always looked on Bobby's horse training career as an abandonment of his roots and a betrayal of the Cameron name—but he was wrong. If he could see his son now, so patently overwhelmed with love for the ranch, he'd realize that the boy had always been a cowboy at heart, and always would be.

Sadly, it was more than Wyatt could say for his own son.

"The way I see it," said Bobby, clearing his throat and, with an effort, marshaling control of his emotions, "we've got two choices. Either we keep going as we are, trying to make the cattle business work—"

"And go under," said Wyatt.

"And go under," agreed Bobby. "Or, we try something new."

"Hmmm." Wyatt decided to risk a little teasing. "This 'something new.' I don't suppose it would have anything to do with training Thoroughbreds, now would it?"

"Close." Bobby grinned. "But no cigar."

"Oh?" Wyatt looked suitably surprised.

"Quarter horses," Bobby explained.

"What about them?"

"Training, yes. But not Thoroughbreds. Quarter horses. They're the answer."

"To what?" said Wyatt. "Quit talking in riddles, wouldya? I'm too old for it."

Throwing him his reins, Bobby vaulted down onto the ground, pacing backward and forward and waving his arms around excitedly as he spoke.

"I've been thinking about this a lot. Ever since I got the news in France . . . about Dad." He pushed his hair back out of his eyes and looked at Wyatt directly. "And I've realized: I need to train horses. I need it, Wyatt. Like air, like water, like . . ." he struggled for the best way to put it. "It's not just what I do. It's who I am."

"I know that," said Wyatt gently. "We all understand, Bobby."

"Yeah, well, Dad didn't," said Bobby truthfully. "He never understood. He disapproved like hell, and that's the problem."

"What do you mean?"

"I could open a racehorse training stables here tomorrow," he said, turning back to look at the incredible view below them. "But I know I'd be kept awake at night by the sound of Dad spinning in his grave."

Wyatt chuckled.

"I'm serious," said Bobby. "I could never disrespect his memory like that. Whatever people around here might think of me, Wyatt, I couldn't. I couldn't do it."

Wyatt was silent. Bobby was a better son than Hank had been a father, that was for sure. His loyalty, even after death, to a man who'd never shown him an ounce of affection was touching.

"So that's why I figured quarter horses," he went on. "Okay, so it's not cattle. But quarter horse racing is a cowboy sport, right? No one, not even Dad, could say I was letting the family down or forgetting my roots by training quarter horses. And there's serious money in it these days too."

"I'm sure there is," said Wyatt. "But aren't you overlooking one key point here?"

Bobby looked blank.

"Money," said Wyatt. "We're *this* close to defaulting on our loans as it is." He held up his thumb and forefinger, indicating the tiny distance between their current situation and insolvency. "Where are you planning on getting the cash to start a training business, quarter horse or otherwise? Short of digging the place up for her oil . . ."

Bobby looked suitably horrified.

"Over my dead body!"

"Mine too," said Wyatt. "Mine too. But training facilities don't build themselves, Bobby. You haven't thought this through."

"Sure I have," said Bobby arrogantly. Taking back his reins, he climbed into the saddle for the second time, patting his pony on the neck and rubbing her ears joyfully as he did so. He was a big man these days, thought Wyatt, but around horses he still had the look of a lovesick ten-year-old.

"I'll finish my training commitments for the rest of the year, save up a little nest egg. I have a job in Florida coming up, then an eight-week stint in England. Lord someone or other's offered me a small fortune to work with two of his colts."

"That's great," said Wyatt, trying to sound enthusiastic. "But I still don't think you get it. Six months' wages isn't going to buy you a horse farm. Besides, we already owe whatever money you earn to the bank. That's what I've been trying to tell ya."

"Okay, so we'll find a partner then," said Bobby breezily. "An investor. Some of the owners I've trained for have more money than God. One of 'em'll back me. It'll be a cinch."

Wyatt fought down a gnawing sense of unease. The confidence of youth was all well and good, but it was a poor substitute for experience. In Bobby's mind, clearly, the fantasy of training cowboy horses at Highwood had already taken hold as the perfect compromise solution, allowing him to follow his dreams and stay true to his Cameron heritage. But bringing a stranger into the business was a huge step, and not one to be taken lightly.

"Look," he warned, "I'm not against the idea. And, like I say, you're the boss now. But I do think we should discuss it some more. Bringing an outside investor into Highwood exposes you to a whole bunch of risks. Partnerships can be tricky, Bobby. Things could go wrong."

"Things have already gone wrong," said Bobby bluntly. "We're broke."

Wyatt sighed. Unfortunately, he couldn't argue with that.

"Relax." Bobby grinned. "I may not be a cowboy legend like my father. But I do know horses. And I know I can make this work. Trust me."

"It's not a question of trust . . ." began Wyatt. But Bobby wasn't listening. He'd already nudged his horse in the ribs and was galloping back down the steep hill at breakneck speed, leaving his ranch manager nothing to talk to but a cloud of dust.

* * *

Back at Highwood, it was a veritable hive of commotion. Ranch hands were darting back and forth like worker ants from the cattle pens to the tractor barn, stables, and office, trying to get as much done as they could before the light faded completely.

Tara, the elder of the two McDonald daughters, was manning the phone in the cluttered former barn that served as the ranch office. It had been ringing off the hook all afternoon, mostly with angry or worried creditors wanting to speak to Wyatt, or would-be corporate investors seeking an appointment with Bobby. The Camerons may have vowed never to exploit Highwood for her oil reserves, but the rest of the world was not inclined to let the matter drop so easily. Hank's notorious stubbornness during his lifetime had put off all but the most foolhardy of prospecting companies. But the old man's death had opened a window of opportunity, and now every oil investor from Canada to Texas was trying to be the first to make the new boss of Highland an offer he couldn't refuse.

Seeing Bobby come in, Tara flashed him a harassed smile and gestured for him to sit while she got rid of her current, tenacious caller.

"I will pass it on to him, Mr. O'Mahoney. You have my word on that. No, I don't think there'd be any point in you calling back later tonight. We're not expecting him back till very late. Yes. Yes, I will ask him to call you in the morning. Uh-huh. First thing, I promise."

Putting down the receiver, she leaned back in her chair and ran her hands through her hair in exhaustion. "Holy shit, Bobby," she said, shaking her head. "You would not believe what it's been like in here today. The phone's been goin' crazy."

"I can imagine." He smiled.

She was two years younger than him and Dylan, but somehow Tara had always felt like his big sister. Less pretty and more solidly built than Summer, she was the sensible one of the family. Kind to the roots of her being, she was an optimist like her brother and had inherited the best qualities of both her parents—Maggie's cool temper and Wyatt's easy grace—combining them with her own naughty sense of humor. She might not be the sexiest girl in the world, but she was so much fun to be around that she was never short of boyfriends. Like everyone else at Highwood, Bobby adored her.

"Anything I need to do right away?" he asked.

She shook her head and passed him a neatly typed sheet of paper headed MESSAGES.

"I wrote the most important ones down. That guy at Wells Fargo called again for Dad."

Bobby flinched. Wyatt had just been telling him that the bank had been practically beating the door down since the day the funeral was announced. If they were looking for more repayments, they were shit out of luck, at least until he'd been paid for his work with Pascal Bremeau.

"Tell them they need to deal with me from now on," he said, pulling up a chair and putting both his feet up on the desk. Despite his misgivings and the problems they were facing, he was starting to realize there was also a positive side to being the boss. "And then tell them I'm unavailable. Indefinitely. Anything else?"

"Not really." She rubbed her eyes. It had been a long day. "Bunch of lawyers, bunch of oil companies." Bobby waved his hand impatiently as if swatting a fly. "Oh, and the guy called from the rodeo about that bull."

"Hell, I totally forgot about that," said Bobby. Most bulls ended up being slaughtered for low-quality cuts of beef, but every now and then Highwood would retire one of its most lively, aggressive males to the local rodeo, so some lunatic could risk life and limb trying to ride him. "Did they send someone to pick him up?"

"Dyl's out there now," said Tara with a grin. "It took him and Willy all afternoon to pen him, and now he's mad as hell."

Taking this as his cue, Bobby wandered back outside and across the yard to the cattle pens, where a small crowd of hands had gathered to watch Dylan struggle to drive two thousand pounds of angry, bovine muscle into a waiting cattle trailer.

Whoever ended up trying to ride this fella was going to have one hell of a fight on his hands. Dylan, his brow knitted in deep concentration, danced around the furious animal on horseback, trying to direct him to a gate that led first into a smaller pen and then into a narrow, wooden-fenced chute that would eventually channel him into the waiting trailer. So far, he was getting precisely nowhere.

"Come on now, big fella." He chuckled as the bull flared his nostrils ominously and lowered his head for another charge. "That's just bad manners."

For a boy whose only ambition in life was to become a painter, Dylan was cursed with being naturally brilliant at ranching. If Bobby was a genius at calming difficult horses, then he had the same gift with cattle. Totally fearless, he was astonishingly skilled as a hand, as sure and steady as he was fast at his work. On branding days, he'd been known to handle two calves a minute, holding and clamping each frightened animal as he swabbed them, wormed them, and finally white branded them with the distinctive, curled *HD* for Highwood on their left flank.

"Is that the best you can do?" yelled Bobby, earning himself a quick flip of the bird from Dyl. Though devoted, the two boys had always been competitive in everything. Bobby was trying to throw him off his stroke, but it wasn't going to work. If anything, his presence only served as added motivation.

Dylan's horse, an aging mare called Helena, knew exactly what she was doing when it came to herding stubborn cattle and could still turn on a dime in the pen, despite her advanced years. Easing her forward toward the bull's rear end, Dylan finally managed to nudge the vast animal through the gate and into the smaller pen, where Willy, a sprightly leprechaun of a man in his early forties, was waiting to close the gate behind him. A few seconds later the bull sauntered casually up into the trailer, with a look in his eye that seemed to imply that was exactly what he'd intended on doing all along, if only they'd all left him alone to get on with it.

Dylan turned triumphantly to Bobby. "You were saying?"

"All right, all right, I admit it." Bobby smiled. "You're good."

"Good?" Dylan raised his eyebrow in mock surprise. "How about brilliant?"

"Well, I wouldn't go that far," said Bobby. "Helena was brilliant." Reaching into his jeans pockets for a couple of the mare's favorite hard candies, he held them out to her in his open palm while Dylan dismounted. "She just took you along for the ride."

"Oh, that's right, go ahead." Dylan rolled his eyes. "Give the horse all the credit why don't ya."

It felt good to share a joke, and even better to get his feet out of the stirrups at last, knowing that he was finally done for the day. Since Hank's death, his father had been so distracted that Dylan's own workload had effectively doubled, leaving him even less time than usual for his beloved painting. He wouldn't mind, but he suspected that once Bobby disappeared off training again, things would only get worse. Wyatt would be bogged down with the finances, which meant even more of the day-to-day ranch management would fall to him.

"Long day?" asked Bobby, clocking the bags under his eyes.

"Long? Oh, sure." Dylan shrugged, trying not to look as depressed as he felt. "Aren't they always?"

"Wanna talk about it?" Despite the brave face, Bobby could read him like a book. He knew how trapped his friend felt at the ranch, unable to pursue his art, and he sympathized, although there was not much practical help he could offer. In the end it was only loyalty to Wyatt that kept Dyl here. And no one could argue with that, least of all Bobby.

"Nope," said Dylan. "Nothing to say, is there? Anyway"—he smiled again, his natural good humor reasserting itself—"enough about me. How was your day?"

"Fine," said Bobby. "I had a good talk with your dad."

Both boys had taken off their hats and carried them in their left hands now as they walked up toward the McDonalds' house. Bobby still had his room in the big house, across the far side of the ranch beyond the corrals, but it was so vast and echoingly empty, particularly now with his father gone, that he ate supper most evenings over at Dylan's. Dressed identically in dirty jeans and spurs, they still managed to look as different as chalk and cheese: Bobby with his long legs, loping gait, and hair as bright white-blond as a Swedish three-year-old's; and Dylan, solid, stocky, and dark, walking double time beside him just to keep up.

"If you crack us open a couple o' beers, I'll tell you all about it," said Bobby.

"Sounds good to me," yawned Dylan. He hoped, for all their sakes, that Bobby and Wyatt's "good talk" had resulted in the formulation of some sort of plan. Because right now, much as he might hate ranching, it was his entire family's livelihood. If Highwood went under, so did their home and his parents' pension, not to mention Summer's college fund.

All of their futures were in Bobby's hands now.

CHAPTER SIX

The weeks that followed the debs' ball fiasco were like hell on earth for Milly.

Cecil, who usually made it his policy to stay out of the all-too-frequent mother-daughter disputes at Newells, had for once backed Linda to the hilt when he heard what had happened in London.

"After all your mother's hard work," he told Milly reproachfully at breakfast the morning after the ball. "That was a terrible thing to do. Terrible."

"Well, it wouldn't have happened if you hadn't forced me to be a stupid deb in the first place," she snapped back, defensive because she knew she was in the wrong. "If I'd been riding at Epsom, instead of Mr. Muppet head here—"

"Change the record, Mill, before we all get a headache," said Jasper from behind his *Racing Post.* Having spent the night over at Rachel's, he'd rolled in at eight this morning, looking like the cat that got the cream, and proceeded to wax lyrical about his new girlfriend, deliberately rubbing his sister's nose in it. "You've not been on horseback in two years. How out of your depth do you think you'd have been in the Oaks, hmm?" Smiling smugly, he shamelessly trotted out the expression Dominic had chastised him with yesterday: "It was Epsom, for God's sake, not the Pony Club egg and spoon."

Though still sore about his performance and the public dressing-down he'd received from O'Reilly's trainer, his successful seduction of Rachel had left him on a high that nothing could spoil. After that first time in the trailer yesterday, they'd done it twice more, at her request: once on the backseat of his Range Rover on the way home, pulled over on the hard shoulder of the M11, and then again in her bedroom at

Mittlingsford, the Delaneys' exquisite Georgian rectory a couple of villages away from Newells.

Given that she was only eighteen—just a year older than Milly—Jasper was delighted to find that Rachel was incredibly precocious in bed, voracious almost to the point of nymphomania. Not only was her naked body even more magnificently voluptuous than he'd imagined—she had tits that made Pamela Anderson look like Kate Hudson—but she knew exactly what to do with it, contorting her lithe limbs into every possible position in pursuit of his pleasure and her own.

Sipping at his much-needed coffee this morning, a mental picture popped into his head of those fabulous, melonous breasts bouncing up and down in front of him, the hard candy-pink nipples brushing teasingly against his lips, and he soon found himself struggling to fight down yet another erection. By anyone's standards, Jasper had slept with a lot of women in his time—racing groupies were ten a penny in Newmarket—but Rachel Delaney was without doubt the best shag he'd ever had. And now he'd have her on tap, permanently.

How fucking fantastic was that?

And if pulling Rachel wasn't cause enough for celebration, he'd arrived home to find Milly being torn off a strip by Cecil for disgracing herself at the debs' ball. Well, well, well. So Daddy's golden girl had screwed up at last, had she?

How immensely gratifying.

Jasper hated Milly because she refused to take him seriously as a jockey and was constantly showing him up in public. Terminally pompous, he lacked any ability to laugh at himself, taking all her childish jibes as serious offenses against his dignity. He particularly disliked it when she criticized him in front of girls he was trying to impress. Never would he forget, or forgive, the time when she'd told Becca Davies, a gorgeous groom he'd been on the point of seducing last Christmas, that his nickname at Pony Club was Johnny Fart Pants. Mortifying! Even now the thought of it made him blush to the roots of his hair, something he hated doing because it spoiled his perfect complexion.

His father rarely lost an opportunity to remind him how wonderful his little sister was. It was always "Milly does this" and "Milly helped with that" and "why can't you be more like Milly?" But this morning, he felt like quite the prodigal son returned. The calf was being fattened for him for a change. And, boy, did it smell good.

Linda was adamant that Milly wasn't to be allowed near a horse for the next month, which meant that she would finally be out of his hair at the track. Better still, Cecil was talking about packing her off to some cookery and flower-arranging course in Cambridge during her month-long ban. For the tomboyish Milly, a whole month of feminine pursuits would be tantamount to torture.

As a punishment, Jasper thought gleefully, it was nothing short of inspired.

Ignoring his jibe about her riding, Milly turned back to her father. "Can't you give me some other punishment?" she pleaded. "It's crazy to ban me from the stud, Dad, you know it is. June is one of our busiest months. Who's going to help Pablo and Nancy if I'm not around? Jasper?"

Cecil sighed. The thought had occurred to him that J. would be a poor replacement for Milly during their busy time, but he was not about to admit it now. She'd gone too far this time. She had to be punished.

"We'll manage," he said firmly.

"Of course we will," said Jasper, bridling at the implication that he'd be about as welcome at the stud as a psychiatrist at a Scientology convention. "You're hardly irreplaceable, you know."

"Frankly, Milly," said Linda, through thin, furious lips, "I'm surprised you have the nerve to ask your father for anything after your disgraceful performance in London." Looking pale and tearful in her pink frilly dressing gown after a sleepless night, she'd walked in just in time to hear Milly trying to wangle her way around Cecil as usual. Well, it wasn't going to work. Not this time.

"Yes, really, Mill," chipped in Jasper with ill-concealed delight. "You could show poor Mummy a bit more respect."

Slumping back in her chair, Milly shot him a filthy look, but she knew better than to push it any further. Obviously no amount of begging was going to change either of her parents' minds.

The thought of a month away from her horses was worse even than the thought of Jasper and Rachel's new "romance"—and that was saying something. But what could she do? She'd well and truly burned her bridges this time. She'd just have to suck it up.

Two weeks after this depressing breakfast, she was enjoying a Sunday morning lie-in—her first since she'd had to start getting up at seven to catch the bus into Cambridge for her eight-fifteen start at the horrific Madeleine Howard Home Skills course—when she was woken by a deafening crash from outside her window.

Bolting out of bed, she saw Radar, one of her father's newer stallions, staggering backward against the side of his trailer, mucus pouring from his nose, his knees shaking and spasming grotesquely while Cecil and Nancy struggled to prop him up.

"Mill, get down here!" shouted Cecil, catching sight of his bleary-eyed daughter at the window. "We need some help."

Thrusting her bare feet into a pair of trainers, she was downstairs like a shot and running out into the yard, still in her pajamas.

"Stand here, where I am," panted Nancy. Her thin blond hair was stuck to her forehead and cheeks with the sweat from her exertions. Although strong for her size, the vet was only five foot three, and trying to hold up an animal the size of Radar was no joke. "Push your shoulder as hard as you can into his side," she said. "I'll run and get his shots."

Milly obeyed wordlessly, bracing herself against the frightened animal with all her strength. She could see her dad grimacing with effort at the stallion's rear quarters, and tried to shoulder as much of the fourteen-hundred-pound weight as she could to help him.

"Has he done this before?" she asked.

"Twice," Cecil panted. His face was beet red already, and he was sweating like a gladiator in a heat wave. Her dad has always been a bit overweight, but now Milly noticed he was looking worryingly out of shape. "Nancy's run every test in the book. Other than a slightly raised temperature, we can't find anything physically wrong with him. It's strange, but it only seems to happen when he gets sight of a trailer. Almost like a mental trigger."

"Maybe he's scared. A bad memory or something from when he was younger?"

"Maybe," grunted Cecil. "But short of getting him a horse shrink, I don't know what the fuck to do about it."

The horse continued shaking uncontrollably, his eyes wide and wild with terror. After what seemed like an age, Nancy came running out from the house with her battered leather vet's bag and pulled out a long silver syringe. Filling it with clear liquid from a 30-cc vial, she emptied the whole thing into his neck. Within a few seconds, his tremors slowed and then eventually stopped. Father and daughter gingerly released their pressure and stepped back. He was still unsteady on his legs and swaying a little bit, but he was standing on his own.

"All right. Take him back to the barn," said Cecil, nodding at Nancy. "He's clearly not fit to travel, is he?"

She shook her head, leading the bewildered Radar away and leaving her boss and his daughter leaning, winded with exertion, against the aluminum trailer.

"Thanks," said Cecil with a small smile at Milly. The two of them had barely been on speaking terms since the whole debs' ball disaster, and he was as glad as she was to finally be breaking the ice. "I don't know what happened to Davey and Pablo. Or your brother for that matter. He was supposed to be helping me out here this morning. It's a good job you were around or God knows what we'd have done."

"Where were you taking him?" asked Milly.

"Cedarbrook Farm," said Cecil. It was another, rival stud about twenty miles north of Newells. "Anne Voss-Menzies is thinking of buying him." He shook his head, disappointed. "Or was thinking of buying him, I should say. I'll have to tell her what happened and that we're not coming. Come on." He put his arm around her and started back toward the kitchen. For all their battles over her riding, he adored his daughter and had been almost as miserable these past two weeks as she had, watching her set off into Cambridge every morning. "Let's give the old dragon a ring and then I'll make you some brekka."

The Lockwood Groveses' kitchen was part family gathering place and part farm office. Piles of stud-related paperwork littered the old oak table, and yellowing copies of the *Racing Post* could be found cluttering up the window seat and most of the available space on the sideboards that wasn't taken up with Linda's recipe books or jars of exotic spices. Milly's mother was an exceptional cook—yet another feminine skill her daughter had failed to inherit. Cecil was only ever allowed near Linda's beloved cobalt-blue Aga if he was making one of his famous Sunday fry-ups.

Milly watched him as, battered old portable phone glued to his ear, he set about one-handedly scrambling a bowl of eggs while placating a difficult Anne Voss-Menzies. She smiled, remembering the fateful Sunday morning when her granny Mellon, Linda's prissy and persnickety mother, had picked up what she'd thought was a jar of egg whites and poured it into a bowl for whisking only for a horrified Cecil to come in and announce that she'd just contaminated a semen sample worth twenty thousand pounds from one of his premier stallions. It was the last time Granny Mellon ever made breakfast at Newells—or so much as looked at a plate of scrambled eggs.

"Silly old bat," said Cecil, hanging up and pouring the eggs into a pan of melted butter. The indomitable Mrs. Voss-Menzies was not an easy woman at the best of times and had been furious about Radar's setback this morning. "She gave me a right ear bashing. It's not my fault if the horse won't travel."

"Are you disappointed?" asked Milly, cutting two industrial-sized slabs of fresh granary bread to go with the eggs and opening the cupboard for plates.

"Nah." He grinned at her. "I never really wanted to sell him anyway. His first crop of foals weren't fabulous, but I still think, you know, with the right mares . . ."

Milly loved the way her dad always loyally blamed the mares if any of his stallions' offspring proved disappointing.

"Anyway, love, how are things with you?" Pouring the steaming eggs onto two plates, he ground on some fresh pepper before setting them down with a flourish and sitting down to join her. "How's it going at Madeleine Howard?"

Milly rolled her eyes to heaven. "Terrible," she said, through a mouthful of egg and bread. "Can't you do something? Ask Mum to back off? I mean, it's really awful, Dad. The flower-arranging classes are enough to make you lose the will to live."

Cecil shrugged, biting hungrily into his breakfast. "It's your own fault."

"I know," she said. "But come on, Dad, flower arranging? It's bad enough that you won't let me ride, but now you've got me sticking bloody petunias in vases and laying out place mats! I mean, *hello?* This is not eighteen fifty. Queen Victoria is *not* still on the throne."

Cecil laughed at her indignation and the cynical, questioning upward intonation that all the teenagers seemed to be afflicted with these days, the result of a constant TV diet of American sitcoms and Aussie soaps. She drove him up the wall at times, particularly where her riding was concerned, but he couldn't help but admire her tenacity. He himself wasn't one to give up on a challenge easily—but Milly never gave up at all.

He also adored her seventeen-year-old's knack of having an answer for absolutely everything.

"You really upset your mother, you know," he persisted. "That ball meant the world to her. And she did it for you."

"I know," said Milly. "I understand Mummy being angry. But that course is torture, it really is. And I haven't been anywhere near a horse for fifteen *days*."

She gave the word the same emphasis that a newly jailed prisoner might give the word "years." Perhaps she *had* been punished enough? Sitting opposite him, her hair still a tangled mess from bed and wearing an old, shrunken pair of his stripy blue pajamas, she looked about twelve. Cecil could feel his resolve melting.

He thought briefly about Jasper. If only his son would show even half Milly's dedication to the stud. The boy was almost twenty-five, but he still behaved as if the world owed him a living. He was supposed to have been at the yard at eight this morning, to help get Radar ready to travel. But instead he'd disappeared off to some party or other with the Delaney girl, and Cecil hadn't seen hide nor hair of him since. His bed had clearly not been slept in.

"Look," he said to Milly, who was still gazing across at him with her big pleading eyes. "I'm not making any promises. But I'll have a word with your mother about this Madeleine Howard course. The fact is, with J. away racing so much between now and October, I *could* use some extra help around the yard."

Milly's face lit up like a camera flash.

"Just temporarily," Cecil covered himself hastily.

"Of course." She nodded furiously. With her father on her side, her mother was bound to come around eventually. "I understand."

"Michael Delaney's about to fly some specialist trainer over from California, to work with those new colts he bought back in April," Cecil went on. "You remember?"

Milly nodded. She never forgot a horse.

"Apparently Lady D.'s flatly refused to put the fellow up," said Cecil. "Some bollocks about having the builders in at Mittlingsford or something. Anyway, the long and the short of it is, I offered to have him stay here. Which is fine, except that it means I'll have to spend some time playing the gracious host, so we'll be even more short-handed than usual at the yard."

"Oooo." Milly raised an eyebrow. "Specialist trainer, eh? Victor won't be very happy about that." Victor Reed was Sir Michael Delaney's trainer, who spent four days a week working his horses up at the Newells gallops.

"No," said Cecil, unable to suppress a smile. He had never been particularly fond of the strutting, self-important Reed. "He won't be. And actually nor am I. I've got better things to do than babysit some bloody Yank for Michael. But it can't be helped. So I could use having you around, as long as your mother's agreeable . . ."

"Oh yay, hallelujah!" squealed Milly, jumping to her feet and flinging herself onto his lap, wrapping her arms around him like a little girl.

"I told you, I'm not promising anything," said Cecil, trying to look stern but not succeeding remotely.

"I know," said Milly sweetly, with all the gracious diplomacy of a child who knows the battle is already won. "Just as long as you talk to Mummy. That's all I ask."

Bobby squatted down lower on his haunches to examine the filly's fetlock more closely. "It's not good," he said, shaking his head.

He was in Florida, at the Palm Beach estate of the billionaire paper magnate and racehorse owner Randy Kravitz. Randy had hired him to work with the beautiful young horse whose leg now rested in Bobby's hand. But if he'd realized how badly injured she was, he would never have come.

In the stable with him was the filly's ever-attentive groom, looking sick with nerves, and Sean O'Flannagan. An outrageous, hard-partying Irishman a few years Bobby's senior, Sean also happened to be one of the most respected horse vets on the West Coast and one of Bobby's few real friends on the racing circuit.

"Stand back, would you?" he asked Bobby, who complied. "Let me take another look."

Pacing up and down the pristine, air-conditioned stable, Sean inspected the horse's injury again from every conceivable angle.

"I'm telling you, it was barbed woire," he asserted for the third time. "There's no doubt in my mind."

Like Bobby, Sean had a reputation for arrogance, although he tempered it with so much charm that people tended to be more forgiving than they were of his friend.

"Bullshit," retorted the furious groom. "You can keep on sayin' it, but it's not gettin' any more true. She hasn't been out of my sight for the last three days. And even if she had, there is no wire at Manley Falls. This isn't some goddamn ramshackle joint in County Kildare, buddy."

While the two men glared at each other, Bobby stepped forward again and ran his hand gingerly along the length of the wound. He felt the filly start a little, but she seemed to know she was being helped and refrained from lashing out at him in her obvious pain.

"Whatever it is, it's deep," he said quietly. "I don't think she should be putting any weight on it for the next three weeks at least. Sean?"

Sean grimaced. It was a tricky one.

He'd come along today only as a favor to Bobby. He was in town on a trip with his boss, Jimmy Price, one of the few owners even wealthier than Kravitz. If Jimmy found out he was moonlighting for his competitor, he'd have him fired faster than you could say breach of contract. Randy had promised to keep quiet about today's visit, and had also paid him a small fortune for his opinion, which had gone some way toward easing Sean's nerves. But it was still a tough call.

On the one hand, the cut was undeniably deep. But on the other, Kravitz clearly wanted the horse declared fit for the upcoming Kentucky Oaks, the fillies' version of the Derby. He'd flown Bobby in especially to prepare her for it. If Sean ruled her out now, he was basically flushing hundreds of thousands of dollars worth of the guy's investment down the toilet.

"I don't know," he said, shaking his head. "If we poultice it and rest her completely this week, then bring in the physio next week, there's a chance she could still make it."

"Of course she can make it!" snapped the groom. "It's a fuckin' scratch, for God's sake. Give me a break, you guys."

Bobby straightened up and shrugged his shoulders. There was no way that horse should race. But at the end of the day it wasn't his problem or his reponsibility. He felt sorry for her groom, who would almost certainly be fired, despite his protestations of innocence and due care. It must be heartbreaking after so many months of work. But there was nothing he could do about it.

"Your call," he said to Sean, reaching for his Stetson and placing it back on top of his blond head. "But I'm not training her. I'll let Kravitz know tonight."

He walked out into the pristine stable yard, leaving Sean and the groom to fight it out between themselves. Leaning forward, he stretched out his sore neck till it gave a nice, satisfying crack. He was disappointed. He'd been looking forward to training this filly for weeks now. The stallions he'd been working with in Dubai for the past two weeks had been nothing to write home about—although he'd been paid top dollar for his efforts and was certainly grateful for the money.

Looking around him, he wondered how much Kravitz had spent on this place in the last decade. Twenty million? Maybe thirty? Manley Falls, named after a camping resort in Montana where Kravitz used to spend his summers as a kid, was the kind of farm that more modest owners fantasized about owning one day. It had none of the natural beauty or grace of a ranch like Highwood. The whole place was designed to be as efficiently functional as possible, with temperature-controlled stables and barns; flat, floodlit paddocks; and long stretches of immaculately maintained gallops, shaded from the punishing Florida sun by carefully planted lines of palms. With its serried rows of white-washed, clinical-looking outbuildings, it reminded Bobby more of a factory than a horse farm. But still, it was impressive.

And whatever they were doing at Manley Falls, it was working. Kravitz had trained two Kentucky Derby winners here, as well as winners of the Dewhurst, the Aga Khan, and the National Stakes in Europe. He was an owner to be reckoned with; to be invited to work with one of his horses was a rare privilege, and Bobby knew it.

"I'm giving her another day," said Sean, wandering into the yard to join him.

"Waste of time," said Bobby dismissively. "She'll never make the Oaks and you know it. She's in pain."

"Not as much pain as I'll be in if Jimmy finds out I was here today," said Sean with a grin, pulling a finger across his throat like an imaginary knife and making melodramatic gurgling noises.

Bobby laughed. He'd known Sean for years and they'd always gotten on well, although the Irishman was far more hardheaded than he was when it came to horses. At the end of the day, Sean believed a racehorse was an investment, not a pet. His job was to get his animals up and running, not to mollycoddle them.

Bobby called him a heartless bastard. Sean called Bobby a sentimental fool. But beneath the insults, they both respected each other's expertise and professionalism.

"Anyway, enough about work," said Sean, changing the subject. "I take it you're still planning to stick around for the party tonight?"

One of Palm Beach's biggest polo patrons was throwing a huge bash that evening and all the staff from Manley Falls had been invited. Most of them had been in a frenzy of excitement about it for the past three weeks. Sean, having only just gotten into town, was not invited—but he had every intention of tagging along with Bobby anyway. The girls in Palm Beach were always spectacular, and there was no way he was going to miss out.

"Of course," drawled Bobby. He'd been so distracted and depressed by all the problems back at Highwood since his dad's death, it was about time he allowed himself a little fun. "If you ask me very nicely," he added with a grin, "I may even leave a couple of girls free for you."

"Ha!" said Sean. "As if you stand a chance against the mighty OLM."

"OLM?" said Bobby.

"O'Flannagan Love Machine," said Sean, with a James Bondesque lift of the eyebrow that made Bobby roar with laughter.

"Love Machine" might be pushing it, but with his jet-black, curly hair, soulful gray eyes, and knicker-droppingly gorgeous Irish accent, Sean had always had a way with the ladies to rival Bobby's. Though only five foot eight, what he lacked in height he more than made up for in blarney, and his reputation as an animal in bed preceded him across California and beyond.

"You do realize you're delusional?" said Bobby.

They'd crossed the yard now to where Sean had parked his hired bright-red BMW. Chucking his vet's bag onto the passenger seat, he climbed in behind the wheel.

"We'll see," he said. "A hundred bucks says I score some action before you do."

"Oh, please!" said Bobby. "You're on. Just make sure you're here by seven," he yelled over the roaring revs of the engine, "or I'm leaving without you."

By the time seven o'clock rolled around and they were on their way, Bobby's earlier enthusiasm was already waning.

Kravitz had been less than pleased when he'd announced he couldn't train his filly and that he would be leaving in the morning. Their difficult conversation had put a damper on his spirits, and though the lure of the girls was still strong, after a late afternoon siesta he'd woken to find himself feeling unaccountably tired and low.

Perhaps the stress he'd been under since Hank's death was finally catching up with him? Whatever, the thought of having to make cocktail party small talk with a bunch of Floridian polo nuts suddenly seemed about as much fun as as eyeball acupuncture.

"Cheer up, for God's sake," said Sean, taking another corner on the coast road at spine-tingling speed. "It's a party we're going to, not a focking wake."

"Sorry," said Bobby. "I'm just distracted, I guess."

"Dreaming about your quarter horses at Highwood, are you?" said Sean. "Well, you never know, you might meet a potential investor tonight."

"I doubt it," said Bobby. "Most polo patrons wouldn't know a quarter horse from a Quarter Pounder."

Sean laughed. "Well, that's true," he admitted. "But the women out here are loaded. Land yourself a rich wife in Palm Beach, my friend, and you can buy as many quarter horses as you like. Ship 'em back to California on a private jet!"

"It's a thought," said Bobby.

"And if not," said Sean philosophically, "you can just get laid and enjoy yourself, can't you? It's what they call a win-win situation."

"I dunno," said Bobby gloomily. "I'm not really in the mood."

"*Not in the mood?*" Sean looked incredulous. "Jaysus, what's wrong with you? Oh, lord. You're not gay or something, are you?"

"No," said Bobby indignantly, "I am not *gay*, thanks for asking. My God! Just because I occasionally have an impulse that does not originate from my pants."

"Ah, but that's not natural, now is it?" said Sean, apparently without irony. "Have you slept with any girls since you've been here? Any at all?"

"Sean. It's been two days."

"Exactly!" He sounded triumphant, as though Bobby had just proved

84

his point. "So quit your whining like an old woman, would you? This is going to be fun. Remember fun?"

Dimly, thought Bobby.

When they walked into the party twenty minutes later, every female head turned to gawp at them. Both wearing formal black blazers and both deeply tanned, Bobby from two weeks in Dubai and Sean from his long season's work in California, they cut figures every bit as fine as those of the handsome Argentine polo players who usually got top billing among the women at Palm Beach social events. They also had the advantage of being new blood—although a surprising number of girls seemed to recognize Sean.

A particularly brazen blonde, her enormous breasts squeezed into a black Gucci corset dress, accosted him the moment they walked through the door.

"You bastard."

"Dana." Sean didn't miss a beat. "Lovely to see you too. Have you met my friend Bobby?"

"How come you never called?" She pouted. "Two weeks I waited, and not a peep out of you, O'Flannagan."

She sounded angry, but Bobby couldn't help but notice an incipient smile playing at the corners of her mouth. A few seconds later and she had her arm wrapped around Sean's waist in a manner that could only be interpreted as flirtatious. Perhaps OLM wasn't so wide of the mark after all?

"Oh, but I did, sweetheart, I did," Sean protested, utterly unconvincingly. "Didn't you get my messages? Anyway, don't be angry. Meet Bobby. He's a cowboy."

"A cowboy, eh?" said the girl, turning her attention in Bobby's direction, blatantly checking out his powerful arms and torso, like a buyer at Keeneland giving the once-over to a new horse. "Interesting," she purred. "So what brings you to Palm Beach, cowboy? You lost?"

"No," said Bobby without even a hint of a smile. Flirtation bored him. He couldn't see the point. Anyway, he already knew he didn't want to fuck this girl. He wasn't a big breasts man, and the rest of her was nothing to write home about. "I'm working."

"Hmmm. Friendly," she said sarcastically. "But you." She turned back to Sean. "You come find me later, okay? Maybe you took my number down wrong. I might give it to you again if you ask me nicely."

Bobby watched as she brushed her hand against the bulge in his friend's pants before winding her way back through the crowd to join her girlfriends, her backside jiggling in the tight black confines of her dress as she did so.

"Well," said Sean, once she'd gone. "I reckon you owe me a hundred bucks. That's a dead cert, right there."

Bobby didn't argue.

"Why were you so rude to her, anyway? It's not much of a bet if you don't even try."

"Not my type," he said simply, reaching out to relieve a passing waitress of a flute of champagne. "Besides, it was you she wanted."

"Only 'cause you gave her the brush-off," said Sean. "What did she have to do, strip you naked and pin you to a bed?"

An image of Chantal Bremeau, her long dark hair spilling down over her perfect, high brown breasts, suddenly popped into Bobby's head. It was disturbingly arousing.

"No." He smiled to himself, savoring the memory. "I don't like aggressive women, as it happens. Not usually, anyway."

"Suit yourself," said Sean. "All the more for me, I suppose." And with that he disappeared into the heaving throng, like a one-man, pussy-seeking missile.

Looking around, Bobby tried to get the measure of the other guests. It was an eclectic bunch: everyone from low-paid Hispanic grooms to billionaire playboy polo patrons milled around the lavish Moroccan pool and spa, trying their luck with the various scantily clad women, most of them the wives or girlfriends of the Palm Beach horse fraternity but one or two of them players in their own right. Carlo Walger, the dashing ten-handicap hero of Argentine polo, was apparently engrossed in conversation with his patron's stunning twenty-two-year-old wife, Brandi, although judging by his eye contact her breasts seemed to be doing most of the talking. Elsewhere, Bobby noticed, a number of famous flat race jockeys had turned up to compete with the polo crowd.

Rising star Connor Hargreaves was propping up the bar, looking even more deeply tanned than usual after his recent triumphant visit to Dubai, riding for Sheikh Mohammed.

Next to him was Barty Llewellyn, a trainer from one of the big Kentucky farms whose horses Bobby had worked with for a month last summer. Barty was one of the few trainers self-assured enough in his own talent to have actually welcomed Bobby's help, and the two of them had always gotten on well.

"Hey, look who it isn't!" he said, catching sight of Bobby as he battled toward him through the crowd. "Bobby Cameron, as I live and breathe. How the hell are you, kiddo? And what brings you to this den of iniquity?"

Barty was in his early sixties, a tall, wiry, urbane guy with closely cropped gray hair and a natty line in beautifully tailored linen suits. He'd never married and it was generally assumed that he was gay, although no one could ever recall him being romantically involved with anybody, male or female. Like so many at the top of his profession, Barty's whole life was his horses. He used to tell Bobby they were like his children. Having watched him in action in the training ring, Bobby had no trouble believing it.

"I'm good," he said. "I came out a couple of days ago for a job."

"Oh?" said Barty.

"One of Kravitz's fillies," said Bobby, lowering his voice, "but between you and me, the horse isn't up to it. I'm flying back home tomorrow. No point sticking around."

"So it's true then?" A hugely fat man with a hideous bouffant helmet of red hair combed forward over his forehead like Donald Trump, and an unlit cigar clamped Al Capone style between his teeth, interrupted them. "I'd heard a rumor that horse was lame. But it's nice to have it confirmed."

"Hello, Jimmy," said Barty. "Bobby, may I introduce Mr. Jimmy Price. Jimmy, this is Bobby Cameron, a friend of mine."

Reluctantly, Bobby extended his hand. He knew who Price was, of course, though they'd never met. Quite apart from the fact he was Sean's boss, the man was a legend in California racing circles. A newspaper mogul with a well-documented ruthless streak—he had left his first wife all but penniless after a bitter divorce, eventually driving the poor woman to suicide—he also had the Midas touch when it came to buying horses. Unusually for an owner, he didn't restrict himself to Thoroughbreds and had dabbled successfully in polo and quarter horse racing as well. Jockeys tended to fawn over him, hoping to be sponsored by the man who had launched so many racing careers, Connor Hargreaves's among them. With his vast wealth, stellar horses, and unrivaled clout in the press, Jimmy Price's patronage was enough to boost his chosen mentees' profiles into the media stratosphere.

Nevertheless, Bobby wasn't a fan. He himself might be a womanizer, but he would never deliberately set out to hurt anyone, the way Jimmy had his ex-wife. The guy evidently believed that if you had enough money, you could buy your way out of the rules that applied to other, lesser mortals—decency and loyalty among them. Somewhere along the road to success, Price had had a complete compassion bypass. And Bobby had no time for that.

"Do you always eavesdrop on other people's conversations, Mr. Price?" he asked frostily.

If Jimmy was fazed by his bluntness he didn't show it. Instead, he responded in kind. "Sure." He shrugged. "If they're interesting enough. If you don't want people to listen to you, kid, my advice is to keep your mouth shut. Especially when it involves your boss's horses. If you'd been working for me, I'd've fired your ass for loose lips like that."

Bobby's upper lip gave an involuntary curl of distaste as he watched Jimmy pick up a vol au vent with his fat, sausagelike fingers and dispatch it to its doom in the dark wet recesses of his mouth. Even the way he chewed was objectionable. How could Sean stand working for him?

"Kravitz is not my boss," he said haughtily. "I work for myself. And, believe me, it'll be a cold day in hell, Mr. Price, before I'll ever work for you."

Barty laughed nervously. He'd always liked the Cameron kid, but at times he could be his own worst enemy. Jimmy Price was not the sort of man you wanted to make an enemy of, particularly if you lived in California and had ambitions in the racing world.

"I was sorry to hear about your father," Barty said, hastily changing the subject.

"Thanks," said Bobby. Under other circumstances he'd have liked to open up to Barty about his apparent inability to grieve for Hank and the problems he was facing at Highwood. Beneath that dapper, wry exterior, Barty was a kind, sensitive man, and Bobby felt instinctively that he'd have understood. But he was damned if he was going to show an iota of vulnerability in front of Jimmy Price. He'd only known the man for about twenty seconds, but every one of his prejudices and preconceptions about him had already been confirmed.

Reaching into his jacket pocket he pulled out one of the new business cards that Tara had had made up for him while he was in France and handed it to Barty. "I'm flying out to England in the next couple of days," he said. "But we should talk when I'm back. These are my numbers."

Barty nodded, pocketing the card.

"I'll be completely snowed at the ranch till Christmas, so I'm not sure when I could get out to Kentucky . . ."

"The ranch?" Jimmy's ears had suddenly pricked up. "You a breeder, son?"

"Bobby's from an old cowboy family," explained Barty. "His father, God rest him, passed away a few weeks ago, so my man here is taking over the family cattle ranch. One of the most beautiful properties on the West Coast, so I've heard."

Bobby tipped his hat in gratitude for the compliment.

"A cowboy?" sneered Jimmy, lighting his cigar and ostentatiously blowing a puff of smoke right into Bobby's face. "You're kidding me, right? Like, cattle drives and corrals and all that shit? You still do that?"

Bobby felt his knuckles tightening. Who the hell did this asshole think he was?

"Yes, Mr. Price, I do." His tone was ice-cold. "Why? Do you find that funny?"

It was one thing for him or Dylan to complain about ranching and how much more there was to life than raising cattle. But for an outsider like Price to disrespect the cowboy culture, that was something else entirely.

Jimmy noticed Bobby's aggression, but he wasn't a man to be easily intimidated. Taking a long, slow lungful of smoke, he blasted it out through his nose like a dragon before replying.

"I guess I find it quaint. You don't expect to meet many cowboys out here in Palm Beach, do you, Bart? Unless of course you count the real estate developers!"

He threw his blubbery head back and laughed at this, unashamedly impressed with his own brilliant wit, his fat jowls shaking like Jabba the Hutt.

"I'll call you," said Barty. He'd sensibly stepped forward, inserting himself between the two men before, heaven forbid, they should come to blows. "As soon as you're back from Merry Olde, okay?"

"Yeah," said Bobby, backing away but allowing himself one more scowl at Price before he left. "Do that."

A couple of minutes later and Sean had reappeared at his side out of nowhere, like a drunk Irish genie of the lamp. He had two girls with him, one on each arm, both of whom looked Argentine. That almost certainly meant they were here with polo players; which meant they were strictly off-limits for anyone who didn't want to be beaten to a pulp by their jealous husbands before daybreak tomorrow.

"What was all that about with Jimmy?" he asked nervously. "You didn't let the cat out of the bag about me being at Kravitz's, did you?"

"No," said Bobby tersely. "I almost took a pop at him though. The guy's a jerk. Makes my flesh crawl. How can you stand to work for him?"

"If you'd seen his horses, you wouldn't need to ask me that question," said Sean, ever the pragmatist. "I'd work for Adolf Hitler if he had stables like Jimmy."

"You don't mean that," said Bobby.

"Oh, I'm afraid I do," said Sean. "But enough about my prostituting my talents. You must meet my friends. Maria, Conchita"—he turned to the two Latin lovelies beside him—"this is my good friend Bobby Cameron." The girls nodded and smiled. Clearly neither of them spoke a word of English. "I'm afraid Bobby suffers from a very serious

90

case of principles. He only works for the good guys, you see. He's actually been diagnosed torminally morally uproight. Isn't that roight, Bobby?"

Before he had a chance to clip Sean around the ear, Bobby found his arms full of nubile Argentine woman. One of the girls, taking Sean's speech as her cue to introduce herself, had bounded into his embrace like an affection-starved Labrador.

"Pleased to meet you." He laughed. He noticed that her friend had thrust one red-taloned hand quite blatantly down Sean's pants and was rummaging around down there now, in full view of all the other, passing guests. "Not shy, are you?"

Allowing himself to be smothered with kisses, he had almost forgotten his annoying encounter with Jimmy Price, and was finally starting to enjoy himself when he felt a tap on his shoulder.

"Husbands, to your left, forty-five degrees," Sean hissed.

Spinning around, Bobby caught sight of two Argies, both built like brick shithouses, advancing menacingly toward them.

"Sorry, sweetheart," he said, disentangling himself from the girl and making a somewhat undignified bolt for the door. "Gotta run."

Crouched down behind Sean's BMW a few minutes later, gasping for breath, both boys waited in the shadows until the irate polo players finally gave up the chase and went back inside.

"Fuck, that was close!" said Bobby, laughing now that the danger was past. "How much steak do those sons of bitches eat? The one on the left looked like a sumo wrestler."

"Soch a shame, too," Sean sighed. "Gorgeous girls, those two, and up for anything. We could have shared them."

In the darkness, Bobby's eyes widened. "Nice thought," he said, "but I'll leave the gang bangs to you. One girl at a time is more than enough for me."

Sean shook his head ruefully. "You need to start broadening your horizons, Dorothy," he said. "You're not in Kansas anymore."

Bobby chuckled, brushing the dust off his sleeves. He tried to imagine what his father or Wyatt or any of the hands back home would have thought of the idea of four-in-a-bed sex with other people's wives—but it was literally beyond imagining. Things like that simply didn't happen in the Santa Ynez valley.

"No, I guess I'm not," he said. Helping Sean to his feet, a wave of tiredness washed over him. Suddenly he felt fit to drop. "And sorry to disappoint you." He yawned. "But the only bed I want right now is my own."

CHAPTER SEVEN

Jasper sat scowling in the passenger seat of his father's dark blue Range Rover, halfheartedly rearranging his hair in the rearview mirror. He'd recently taken to growing his fringe out longer and gelling it into semi-rigid spikes, boy-band style. Most of the girls who hung around the jockeys' changing rooms seemed to dig the new look. But ever since Rachel had told him two nights ago during sex that it looked like a hedgehog had crawled onto his head and died there, he'd started to feel a bit self-conscious about it.

He and Cecil were on their way to Heathrow to pick up Michael Delaney's much-hyped Californian trainer, their soon-to-be houseguest.

"I don't see what's so special about this bloke anyway," he complained bitterly for the third time in as many hours. He resented the fact that his dad had dragged him all the way out to the airport just to do a meet and greet. Bobby bloody Cameron was already becoming a right royal pain in the arse. Rachel had been boring him to tears for weeks about how brilliant the guy was supposed to be with horses. As if he gave a shit!

"Truthfully, Jasper," said Cecil, "nor do I." Pulling back out into the fast lane, he overtook the filthy, fume-belching lorry in front of them. "Michael's already got one of the best trainers in the country, and all his colts have performed well this season. Why he thinks he needs to fly John Wayne over, I have no idea. But the bottom line is, we make a lot of money from Delaney's stallions. It won't kill us to put the lad up for a few weeks."

"Hmmm. Well, I think it's damned cheek," grumbled Jasper. "I haven't got time to babysit some fucking self-styled horse whisperer mid-season. He's bound to get under our feet around the yard, isn't he?

Fannying about with his lasso up at the gallops, or whatever it is he does."

Cecil bristled silently. Under *our* feet? That was a joke. The only time J. showed his face around the yard was if he needed money or wanted Cecil to pull even more strings with his clients to try to get him rides. He'd even had the nerve to make a fuss this morning about coming along to Heathrow. As if he had anything better to do.

"Well, let's give the fellow a chance, shall we?" was all he actually said. "If he's as good as Michael says, you might actually learn something from him. Let's face it, your performance hasn't been as good as it could be lately."

"Learn something? I doubt it," said Jasper with breathtaking arrogance, re-forming his spiky fringe in the mirror for a fourth and final time and pouting at his improved reflection. "I'm not interested in making lonesome treks across the open plain, am I? I'm interested in winning races. I don't see how some jumped-up, mustang-riding cowboy from hicksville is going to help me do that. Do you?"

Back at Newells, Linda was busy preparing the Sunday welcome roast for their illustrious new houseguest. (In her eyes, Bobby was illustrious by association, as indeed was anyone connected with Sir Michael and Lady Delaney, however loosely.)

Milly had come in from the stallion barn with only muted complaints, anxious to keep on her mother's good side since their uneasy truce had been reached. She was upstairs now, making up the guest bed with fresh sheets and putting the best matching blue towels in the bathroom.

With an inward wince of shame, she noticed the strategically positioned pictures of her parents meeting the Queen at Ascot, and the Queen Mother at Goodwood, shoved right to the front of the dresser. Her mother must have moved them from the drawing room, to make absolutely sure that these two snapshots of social triumph would not be overlooked by their American guest.

And, oh God, what was *that* doing there?

Shuddering with horror, Milly removed the black-and-white picture of herself as one of the chorus in last year's ADC carol concert and shut it in a bedside drawer. The camera had captured her in a truly vile peach velvet dress, mouth wide, belting out "Once in Royal David's City." If she were to have any chance at all of getting this hotshot trainer to see her potential as a jockey, she didn't want that to be the first image he had of her.

Ever since her dad had told her that Bobby would be staying with them, a plan of sorts had begun forming in Milly's mind. Cecil had as good as admitted that he didn't have time to spend babysitting the American. So it should be the easiest thing in the world for her to assume the role of hostess, out at the stables, anyway. Which would mean plenty of unsupervised time with both her father's and Delaney's horses. She could acquaint Bobby with Sir Michael's colts, smooth things over between him and Victor, and generally make herself useful—in return for which, she hoped, he would turn a blind eye to her riding and perhaps even agree to give her some secret training sessions. If he thought she was good enough, of course.

But he would. She'd make sure he would.

Perhaps an outsider could succeed where she had failed and convince her father that it was safe for her to ride?

She'd finally made the decision—to take the forbidden step and defy her parents' ban—about ten days ago. Arriving home exhausted from her hated flower arranging course, she'd walked into the kitchen to find Rachel Delaney sitting in *her* favorite chair, chatting away chummily to *her* mother about the day she'd spent riding *her* horses. Milly would never forget the look of spiteful triumph in Rachel's eyes that day—a look that seemed to say: Face it, Milly, you've lost. I've got everything you've ever wanted. Even your own mother loves me! And there's nothing you can do about it.

Well, she was damned if she was just going to roll over and take it. If Rachel wanted war, she could have it. Milly was going to ride again, and she was going to ride the pants off that bitch too. Somehow.

All she needed was an opportunity. And Bobby Cameron's visit, she'd decided, might be just the thing to provide it.

Having finished making up the bed, she began carefully arranging the assortment of lilies and white roses that Linda had brought back from the flower shop in Newmarket. After two miserable weeks at Madeleine Howard Home Skills, she at least knew better than to plonk them willy-nilly into a vase.

"Oh, Mill, those look lovely." Linda had come upstairs to check on her progress, and beamed when she saw the flowers. Happily she had failed to notice the missing picture. "And so does the room. Thank you, darling. Now I think you'd better go and get changed." She glanced at her watch. "Dad called me from the M11 about five minutes ago, so I'm expecting them back fairly soon."

"Changed?" Milly frowned. She'd been hoping to get back out to the barn and check on Easy before lunch. "Can't I just wear this?"

"Absolutely not," said Linda, giving a little shudder at her daughter's grimy jodhpurs and shapeless, graying T-shirt. "Go and change. And do try to find something vaguely feminine."

For fuck's sake, thought Milly a few minutes later, rummaging through her messy drawers for something clean to put on. As if Bobby Cameron was going to give a shit whether she looked "feminine" or not. Grudgingly she washed her face with soap and water and rubbed in some of the moisturizer her mother had bought her. She drew the line at makeup, but she did at least brush her hair, tying it back neatly in a ponytail, and sprayed some Penhaligon's Victorian Posy on her neck and wrists.

No way in the world was she wearing a dress. It was bad enough having to do it for parties, but she wasn't about to start at home too. Still, she didn't want to antagonize her mother too much at such a crucial juncture. Gritting her teeth, she plumped for a compromise option of white Top Shop trousers and the flowery blue shirt from Ralph Lauren that Cecil had bought her two birthdays ago and which she had never yet worn (it still had its price label attached). Biting through the plastic tag, she ripped it off and, without bothering to undo the buttons, pulled the offending garment on over her head.

A few minutes later and a cacophony of barking from Cain and Abel, the Lockwood Groveses' two ancient, arthritic Jack Russells, announced that the airport welcoming committee had returned.

Linda had already opened the front door and was kissing the tall, blond figure of their new guest on both cheeks when Milly appeared at the top of the stairs.

"Bobby, this is my daughter, Millicent," she said, stepping aside so that the two of them could see each other.

Milly stood frozen at the top of the stairs like a statue, her fingers locked around the banister rail. It wasn't like her to be shy or to pay much attention to members of the opposite sex. But for once she found herself wishing fervently that she'd worn something sexier or put on some makeup. At the very least, she should have washed her hair! Because standing below her was, without doubt, the most handsome, exquisite-looking man she had ever laid eyes on. And here she was, dolled up like a poster girl for the Women's Institute, complete with huge flowery bosom and shiny cheeks. Why did these things always happen to her?

"Hello, Millicent." Stepping toward the foot of the stairs, Bobby extended his hand, his big, open smile flashing up at her like a beacon.

She knew from Jasper, who knew from Rachel, that Bobby was twenty-three. That was only three years older than poor little Harry Lyon. But the Adonis in front of her seemed far, far older than that: a real, grown-up man. Suddenly the whole idea of winning him over as an ally against her father seemed far-fetched and ridiculous. Childish, even. And Milly realized in that instant that the last thing she wanted this man to see her as was a child.

"It's Milly, actually," she stammered. She wanted to sweep downstairs with all the poise and elegance of Grace Kelly, but her lower body seemed to have developed a mind of its own and remained stubbornly rooted to the spot. "Everyone calls me Milly."

"I'm Bobby." Oh, that smile again! "Pleased to meet you."

"Yes. Very good. Hello. Excellent." To her horror, the words came spilling out of her mouth at random. She sounded like one of those awful, pull-string talking dolls she'd had as a girl. Feeling her cheeks burning, she prayed she wasn't blushing quite as violently as she imagined.

Bobby smiled inwardly. The poor kid looked terrified. And she'd obviously gotten dressed in the dark. Cecil had told him in the car that he had a horse-crazy seventeen-year-old daughter, but this girl looked much younger.

"Shall we go through for lunch?" trilled Linda brightly. "You must be famished, Bobby." She seemed oblivious of the trouble Milly was having putting one foot in front of the other as she staggered downstairs to join them. "Jasper can show you up to your room afterward."

"And then I can give you a tour of the stud. If you're up to it, of course," said Cecil.

"Sure," said Bobby. "That'd be great. Something smells absolutely delicious."

"Thank you." Linda flushed at the compliment like a schoolgirl. Apparently Milly wasn't the only one to have fallen for Bobby's charms. "I only hope it tastes as good as it smells. You can never be sure with lamb."

Offering Bobby her arm, she led him through into the dining room. "Shall we?"

Lunch was, predictably, delicious, although Bobby found he was too tired to muster much of an appetite. In any case, he was a lot more interested in figuring out his hosts than in the food.

He'd be in England for six weeks, the longest he'd ever spent on a single job. The thought of not seeing his beloved Highwood again till mid-fall was keeping him awake nights, but he'd have been crazy not to take the obscene amount of money Sir Michael Delaney was offering. Wyatt would have hit the roof if he'd turned the job down. Besides, he'd heard amazing things about Newells Farm from some of the Kentucky breeders. The chance to stay there and check out Lockwood Groves's horses for himself was too good to pass up.

Cecil seemed like a good guy. He had a certain brusqueness to him that reminded Bobby of his own father, but, unlike Hank, Cecil tempered his plain speaking with a tangible warmth. On the long drive back from the airport he'd been friendly and funny and avuncular, going out of his way to put Bobby at his ease. He could talk naturally and for hours about his horses, and had clearly forgotten more about their bloodlines than most breeders ever knew in the first place. And he was polite, too, something Bobby had been raised to value very highly but found he encountered less and less the farther he traveled away from Highwood with its strict cowboy code of courtesy.

Cecil's son, on the other hand, was a card-carrying jerk. As sullen and moody as a teenage girl with PMS, Jasper had made no effort whatsoever to hide his dislike of Bobby from the moment he stepped off the plane. Used to hostility and resentment from trainers, Bobby couldn't figure why this small-time British jockey with the ridiculous haircut should feel so threatened by him. But threatened he clearly was. The only time the guy had broken off his pout-a-thon to speak on the journey home was to boast about his own prowess in the saddle, which made him come across as both boorish and insecure. He seemed to know absolutely nothing about his own father's stallions, odd for an only son who was set to inherit the stud. All in all he was a spoiled, self-absorbed pain in the ass.

"Jasper, darling. More potatoes?" Linda leaned across the table, proffering the steaming bowl of Jersey Royals like a peace offering, as though it were her fault her son was in such a gruesome mood.

Hmm. No doubt about it. There was some serious oedipal shit going down there. Obviously Jasper was the apple of Mommy's eye.

But it was the poor, neglected daughter who interested him most. At first he thought she was going to be too shy to say anything. Every time he glanced at her she blushed like an overripe tomato, poor thing. But as soon as the conversation turned to her father's stallions, she was like a different person. Shaking off her gaucheness like a phoenix rising from the flames, she displayed a knowledge of each animal's bloodlines, offspring, track performance, health, and training regimen that was positively encyclopedic. He was impressed.

"I'm taking a wild guess here, Milly, and assumin' you ride a little yourself?" he commented, after listening to her catalog the running problems of one of Sir Michael's new colts in minute detail. Evidently her knowledge of horseflesh did not stop at her father's animals.

"Actually, no," said Jasper snidely. "These days Milly's interest in horses is purely academic. Isn't it, Mill?"

Bobby noticed the thunderous look she shot her brother and wondered what sort of family minefield he'd inadvertently wandered into.

"These days?" He raised a questioning eyebrow at Milly, but this time it was her father who answered for her. Did no one ever let this girl speak?

"Milly's a wonderful horsewoman," said Cecil, choosing his words carefully. "But she had to give up her riding for medical reasons."

"Made-up reasons," Milly muttered under her breath, just loud enough for Bobby to hear and flash her a grin that turned her insides to goo and sent the color rocketing up her cheeks yet again.

Deciding to ignore her, Cecil went on. "Racing's loss has become Newells's gain, though," he said. "My daughter's an invaluable asset at the stud."

"I can imagine," said Bobby.

Milly felt her heart give a little leap of delight. He likes me! He actually likes me!

"Jasper rides professionally," interjected Linda, offering Bobby some more sautéed courgette. "He rode in the Oaks at Epsom last month, didn't you, darling?" she couldn't resist adding.

"Oh really?" Bobby's ears pricked up. "That's impressive. How'd you do?"

A small vein at Jasper's forehead had begun twitching and his upper lip gave an involuntary curl. He could have shot his mother.

"Badly," said Milly triumphantly. "He came in ninth. Out of ten."

Ah, thought Bobby. Not shy then. Just squashed. Evidently there was no love lost between brother and sister. He already knew whose side he was on.

"His horse was terribly overtrained." Linda leaped instantly to Jasper's defense. "He actually rode very well."

Milly spluttered so hard with laughter at this that she choked on her red wine.

"Milly. Make yourself useful and start clearing away the plates," snapped Linda.

Mortified that she'd just sprayed a mouthful of wine all over herself in front of the gorgeous Bobby, Milly was only too happy to have an excuse to leave the table. Gathering up the plates in a flash she bolted out into the kitchen to clean herself up.

She wondered if she'd have time to nip back up to her bedroom and put on some makeup? At least tone down her raging, reddened cheeks before pudding . . .

Once she'd gone, Bobby turned back to Cecil, his curiosity piqued.

"These 'medical reasons,'" he said. "Is it something serious?"

Cecil frowned, and Bobby instantly regretted having pushed the point. "She had an accident," he said brusquely. "A long time ago. But it's all in the past now. Milly's perfectly happy."

Right. And I'm the queen of Sheba, thought Bobby.

"You know what teenage girls are like," chipped in Linda. "Terribly easily bored. Any day now it'll be out with the horses and in with the chaps!"

Milly, who had walked back in just in time to hear this toe-curling pronouncement from her mother, almost dropped the stack of china pudding bowls she was carrying.

"I'll never be bored of horses!" she said vehemently. "Never! And I'm not at all into boys, Mummy, you know I'm not."

"Really?" said Jasper cruelly. "Because that looks an awful lot like face powder on your nose. What did you do, slap it on with a trowel?"

"I don't know what you're talking about," she snapped back at him, keeping her dignity even through her blushes and setting the bowls down on the table in front of Linda's steaming apple and blackberry crumble. "Your hair gel must have seeped through your scalp and given you brain damage."

Bobby chuckled and for the briefest of moments caught Milly's eye.

Oh please, please, God, Milly prayed silently, let him be as nice as he seems. And if it's too much to ask that he should fancy me, then can we at least be friends?

If he backed her up with her father the way he already had with Jasper, he might just turn out to be her savior after all.

Later that afternoon, once Bobby had unpacked, Cecil took him off for an extensive tour of the farm. It was still August, but the weather seemed to have decided that autumn was already upon them. It hadn't stopped raining all day, although this morning's torrential downpour had now been replaced by a steady, gray drizzle that blew like a fine mist into their faces as they walked.

"I'm impressed," said Bobby, as he was led from the stables to the stallion barn and breeding shed, then up the hill in Cecil's shabby old farm truck to the gallops and the huge, indoor training ring. "I hadn't realized you operated on such a grand scale. This place reminds me of Overbrook."

Cecil laughed. "Well, I wouldn't go that far." Overbrook was one of the biggest, most prestigious stud farms in Kentucky. "But we're not as much of a backwater as most Americans seem to think."

"So you're what, half stud, half training stables?" said Bobby, gazing in awe at two exquisitely lithe chestnut geldings being put through their paces on the slippery grass of the gallops by their respective stable lads.

"No, no," said Cecil firmly. "We're a stud. That's the core business, always has been. I got a racing permit a few years ago, just for fun mind you, and I train a few of my own horses on the side. But that's as far as it goes."

"Oh." Bobby looked surprised. "So, none of your clients train here then?"

"Well, not officially," said Cecil with a wink. "But let's say certain close friends might unofficially use the facilities from time to time."

"Like Delaney, you mean?"

"Sometimes," said Cecil. "Yeah, Michael's been a very loyal client, so I'm happy to accommodate him. Victor Reed, his trainer, works up at our gallops four days a week."

"What's Victor like?" Bobby tried to make it sound like a casual inquiry. In fact he was desperate to find out as much as he could about the famously prickly Victor before their first meeting tomorrow.

"Truthfully?" said Cecil. "He's a total wanker."

Normally he would be far too professional to let his guard down and speak so candidly in front of one of his clients' employees. But something about Bobby seemed to invite confidences, and he found himself talking more freely than he'd intended.

"Is that so?" Bobby nodded thoughtfully. He was disappointed but not surprised. Just what he needed, another resentful trainer to contend with.

Suddenly he felt cold, wet, and overwhelmingly tired as the full force of his jet lag started to hit him.

"Cheer up," said Cecil. He hoped he hadn't scared the poor boy off. "You'll be all right. I'm sure you've worked with tougher customers than old Victor."

"Yeah," said Bobby, thinking of the tyrannical Henri Duval. "I'm sure I have."

Climbing gratefully into the dry warmth of the truck, they drove back to the house.

"Ah, there you are," said Linda, swooping down on them as they walked into the kitchen and helping them both out of their wet coats. "Cecil, what have you been doing to the poor boy? He looks done in. Milly, show Bobby up to his room, would you? And make sure he has everything he needs."

Bobby looked up and saw Cecil's daughter, deep in the latest issue of the *Racing Post*, warming her back against the Aga. She'd changed into an old pair of cords and a V-necked sweater, a distinct improvement on that flowery effort she'd been wearing earlier. She actually had quite a decent figure in a petite, almost boyish sort of way.

"Hmmm?" Tearing herself reluctantly away from the piece on the Oaks, Milly did a double take when she caught him staring at her. She'd been so engrossed, she hadn't heard him come in. Suddenly she had no idea what to do with her hands and found herself dropping the paper in a fluster. "Sorry, Mum, what did you say?"

"Our guest, darling." Linda sighed wearily. "Could you take him upstairs?"

"That's okay," said Bobby. "I know where I'm going."

"No!" said Milly rather louder and more urgently than she'd intended. Both her parents looked at her oddly. "I mean, that's all right," she explained, blushing. "I can take him. I can take you."

Looking at Bobby, she risked a small smile, which he returned. She was a nice kid, this one.

Up in the guest room, she made a monumental effort to stay cool as she showed him around. "The shower's a bit dodgy, but if you leave it for five minutes the water will get hot," she said, staring resolutely at her shoes whenever she spoke to him. "And the towels are on the bed, and if you need more hangers there are plenty in Jasper's room, also soap and stuff like that, if you need it, I can always get some more. . . ."

"I'm fine," said Bobby, laying a hand on her shoulder to stop the flow of nervous chatter. "Thanks."

Milly froze, too overwhelmed at being touched by him to move, let alone speak. Even after he removed his hand she couldn't seem to regain her composure.

"Perhaps tomorrow," he said, "you can talk me through the problems these colts have been having? Your father tells me you know them better than anyone else. If you're not too busy, that is?"

Milly nodded mutely. It was the best she could do.

"Great," said Bobby. "Well, er . . . I'll see you later, then?" He raised an amused eyebrow as she still failed to move. He decided to spell it out. "I kinda need some sleep now."

"Oh!" said Milly, coming to her senses at last like a tortoise stumbling out of hibernation. "Of course. Sorry. I'll leave you to it."

Bolting out of the room, she shut the door behind her and was halfway down the corridor before embarrassment finally gave way to elation.

She was going to spend the day with him tomorrow! He'd asked her for help with the colts. She hadn't had to do anything!

Skipping into her own room, she climbed up onto the chair and ripped down her posters of Robbie Pemberton and Frankie Dettori. Who needed posters when she had a living, breathing fantasy sleeping right down the hall? Then she got her under-sixteens eventing cup down from the shelf above the bed and clasped it to her chest, spinning around and around till she felt dizzy.

Jasper and Rachel could be as hateful, and her parents as stubborn, as they liked.

She was going to ride again. That was all that mattered.

And beautiful Bobby Cameron was going to help her.

CHAPTER EIGHT

"All right, now back, back, back!" Bobby yelled into the echoing emptiness of the indoor school, holding on to his hat with one hand while waving the other at a blissfully oblivious Milly as she cantered past him. "Lean back!"

It was three weeks since he'd first shown up at Newells, and already she could barely remember the time before he came. "I'm going to call it BC," she'd told him gleefully, the night after their first training session together. "Before Cameron." After all her scheming and hoping, winning him over as an ally and mentor had been far easier than she'd expected. Winning his love, sadly, was proving a lot more complicated. But for now his friendship, and the sheer delight of riding again, were enough to put her in a state of semi-permanent ecstasy.

"Hell, girl." He shook his head in exasperation. "What part of the word 'back' do you not understand?" Thundering over to him on Elijah, one of her father's most valuable colts, she was standing high in the stirrups, knees up, her upper body jutting so far forward over the horse's ears she looked as though she might topple off him at any moment.

"What?" she said, her face a picture of wronged innocence as she reluctantly dismounted. "I was only giving him a bit of encouragement. How can I talk to him or tell him what a good boy he is if I'm not allowed near his ears?"

Bobby tried not to smile, but it was impossible. She reminded him so much of himself at her age, it was frightening. At first he'd been annoyed by the way she followed him around like a shadow. Every morning like clockwork, she was up at the school before he was, brushing the horses, polishing tack, even making coffee for him and Victor. He'd done his best to put her off politely—the last thing he needed when training was some bright-eyed, bushy-tailed kid distracting him. Finally he'd resorted to his usual, blunter tactics and told her in no uncertain terms to get the hell out from under his feet.

But Milly had steadfastly ignored him, popping back up like one of those candles you can't blow out, always cheerful, always there. And in the end, he had to admit she made herself useful. No job was too menial, or too demanding, and both her knowledge and natural instincts around Delaney's colts made her handy to have around.

For the first time ever, he'd met someone whose bond with horses rivaled his own. And she was single-minded too—stubborn as a mule, in fact—a trait he had always admired. The more time they spent together, and the more he got to know her, the more sympathy he felt for her situation.

Silently, he'd watched the bitchy way that Sir Michael's daughter treated her: Rachel had also taken to hanging around the yard like a bad smell since he'd arrived, prancing around in her sexed-up riding gear trying to get his attention and make Jasper jealous. Even worse was the way that both of Milly's parents stifled their daughter's ambitions—this whole riding ban, once Milly had explained it to him, was as crazy and unnecessary as it was cruel. And as for that horrific brother of hers, there was nothing wrong with that asshole that a good horsewhipping couldn't fix.

He'd had his misgivings at first when she'd asked for his help. Her father was, after all, his host, and he'd hit the roof if he knew Milly was riding and that he, Bobby, was complicit in it. But after she'd persuaded him to watch her in the saddle just once, all his doubts evaporated.

She was good. Better than good. In fact, considering that she hadn't ridden at all in two years, she was phenomenal. What struck him most though was how good she was over short distances. Like Jasper, she was an aggressive rider. But unlike him she wasn't aggressive *toward* her mount. Instead, she allowed her infectious competitiveness and fearlessness to push horses to the absolute limit of their endurance, turning in some quite astonishing times on short, flat sprints.

It was kinda ironic, for an English breeder's daughter. But Milly was, in fact, a natural quarter horse racer. What had Cecil been think-ing, to squander a talent like that?

For the first time since Hank's death, Bobby found himself focusing on something other than Highwood and his own problems. In a funny way, it was kind of a relief.

"I'll ride him back to the yard," he said, lengthening Elijah's stirrups by about a foot before vaulting up into the saddle himself. "You'd better stay here and help Pablo rub down Kingdom." Keys to the Kingdom was the trickier of Delaney's two colts, and the one they'd been working with the most in the last couple of days. "Oh, and I need you to finish filing Victor's training notes before tomorrow. I'm going to Jonny Dav-enport's party tonight, so I won't have time."

"Okay," said Milly, her face falling. Desperate to please him in any way she could, she never complained when Bobby palmed work off onto her. It was the thought of him disappearing off to yet another party that upset her.

Having always thought of the English as standoffish and reserved, no one was more surprised than Bobby by the warm reception he'd re-ceived among Newmarket's hostesses. No one, except possibly Jasper, whose fury at the way the cowboy wonder had steamed in on his terri-tory knew no bounds.

"The guy thinks he's God's gift," he complained endlessly to Rachel and anyone else who would listen. "All that 'yes, ma'am-ing' and calling everybody 'sir.' And that ridiculous Clint Eastwood hat he wears around the yard He's so *faux*, he makes me want to throw up."

But his irritation was as nothing compared to the anguish suffered by poor Milly. Watching Bobby head off to parties night after night, knowing that every predatory racing groupie in Newmarket would be throwing herself at him, made her want to weep with frustration. Worst of all were the nights when he'd bring a girl home. Lying awake in her single bed, teeth grinding with misery, she would try to block out the sound of drunken giggling, followed by the hideous click of his bed-room door that always plunged her aching heart into an even deeper abyss of despair.

Couldn't he see how much she loved him? And how much better she'd be for him than the awful sluts he brought back to the house?

With each passing day her love for him grew like an out-of-control weed. But the affection he had for her remained steadfastly of the paternal variety. She'd tried everything to get him to notice her sexually, even investing six weeks' worth of her allowance on a pair of skintight, Rachel Delaneyesque jodhpurs to wear to their secret training sessions. But he hadn't paid a blind bit of notice. Sometimes she thought she could turn up naked, like Lady Godiva, and all he'd do would be to bleat on about form and how she needed to lean back more in the saddle. His indifference drove her crazy.

The only faint silver lining to the depressing cloud of her unrequited obsession was that he seemed equally oblivious to Rachel's charms as to her own. Jasper was too vain and self-satisfied even to register the outrageous way that his girlfriend flirted with Bobby, but to everyone else it was painfully obvious.

When Milly had asked him, with her heart in her mouth, what he thought of Rachel, he'd replied with the three immortal words: "a bit desperate."

Just when she'd thought she couldn't possibly love him any more.

One Sunday evening, a few days after her training session with Elijah, Milly walked into the drawing room to find Bobby alone, staring into the dying embers of the afternoon's fire.

"Penny for them?"

"Hmmm?"

He looked up, startled, but smiled when he saw it was her.

Not usually a big drinker, he'd been to a cocktail party at a famous jockey's bachelor pad yesterday and had rather more tequila shots than he'd intended. Suitably loosened up, he'd been persuaded to spend the latter part of the night in the back of a trailer with a very friendly young lady named Deborah—an enjoyable experience, certainly, but one that he was paying dearly for today.

So far England had been a blast, way more fun than he'd expected—

even Sean O'Flannagan would have been proud of his pulling rate since he'd gotten here—but today he found himself in a melancholy mood. With an epic hangover and more aches and pains than a losing prizefighter, his mind had begun to turn back to the ranch and all the problems awaiting him at home. Milly's training, and the progress he'd been making with Sir Michael's colts, had distracted him for weeks now. But much as he might like to, he couldn't put Highwood's problems off forever.

"Sorry," he said, "I was miles away. Back home, actually. Thinking about the future."

Milly frowned. Coming from Bobby, "future" had become a dirty word, reminding her as it did that he would soon be leaving Newells, and her, forever. On the other hand, she loved it when he talked to her about his life back in America. Knowing he never spoke about these things to anyone else at Newells, it made her feel special to be the one he confided in.

Curling her legs beneath her on the worn leather sofa, she artfully leaned forward just a little, so that a hint of cleavage peeped out beneath the undone top buttons of her new Miss Selfridge peasant blouse. Despite everything, she still hadn't given up hope that he would wake up one morning and realize that she was, in fact, a woman.

"The future? You mean your plans for the ranch?" she asked tentatively. "The quarter horses?"

A glow of excitement spread over Bobby's features, making him look even more ridiculously handsome, if that were possible. He was wearing faded jeans today and an old green T-shirt that clung to his biceps like shrink-wrap. Despite the shadows under his eyes and day's growth of dark-blond stubble, he still looked as beautiful as a Michelangelo sculpture, with those hypnotic hazel eyes that could make Milly crumple from twenty paces.

Picking up one of Linda's overstuffed pink cushions, he chucked it over to the other side of the room and sat down beside her, his physical proximity making her organs liquefy with longing.

"Quarter horses are so damn beautiful," he said, warming to his theme, knowing that in Milly he'd found the world's most receptive audience. "You'd be amazed. I swear, they're the smartest, finest, most versatile horses you've ever laid eyes on."

He was so close, the urge to touch him, to reach out and stroke the rough shadow of stubble along his jaw, was almost overwhelming.

"Did I tell you that the whole breed, all of 'em, are descended from just *one* Thoroughbred chestnut?" said Bobby.

"No," lied Milly, who never tired of hearing him talk. He'd already told her the story of Janus at least twice, but she didn't care.

"A planter named Mordecai Booth brought this stallion, Janus, over to Virginia from England," he began again. "Started breeding him to quarter racing stock. That's what started it all."

He brought his face even closer, till she felt the warmth of his breath against her cheeks. Oh, God, she loved him so much, she couldn't bear it. How come he could talk to her like this, share his passions, his hopes, and his dreams, but not share himself?

Agonizingly conscious of her chest heaving under the peasant blouse, she wondered if men could smell one's desire the way that stallions could and prayed fervently that they couldn't.

"Of course, most Thoroughbred trainers reckon themselves 'above' quarter horses," Bobby went on, apparently unaware of the turmoil he'd plunged her into. "But those guys are just idiots."

He shook his head incredulously at the thought of such philistinism, and Milly shook hers too, desperate not to be tarred with the same brush as those other Thoroughbred snobs.

"Of course they are," she said, showing admirable passion for someone who, until a few weeks ago, had never heard of quarter horses. "Complete idiots."

"But what they don't realize," Bobby insisted, "is that there's really a lot of money in it. And I mean a *lot* of money. The All American Futurity—that's kinda like the Derby for quarter horses—has a purse of over two million dollars. Two million! Imagine? If only we weren't in so much debt and I could start training at Highwood right away . . . I could make a fortune, I know I could."

Overcome with excitement, he seized her hand. Milly could have sworn her heart stopped in that instant. It was with some difficulty that she regained enough composure to speak.

"You're so lucky," she sighed, eventually. "You get to train horses, to do what you love, and no one can stop you."

"Well, not quite," he said, releasing her hand at last to her great disappointment. "I know it might seem that way, but I have a lot of responsibility too. I have to get Highwood out of the financial shit before I can do anything."

"Yeah, whatever," said Milly gloomily. "But you will, won't you, in the end?"

"I hope so," said Bobby.

"And then you can train. But I bet you'll still be stuck in Newmarket, not riding. Probably *married* or something, if Mummy gets her way."

She said the word with such disgust, it made him laugh out loud.

"Would that be so bad?"

"Yes!" she said fervently. "Of course it would." Then, belatedly realizing the implication of what she was saying, she started to backtrack: "Well, I mean, I suppose it depends. You know, on the boy. I mean, the man." She blushed furiously. "But not riding would be awful anyway. You know it would."

Bobby stood up and turned away from her, back to the fire. He didn't know what it was about Milly—how she managed to make him feel sympathetic and guilty and responsible all at once—but he couldn't shake the niggling feeling that he really ought to do something to help her. Even with his father's death and the problems at Highwood weighing heavy on his mind, somehow this girl—with her determination and her spirit and her sheer single-mindedness that reminded him so much of himself—tugged at his heartstrings harder than anyone had a right to.

A long minute of silence ensued, during which Milly tortured herself wondering if she'd said something wrong and if so, how she might undo the imaginary damage.

"I could train you," Bobby said at last.

She looked at him blankly for a moment, before managing a strangled, "What?"

"You could come back to California with me," he said, as though it were the most obvious, normal suggestion in the world. "You'd work on the ranch in return for room and board. And evenings and weekends, when I'm not traveling, I'll train you. I'll train you to race quarter horses."

Now it was Milly's turn to laugh. "Yeah, right," she said. "And I'll get there on a magic carpet by clicking my heels together three times and saying, 'There's no place like Highwood,' right?"

It was only when he didn't laugh back that she realized he was serious.

"But, Bobby, my parents," she said. "They'd never agree. Would they? I mean—of course they wouldn't." She mustn't allow herself to hope. "Why would they agree?"

Bobby shrugged. "Because it makes sense? Because deep down, your dad knows he's in the wrong about your riding? Hell, I don't know. But we won't know for sure unless we ask them, will we?"

He was torn. Maybe he shouldn't be getting the kid's hopes up? After all, there was every chance that Cecil would tell him to take a hike. He'd probably be furious that he'd allowed Milly to ride with him in secret these past few weeks. He might even kick him out of the house. Even if he didn't, letting his overprotected seventeen-year-old daughter fly to the other side of the world was a lot to ask of a man who'd already showed himself to be terrified about her welfare.

But he had to do something, if only to let Milly know that she did have a talent worth fighting for. He knew better than most what it was like to have your father stand in the way of your talent. If he didn't stick up for her, now, while he had the chance, who else was going to do it?

"What do you think?" he said. "Is it worth a shot?"

What did she think? Jesus. What would a starving refugee think if you offered him a bowl of soup? What would Michael Jackson think if he landed a job in a nursery school? It was too good to be true, that was what she thought. To be living and working with Bobby, in California? To escape from the claustrophobic nightmare of her life at Newells, from Jasper and Rachel, from her mother and the Newmarket ADC? To be trained properly, professionally trained as a jockey, even if it was with horses she'd never heard of?

She felt like shouting from the rooftops. He'd really do this? For her?

But reality crushed the fantasy almost before it had begun.

"It's a lovely idea," she sighed. "But it won't work. Even if you talked my father around, Mummy will never let me go. Not in a million years."

"You might be right," he said, "but let me talk to Cecil anyway. You've nothing to lose, after all." He was right there. "And even if they do say no, I want you to promise me you won't lose faith in yourself. You're a terrific jockey, Milly. Ultimately no one can decide your future but you. You know that, right?"

At that moment, all she knew was that she would never, ever love anybody a zillionth as much as she loved him. Standing in front of her, so tall and strong and reassuring, she could almost believe that he would make Cecil see sense, that he would be able to rescue her like some white-chargered prince showing up at the foot of her tower.

If only life worked like that.

"Absolutely not."

Slamming the door of the stallion barn behind him, Cecil stalked off toward his car. It was three days after Bobby's conversation with Milly, and he'd finally found the right moment to raise the subject of taking her back to Highwood with her father. So far, their little chat wasn't going too well.

"But why not?" Bobby pursued him. "Keeping her here makes no sense, sir. I'd take good care of her."

"What, by putting her back up on horseback where she could risk her neck?" Retrieving a half-smoked cigar from his pocket, Cecil relit it as they walked on. "I don't think so, sunshine. If I wanted her to ride, I'd have her do it here. But I don't, as you well know."

The roar of fury he'd emitted when Bobby confessed to his secret training sessions with Milly could be heard echoing halfway around Cambridgeshire, but Bobby had taken his life in his hands and floated the idea of her coming out to Highwood anyway. Having pissed his host off this much, he might as well see the thing through.

Angry as he was, Cecil admired the boy's tenacity, and Milly's. How long had she been cooking up this little scheme? he wondered.

"Look, Bobby," he said, relenting slightly, "I appreciate what you're

113

trying to do. I know you and Mill have been getting on well, and she clearly adores you."

"This isn't about me liking her, sir," said Bobby truthfully, "although of course I do. She's a great kid."

"She is." Cecil nodded and billowed out a cloud of acrid cigar smoke in agreement.

"It's about her being a potentially world-class rider. Believe me, I've worked with some topflight jockeys in my time. Milly's got what it takes. I'm certain of it. Given a little tweaking her technique would be perfect for quarter horses. She could be the next Joe Badilla, Jr."

"I'm sorry, Bobby, but I'm not so certain," said Cecil, frowning. He had no idea who Joe Badilla was, nor was he in any hurry to find out. "She hasn't ridden for two years—at least I bloody well hope she hasn't. She can't be that good."

"She is, sir," said Bobby flatly. "Watch her."

Cecil felt his anger bubbling up again. He didn't want to "watch her." Nor did he take kindly to being lectured by a womanizing American trainer he'd only known for five minutes on what was or wasn't best for his daughter. He liked Bobby. But this was going too far.

"What makes you so concerned about Milly, anyway?" he asked, his eyes narrowing. "Are you quite sure your interest is purely professional?"

Bobby threw his shoulders back and gave a short, arrogant laugh that would have crushed Milly had she heard it. "If you're implying what I think you're implying," he said, "you're way off. I may be many things, Mr. Lockwood Groves, but I'm not a pedophile."

"Hmmm." Cecil sounded unconvinced. "Well, anyway, I'm afraid it's out of the question. And your little sessions up at the school have got to stop as well."

Climbing into his Range Rover, he slammed the door shut with what he hoped was unmistakable finality. But Bobby wasn't through yet. He'd promised the kid he'd do his best to help her, and he had to try.

"She's not happy here," he said, thrusting his head through the open passenger window. "And I think you know it. Stevie Wonder can see that she can ride the pants off her brother, but she never gets the chance to show what she can do. Hell, if your wife had her way, Milly wouldn't even get to help out at the stud; even though she's brilliant with your stallions, better than any of you give her credit for."

"All right, that's enough," said Cecil with a face like thunder. "Where the hell do you get off criticizing Linda? Do I have to remind you that you're a guest in this house?"

Bobby stepped back from the car. For the first time, he felt slightly chastened. He'd given it his best shot, but he obviously wasn't going to talk Cecil into it.

"Look, I'm sorry," he said. "I don't mean to be rude. It's just that . . ."

"Well, you *were* rude," said Cecil furiously. "This is none of your business. You had no right getting involved in the first place."

Watching him speed out of the driveway, churning up gravel like angry machine-gun fire, Bobby was surprised to find himself feeling intense disappointment.

He really didn't know why he cared so much about Milly. But he did. The thought of her talent being left to wither away on the vine was just plain wrong—it bothered him more than it ought to.

But his disappointment was nothing compared to hers.

"It's okay," she said bravely when he caught up with her later and told her how the talk with Cecil had gone. She was in Easy's stable—he'd been off his feed earlier in the day and she wanted to check up on him—and was making a valiant effort to sound cheerful. "I knew he wouldn't go for it. I appreciate you trying, really."

But she couldn't fully hide the tears in her eyes, and Bobby saw the way her shoulders shook when she buried her face in the horse's neck, trying to comfort herself the same way that he did when things went wrong.

Poor little thing.

He should never have gotten her hopes up.

"Maybe he'll come around?" he said. "Maybe he just needs time to get used to the idea?" But the words sounded hollow, even to himself. They both knew that Cecil wouldn't budge, however much time they gave him.

"Maybe," said Milly despondently. "At least he wasn't too mad about the sessions we've already had."

"Yeah." Bobby tried to remain upbeat. "That's something, right?"

Despite her best efforts, a single, fat tear began rolling down Milly's cheek.

"Aw, shit," he said. "C'mon now. Don't cry." Not knowing what else to do, he walked over and, pulling her gently away from Easy, enveloped her in a hug.

Burrowing into his chest, Milly breathed in the smell and warmth of him and dried her tears on his shirt, all the while trying desperately to lock the memory into her brain forever. He was holding her! He was actually holding her! But, at the same time, she knew he might never hold her again. Soon he would be gone, back to America, and all her hopes of riding again would be getting on that plane with him.

Before he came she wouldn't have thought it possible to feel such crushing disappointment and such intense joy at the same time. That must be what all those love songs were referring to: about love being confusing and painful even though it was wonderful. She'd never understood them before, but now she did. That was exactly the way she felt with Bobby. It was love, it had to be.

"You are coming to my play tonight, aren't you?" she asked eagerly.

"Your play? Of course," Bobby heard himself saying. "Wouldn't miss it." In fact he'd forgotten all about Milly's little "turn" at the local am-dram event, and had been planning a hot date with Deborah, the same girl who'd so wonderfully redefined the concept of British hospitality for him last Saturday night. But one look at Milly's huge, tear-glossed doe eyes turned hopefully up at him, and it was all over. He hadn't the heart to let her down twice in one day, not even for a night with Newmarket's answer to Pam Anderson.

"Yay," she said, and smiled.

She had the sort of smile that cracked her face in two like a scythe, the sort you couldn't help but smile back at. For a split second, she looked so beautiful, he felt the beginnings of a familiar stirring in his groin. Horrified, he stamped it down.

What the hell was he thinking? She was only a child, for Christ's sake. Maybe Cecil knew him better than he knew himself? It was an uncomfortable thought.

"I'd better get back to work," he said, pulling away from her and heading for the stable door before he got himself into any more trouble. "I'll see you tonight. Okay?"

"Sure," said Milly, turning back to Easy. Still reeling from Bobby's unexpected embrace and the disappointment of her dad's reaction, she didn't know whether to laugh or cry. All she did know was that he would be there for her tonight.

For the moment at least, that was enough.

Some twenty odd miles away at the Delaneys' manor in Mittlingsford, Rachel and Jasper were upstairs in Rachel's bedroom, fucking.

"Do you like that?" Jasper grunted, thrusting deeply into her from behind, admiring his own shoulder muscles and tight, toned backside in the mirror as he did so. Recently they had taken to doing it with Rachel's wardrobe door propped open, ostensibly so that he could watch her while he screwed her, although in reality he spent more time gazing at his own physique than hers.

"Mmmmm," Rachel murmured. Actually, she was deeply involved in a fantasy involving Bobby Cameron and a riding crop and *was* rather enjoying herself. So far the real Bobby had been disappointingly impervious to her charms—all he seemed interested in was babysitting bloody Milly for reasons she couldn't begin to fathom. But she hadn't given up hope of seducing him before he left.

In the meantime, she looked on Jasper as a useful human dildo.

Feeling the rhythm of his thrusts increasing, and little droplets of sweat falling onto her back as his moans got louder and louder, she assumed he was about to come and squeezed her own muscles tightly around him.

"Oh, J., yes! Please, don't stop," she panted. Happily, she was on the point of climaxing herself. As tiresome and vain as he was, she had to admit that Jasper had marvelous timing in bed. "I'm almost there!"

A few seconds later and she came violently, her spasms of ecstasy pushing him over the edge as well. It was only with an effort that she managed to prevent herself from calling out Bobby's name, turning it instead into a sort of drawn out "oh boy!" that Jasper naturally took as a compliment.

"Not bad, eh?" he said, easing himself out of her with a look of smug satisfaction on his face. She didn't deign to reply but shot up out of bed and straight into the shower. She'd never been one for chitchat after the deed was done, and wasn't about to break the habit of a lifetime for Jasper Lockwood Groves.

Emerging a few minutes later, naked and dripping, she started drying her hair.

"So he's definitely coming then, is he?" she shouted, through the whirr of the dryer.

"Who?" asked Jasper, frowning. "Coming to what?"

He wasn't used to being ignored by girls, and Rachel's sangfroid really pissed him off. Most of the racing groupies he slept with were more than happy to wax post-coitally lyrical about his lovemaking prowess. To be honest, he often enjoyed the post-shag praise fest more than the bonking itself. But Rachel could never be bothered. It made him feel insecure, as did the fact that all the exertion had made his nose go horribly red and shiny. If she'd have taken a little longer in the shower he could have swiped some of her face powder from the dresser and toned himself down a bit before she noticed. Now he'd be forced to talk to her looking like bloody Rudolph.

"Bobby," she said, whipping the towel down from her head and drying herself between the legs quite unself-consciously. "He is coming to Milly's play tonight, right?"

"I doubt it," said Jasper. He was starting to feel well and truly fed up. He was sick to death of all the attention Bobby had been getting from everyone at Newells, not to mention the local female population. And now even his own girlfriend seemed to want a piece of him. "He had a bust-up with Dad the other day about Milly." He pouted. "Apparently he's been letting her ride with him in secret, and Dad went ballistic. What do you care, anyway?"

His lower lip was sticking out so far he looked like a five-year-old who'd just dropped his lollipop in the sand. Sighing inwardly, Rachel turned off the dryer and climbed back into bed, straddling him as she leaned forward and planted a long, lingering kiss on his mouth.

"No reason," she simpered between kisses. "Just curious, that's all."

His jealousy was pathetic, but she had to be careful. Even Jasper had his limits, and the last thing she wanted now was for him to dump her in a huff. She'd barely begun the tortures she had planned for Milly. For the time being, at least, she needed him.

Still, she hoped he was wrong and that Bobby would put in an appearance tonight. It was the only reason she'd agreed to go to the tedious production of *Romeo and Juliet* that the ADC were doing at Mittlingsford Commemoration Hall. That and the fact that she knew it would infuriate Milly that Linda had invited her. Jasper's mother had gone into social-climbing overdrive the moment she'd heard that little Johnny Ashton—Lord Ashton to be—was playing Tybalt. Despite Milly's protestations that his breath smelled of cat food and he had more spots on his face than a ladybug, Linda hadn't given up hope of fostering a "friendship" between her daughter and "The Hon John" as she cringe-makingly referred to him.

"Good," said Jasper, ramming his tongue in and out of her mouth like a lizard trying to catch flies. Grabbing her hand, he yanked it down and wrapped it firmly around his erection. "Because if I see you anywhere near the Lone Ranger, I swear to God . . ."

"Shhhh," Rachel cooed soothingly in his ear. "Why would I want him, when I have you?"

Mollified, Jasper got back to what he liked to think he did best: screwing her. Bobby might have every other girl in Newmarket flinging their knickers at him. But Rachel, the one they all wanted, was his. And she was damn well going to stay that way.

Mittlingsford Commemoration Hall was typical of postwar village architecture. An ugly brick structure with a green tin roof, it was as dour and utilitarian inside as it was outside, with a small wooden stage facing rows of uncomfortable-looking metal and canvas chairs and a pervasive smell of disinfectant lingering in the air.

Backstage, Milly was intermittently sneaking glances through the curtains into the dimly lit audience looking for Bobby and surreptitiously devouring the latest edition of the *Racing Post* which she'd hidden between the pages of her script.

Johnny Ashton sat a few feet away, looking green. His pimply features were so taut with fear that even Milly couldn't help but feel sorry for him. The rest of the cast called it his firing-squad look and it was at its worst tonight, due to the fact that both his horribly overbearing parents, Lord and Lady Ashton, were sitting in the front row, waiting to pounce on the slightest mistake he might make. The Ashtons were the sort of parents that made Milly feel grateful for her own, and that was really saying something.

Her crowded thoughts left little room for Johnny, however. All she could think about was Bobby and their encounter in Easy's stable earlier. She knew he didn't love her—at least not in the crazy, desperate, passionate way that she loved him. But he liked her. He definitely liked her. It was a start.

Where was he, anyway? He'd promised he'd be here, and they were going to start in a minute, but so far he was nowhere to be seen.

"Oh, no way," she seethed under her breath. For there, making her way to the empty seat next to her parents—Bobby's seat—was Rachel. She was turning heads in a pink baby-doll dress that, if it were possible, made her tits look even bigger than usual. What the fuck was she doing here?

So far, miraculously, Bobby had shown no sign of sexual interest in Rachel. But unlike her boneheaded brother, Milly could see quite plainly that Rachel fancied *him*. And as she knew to her cost, Rachel had an uncanny habit of getting what she wanted.

"Five minutes everyone!" William Best, Newmarket Drama Club's neurotic director, clapped his dry, flaky hands for attention, and the low hum of backstage conversation immediately ceased. Milly hastily stuffed her *Racing Post* down the side of the back stairs and peered into the audience one last time.

Thank God! There he was.

Her heart skipped a beat as she glimpsed Bobby making his way toward her parents. Evidently he and her father had had some sort of rapprochement, as Cecil smiled and immediately instigated a hurried shuffling of chairs, pinching a vacant seat from the row behind and squeezing it next to his own. It was only when Bobby sank down into it, all long legs and tan, that she realized with horror that Rachel was now on his other side.

Bobby, though he didn't look it, was almost as stressed as Milly was. Pissed about missing his date with Deborah, and still bothered by the fleeting flash of lust he'd felt with Milly earlier, he'd thrown himself into work this afternoon to take his mind off things. As always when engrossed with his horses, he'd lost track of time and set off late for Mittlingsford. Needless to say he'd then promptly gotten lost in the brain-aching maze of country lanes that led to the village. He was starting to panic that he might miss the damn thing altogether by the time he finally stumbled upon the hall.

"Sorry. Excuse me," he said, sweat pouring off his forehead as people got to their feet to let him through.

"You're cutting it a bit fine, aren't you?" hissed Jasper as he slid by. Annoyed he'd been bullied into coming tonight by his mother, and even more annoyed that Bobby and his father appeared to have buried the hatchet, he was not in the warmest of moods.

Ignoring him, Bobby turned to Cecil.

"Those lanes were a nightmare in the dark," he whispered. "Sorry."

"Not to worry," said Cecil, as the lights began to dim. "You're here now."

"Hello. Remember me?"

Great. That was all he needed: Sir Michael's slutty daughter leaning over him in what looked like a whore's nightgown, sticking her grand canyon of a cleavage in his face. Why did so many pretty girls dress in a way that left nothing to the imagination? It was so unsexy.

"Rachel," he said coldly. He'd seen firsthand what a bitch she was to Milly, and had no intention of making nice. But she seemed to have missed his unfriendly tone, dissolving into a flirtatious, girlish giggle and, as soon as the lights dimmed, reaching over and brazenly grabbing his hand.

Was he imagining things? Or did she just caress the inside of his wrist with her thumb?

Before he had time to react, the curtain went up. A ripple of applause spread around the auditorium as the cast filed onto the stage to take their places. Milly beamed at Bobby and, forgetting herself in her excitement, waved, like a four-year-old spotting her mother at the Nativity play.

"Oh, do look, she's waving," Rachel whispered patronizingly in his ear, leaning in so close that he was knocked sideways by a waft of her Chanel 19. "I think somebody has a little crush on you."

Snatching away his hand, he hissed back at her, "Milly and I are friends. She's only a kid."

"Exactly." Once again, Rachel had failed utterly to pick up on his hostility, or register that she had inadvertently touched a nerve. "I expect you prefer real women, don't you? Women with a bit of experience?"

Hiding the gesture behind her purse, she stretched out her arm and allowed her hand to graze his thigh in a definite come-on. In other circumstances he might quite have enjoyed the thrill of doing the dirty on Jasper while he sat just a few feet away. But everything about Rachel Delaney made his hackles rise. A wave of revulsion poured over him like ice-cold water and he pried her hand firmly away.

"I prefer women I can trust," he said flatly. "I could never respect a promiscuous girl. Never."

Rachel's eyes narrowed and her full, pouting lips puckered into a little purse of fury before she recoiled, stung, into her seat.

"Is he bothering you?" asked Jasper, who couldn't hear what they were saying but had witnessed some sort of exchange.

"No," she said, collecting herself, grateful that he couldn't see the hot flush of her cheeks in the darkness. "You're right about him, though. He is arrogant. And distinctly average looking. I have no idea what people see in him."

Snaking his hand up under her dress, Jasper began stroking proprietorially beneath her panties. "Course I'm right," he said, nuzzling her neck. "He could never satisfy you like I can, Rach. Nobody could."

The first act was groaningly awful, a litany of missed cues and wobbling sets that left much of the audience, including Bobby, struggling to stay awake. His legs were also killing him, squashed into a seat so small it would have shamed an economy cabin on American Airlines. The moment the interval was announced, he shot to his feet in relief.

Cecil made his excuses and nipped outside to make a phone call. Rachel and Jasper were also quick off the mark, dashing off for a cigarette, leaving Bobby to make small talk with Linda at the makeshift bar in what was optimistically termed "the foyer." Everything about the place—the chairs; the 1960s windows; the hideous, shit-brown linoleum floor—reminded him of his old school auditorium back in Solvang: not a place that held many happy memories. He gave an involuntary shudder now at the thought of it.

"What did you think?" asked Linda, handing him an unwanted warm beer in a plastic cup. She was dressed, conservatively for her, in an electric blue shirt-waister offset by thickly caked blue eye shadow that stuck to her crow's feet like Polyfilla whenever she smiled. "Wasn't Milly a dream?"

"She, er, was one of the best actors in it," he said truthfully, choosing his words with care. "You must be very proud."

"Oh, I am." Linda smiled knowingly. "And did you see the way the Hon John was staring at her whenever he didn't have a line?"

"I'm sorry, the on who?" asked Bobby.

"Johnny. The future Lord Ashton," Linda gushed. "He's quite smitten with our little Milly, I should say. Quite smitten!"

Bobby found himself feeling more than a little put out at this information. If some dirty little kid was after Milly, surely her mom should be against it, not for it? Maybe he should talk to Cecil. Then again, maybe he'd already shot his bolt on that score.

"What are you bending his ear about now, Mummy?" Milly, still dressed in her costume of long black skirt and ruffled, burgundy blouse, had snuck up behind them.

"What are you doing out here?" Linda sounded aghast. "You should be backstage with all the others. Go on, off you go." She made shooing motions with her hands. "Go and chat to Johnny, darling. I'm sure he could use the company."

"I doubt it," said Milly, matter-of-factly. "He's been chundering his guts out in the bogs ever since the curtain came down. His parents are such fucking tyrants, he's a nervous wreck. Anyway, I only popped out for a sec to say hi to Bobby."

She beamed up at him, a picture of innocence, cheeks flushed and eyes blazing, and Bobby felt another stab of guilt, both for the way he'd let her down and for wanting her earlier, however briefly. There might be only six years between them, but at this age they were like six light-years. Only days ago he'd been telling her father that he wasn't a pedophile. Now he wasn't so sure.

That was it. Tomorrow he'd take the morning off, drive over to Deborah's, and have sex till he couldn't see straight. One marathon session with a real, grown-up woman should sort his head out.

"You did a great job," he said, showing Milly no hint of his inner misgivings. "I'm looking forward to act two."

"Huh," she sniffed. "I wouldn't hold your breath if I were you. It'll be super boring. I saw you chatting to Rachel earlier," she said, trying to keep her voice casual.

"Not by choice," he reassured her, and was rewarded with a second enormous grin.

"Milly, darling." Linda, sensing her matchmaking window with Johnny Ashton slipping inexorably away, was getting anxious. "You're really being terribly rude. You must go backstage."

"In a minute," said Milly. "Ooo, is that for me?"

Cecil had returned from the bar bearing ice creams. Handing one each to his wife and daughter, he reached into his inside jacket pocket and pulled out his vibrating mobile.

"Lockwood Groves," he said, ignoring a frosty glance from Linda. But her expression changed when, a few seconds later, she saw the color drain from his cheeks and his brow knotting into a frown of deep concern. "Jesus Christ," he whispered. "Are you sure?"

Jasper and Rachel had wandered back in, and were now staring at him along with the others.

"When did this happen? Have you asked for help?"

Milly felt her own heartbeat speeding up to a gallop. She couldn't remember ever having seen her calm, collected father looking so panicked. Something must be really wrong.

"Yes. Okay. Okay." Cecil nodded gravely. "I'm on my way."

"What is it?" asked Linda as he hung up. "Is everything all right?"

"No," said Cecil. "It's not. That was Nancy." He looked ashen. "Radar collapsed about twenty minutes ago. She says it doesn't look like he's going to make it."

Milly's eyes widened and her hand flew to her mouth in shock. Instinctively Bobby put his arm around her, but she was too upset even to register it and pulled away, pacing back and forth.

"What's wrong with him?" Her voice quivered.

"Equine influenza," said Cecil bleakly. "A particularly virulent strain, it would appear. And I'm afraid it gets worse. Some of the other stallions have been affected."

Milly stopped her pacing. "Which stallions?"

"Easy's already running a temperature of a hundred and four," said Cecil, confirming her worst fears. "He's in a bad way." He turned to Linda. "I'm sorry. I have to get straight back there."

Without thinking, Milly reached for Bobby's hand, which he gave her, instinctively squeezing his support. He knew how much she loved that horse.

"I'm coming with you," she announced to her father.

"Me too," said Bobby.

"Don't be ridiculous, Milly," said Linda. "You have a play to finish. It's out of the question. Jasper can go and help your father if need be."

Releasing Bobby's hand, Milly spun around to face her mother, her features set in a mask of such pure determination that even Linda was caught off guard.

"Fuck the stupid play," she said. "I'm going back to the stables, and I'm going right now. Easy needs me."

CHAPTER NINE

Back at Newells, the entire yard was in chaos.

Under the full glare of the floodlights, a veritable swarm of vets, grooms, and handlers ran back and forth from the house carrying syringes; buckets of water; and a variety of towels, blankets, and bandages. Seeing Cecil's 4x4 screeching into the graveled driveway, Nancy rushed forward to greet him, her pixie-like blond figure followed closely by a harassed-looking man who had evidently just been dragged out of bed. He still wore his pajama trousers—tucked into riding boots—and his upper body was covered with a thick Guernsey sweater that had been pulled on inside out.

"I drove like a maniac, but it takes forever on those fucking country roads," said Cecil, glancing apologetically from his watch to the vet and back again. "How are we doing?"

"They're both still alive," said Nancy, nodding a brief hello to Bobby and Milly, who she was pleased to see Cecil had brought back with him. If anyone could help calm and comfort these two stallions it was them. "But it's not looking good. Radar's up to a hundred and five and a half, and Easy's not far behind. His nose looks like Niagara Falls."

"Can I see him?" Milly stifled a sob.

"Sure," said Nancy kindly. "Follow me. This is Drew, by the way, from the EDRI." She introduced pajama man as the five of them hurried over to the stable where Radar and Easy had been isolated. The Equine Disease Research Institute was well-known in Newmarket, its vets and scientists some of the most respected in Europe. "I brought him in in case there was anything we'd missed."

"And?" asked Cecil. "Was there?"

"I'm afraid not," said Drew in a soft Scottish burr. "It's a clear-cut case of the flu, although one of the most virulent I've seen in a long while. Unfortunately, as with all flu viruses, it's highly contagious. We won't know for sure how many animals have been affected for a day or so, although judging from the severity of the two cases you have, I would expect to see symptoms emerging within hours if it has spread."

"But we immunized them all, for God's sake," said Milly. "I watched Easy get his flu jab myself."

"New viral strains pop up all the time," said Bobby. "That's the problem."

"Exactly," the vet agreed. "All it takes is contact with one unknown horse who might have traveled abroad, say, or been exposed to a new, mutated strain. And the thing can spread like wildfire."

"It isn't fatal, though, is it?" Milly asked, unbolting the door to the temporary quarantine.

"Usually, no," said Drew, following her inside. "But, like I say, this is an unusually bad case. And as with humans, it's the elderly and the very young who are most at risk. Radar has a better chance than your old man here." He pointed to Easy, who lay in the corner of the stall, curled into a shivering, sweat-drenched ball. Too tired to lift his head, his eyes rolled up at the sound of Milly's voice and he gave her a hopeless, exhausted look of recognition. Already he seemed smaller somehow, diminished by the awful virus that had struck him down so suddenly.

"Poor baby." Kneeling down beside him, Milly flung her arms around his neck. It was like pressing herself against a wet radiator, he was so hideously hot. "Can't we do anything? I mean, we can't just leave him here like this."

"Can I help?" asked Bobby. He felt so useless, standing there like a spare part. It had already been a tough week for Milly, but he knew that her other disappointments meant nothing compared to the prospect of losing Easy. He wished there were something he could do.

"Thanks, but not really," said Nancy. "He's had a shot of painkiller, but too much weakens his ability to fight it. We've been using towels and water to cool him. Other than that, there's not much we can do except to let it run its course."

Cecil ran his hands through his hair in despair. Like Milly, he was fond of his horses, particularly Easy, the old man of the yard. But unlike his daughter, he could also look at this devastating disease from a business perspective. Easy Victory was by far the stud's most profitable stallion. To lose him alone would be a serious blow. But if the rest of his stallions turned out to be affected, the business that he'd spent the last twenty years building up would be decimated, perhaps even finished for good. He was insured against the loss of his own animals. But once a stud got a reputation as being unsafe or disease prone, that was it. Not even long-standing clients and friends like Michael Delaney could afford to take that sort of risk with their racehorses or their sires.

"I know it's not what you want to hear," said Drew, echoing Nancy. "But the best we can do for these two now is to keep them cool, give them some peace and quiet to try to rest, and keep them well away from the others."

Milly looked at Bobby despairingly.

"What are their chances?" asked Cecil. He had not expected either horse to look quite as ill as they both did. "Honestly."

"Honestly?" said Drew with a sidelong glance at Nancy. "Fifty-fifty. At best, I'm afraid."

The night was one of the longest of Cecil's life. Heeding the vets' advice about letting the two sick animals rest, he spent most of his time in the stallion barn and the other livery blocks, checking on the progress and temperatures of the other horses. Early signs of equine flu included nasal discharge, depression or listlessness, and loss of appetite, although with a strain this strong he would expect the symptoms to become acute very quickly and, in particular, for body temperature to shoot up out of the blue, as it had done with both Radar and Easy. By daybreak, hope was rising that somehow, miraculously, the rest of the stud remained unaffected. Some of the stallions were irritable, baffled, and annoyed by all the unusual nocturnal comings and goings—but none of them were showing significant temperatures.

It was a long night for Bobby too. Having spent the night fetching wet towels and making everyone endless cups of coffee, he finally decided to catch an hour or so's sleep at around five A.M. Yawning and stretching out his aching arms as he headed back to the house, he made one last stop by the barn where the two sick animals were being isolated to check on Milly. Sticking his head around the door, he found her curled into a fetal ball in the straw behind Easy's forelegs, one hand extended behind her to rest gently against the horse's sweat-soaked flank. Radar appeared to be sleeping soundly in the far corner. Still in the black skirt and burgundy ruffles she'd been wearing at the play, both now muddied beyond repair and covered with horsehair and straw, she had kicked off her formal black court shoes, tucking her bare feet in behind her.

For the second time that day, Bobby felt a rush of tenderness toward her. He knew what it felt like to lose an animal you loved as much as Milly loved Easy. It would be so easy to go and lie down beside her. To pull her to him. Comfort her.

And he wanted to. Fuck, he wanted to so much it hurt. But with a titanic effort, he held himself back. God knew he wasn't the most scrupulous of men when it came to sex. But to take advantage of a young girl's childish crush, when she was at her weakest and most vulnerable? Even he couldn't live with himself after that.

Kneeling over her, he gently stroked her cheek until her eyes flickered drowsily open.

"Hey," he said softly. "Sorry. I didn't mean to wake you. I just wanted to see if you were okay?"

"I'm fine," she whispered unconvincingly. Her eyes were puffy and red from crying, and her nose was almost as inflamed as Easy's. "I wasn't asleep. You going to bed?"

"I was going to," he said, standing up and rubbing a tired hand across the back of his neck. Even in her misery, Milly found herself wishing it were her neck he was touching instead. "Nancy and your dad say there's not a lot that can be done right now."

She gazed up at him. Standing above her, his silhouette dimly illuminated by the milky glow of the moonlight, he looked as handsome as he ever had.

Guiltily, she turned her thoughts back to Easy. How could she even *think* about anything else while he was so sick?

"How's he been?" asked Bobby, as if reading her mind.

"Like this." She ran a loving hand over his rump. "His breathing's so shallow, and he's shivering all the time."

"Do you want me to stay with you?" he asked, half hoping and half fearing that she'd say yes. "I'm happy to, if you need the company."

Milly thought miserably that she'd never wanted anything quite so much in her entire life. But she knew that these might be her last few hours with Easy. He needed her more than she needed Bobby.

"No," she said, nuzzling back into Easy's side. "You go get some sleep. I'm fine on my own."

"Okay." He tried to hide his disappointment, taking off his leather jacket and laying it gently on top of her. She was curled up into such a tight ball that it covered her body almost completely, like a blanket. Only her beautiful, pale, freckled face could be seen poking out at the top. "You know where I am if you need me," he said. And he left, softly closing the stable door behind him.

Cecil came into the barn about an hour later, at just after six. Milly was still curled beneath Bobby's jacket, sound asleep. Radar, to his surprise and delight, was on his feet. He pricked his ears up at the sound of footsteps, shaking his head from side to side, like a passenger trying to uncrick his neck after a long plane journey, and blinking at Cecil as if to ask him what all the fuss had been about.

"Well, hello there, you old troublemaker." Cecil smiled as he scratched the horse between the ears and stroked gently along the length of his narrow white star. "Welcome back."

Radar nuzzled him affectionately in response, seemingly oblivious to Milly's presence—and that of the prone, lifeless form of his stable mate and onetime companion on the straw behind them.

Turning around, Cecil sighed heavily. He'd just been given a tentative all clear on the rest of his animals by the veterinary team and had been on the point of allowing himself a small taste of relief. But now his heart sank again as he confirmed for himself the news that he'd been both dreading and expecting: Easy Victory was dead.

Crouching down on his haunches, he gently shook his daughter awake.

"Mill," he whispered. She barely stirred. "Milly," he tried again, more loudly this time.

"It's all right, Dad," she said wearily, her eyes still firmly closed. "You don't have to tell me. I know. He's gone, isn't he?"

Hearing her trying so hard to be brave, exhaustion battling with the sorrow in her voice, he felt close to tears himself. Easy had been a once-in-a-lifetime stallion. They would all miss him. But Milly had had a special bond with him, closer than anyone else's.

She'd changed so much in the last few weeks, since Bobby had arrived. It was almost as if the old, preaccident Milly had come alive again. As angry as he'd been when Bobby confessed they'd been riding together behind his back, looking at her now Cecil realized how much he'd missed his happy, carefree daughter; the one whose eyes lit up the moment she climbed up into the saddle. These days, he also recognized, with a stab of paternal concern, they also lit up every time Bobby Cameron walked into a room.

His little girl was growing up. Or rather she would be—if only he'd let her.

The thought of Milly riding again, of taking that risk, still filled him with a terror that made his breath catch in his throat. But deep down, ever since his row with Bobby, he'd had a gnawing awareness that maybe the boy was right: maybe Milly should go with him to California?

Bobby's words kept coming back to him, like an endlessly playing tape in his head: "She's not happy here." With Bobby leaving, and now with Easy gone, she'd be even less happy.

Would she forgive him, he wondered, if he didn't let her go?

Should she forgive him, if he continued to let his own fears blight her life and stifle her talent?

Reaching beneath Bobby's straw-covered jacket, he found her hand and squeezed it, pushing his doubts and fears about her future to the back of his mind for now. Whatever mistakes he might have made as a father, he loved her more than anything. Right now, he simply wanted her to know it.

"Yes, sweetheart" was all he said. "I'm so sorry. He is gone. Easy's gone."

* * *

Far away in Solvang, Wyatt McDonald tried in vain to shake himself free of the black mood that had gripped him since daybreak as he hurried down Main Street.

The early fall sky was as blue and cloudless as a tourist-board postcard, and even at this relatively early hour the sun's rays were warm enough to bake his back as he made his way through town. He was headed to the bank to meet with the manager, his old friend Gene Drummond. Friendship aside, it was not likely to be an enjoyable meeting, and the prospect of it was causing his brow to knit with stress as he walked.

"Mornin', Wyatt." Mary Lonsdale, the sweet-natured, hugely overweight clerk from the post office, waved at him as she emerged from Devon's Pharmacy.

"Mary." He tipped his hat at her, smiling despite his inner gloom. Wyatt had known Mary for going on forty years now. She was one of the gentlest souls he'd ever met.

One of the nice things about Solvang, like any small town perhaps, was that neighbors still knew and cared for one another. A popular local figure like Wyatt could barely expect to walk twenty yards through town without somebody rushing out to greet him or wave or ask him how the kids were doing or how they were all getting on up at the ranch since poor Hank's passing. Being September, the worst of the tourists had gone but he still passed a couple of groups of sightseers on his way to Wells Fargo at the far end of town, their LA tour bus sticking out like a sore thumb in the central village parking lot.

Founded by Danish settlers, educators from the Midwest who came out to California looking to establish a new colony in the early nineteen hundreds, Solvang had always been a big draw on the Western tourist trail. The name itself means "sunny valley," and that it certainly was. But it was the unique Danish architecture, a token of the old European way of life frozen in time up in the California mountains like a fossil in amber, that kept the crowds of visitors coming back here summer after summer, year after year. With its cobbled streets, gas lamps, tiled gable roofs, and no less than four windmills, the place looked like a Disneyland Denmark. But behind the tourist façade of the Happy Windmill Hotel, where Bobby's mother, Diana, had once worked, and the endless gift stores selling Danish flags and peasant dolls, there existed a real living, working community. Some of the families—with names like Sorensen, Rasmussen, Skraedder, and Olsen—had lived here now for four generations, and took their Danish ancestry and heritage very seriously. Inevitably, they had intermarried with even older local families, some of whom, like the Camerons and the McDonalds, had ancestors who had lived and worked as cowboys in this valley for almost two centuries.

Walking up the white wooden steps into the old bank building, Wyatt took off his hat and brushed the dust from his feet before approaching the teller.

"Mornin', Phyllis." He smiled.

"Wyatt." The old woman flashed an almost toothless grin back at him. "Gene's expectin' ya. You wanna go straight through?"

His old friend got up from behind his desk and walked around to greet him as he came in.

"Wyatt. Good to see you, buddy. How you been?"

It was an odd question, given that they'd spent half an hour together only last Tuesday at the high school PTA meeting, chewing the fat about Highwood and life in general. Still, maybe he was just nervous and looking for something to say.

"Good," said Wyatt, sitting down in response to a gesture from Gene. "But somethin' tells me I may not be feelin' quite so good once this meetin's over. So come on. Don't keep me in suspense, Gene. What's on your mind?"

"Well, firstly, I want you to know that none o' this is my doing, Wyatt." He shifted awkwardly in his seat. "This comes from the powers that be. I'm just the lowly messenger boy."

"I know that," said Wyatt kindly. "Go on."

"Well, second thing is, I really ought to be havin' this conversation with Bobby. Highwood's his property now. . . ."

Wyatt held up his hand to stop him.

"Gene, I've told you. Bobby's away in England. But he's given me full authority as ranch manager. I'm authorized to have access to all the relevant financial information. I can bring you in the signed documents if you'd like?"

The other man shook his head, his brow furrowing like buckled metal.

"Jeez, Wyatt, no. That's not necessary. I hope I can trust your word."

"Well, I hope so too, Gene," said Wyatt, bristling slightly at the turn the conversation was taking. Still, there was no point falling out with such an old friend over something like this. At the end of the day the guy was only tryin' to do his job.

"I'll cut to the chase then," said Gene, looking as miserable as such a naturally jovial man could ever look. "You're behind on the interest payments, almost six full months now."

Wyatt winced. "I know. But the last three months we've been makin' it up. Bobby's earnings—"

"Aren't enough," said Gene. "Hank knew that he was in real danger of foreclosure last year. Now, true, at the time that extra money from Bobby persuaded the bank to hold off. The problem though, Wyatt, is that usually it's in their—in our—interest to work something out, especially where we can see the borrower is trying to pay and has systems in place to work on reducin' their debt."

"Which we do, and we have," said Wyatt, raising his voice in frustration.

"Maybe. But you know as well as I do, with that oil sitting there . . ." Gene left the sentence hanging. There was no need to spell it out. Wyatt knew exactly what he meant: It was in the bank's interest for Bobby to default on his payments. That way they could gain legal possession of Highwood and, by extension, her oil rights.

"What exactly are you tellin' me here, Gene?" he asked him matter-of-factly. "What's the bottom line? How much time do we have?"

"Well, that's what I'm tellin' you, Wyatt. You don't *have* time. Not more 'an a few weeks anyhow. The bottom line is, you need to make good on those back payments, in full, and you need to keep the interest a-comin'. One slip—one late payment—and these guys are gonna come down on you like a plague of locusts. And they'll be bringing their drills."

Wyatt ran his hand through his hair slowly, squeezing his temples as if trying to dredge up some inspiration.

"How about if we brought in a partner?" he said, remembering Bobby's suggestion. "An investor of some kind? Somebody with cash flow."

Gene nodded approvingly. "That would be perfect. But, Wyatt, I can't stress this enough to you and Bobby: Time is of the essence here. If you've got some white knight in mind, I suggest you get on the phone and call him. Because unless you come up with something pretty soon, my friend—"

"I know, I know. Don't say it."

"It's my job to say it," said Gene. "As your bank manager and as your friend. Find that money, Wyatt. Find it. Or your boy Bobby's gonna lose that ranch."

Todd Cranborn stepped out onto the deck of his sprawling Bel Air mansion and gazed down with satisfaction at the view beneath him.

Yet another brilliant, cloudless day: perfect LA sunshine. The morning mist that rolled in off the ocean had already been burned away so that it was warm enough to be outside in shorts and a T-shirt even at this early hour. Directly below the house lay the manicured greens of the Bel Air golf club, where tiny figures in plaid pants could be seen whizzing back and forth in their golf carts, too lazy to walk the hundred or so yards to the sandy bunkers and retrieve their errant balls themselves.

Todd hated golf. To him it was like living death. The rich old men who tottered out onto the greens every afternoon made him shudder, content to fritter away their retirement years hitting a ball into a hole or knocking back bourbons in the clubhouse, anything to avoid the company of their hard-as-nails, stretched-faced Beverly Hills wives back at home. Horrific. He did, however, like living above the golf course. Homes in this part of Bel Air were some of the most prestigious and sought after in the whole of LA, for their proximity to the country club and their panoramic views across the city, right out to the ocean and, on a clear day, Catalina beyond. These homes were the best. And Todd Cranborn liked to be the best.

Born in Boston some thirty-seven years ago, the youngest of three sons of blue-collar parents (his father, Bob, spent fifty years on the assembly line at an out-of-town plastics factory and his mother, Siobhan, was what is now euphemistically known as a homemaker) Todd made his first million, in property, before his twenty-fifth birthday. The first of his family to go away to college, he dropped out of NYU at nineteen, much to his parents' dismay, and went into business with a local developer, buying up small units in suburban minimalls in New Jersey and leasing them out at a vast profit. Soon he had progressed to time-share condos, always focusing on volume, always at the lower end of the market.

After a few years, he had made enough to ditch his partner and strike out on his own. With remarkable business instincts and ruthless self-discipline—he never overreached himself financially to stretch for a dream property but stuck rigidly to what he knew: keeping within his budget, borrowing conservatively, cutting his losses when necessary—he had soon netted himself a fortune in the high tens of millions.

To his credit, the first thing Todd did when he got rich was to reach out to his family. He offered to buy his parents a new house, and dangled gifts of new cars and holidays in front of his elder brothers like Santa Claus. But, happy as they were about his success, a deeply ingrained sense of working-class pride made it impossible for them to accept his generous offers.

Todd couldn't understand it. Was his money not good enough for them or something? Did they hate him because he was educated? Misinterpreting their pride as straightforward jealousy and pigheadedness, he retreated, wounded, into his shell. Within a few years contact with his brothers had dwindled to cards on Christmas and birthdays. Not long afterward, it ceased altogether.

The estrangement from his family had a profound effect on Todd.

It left him with an inability to trust those closest to him as well as a passionate hatred of class prejudice in any of its forms.

Far from hurting his career, however, his newfound bitterness seemed to spur him on to even greater heights of achievement. He expanded his business out to Florida and, later, California, where he quadrupled his wealth, thanks to shrewd coinvestments with Native Americans that enabled him to sidestep state planning and building regulations, not to mention taxes.

"Baby? Are you out there? Where'd you go?"

Catherine, the slutty brunette from the Valley he'd picked up at Louis Frampton's party last night, padded out onto the deck. She was wearing one of his favorite, indigo-blue Interno Otto shirts, and her massive silicone breasts were stretching the fabric dangerously close to breaking point.

Todd's heart sank. Why couldn't these girls just do the decent thing and leave in the morning? Her raspy, smoker's voice had a practiced sexiness to it that had turned him on like hell last night, after five martinis and some truly exceptional coke. But now it grated like fingernails on a blackboard.

"Hi," he said coldly. "I have a lot of work to do this morning, sweetheart, so I thought I'd get an early start." He looked at his watch and frowned. Shit. It was after nine already. "Can I get you anything?"

This last offer was made with such palpable impatience and bad grace, it was a miracle that the girl missed it. But not being the sharpest tool in the box, she took his offer at face value and, sidling up to him, wrapped herself around him like ivy, her red-taloned hand reaching down his shorts for his cock.

"Sure. You can get me something," she whispered breathlessly, looking up at him with what she erroneously believed to be a sexy, come-hither gaze as she rubbed his groin. Last night he'd hardened to iron almost instantly at her touch. Now he was limp, bored, reactionless. Wrinkling his nose in distaste—she still smelled of sex and sweat, and the warm, fishy scent of her was unpleasantly overpowering in the still morning air—he removed her hand and flashed her a curt, businesslike smile.

"I was thinking more in terms of a cab."

Todd liked sex, but he did not like women. As a rich, single guy in LA, he could have his pick of some of the most beautiful girls in America—it was one of the main reasons he had chosen to settle in this most beautiful but shallowest of cities—but rarely did he sleep with any of them more than once.

It wasn't just his money that had the women swarming around him like flies on shit. He was a looker too, stockily built like a boxer, with thick, wavy chestnut hair. His features were strong: solid, square jaw; a big broken nose (it suited him somehow); and a wide mouth with very thin, slightly curling lips that gave him a permanent semi-sneer. Some girls told him he reminded them of Jack Nicholson, a resemblance of which Todd was secretly very proud.

Like Nicholson, he was a womanizer. But unlike Jack, he wasn't the kind that adored women so much they just couldn't seem to help themselves. Instead, his awesome sex drive was fueled by something else—anger, bitterness even—that left him with a bad taste in his mouth even after the most enjoyable of erotic encounters. He could feel it now, with Catherine. He wished she would evaporate and leave him in peace.

Instead, offended by his rejection, she started pouting and whining like a spoiled child. It was all he could do to restrain himself from smacking her. Finally she agreed to let him call her a cab, but only after numerous assurances on his part that he would call her later once his work was finished and they would definitely hook up again soon. Did these girls really believe that shit? he wondered. It was only after she'd gone, when he sat down at the PC in his study to check his e-mails, that he realized she'd driven off still wearing his expensive Italian shirt.

Goddamn it. Why did these stupid sluts always go for the best stuff? He really must get Luigi to put a lock on his closet door before he brought another one home.

Glancing down his new messages—his inbox, as always, was full to bursting—he focused in on one from his lawyer in Santa Barbara and double clicked it open.

"Fuck," he muttered to himself as he started to read. Some of the local residents had gotten up a petition, protesting against his acquisition of some land near Buellton with a small syndicate of local Native Americans. By ensuring they had a 51 percent stake, he would be able to build the huge tracts of cheap residential units that he wanted without interference from state government. The locals rightly suspected he was about to deface their pristine valley.

Smug, middle-class cunts. Todd had no time for these people with their committees and their envy and their small-town, middle-American mentality. If they wanted to protect the land so badly, they should have bought it up themselves. He wasn't doing anything illegal, so they could stick their petition up their self-righteous Waspy asses.

Reading on further, he stopped at the last paragraph of the e-mail, forgetting about the Buellton land for a moment.

"You may or may not have heard," it read, "but Hank Cameron finally bit the dust a couple of months ago. The Highwood ranch now belongs to his son, Bobby."

Interesting. Todd had had abortive dealings with Hank some six or seven years ago about acquiring a stake in his ranch. Total no go. Years later, he had run into the son out in Florida. The boy was brilliant with horses apparently, although it was his arrogance that Todd remembered him for. Bobby had looked right through him like he was nothing when they met at a party. Then later he added insult to injury by leaving with a gorgeous redhead that Todd had had his eye on himself. Needless to say, he wasn't Bobby's biggest fan.

But the Cameron ranch, bursting as it was with more oil than Texas—now that was something else. What wouldn't he give to get his hands on even a tiny piece of Highwood and her oil?

"Before you ask, the boy's not selling," the message continued. "But I gather from various sources here that he's struggling financially. There's some talk about him training quarter horses for income, but apparently he can't raise the cash to get started. Anyway, you asked me to keep my eye open, so I thought you'd like to know."

He was good, this new lawyer. Sharp. Leaning back in his chair,

Todd closed his eyes and tried to picture the Cameron land. He was no nature lover, but Highwood had been beautiful enough to stick in even his memory. Unfortunately the idyll was ruined for him by the knowledge that all that untapped oil was being wasted. Just how dumb were these cowboy bastards? When he closed his eyes, he could almost smell the money burning. It made him feel sick to his stomach.

Picking up a squishy purple executive stress ball from the desk—an eons-old Christmas present from his mother—he squeezed it in frustration. There must be some way for him to reinitiate a contact there.

From the way that he'd ignored him in Florida, he was pretty sure that Bobby wouldn't remember him. That gave him an advantage. As did the fact that the boy needed to raise cash for his quarter horse venture: One thing Todd had plenty of was cash. The trick would be to approach Bobby gently so as not to scare him off. Because the moment he sensed that oil was what he was after, he'd run for the hills every bit as fast as his daddy had, Todd was sure of it.

Racking his brains, he tried to dredge up the name of Hank's old ranch manager. Willie, was it? Or Wes? Something like that. A real, salt o' the earth cowboy, like his boss, both of them stuck in some sentimental, working-class time warp. They had no business sense, none at all, but they also had no greed. That made them tricky customers on two counts.

Hmmm. He'd have to give it some thought.

In the meantime, he picked up the phone and settled in for what was to be a long day of business calls to the East Coast. The fact that it was Sunday, or that outside a jewel of a California day was unfolding around him, meant nothing at all to Todd.

His whole life was his work.

And that was just the way he liked it.

CHAPTER TEN

The atmosphere at Newells in the weeks after the flu outbreak was extremely tense.

The death of a famous stallion like Easy Victory was always going to be big news in Newmarket. Scare stories about a fatal superstrain of equine influenza soon began spreading faster than the disease itself, plunging Cecil into a state of code-red damage control overnight. He spent his days driving all over the country with his veterinary team, trying to reassure his various clients in person that his stables were safe. The long hours and intense stress involved in such a full-scale PR effort were grueling, and on the rare occasions when he was home he was unusually snappy and irritable with everyone from Linda to the grooms.

About three weeks after Easy's death, he walked into the kitchen looking even more strung out than usual.

"Have you seen Jasper?" he asked Linda, cursing under his breath to see that the sugar bowl was empty and noisily opening and shutting cupboards to hunt for a new package. "He was supposed to be exercising Danny and Caligula this morning, but he's done a runner again, the lazy little bastard."

"He's at Mittlingsford I think," Linda said calmly, retrieving the sugar from the larder and filling the bowl for him while he sat down grumpily at the table. "Julia Delaney needed some help setting up for the party, and he offered. You shouldn't be so hard on him, you know."

"Shouldn't be so hard on him?" grunted Cecil, then promptly scalded the roof of his mouth with a gulp of too-hot coffee. "I'm fighting to keep our heads above water here, Linds," he said. "And our son would rather be folding napkins for his bloody girlfriend than pitching in."

Tonight was the night of the Delaneys' annual end-of-summer

party, the most eagerly anticipated social fixture in Newmarket. Linda was in a frenzy of excitement about it, especially since this year, with Jasper and Rachel walking out together, she'd be part of the inner circle of favored guests, the ones that got to spend the most time with Sir Michael and Lady D.—or Julia, as she now knew her.

"I can take Caligula out if you like," said Bobby. He'd just walked in in dirty jeans and an old Lakers T-shirt soaked through with sweat after an early morning training session up at the gallops. "I'm free this afternoon, as it happens."

"Really?" said Cecil, perking up slightly. Bobby had been a lifesaver since the flu, pitching in well beyond the call of duty. Their earlier spat over his secret training sessions with Milly was now well and truly forgiven and forgotten. Which was just as well, seeing as Bobby appeared to be the only person who could get through to Milly at all since Easy's death. With the rest of them she'd retreated into her shell completely, spending hours alone in her room staring into space, locked up in her own, private grief. She wasn't even moaning about not being allowed to ride anymore, which was so deeply out of character that it worried Cecil more than anything else.

It scared him to think that Bobby would be on a plane back to California in less than a week. If Mill hadn't snapped out of her depression by then, he had no idea how to help her.

Just then, Milly shuffled gloomily into the room looking not unlike a human version of Eeyore in a shrunken pair of Cecil's stripy pajamas. With only the briefest of nods to Bobby, and not a word to her parents, she started making herself a piece of toast.

"Ah, there you are," said Linda briskly. Unlike Cecil, she had no time for Milly's theatrical sulking and thought the whole hoo-ha over one dead horse absolutely ridiculous. "I hope you haven't forgotten it's the Delaneys' party tonight?"

Milly groaned and rolled her eyes.

"Finish that quickly," said Linda, ignoring her, "and I'll take you into town with me. Your hair needs a trim and— Good God, darling, your *feet!* You look like a hobbit. I'd better see if they can fit you in for a pedicure too."

"Don't bother. I'm not going," said Milly, getting herself down a plate.

"Of course you're going," said Linda firmly. "I've already accepted for all of us. It would be unspeakably rude to pull out now."

"Well then, I'll just have to be unspeakably rude, won't I?" Grabbing the hot toast, Milly sat down next to Cecil. "Besides, I never accepted anything. You accepted for me because you're still trying to pimp me out to John Ashton like a bloody geisha."

"Don't be rude to your mother," said Cecil on autopilot.

"It's not up for discussion anyway," said Linda."You're coming if I have to drag you there myself. And you're getting your hair done too."

Pushing her chair back with a clatter Milly leaped to her feet, glaring at her mother. "I hate you!" she sobbed. "I don't want to go to a stupid fucking party. Easy's dead. Don't you get it? Dead. I loved him. Doesn't that mean anything to you?"

"We all loved him," said Linda frostily.

"You?" Milly shook her head in disbelief. "You never loved him. You couldn't have picked him out in a two-horse lineup, and you know it!"

"Milly, that's enough," said Cecil. But she'd already stormed off, slamming the kitchen door with an earthshaking thud behind her.

"Maybe I should go and talk to her," he said, pushing away his coffee cup with a worried frown.

"Don't you dare," said Linda. She was sick of everyone pandering to Milly and dignifying her tantrums with concern. "It's straightforward bad behavior, that's what it is. I don't know how you can be so down on poor Jasper, when Milly's the one behaving like a spoiled child. If anyone's not pulling their weight, it's her."

Sensing a marital storm brewing, Bobby snuck out of the room and made his way quietly upstairs.

"Knock knock," he said softly, opening Milly's bedroom door a fraction. She was lying facedown on top of her duvet, her whole body shaking with sobs.

"Go away!" Her yell was muffled by the pillow.

She was grateful that he'd come after her, but much as she longed to fling herself into his arms, she didn't want him to see her looking all red faced and snotty. She hadn't even had time to clean her teeth yet this morning, so she probably smelled awful too.

"Come on," he said, ignoring her and perching on the edge of the bed. He smelled of sweat and horsehair, a heady combination that made Milly's senses reel. "Talk to me. You know I'm not leaving until you do."

Reluctantly, she rolled over. Her eyes were red around the edges and still watery, and her glorious mane of hair was sticking up at all angles in a tangled thatch, as though someone had rubbed her head with a balloon. Her wide, pale lips were trembling, whether with anger or sadness it was impossible to tell. All Bobby knew was that he didn't think he'd ever seen her looking more adorable.

She's a kid, he told himself firmly. The sooner he got back to Highwood, and got over this infatuation, the better.

"I don't care what Mummy says," Milly sniffed defiantly. "I'm not going. I'd rather eat snakes."

"Uh-huh." He smiled. "Well, that's a shame. I was kinda relying on you to help me get through the evening. And I have to go. Rachel's dad is paying me."

Milly sat up in bed, wiping her nose on her pajama sleeve.

"You don't need me," she said, unable to keep the bitterness entirely out of her voice. "There'll be girls galore there happy to take care of you, I'm sure. Deborah'll be there," she added pointedly.

"Maybe," Bobby said. "But I can't talk to her the way I talk to you."

Milly flushed with happiness. It was the most directly affectionate thing he'd ever said to her. Ever since their hug in Easy's stable, he'd pulled back from her in some indefinable, and yet undeniable, way. The easy friendship and camaraderie they'd enjoyed before seemed to have disappeared, replaced by an awkwardness that she had no idea how to bridge.

There were moments, like that moment in the stable, when she could almost believe he felt something for her. But then he'd go back to being grown-up and distant, back to Deborah and all the other sophisticated, sexy girls who could evidently give him something that she couldn't. God, how she hated them all.

It was nice to be the one that he could talk to. But she'd so much have preferred to be the one he couldn't keep his hands off.

Standing up, Bobby moved over to the window and stared outside. It was a cloudy morning and the wind was blowing already-brown leaves all over the yard, making them dance like autumn sprites across the concrete.

"I'm leaving on Thursday, you know," he said. "Back to the States."

"This Thursday?" Milly looked horrified. "But that's only six days away! I thought you were going to be here for six weeks?"

"It's been six weeks," he said with a shrug, feigning a nonchalance he was far from feeling. "Actually, it's been seven. And I have a ranch to run. Folks back home'll have forgotten what I look like."

"No they won't," said Milly. She was biting her lower lip to keep the tears from flowing, but he could see how upset she was that he was going. Maybe that was part of what drew him to her so strongly? Other girls wanted him, but none of them really cared about him the way that she did.

"You can come visit," he said, taking her hand in his and stroking it gently, trying his utmost to feel paternal, "once I've got my quarter horses."

"Yeah, right," said Milly, entwining her fingers with his and wishing more than anything that she never had to let him go. "I can't see my parentals agreeing to that in a hurry, can you?"

"You never know," said Bobby. Although privately he agreed with her. Cecil and Linda would want her to forget all about him. But maybe that wasn't such a bad thing. She should find a nice English boy her own age. Make her mom's dreams come true.

"If you really want me to come tonight, I will," said Milly. "But I'm only doing it for you, not bloody Mummy."

"Understood," he said, turning away from the window at last. "Who knows?" he added brightly. "We might even have fun."

It was seven fifteen before they were all, finally, in the car.

Jasper was usually the prima donna of the family, but tonight he'd gone on ahead with Rachel, and for once it was Milly who held every-one up, insisting on changing her outfit at the last minute.

She'd planned to wear a slinky red number, that went with her new, sophisticated, swept-up hair. But she'd suddenly panicked that it was too Ivana Trump and decided to change into a more subdued, olive-green von Furstenberg wrap dress instead.

She was pleased with the result, though. For once, Bobby was going to see her looking sexy. It was almost enough to make her glad she'd de-cided to come to stupid Rachel's stupid party after all.

Skipping out to the car, full of hope and anticipation, she twirled around in front of Bobby like a ballerina. "Ta da!" She giggled. "What do you think?"

He frowned. "You look different."

Milly's face fell. It was hardly the rapturous response she'd been hoping for.

"Don't you like it?"

"Come on, chop-chop," said Cecil impatiently before Bobby had a chance to answer. "Get in, you two. We're late enough as it is."

Climbing miserably into the backseat beside Bobby, Milly felt ut-terly deflated. So much for impressing him. He'd made her feel about as attractive as a foot fungus.

Shifting uncomfortably in his own seat, Bobby steadfastly refused to look in her direction. That green dress clung to her curves so sexily, it unnerved him. No, you know what, screw "unnerved." He hated it. She didn't look like Milly. How was he supposed to desexualize her and respect her innocence when she dolled herself up like Audrey fucking Hepburn? And what was with all that goddamn makeup covering her freckles? He longed to lean over right now and wipe it off with his bare hands. But instead he made do with staring moodily out of the window all the way to the Delaneys'.

"Wow," he said, whistling through his teeth as Cecil finally swung the Range Rover through the lichened stone gates of Mittlingsford Manor. For a moment he forgot all about Milly as they rattled down the bumpy track that led to the Delaneys' red-brick, ivy-clad gem of a house.

"Gorgeous, isn't it?" said Cecil.

"No kidding."

He'd heard a lot about the manor from various people, but this was the first time he'd seen it for himself. Lady Delaney had refused point-blank to entertain any visitors till their building works were finished, and all his meetings with Sir Michael had been at Newells. But people were right: It was a stunning house. Its faded Queen Anne grandeur set it apart from the thatched quaintness of the rest of Mittlingsford village, with its elegantly symmetrical façade of huge sash windows and its closely cropped, dark yew hedges bordering the formal lawns like the velvet trim on a smoking jacket. Tonight, lit from the front by hundreds of flickering candles lining the driveway and hung from the lower branches of the trees—Julia Delaney had really pushed the boat out this year—it looked more spectacular than ever.

"Let's find the bar, shall we?" said Cecil. Like his daughter he'd been dreading tonight's party—with the stud in crisis, the last thing he felt like was being sociable—but now that they were here the prospect of an imminent drink had lifted his spirits.

Milly, on the other hand, felt lower than ever as she clambered miserably out of the car. Bobby was still ignoring her. It was almost as if she'd offended him in some way, although she couldn't for the life of her think how. Why had he asked her to come tonight, if all he was going to do was sulk?

Watching him stride into the house without so much as a backward glance in her direction, she steeled herself for a miserable evening ahead. A couple of hours ago she'd felt awash with confidence. Now she felt like Cinderella at a minute after midnight—drab, dreary, and out of place.

"Milly. How are you?" Rachel descended on her the moment she walked through the door, bursting with pseudo-warmth, no doubt for Linda's benefit. Even Milly had to admit she looked ravishing in a starkly cut, backless black dress with a sexy fishtail, her blond hair flowing over her bare shoulders in heavy, cascading waves, like clotted cream glugging slowly out of a jug. Standing next to her, Milly knew she must look frumpy by comparison and felt the last vestiges of her good mood draining away, like used bathwater.

147

"Fine, thanks," she said frostily.

"There are soft drinks for the younger guests in the library," said Rachel in an audible aside to Linda, "if you'd rather Milly didn't drink. And videos and things in there too, if she's bored."

"I'm not a fucking child," Milly snapped, realizing too late that her petulant tone made her sound like one. Bobby turned to look at her, the first time he'd done so since they got in the car. But he had such a pained expression on his face she wished he hadn't. What was *wrong* with him tonight?

"Rachel was only trying to be helpful, dear," said Linda. "Darling!" Her face lit up as Jasper came over. "Don't you look handsome!"

"Hullo, Ma," he said, kissing her on both cheeks. "Dad."

Glaring at Bobby, he snaked a proprietorial arm around Rachel's black-sequined waist. Though she professed to have no interest in Bobby, Jasper had learned long ago that when it came to potential sexual rivals it paid to keep your friends close and your enemies closer.

"What the fuck happened to you this afternoon?" Cecil found his bad mood returning as soon as he saw his son. "We needed you at Newells. Bobby ended up taking the horses out. Doing your job for you. Again."

"I was busy," said Jasper, looking down at his perfectly manicured nails with a practiced boredom that drove Cecil up the wall. "But, thank you, Bobby. Riding to the rescue as usual. Quite the hero, aren't we?"

Bobby felt his fists twitching. Milly's outfit had already plunged him into a foul mood, but Jasper's snide bullshit was the icing on the cake. What he wouldn't give to plant a punch right in the center of the smug asshole's face.

"I do what I can," he said, through gritted teeth.

"Shouldn't you have been working with my horses this afternoon?" Rachel asked haughtily. She hadn't forgotten the way that Bobby had dissed her at Milly's play, and was still looking for an opportunity to get her own back. "That is what Daddy pays you for, after all."

"They're your father's horses, Rachel, not yours," said Bobby brutally. "And I've already taken them as far as they can go. But I appreciate your concern."

Milly grinned. He might be being a jerk to her, but Bobby was still the master when it came to putting Rachel down. Served her right, the patronizing cow.

"What a ridiculous thing to say!" Rachel snapped, losing her cool at last. She looked like someone had just squeezed a lemon into her eye. "Horses can always improve. Victor's been training those colts for a year, and he's still working at it."

Bobby shrugged. "I'm better than Victor," he said, before elbowing past her toward the bar.

"Arrogant son of a bitch!" spluttered Jasper.

"He may be arrogant," said Cecil, "but at least he's always bloody there when you need him."

Not when I need him he isn't, thought Milly, watching Bobby's back disappearing into the throng.

In a few days he'd be gone for good. Tonight was supposed to have been their special night together. How had it all gone so wrong already?

Walking into the drawing room, Bobby was overwhelmed by the crush of guests and heavy miasma of cigar smoke. The room itself reminded him of something out of a history book: all parquet floors and high ceilings with double doors at the far end opening out onto the veranda. Grabbing himself a glass of Pimm's from the bar, he stepped outside. Inhaling the warm evening air, heavy with the scent of honeysuckle, he tried to relax.

Rachel Delaney was a bitch. Meaner than a rattlesnake and spoiled as hell to boot. She and Jasper deserved each other.

Walking down the sloping lawn toward the stream that wound its way along the bottom of the garden, he tried not to think about them, or Milly. Two giggling blondes who passed him gave him the eye and he smiled back, but his heart wasn't in it. For a moment he wondered if he'd slept with one of them a few weeks ago, the shorter one, but as he got closer he could see it was a different girl. Just as well. He couldn't remember the name of the one he'd fucked, anyway.

He reflected how much fun his first few weeks in England had been, screwing around with all the carefree abandon of a sophomore on

149

spring break. But that was before he'd fallen for Milly. Before things had all gotten complicated.

Looking around, he recognized a number of pretty faces from those first weeks, as well as a bunch of jockeys and trainers he'd met through Cecil. The Delaneys' drinks party was an annual fixture on the British racing scene, and everyone who was anyone in the horse world had shown up to enjoy Sir Michael's legendary hospitality.

Milly's old idols Frankie Dettori and Robbie Pemberton were both there, the latter having arrived with a stunning six-foot redhead who towered over him like Helen of Troy on stilts. Bobby recognized the great American rider Jakey Forster and a slew of British flat racing stars, as well as a couple of jump jockeys who'd made the cut. As usual, they were the rowdiest of the lot, whooping it up at the bar with their Sloaney girlfriends or running around squirting the bigwigs from the Jockey Club headquarters in Portman Square with giant water pistols that they'd filled with Pimm's from the jugs at the bar.

After seven weeks in England, Bobby was just beginning to grasp the rudiments of the complex social divisions in British racing. As far as he could tell, the Newmarket flat racing crowd generally considered the jumping crowd to be amateurs, a lot of horsey Hooray Henrys from Gloucestershire, rather than serious, professional sportsmen. For their part, the jump jockeys looked down on their flat racing rivals as "nouves"—nouveau riches—and rarely mingled with them socially. It was kind of like the way the Kentucky owners and breeders looked down on the quarter horse crowd. But tonight both parties seemed to have called a temporary truce.

"Mr. Cameron!" Michael Delaney came marching across the lawn, all smiles and open arms. "Glad you could make it." He had a large glass of punch in his hand, which judging by his ruddy complexion, Bobby reckoned must be his fourth or fifth. His swelling paunch was already stretching his silk cummerbund dangerously close to breaking point.

"Wouldn't have missed it," said Bobby. "Your gardens are incredible, by the way."

"Thank you." Sir Michael looked genuinely gratified. "We like them.

Although, from what I gather, you have a pretty lovely spread waiting for you back in California."

"Yeah,"said Bobby, smiling properly for the first time that evening. "Yeah, I do."

He was ashamed to admit that recently Milly had pushed Highwood right out of his head. But now that he was going home, reality had begun to reassert itself at last. Wyatt's phone calls had become more and more anxious. If he still wanted to start his quarter horse farm— and he did, more than ever—he was going to have to come to some arrangement with the bank, and quickly.

"You must miss it."

"I do," said Bobby truthfully. "But there are things I'll miss here too, when I go." He glanced around the garden, looking for Milly, but she was nowhere to be seen.

"Well, I for one will be sorry to see you go," said Sir Michael. "You've done an incredible job with my horses. Just incredible. Andy!" He waved to an elderly man, deep in conversation with two equally elderly women a few feet away. "Come and meet my friend Bobby Cameron. He's the American trainer I've been telling you about."

While Bobby was distracting himself basking in praise at one end of the garden, Milly sat alone under a willow tree at the other end, getting steadily drunker.

"Oy. OY!" she yelled at a passing waiter. "I'll have one of those. Pleashe."

He brought over a silver platter of mini-sausages wrapped in bacon and looked on disapprovingly as Milly scraped the whole lot onto her empty plate. After he'd gone, she took another swig of champagne from the bottle she'd purloined earlier and stuffed a handful of the hot, greasy food into her mouth. Depression seemed to have given her an appetite. Or perhaps that was the alcohol?

Kicking off her high heels—stupid bloody things were giving her blisters, and Bobby obviously didn't find them sexy anyway—she unpinned her hair while she ate. The hairdresser had pulled her updo in so tightly it was making her face ache. After her seventh sausage, she started to feel a bit queasy and thought perhaps a walk might clear her head. She could see Bobby still holding court by the stream, so she headed in the opposite direction, staggering aimlessly toward the rhododendron bushes.

They were far enough away from the house that there was very little light, and even in bare feet she had difficulty picking her way over the bumpy ground. Suddenly, she heard a noise through the bushes, a sort of half groan, half pant. It sounded as though someone might be in trouble.

"Hellooo?" she called tentatively into the darkness. "Is anyone there?"

No answer.

"Are you all right?"

Silence. Then, there it was again. The noise. With courage that owed more than a little to all the champagne she'd just drunk, she fought her way through the leafy branches of the rhododendrons toward the sound. Her dress was snagging horribly on all the twigs and would probably be ruined, but if someone were lying back there, injured, and she hadn't done anything she'd never forgive herself.

"Helloooo?"

"Jesus Christ! Milly!"

It was Jasper. Not injured but standing, with his knees bent and his trousers around his ankles, receiving what looked to be a very enthusiastic blow job from Lucy McCallum, one of Rachel's closest so-called friends. In fact, Lucy was so focused on the job in hand (or rather in mouth) that she'd failed to hear Milly's approach and continued bobbing her sleek brunette head backward and forward like a clockwork woodpecker.

Screaming, Milly turned and ran, stumbling onto her hands and knees more than once in her desperation to get away. She didn't think she'd ever seen anything quite so revolting. Just knowing that J. was already cheating on Rachel might have cheered her up, but having to actually *watch* him, *naked,* doing *that* . . . the thought of it made her stomach churn. She began regretting the sausages even more.

Without stopping, she ran mindlessly, back up the lawn onto the veranda, and bolted through the French doors into the drawing room.

Through the combined fog of panic and drunkenness, it took a moment or so for her to realize that the entire room had turned to stare at her.

Rachel, ironically, was one of the last to notice Milly's sudden, bedraggled, barefoot arrival. Since Jasper had wandered off she'd been having a whale of a time being chatted up by a permatanned, white-toothed cockney sports agent called Desmond Leach.

"No doubt abaht it," Des had been assuring her in his smooth, cockney patter, "you could be makin' a lot more dough than you are at the moment. It's all about finkin' big picture, innit?"

He wasn't the first person to tell her that she ought to be making more of the small flurry of press interest she'd received as a sexy female rider. Although she pretended to scorn publicity, secretly Rachel adored the attention and had often fantasized about becoming racing's "It Girl," a sort of Tori Spelling mark II, only in her case riding a horse rather than looking like one.

"You'd look terrific in *GQ*," Des went on, edging ever closer toward her on the sofa. "I'm finkin' lovely, sexy shots, you in your undies in the stables. All very tasteful though, o' course."

Rachel had barely begun to lose herself in this intoxicating idea when who should come staggering in but bloody Milly, looking for all the world like she'd just been molested. Her hair was everywhere; her hands, knees, feet, and face were all smeared with mud; and her dress was cut to ribbons.

"What on earth happened to you?" Extricating herself from Des's advances, she looked her up and down with distaste.

"What?" said Milly, confused. She'd been so desperate to get away from Jasper she hadn't given a thought to how she must look, but looking down at her shredded dress now, it finally dawned on her why everyone was staring. "Oh, that. Sorry. Nothing. I fell. Over. I fell over." God, it was hard trying to string a sentence together after a bottle of Dom Pérignon.

"Jesus. Are you okay?" The next thing Milly knew, Bobby was beside her, wrapping a strong arm around her shoulders, his concern in sharp contrast to Rachel's hostility. She felt a brief flicker of happiness—

he seemed to have gotten over whatever it was that had been pissing him off before—but it was soon replaced by horror when she realized what a sight she must look, especially standing next to Rachel in full-on goddess mode.

"What happened, Mill?" he pressed her, his voice loaded with a tenderness that for some reason made Milly want to cry. "Did someone hurt you?"

"No." She shook her head. "Nothing like that. I'll tell you later."

"Uh-uh, I don't think so." He bundled her outside as people gradually drifted back to their prior conversations. If anyone had touched her . . . if anyone had laid one finger . . . "Tell me now."

"Look, it was nothing, okay?" she snapped. Perhaps it was Dutch courage, but she was getting sick of the way he kept running hot and cold with her: loving and sweet this morning, moody and withdrawn all evening, and now apparently back in knight-in-shining-armor mode. "I was down in the bushes—"

"What?" Bobby's face clouded over. "Why? Who with?"

"With no one," said Milly, exasperated. "By myself. At least I thought I was by myself."

Before she could get any further, Jasper came running up the hill, his face flushed with what looked to Bobby like exertion but Milly recognized as panic. Ignoring Bobby, he made a beeline for his sister.

"Have you said anything?" he asked breathlessly, adding, when she didn't reply instantly, "You'd better bloody not have or your life won't be worth living, I can promise you that."

"Oh, up yours," said Milly. The champagne was definitely helping. "What do you think I'm going to do? Walk into the party and announce to the world that I caught you playing hide the sausage with one of Rachel's best friends? As if I care!"

"I'm sorry," said Bobby, grinning as he began to piece together what must have happened. "Hide the sausage? I don't think I know that game."

"Bollocks," said Jasper bitterly. "You're Olympic bloody champion at it, so don't go getting on your high horse with me, Cameron. And you'll keep your mouth shut as well, if you know what's good for you."

154

"Oh yeah?" said Bobby, bristling at the implied threat. "And what if I don't?"

"I'll—I'll—you'll see," Jasper blustered lamely. "I'll make sure you regret it, that's all."

"To be honest, I doubt Rachel will even care," said Milly, who was enjoying seeing her brother on the back foot for once. "She looked *very* cozy with that good-looking sports agent on the sofa a few minutes ago. I think she's forgotten all about you."

"Rubbish," Jasper said. But he looked intensely worried and quickened his pace as he left them and headed up toward the house.

"Did you really catch them at it?" said Bobby, laughing, after he'd gone.

Milly nodded. "Loose McCallum was giving him head in the rhododendrons. It was the grossest thing I've seen in my entire life."

It felt nice to be talking together like this, relaxed, the way they used to be.

"No wonder you look like you've been through the wars," he said.

"Oh, God." Instantly self-conscious again, Milly brought her hands to her tangled hair, and she began frantically rubbing at the smeared mud on her face with the back of her hand. "I must look awful."

"No," said Bobby, grabbing her hand and pulling it away from her face. "Don't. You look so much better. Natural. I didn't like how you looked before. It wasn't you."

Milly stood there, achingly conscious of the warmth of his hand enveloping her own, until her reverie was shattered by a piercing cry from the terrace behind her.

"Help!" Her mother's voice was unmistakable, but the panic in it was unfamiliar and frightening. "Somebody help here! Quickly!"

Pulling free from Bobby's grip, Milly raced up the stone steps to where Linda was kneeling, leaning over what looked like a body.

"Julia, call an ambulance." Sir Michael's authoritative voice cut through the night air like a foghorn.

"Mummy?" With huge trepidation, Milly pushed her way through the gathering crowd. It was only as she got right next to her mother that she recognized the figure sprawled out on the stone, his head lolling from side to side in semiconsciousness. It was Cecil.

* * *

The drive to the hospital was all a bit of a blur. Linda rode in the ambulance with Cecil, now heavily sedated, and Jasper, who looked absolutely white with shock. It had been quite an evening.

Never one to miss a drama, Rachel had insisted on coming along with him "for support," so by the time Milly got to the ambulance, there was no more room. Reluctantly, she'd agreed to follow behind with Bobby in her parents' car.

"The paramedics told Mummy it was a minor stroke," she said, wringing her hands anxiously in the passenger seat and sobering up by the second as they hurtled toward Addenbrookes Hospital in Cambridge. "Can a stroke really be minor, though?"

"Sure it can," said Bobby, trying to sound reassuring although in fact he hadn't a clue what he was talking about. "Half of his slurring and confusion is probably just booze. You wait and see. They'll run a CT scan and he'll be fit as a fiddle."

By the time they arrived at the hospital, Linda and Jasper were already in the waiting room, looking ashen. Rachel sat between them, her makeup still perfect despite the practiced look of concern that she now wore while she squeezed Linda's hand. Any other day and Milly would have wanted to throttle her. But right now all she could think about was her father.

"How's he doing?" she asked Jasper.

"We don't know yet," he said, forgetting to be rude for once. "They're still running tests. The nurse said it may be a while before anyone can see him."

"I'll do a coffee run then, if anyone wants some," said Bobby. "I figure y'all could use some family time alone. Rachel, you wanna join me? Give these folks some room?"

For a moment the Princess Diana angel-of-mercy mask slipped and Rachel snarled at him silently, her lips puckered into a tiny cat's bum of fury.

"No, thank you," she said tersely. "I think I can do more good here. But I will have a coffee if you're going. Milk, two sugars. And the same for Mrs. LG."

Linda smiled at her gratefully. "How sweet of you to remember, Rachel."

"Don't go." Bobby felt Milly grab his arm. "I want you to stay. Please."

Most of the mud had been wiped off her cheeks, but her mascara was smudged beneath both eyes, making her look like a monsoon-drenched possum, and she was shivering in the flimsy tatters of her wrap dress. The drafty hospital corridor was so cold it made the downy blond hairs on her forearm stand on end.

Bobby hadn't seen her looking so vulnerable since the night that Easy died. Nor had he wanted her as much since then.

"Of course I'll stay," he said, once again resisting the urge to pull her to him. "If that's what you want. I didn't want to intrude, that's all." He looked pointedly at Rachel, who glowered back.

It was over two hours before a smiling Welsh nurse emerged from the swing doors behind the reception desk and announced that "the patient" was now well enough to receive visitors. At Milly's insistence, Bobby followed the family along the brightly lit linoleum corridor with its cloying scent of disinfectant (Rachel didn't wait to be asked) and into Cecil's room, a stark, windowless box with a cast-iron bed on which he was propped up with four large pillows. He smiled sheepishly as they all trooped in.

"Darling," sobbed Linda, rushing straight to his side and flinging her arms around him. "We were all so worried. Are you all right?"

"He's fine," said a voice from behind the door. None of them had noticed the consulting physician standing there, and they all spun around now as one to stare at him. "I'm Dr. Triggs." He introduced himself to Linda, nodding a vague acknowledgment to everyone else in the room. "Your husband has had a stroke, Mrs. Lockwood Groves, which is a serious thing, although thankfully his CT scan and the other tests we've run show no permanent damage to his brain or nervous system."

"See?" whispered Bobby, with a wink at Milly.

"Do you know what caused it, doctor?" asked Rachel.

Now that the worst was over, Milly allowed herself to feel the first small stabs of annoyance at the way Rachel had muscled in on the situation. She shouldn't even *be* here, let alone be asking questions. It wasn't her dad who'd collapsed.

"Well, we can't say for sure," said the doctor, no doubt mistaking her for a daughter. He looked sternly at Cecil. "But his blood alcohol level was shocking, and his arteries look like the M25 in rush hour, so it's a safe bet that an atrocious diet and complete lack of exercise had something to do with it."

"I knew it!" said Linda. "How many times have I warned you about your diet, Cecil? How many?"

"Before you get carried away," said Cecil weakly, "Dr. Triggs also says that stress may have been a factor. So no one's allowed to shout at me or force-feed me lettuce, because I find that very stressful. Isn't that right, doctor?"

The doctor looked at him rather as a strict headmaster might look at a troublemaking fourth former.

"Shouting is perhaps best avoided," he said. "But lettuce sounds like an excellent idea to me."

Linda looked triumphant.

"For the moment, though, you need some rest. So no more than ten minutes visiting, please, and then I suggest you all get some kip and come back and see him in the morning."

"You do look tired, Dad," said Milly, grabbing a plastic chair from the other side of the room and elbowing Rachel out of the way so she could sit right next to the bed. "Do you want us to go now?"

"No," said Cecil. "No. Actually I want you all to stay. I've been thinking about things a lot in the last few hours. Not knowing what was wrong with me. Not knowing if I was even going to make it or not."

"Oh, darling, don't say that," said Linda with a shudder. Rachel put an arm around her, and Milly noticed the way that her mother leaned into it, like an injured bird. Since when had those two become thick as thieves? Some time since Easy's death, she imagined, when she'd been too off the ball to notice. Was there no tragedy the girl wouldn't exploit to inveigle her insidious way into Milly's family?

"Whether or not I say it, it's true," said Cecil, shifting his position against the pillows, trying to make himself more comfortable. "Something like this really puts life into perspective." He smiled weakly at Milly. "I owe you an apology, sweetheart."

"For what?" she asked, surprised.

"For a lot of things," said Cecil, his eyes welling up with tears. The sedatives they'd got him on must be making him overly emotional. "But most recently for standing in the way of you going to America. It's time you got on with your own life, and if that means riding again, so be it. Bobby's offered you a great opportunity. You should take it."

Milly looked at him blankly. It was too much to take in, especially after the roller coaster of emotions she'd been through this evening. It was like your jailer suddenly turning around and giving you not only the keys to your cell but a passport and a blank check too, to start a whole new life. "Thank you" just didn't seem to cut it.

"Darling." Linda laughed nervously. "I hardly think now's the time to be making these sorts of big decisions. We should talk about this in the morning, when you're more yourself."

"She's right, you know," said Jasper, backed up by some enthusiastic nodding from Rachel. The idea of Milly riding competitively again, even if it was going to be in America, racing obscure cowboy horses no one had ever heard of, filled both of them with horror. "You haven't thought it through, Dad."

"Put a sock in it, J.," said Cecil firmly. "I'm talking to your sister. Milly?"

"I don't know what to say," she said quietly, praying that this was real, that it wasn't just the drugs talking.

"You do still *want* to go?" said Cecil.

"Of course, of course I do!" she said. "If you're really serious. And if Bobby's offer still stands?"

Bobby, who'd been hovering at the back of the room, trying to keep a low profile, felt uncomfortably aware of ten eyes swiveling simultaneously in his direction: Linda's, Jasper's, and Rachel's all narrowed in suspicion; Cecil's wide with questioning anticipation; and Milly's dewy and wet with hope.

Even if he'd wanted to change his mind, there was no way he could do it now.

"Sure." He smiled. "Of course."

"All I ask," said Cecil earnestly, "is that you take good care of her."

"The best, sir," said Bobby. "You have my word on it."

So that was that. Milly was coming to Highwood, to his life, his world, whether he liked it or not. Part of him was thrilled not to have to leave her—but another part knew that her presence there would be more of an exquisite torture than a joy.

Romance was out of the question. Apart from the fact that she was far too young and he had a ranch to rescue, he'd just promised her sick father that he'd act in loco parentis. And though he might be guilty of many things, Bobby Cameron didn't break his promises.

Once they got to California, his job was to be Milly's father. And that was exactly what he intended to do.

CHAPTER ELEVEN

Dylan McDonald was up in his room at Highwood, painting. Since Hank's passing, life at the ranch had been so hectic that he'd had even less time than usual to work on his art. But today was Sunday, and the light pouring in through his dormer window when he woke up was so good, he'd decided to skip breakfast and get straight to it.

Perched at his easel in an old pair of Nike sweatpants and a T-shirt, he was adding the finishing touches to the portrait of his father that he'd started in secret some three months ago, working from an old photograph.

He was disturbed by a knock on the door. Hurriedly, he grabbed a towel to throw over the canvas, trying to keep the impatience out of his voice. "Who is it?"

"It's me, Summer. I brought you up some sugar with a little coffee in it. Can I come in?"

Grinning, he opened the door and bundled her inside, relieving her of the steaming cup of syrupy joe, his absolute favorite. Dylan loved all his family, but he felt closest to Summer. Less grown-up and serious than Tara, she was the one he had most in common with. Although looking at his jet-black curls and olive skin next to her Swedish blond complexion, no one would have guessed the two were even related.

"Can I see?" she asked, gesturing to the hastily covered easel.

He frowned. "I guess." He hated, dreaded showing his work to anyone. Like most talented artists he was ridden by neurotic self-doubts, but in his case they were made worse by the knowledge that his dad, not to mention all the other Highwood hands, figured painting was for sissies: the Santa Ynez equivalent of announcing you were moving to

San Francisco, changing your name to Peaches, and planned on performing Barbra Streisand numbers in drag for the rest of your life.

Summer was different, though. She'd always understood.

"Shit, Dyl," she said, whistling with admiration as he tentatively peeled back the towel. "That's amazing. You've really got him. How old was he then?"

He handed her the picture of Wyatt he'd been working from, a battered old black-and-white snap he'd "borrowed" from his mother's album. "It's not dated. But I'm guessin' twenty-two, twenty-three?"

Summer shook her head and laughed. "Handsome son of a bitch, wasn't he? What happened? He looks like a prune."

"Oh, stop it," said Dylan. "You wait and see what you look like in your late fifties, after forty years out in all weather, working the land."

"Me?" She flung herself backward onto his bed, her long, tanned legs dangling down over the edge like two supple sticks of caramel. "I'm not spending forty *minutes* working the land, never mind forty years. I'm going to go to Berkeley, and then Harvard Law." She counted her future achievements off on her fingers nonchalantly. "Then I'll make millions, live in LA, and be so rich I can get my face lifted at the first inkling of a wrinkle. No prune face for me."

She will, too, thought Dylan, looking at his sister's flawless face, awash with the promise and confidence of her youth, as smart as she was beautiful. She'll do all that and more. And I'll be stuck here, driving cattle and breaking horses for Bobby till they carry me away in a box.

"What d'you think she'll be like?" asked Summer, abruptly changing the subject. Milly's arrival had been the hot topic of conversation at the ranch since Bobby called to say he'd be bringing the English breeder's daughter back with him. The plan was apparently for Bobby to train her to race quarter horses, in return for which she'd help out at the ranch.

Dylan shrugged. "I don't know. Bobby says she's a terrific rider."

"Hmmmn." Summer frowned skeptically. "I'll believe it when I see it."

Everyone else was excited to meet Milly, but Summer was distinctly nonplussed. The truth, though she would rather die than admit it to a living soul, was that she had loved Bobby for as long as she could remember. The last thing she wanted was some snotty-nosed English madam waltzing in and stealing his attention.

Not that he had ever showed the slightest romantic interest in her. As far as he and everyone else at Highwood was concerned, Bobby was her big brother in all but genetics. But one day, she meant to change that. And in the meantime, she took comfort in the knowledge that he'd never been serious about any of the many girls he dated. As unsatisfactory as it was, the sisterly bond she shared with him remained his closest female relationship.

This Milly chick was the first girl ever to threaten it. And though they hadn't met, Summer already hated her with a passion she was having more and more trouble concealing.

"You could sell that, you know," she said, sitting up and switching her attention suddenly back to her brother's portrait. "It's very good. Why don't you show it to Martha Bentley's mom? You know she just opened a new gallery in Santa Barbara as well as the place in Los Olivos?"

About five miles further down the tourist trail from Solvang, Los Olivos was a pretty wine-making town that had lately become a haven for artists, writers, and what Wyatt liked to refer to as "hippie types" from across California. There were a number of galleries there, of which Bentley's was just one.

"I don't think so," said Dylan, covering up the picture again with finality. "No one in Santa Barbara is gonna want to buy a picture of Dad. Besides, I'm not that pleased with it. It still needs a lot of work."

Wrapping her arms around his waist, Summer gave him a sisterly kiss. "Bullshit. It's great," she said. Dylan had always been too modest, happy to hang back in the shadows and let someone else shine. She wished he wouldn't put himself down so much.

As for her, lack of confidence had never been her problem. Nor was she one to shy away from a fight. If this Milly whatever her dumbass name was thought she was going to steamroll her way into Bobby's affections, she'd have to get past her first. Summer had her sweet side—she was a loving sister and a loyal friend—but when she put her mind to it, she could also be a formidable opponent.

* * *

Some fifty miles away, Bobby was so exhausted he was having trouble keeping his eyes on the road. But despite his tiredness he was enjoying the drive home from the airport with Milly. She'd spent most of the journey with her head thrust through the window, as eager and alert as an overexcited puppy, gazing rapturously at the California countryside as it unfolded before them.

She could hardly believe that the Delaneys' party, and her father's collapse, had been only a week ago. The intense joy she'd felt after Cecil's spectacular change of heart had been followed by a short, sharp shock of grief as the reality of leaving Newells hit home. Not that she wasn't excited to be going to America with Bobby and, better still, riding competitively again. But Nancy and Pablo and the others had become like family to her over the years. She knew she'd miss them and the horses terribly. In a way, Easy's death had made the break less painful, as had the fact that Rachel's constant presence around the yard made it hard for her to relax at home anymore. But it was still a wrench.

Nor had her mother made things any easier, alternating between anger and tears in the run-up to her and Bobby's departure.

"What will I do without you?" Linda had moaned, the morning they finally left for the airport. "What with Daddy working all hours and Jasper off racing all over the country, I'll be quite on my own here."

She seemed to have conveniently forgotten that for the last six weeks she'd spent more time with Rachel than with Milly, and that on the rare occasions the two of them had been home alone together, they'd fought like cat and dog.

"It's only California, Mummy, not Mars," Milly tried to reassure her, as she heaved the last heavy case into the boot of the Range Rover. "I'll be back before you know it."

But would she? Her invitation to Highwood was open-ended, but despite Bobby's glowing descriptions of the place, she still had no real idea what to expect. All she did know was that her dreams and her destiny lay on the other side of the Atlantic. And it would take a lot more than a guilt trip from Linda to hold her back.

"It's just so beautiful," she said, gasping in awestruck wonder as they turned a corner and yet another lush, green valley spread itself out before them like Eden. "No wonder you love it here so much."

"Wait till you see Highwood," said Bobby proudly. "It'll knock you out, I promise you."

Milly didn't doubt it. She was already knocked out. The scenery was like nothing she had ever seen before. Or perhaps it was more of an amalgam of all the most beautiful places she *had* seen: the lush, rolling hills of the Lake District meeting the awesome splendor of the Swiss Alps, with Normandy poppy fields and a Côte d'Azur sky thrown in for good measure. The neon-bright, undulating greenery was so pristine it almost looked fake, as if God had picked up an enormous flat, manicured fairway and concertinaed it in his hands, crushing and folding it into steep hills and plunging valleys.

"Actually, that's pretty much how it happened," said Bobby, laughing, when she expressed this to him. "It was prehistoric earthquakes that scrunched the land up like that. It would have been flat once."

After another twenty minutes they eventually descended into another valley, and the wild landscape gave way to long stretches of flatter, more cultivated land. Turning off the highway toward Buellton, the long, straight road was lined on either side by sky-high sycamores, giving it the look of a Parisian avenue, and sparkling white fences marked the entrance to lovingly maintained paddocks and stable blocks, horse farms stretching as far as the eye could see.

"I thought you said this was cattle country?" said Milly, surprised.

"It is," said Bobby. "But cowboys need horses too. These are all quarter horse farms."

"I wonder why your dad was so against the idea of you starting a training stables then? You know, if everyone else was doing it."

At the mention of Hank, Bobby's face fell. In England he'd managed to push the specter of his father's death to the back of his mind. It had almost been a relief to be sucked into someone else's world, someone else's problems, and forget his own. But from the moment they touched down at LAX, he could feel a dark cloud descending on him once again: a miasma of paternal disapproval from beyond the grave.

"My dad was against a lot of things, for no particular reason," he said darkly.

Milly was about to giggle and say "mine too," but something about Bobby's face made her think better of it. Obviously his problems with Hank had gone a lot deeper than simply being forbidden to ride. He might not appreciate the comparison.

It wasn't until they finally pulled into the long driveway leading up to the ranch that the smile returned to Bobby's face.

"Hey, boss! Good to see you. Welcome home." Wyatt bounded across the dusty yard with the energy of a man half his age and clapped his hand warmly across Bobby's shoulders as he climbed out of the car. "And you must be Miss Lockwood Groves?"

"Milly, please." She smiled, unfolding her long legs from the cramped confinement of the front passenger seat and peeling her sweaty jeans from the backs of her thighs before offering him her hand. "How do you do, Mr. McDonald?"

Though he looked older than she had imagined from Bobby's description—sort of gnarled, like Yoda—she knew instantly that this must be Wyatt. She'd been told to look for the open, honest smile and strikingly blue eyes. Even with all the wrinkles, she thought, there was something quite handsome about him.

"It's Wyatt." He chuckled at her formality. "And I'm good, thank you, Milly. Welcome to Highwood."

Before she had time to say another word, Milly found herself being swooped upon by the McDonald women. Maggie came running out of the house first, her kindly face looking flustered, still in her dirty apron and with long wisps of graying blond hair escaping from an unruly bun.

"Bobby Cameron, put me down this instant!" she laughed delightedly as Bobby lifted her up in his arms and started twirling her around. "I'll put you over my knee, you hear me?"

Bobby had told her Maggie was like a mother to him, and Milly could see instantly how close the two of them were.

"I'm sorry, honey," said Maggie, offering Milly her flour-dusted hand once Bobby finally put her down. "I'm Maggie. Real pleased to meet you."

"And you." Milly beamed. These people all seemed so *nice*. It was like wandering onto a set of *The Waltons*. She turned to the pretty girl hovering just behind her. "And you must be Summer?"

"Tara," said the girl, relieving her of the jacket and purse she was still clutching in her hand.

That was Tara? According to Bobby, she was the plain sister. What on earth must Summer look like then? Claudia Schiffer?

A few seconds later and her question was answered when a ridiculously leggy blonde in a pair of micro Daisy Dukes that wouldn't have covered even one of Milly's butt cheeks flung herself at Bobby like a groupie at a rock star.

"You're back!" she squealed. "You're back, you're back, you're back!"

While Bobby kissed and embraced her, Milly took a closer look at the famous Summer. She was infinitely more beautiful than Bobby had described her. Flawless skin; insanely high, prominent cheekbones; and perfect, palest-pink Cupid's bow lips were framed by a waterfall of golden hair that would have made Rapunzel weep with jealousy. And as for that figure . . . as far as Milly could tell, 80 percent of her body mass must be made up of femur, and the other twenty was breasts. If Rachel Delaney were taller and willowy and elegant—and about a thousand times more gorgeous—she might look like a pale imitation of Summer McDonald.

Instinctively, Milly felt a small, sharp stab of hostility toward this goddess who was still showering Bobby with kisses in between bombarding him with an endless battery of questions about his trip. In her experience, girls that beautiful were normally serious bitches.

But she mustn't prejudge people. Bobby had described Summer as "a sweet kid" and perhaps she was just that? After all, it wasn't her fault she was beautiful.

Walking around the car, she waited for a lull in their conversation before introducing herself with a smile. "I'm Milly," she said. "I'm going to be training with B—"

"Yes, I know who you are," said Summer coolly. The smile was not reciprocated. "The new quarter horse sensation to be, Bobby told me."

"Oh," said Milly, flustered. Everyone else had been so polite and welcoming that this sudden rudeness had caught her off guard. "Well, er, I wouldn't say that exactly. I just want a chance to learn," she stammered.

"She's gonna do great," said Bobby, apparently unaware that Summer had fired a warning shot in Milly's direction. "Of course, we need to get the training facilities built first," he added wistfully.

"Yeah. We gotta talk about that," said Wyatt. "I spoke to the bank again this morning—"

"For heaven's sake, Wyatt, let the boy in the house before you start talking business," said Maggie. Then, turning to Milly, "And you must be exhausted, poor thing. Tara"—she looked at her elder daughter—"why don't you help Milly inside with her things. You'll be staying in the big house with Bobby," she explained to Milly, "but you'll eat most of your meals with us. And, of course, our door's always open if you feel like company."

"Thanks," said Milly.

Summer let out an audible groan.

Well, fuck you too, bitch. Who cares what you think? She was going to be sharing a house with Bobby. Just the two of them. Alone. It would take more than some pouting blond stick insect with her nose out of joint to take the gloss off that.

With Tara carrying her heaviest suitcase—lifting it as effortlessly as if it were empty—Milly struggled behind into the big house, lugging the smaller case with embarrassing difficulty up the wide wooden stairs to her room.

"So. This is the guest suite." Flinging the suitcase down on the bed, Tara opened the door through to the bathroom, a gorgeous Victorian affair with a freestanding copper bathtub and huge white jug beside the basin. "Your towels are in the cupboard there, and there's soap and toiletries in the basket. But you just let us know if you need anythin' else."

Milly sank down onto the bed and tried to take it all in. The room was exquisite—the whole house, in fact, was like a museum piece, a creaking wooden shrine to Wild Western Victoriana, each of its huge rooms still boasting their original floorboards and cornices and heavy oak doors. There was something slightly sad about the place though, despite its grandeur. It still felt like an old man's house. Perhaps Hank's spirit was not fully at rest yet? Whatever the root of the eeriness, she imagined Bobby must have felt terribly lonely, coming back here after his dad's death.

But he wouldn't be lonely anymore. Not with her here.

He still hadn't made even the faintest hint of a move on her since the night in Easy's stable. If anything, he'd become, if not exactly distant, then at least more big brotherly since Cecil had given his blessing for her to come to Highwood. But she wasn't overly concerned. Before, at Newells, she'd felt the clock constantly ticking. But now she had months, years even, to win him over. Surely here, in this beautiful old house, it could only be a matter of time before he realized that they were meant to be together?

"Supper's at seven, over at ours," said Tara, her voice a softer, more feminine version of Bobby's knee-weakening drawl. "Momma's made apple and walnut cobbler to celebrate your arrival, so I hope you're hungry."

Cobbler sounded nice. But what she really needed, thought Milly, sinking back against the softly plumped feather pillows as Tara closed the door behind her, was a bath. Summer might be a standoffish cow, but seeing her so fresh faced and stunning had reminded Milly how tired and smelly and travel worn she must look. If she was going to get Bobby to fall in love with her—and she was, somehow; she had to—then she couldn't afford to wander around smelling like a pair of Jasper's old socks while Summer shimmered beside her like an ethereal rose-scented Venus.

Wearily, she heaved herself to her feet and wandered into the bathroom. Now, what the hell had she done with that electric razor?

Meanwhile, over at the McDonald house, Bobby was sitting at the kitchen table with Wyatt and Dylan, who'd just gotten back from running some errands in Los Olivos. He was simultaneously sorting through two months of mail, listening to a summarized update of ranch business, and picking at a slice of Maggie's mouthwatering coffee cake.

"I do have one piece of good news," Wyatt was saying, as Bobby read and put aside another angry-red phone bill. "We have a guy comin' up to meet with you tomorrow, first thing. Wants to talk about quarter horses."

Bobby pricked up his ears. "Really? An investor?"

"Could be," said Wyatt. "Name of Todd Cranborn. Says he knows you, or he knew Hank or something. Even claims to have met me before, although I'm darned if I can recall it. Anyhow, he's a real estate guy from the city. Apparently he'd heard you were thinking of starting some sort of training school here and were looking for funds."

"Interesting." Bobby rubbed his chin thoughtfully, scratching the back of his hand on half an inch of blond stubble. "But why would a real estate guy be interested in a quarter horse farm?"

Wyatt shrugged. "No idea. Figured you could get into all that. All I do know is that he's the only fella so far who hasn't mentioned the word 'oil' to me. As far as I can tell he's serious about investing, and he's certainly rich enough to help us out."

"Cranborn," muttered Bobby to himself. "It kinda rings a bell. Dyl?"

"Never heard of him," said Dylan, cramming the last of Bobby's slice of coffee cake into his mouth. "But beggars can't be choosers, right? If he's got the cash—"

"We're not beggars, Dylan," chided his father.

"Not yet," said Bobby. "But let's face it, we're cutting it pretty fine now. If it's a choice between our friend Mr. Cranborn or Wells Fargo foreclosing, I know which horse I'm backin'. And he's interested in quarter horses you say. . . ." Already his mind was wandering off into fantasy, picturing state-of-the-art, air-conditioned stables and an indoor school, with a long, sandy stretch of gallops up on the hill.

"Let's just see what he has to say, shall we?" said Wyatt, cautious as ever. He'd always been more of a pragmatist than Hank, and he wasn't against Bobby's horse training idea. Ranching, like every other business, had to evolve in order to survive. He knew that. As long as they weren't vandalizing the land with oil wells and diggers, and there were still cattle on the hills, he was happy enough.

What worried him was the thought of Bobby leaping into something blind. Or, worse still, trying to build a new business before he'd dealt with the debts crippling the old one. He'd always been an impetuous kid, and he always, but always, thought he was right.

"Enough shoptalk," said Dylan, who was sick to the back teeth of hearing about investors and bankruptcy. "How was England? And what's this Miss Milly really like?"

"She's pretty," said Tara, who had just come in after settling Milly in at the big house. "Small but with an amazing figure."

"Please," said Summer, glancing up from the Steinbeck novel she'd been glued to for the past three days. "She so is not. I think she looks kinda masculine."

"Oh, no, now I wouldn't say that, would you, Bobby?" asked Maggie, joining the debate from the other side of the kitchen where she was sprinkling the last of the topping onto the cobbler.

"I don't know," he said moodily. "I never really thought about it."

Summer positively glowed with satisfaction at this response. She saw the way Milly had been looking at Bobby outside—like a teenage Priscilla Beaulieu drooling over Elvis—but evidently any feelings she might have for him were entirely one-sided.

"You never *thought* about it?" said Dylan. "*You* never thought about it? Bobby love-'em-and-leave-'em Cameron never thought about whether or not she's cute?"

"She's seventeen, Dyl," snapped Bobby. "Okay? She's here to ride and to work. She's a good kid, but that's it."

"Okay. Sure," said Dylan, raising an eyebrow at Tara. Bobby was famously quick to lose his temper but never normally with him; and certainly not over something as innocuous as a bit of teasing about a girl. "I was just curious, that's all."

A couple of hours later, his curiosity was satisfied. He'd spent the tail end of the day out mending fences with Wyatt, and by the time they got home again they were late for supper. His mother was tearing her hair out at the stove, struggling to keep the zucchini from disintegrating into a mess of green, overcooked slime.

"There you are!" she said, frowning. "About time." Lateness for meals was a cardinal sin in the McDonald household.

Lifting up a vast pot of potatoes, she began straining them over the sink, blasting her already flushed face with still more hot steam. "These were ready twenty minutes ago, you know," she said. "Tara, can you bring the butter over to the table, please, darlin'? And where is Milly?"

It wasn't like Maggie to get irritable, but ruined meals were one of her particular bugbears.

"I'm here." Milly appeared in the doorway, rubbing her eyes sleepily. "So sorry I'm late. I had a hot bath and lay down on the bed for five minutes, and I'm afraid I was out for the count. You should have woken me." This last was to Bobby, who immediately found himself trying to banish from his head an image of a flushed and naked Milly sprawled out on her bedspread. The effort seemed to plunge him back into a grouchy mood.

"Sorry," he said gruffly. "I got caught up with work."

"Well, never mind, never mind," said Maggie kindly. She didn't want the girl to feel unwelcome and was already regretting her earlier, abrupt tone. "You go squeeze in next to Dylan over there and we can get started."

Milly smiled nervously. She wasn't normally shy, but the McDonalds all looked so tanned and beautiful and healthy, not to mention completely at ease in one another's company. Sitting next to them she felt like the creature from planet Zog: pale, awkward, and hopelessly out of place.

After waking up so late, she hadn't had time to make as much effort as she'd have liked for her first night at Highwood. She'd opted for the first half-reasonable thing she'd pulled out of her suitcase: a clean pair of white jeans and a dusty pink cashmere sweater, under which she was already starting to burn up in the heat of Maggie's kitchen. She had, at least, been able to wash her hair, and though still slightly damp it already shone like polished wood down her back. For makeup she'd made do with a swipe of mascara and lip gloss, pinching her cheeks on her way across the yard from the big house in place of the blusher that had broken apart in her bag, ruining at least three T-shirts, and had to be thrown away.

"Hi. I'm Dylan." A grinning, black-haired boy moved over to make a space for her. He looked like a boxer, with his broken nose and oddly crooked mouth, as different from either of his sisters as they were from each other. But he did have Wyatt's coloring, and the trademark Mc-Donald electrically-charged smile. Like his father, he shouldn't technically have been attractive, but somehow he just was. If she hadn't been so madly in love with Bobby, Milly could easily have fancied him.

"Bobby tells me you're the next Joe Badilla, Jr."

"Who?" said Milly. Then, remembering Bobby had mentioned this name to her at Newells, added, "Oh, the quarter horse jockey? Yeah. I mean"—she blushed suddenly—"not, 'yeah, I'm the next him,' but 'yeah, I know who he is.' Bobby told me." She glanced across the table at Bobby, wondering if he'd remember, but he was deep in discussion with Wyatt and didn't look up.

After a brief lull in conversation while Maggie helped everyone to chicken pie, leeks, and potatoes, a rapid-fire interrogation of Milly began in earnest.

"So," asked Maggie, once the topics of English fashion, the royal family, and whether or not Milly had ever seen David Beckham in the flesh (she hadn't) had been fully exhausted by Dylan and Tara. "How are you settlin' in over there. Do you like your room?"

"Oh, I adore it," enthused Milly. "I love all that Victorian furniture, the bath, the wrought-iron bed. It's beautiful, like something out of an old Western film. I feel I should be wearing a crinoline or something."

Summer, who'd maintained a stony silence thus far, gave her a withering look. "Trust me," she snapped, "Highwood is nothing like a Clint Eastwood movie. You can forget all your romantic visions of cowboys and Indians. If that's what you've been expecting, you're in for a tough few months."

"That's not what I meant," said Milly, stung. She wondered again why this girl had it in for her. "I wasn't trying to be patronizing or anything." She willed Bobby to stick up for her, or at least look in her direction, but he seemed determined to ignore her tonight. She tried not to mind. After all, he hadn't been home in months and he must have tons of work to catch up on, not to mention seeing all his old friends again. But she still found herself wishing they could be alone again, as they had been on the long journey from England. For the most part he'd ignored her then, too. But somehow she preferred being ignored without an audience.

"Oh, don't mind her," said Dylan, shooting Summer down with a reproachful frown that she pretended not to understand. "She got up on the wrong side of bed this morning, that's all."

Seething, Summer retreated into her shell. First she'd enchanted Bobby, and now the little witch had Dylan sticking up for her too. He'd only known her five minutes! Watching Milly tucking into her mother's potatoes, she said a silent prayer that God might make her choke on them.

Dylan, meanwhile, was utterly charmed. How could Bobby not have let on what a knockout Milly was? Okay, so she was seventeen, but come on! She wasn't seven. That incredible hair, the cute freckles, the pink sweater clinging so tightly to her high, round breasts, like two cashmere grapefruits; from where he was sitting it was all good. He'd love to paint her.

Once the main course was over, he and Summer cleared everyone's plates and returned to the table with bowls filled to the brim with apple and walnut cobbler smothered with lashings of fresh cream. Milly had been too preoccupied trying and failing to get Bobby's attention to enjoy her chicken pie, but now she suddenly realized how famished she was. She didn't think she had ever seen anything quite so fattening in her entire life, and yet all the McDonalds looked like walking gym adverts. They must take an awful lot of exercise.

"My God, I can't eat all that!" she said aghast when she saw the size of her helping. "My mother would have a coronary. I'll turn into a whale."

"I'd taste it first if I were you," said Wyatt. "One bite of Maggie's cobbler and you won't be able to stop yourself. She's a legend in this valley for her cooking."

Milly tried a spoonful and closed her eyes in ecstasy. He wasn't kidding. It was divine.

"And you needn't worry about becoming a whale either," said Bobby.

It was the first unsolicited comment he'd made to her all evening, and for a second her eyes lit up. Was he actually about to pay her a genuine compliment?

"From tomorrow on you'll be working so hard, you'll work it off like that." He snapped his fingers for emphasis. "You're gonna need all the energy you can get."

Milly took another mouthful, trying to hide her disappointment. Was that all he cared about? Her bloody energy levels?

"Hell, she doesn't need to worry about gainin' weight anyway," chimed in Dylan. "She has a beautiful figure as it is, but a couple of extra pounds wouldn't hurt. It's nice to see a woman with some curves."

Milly smiled back at him gratefully. Why couldn't Bobby ever say lovely things like that?

"Well," she said, "it may be nice from a man's point of view. But it's not so great for a jockey. I'm already borderline heavy for racing."

"In that case," said Summer, extending one long, slender arm right across the table and swiping Milly's bowl away, "I'll have yours. I can eat anything. I never gain weight."

"Summer!" hissed Maggie, shocked. Her youngest daughter was behaving very oddly this evening. "Leave other people's food alone."

"What?" Summer threw her arms wide in a gesture of wronged innocence. "She just said she's borderline heavy, didn't she? I'm only trying to help."

Help my ass, thought Milly furiously. Little Miss Cheekbones was really starting to get on her tits.

So much for the sweet little sister Bobby had told her about. Summer was about as sweet as a pit bull.

Later, once everyone else had turned in for the night, Dylan accosted Summer as she came out of the bathroom.

"What was that all about at supper, with Milly?" he asked her.

"All what?" she said innocently. She was wearing one of his baggy, old white shirts as a nightgown, with her feet snuggled into a pair of ridiculous fluffy teddy bear slippers and her hair scraped back into a bun. She looked, in short, like butter wouldn't melt in her mouth, but Dylan knew different.

"You know very well what I mean," he said. "I've never seen you so hostile. What have you got against her?"

Summer shrugged. As close as she was to Dylan, she wasn't about to admit her feelings for Bobby to him or anyone.

"I don't know," she said. "I can't put my finger on it. There's just something about her I don't like. Like the way she was going on about how amazing England is."

"She wasn't 'going on' about it," said Dylan reasonably. "We asked her questions and she answered them."

"She's six months younger than me," Summer went on, ignoring him. "But already she thinks she's gonna be the next big thing in quarter horse racing. I mean, where does she get off, you know?" She was on a roll now. "It's gonna be months till Bobby gets this training idea off the ground anyway. And in the meantime we're gonna be stuck with her, hanging around like a bad smell with nothing to do. You know she's gonna be worse than useless around the ranch."

"All I know," said Dylan, putting his arm around her, "is that you sound like you're seriously jealous."

"Jealous?" Summer tried to look shocked. "Of her? Please! Don't make me laugh. She's got the conversational agility of a retarded toad, and she's been beaten with the ugly stick big-time."

Dylan couldn't help but laugh at that. "She has not!"

"Well, *I* think she has," said Summer, pouting. "Anyway, I bet I can ride the pants off her any day of the week."

"You're not even interested in riding," said Dylan. "You're going to LA to become a billionaire lawyer, remember?"

"I didn't say I was interested," said Summer. "I just said I bet I could beat Milly, that's all. According to Bobby, she's barely been near a horse for two years. And before that she only raced Thoroughbreds. How hard could it be?"

"Well, I think you should give her a chance," said Dylan. "You're not being fair. She's miles away from home, and this place must seem pretty alien to her. At the end of the day she's here for a while, whether you like it or not, so you might as well make an effort to try and get along."

"Hmmmm," Summer grunted grudgingly. "Just as long as *she* makes an effort to get along with *me*. Because so far, I don't see what Bobby or the rest of you see in her."

And with that she flounced off to bed, leaving Dylan to his own, very different thoughts of Milly and what her future at Highwood might hold for all of them.

CHAPTER TWELVE

Todd Cranborn pressed a button by the steering wheel and smiled as the roof of his four-hundred-thousand-dollar Ferrari Marinello peeled back with a satisfying *swoosh,* allowing the bright Santa Ynez sunshine to pour down into the car.

It was a beautiful day and the sun seemed to be shining on him metaphorically, as well as physically. His lawyer had called last night to tell him that the local residents' legal challenge to his acquisition of the Buellton land had finally bitten the dust. Thank God. With his Indian partners, he would now be able to start building the low-cost housing that had made him such a rich man, perhaps as soon as next month. God bless Native America!

Idly, he wondered how much money the petitioners had wasted on pursuing him so far—three hundred, maybe four hundred thousand dollars? He hoped they choked on it, every last small-minded, Protestant, middle-class one of them.

But it wasn't just the property deal that had put him in such a good mood. He also had high hopes for today's meeting at Highwood.

Obviously his primary interest in the place, like everybody else's, was the oil. But he also looked forward to the challenge of outwitting the notoriously arrogant Bobby Cameron. Through his property deals in rural California, he already knew a little bit about the cowboy mentality: their ludicrous pride in their archaic culture, their romantic obsession with ranching and "the land." He knew it would be a mistake to go wading in with a blank check and all guns blazing, and an even bigger mistake to betray an interest in Highwood's oil.

Hank Cameron had been stubborn and stupid as a mule. From the little he knew of Bobby, Todd imagined he would be just as bad, if not worse when it came to business negotiations. The trick would be to use that arrogance to his own advantage. Like a judo master, he must turn his opponent's strength against him.

Quarter horses. That would be the carrot. What the kid *needed*, of course, was to restructure his debt and pull the property out of its current financial quagmire. But what he evidently *wanted* was to build a quarter horse training facility. The Bobby Todd remembered was just the kind of spoiled, arrogant, rebel-without-a-clue type to put his wants before his needs. To put his wants before everything, in fact.

Knowing this, he'd spent the past two days boning up on the breed, and now felt fully equipped to talk about their heavy muscling, sprinter's speed, and the awesome versatility that helped them to excel at everything from flat racing to dressage to rodeo events, as if he actually gave a shit.

Ironically, even this smattering of research had been enough to convince him that there was, in fact, serious money to be made in the obscure, Western sport of quarter horse racing. If he played his cards right, he might even make a profit on it while he waited for a chance to move in on the oil reserves. But that was by the by. What he wanted—what he was determined to get—was some sort of ownership in the property. And today was the day he was going to make it happen.

He decided to approach the ranch via Los Olivos and Solvang, deliberately avoiding the Buellton road. That way he could save the pleasure of inspecting his newest acquisition for the drive home. Pulling over just outside Highwood's gates, he took one last glance at his notes, reminding himself of the Cameron family history and the names of all the key players.

"Wyatt McDonald," he murmured, putting the car back into drive and continuing up the mile-long track to the cluster of adobe houses and ancient outbuildings that made up the Cameron ranch. "Not Willy. Wyatt. Like Wyatt Earp."

He parked directly in front of the big house, making sure his pristine convertible was as far away as possible from the filthy-looking tractors and trucks scattered around the yard, and brushed the dust from his suit pants as he walked up to the front door. There was no bell, just a heavy old brass knocker, which he rapped firmly three times.

"No one's in there," came a voice from behind him.

He spun around to face a smiling, mousy-haired girl of about twenty. She was wearing overalls and both her hands and face were smeared with sticky black streaks of what looked like tar. Obviously some sort of laborer's daughter.

"Are you looking for Bobby or Wyatt?"

"Either. Well, both actually," he said curtly. "I'm Todd Cranborn. I have an appointment with Bobby at twelve."

"Tara McDonald," said the girl, wiping her greasy hand on her overalls and offering it to him.

Damn. A McDonald daughter. Cursing himself for being so quick to leap to conclusions, he turned on the charm in an instant, smiling as he shook her hand and trying not to wince at her dirty fingernails.

"My dad's in the office, over there." She pointed to a red-roofed adobe-style hut. Todd wondered whether it was original, guessed it must be. Those old houses were worth a fortune these days. "And Bobby's still out on the drive, I think."

"The drive?"

"Yeah, you know," said the girl. "They're bringing in a couple stray cattle from the hills up yonder."

A *cattle drive?* And did she just say "yonder"? Jeez, these people really were living in some kind of time warp. He half expected the theme song from *Rawhide* to start blaring out through the trees.

"Well then," he said. "I guess I'd better go see your father. You wanna let him know I'm here?"

"Sure," said the girl, who was already striding off toward the office. "Follow me."

Meanwhile, up in the hills, Milly was holding on to the front of her saddle for dear life, holding her breath as her horse slipped and skidded on loose stones and briars beneath her, struggling desperately to scrabble to the top of a lethally steep incline. She had always considered herself a fearless, confident rider. But she had never done anything like this before, and she had to admit she was scared shitless.

They were up in the overgrown wilderness that bordered the north side of the property: "they" being Milly, Bobby, and six other hands, including Dylan, although he was on the other side of the ridge. A few stray cattle had been cunning enough to evade capture during the big drives of the last few weeks, and Bobby thought it would be a good initiation to ranch life for Milly to come along and help round them up.

She might have made a slightly better fist of it if she'd gotten a wink of sleep last night. As it was she'd lain awake for hours after supper, a combination of jet lag and annoyance at all the witty put-downs she could have used on Summer if only she'd thought of them sooner, keeping her from getting the rest she so badly needed.

At about two, wide-eyed and desperate, she staggered out into the hallway to retrieve some melatonin from her handbag and collided head-on in the darkness with Bobby.

"Jesus!" she said, jumping out of her skin. "You scared me. What are you doing up?"

"Sorry," he said. He noticed that she was barefoot and wearing an old Snoopy nightshirt. And as if that didn't accentuate her childishness enough, she actually appeared to be carrying a mangled old teddy bear in her left hand too.

Catching him looking, she blushed.

"Mr. Ted," she said sheepishly. "I know it's silly, but he's always slept with me, since I was little."

Lucky Mr. Ted, thought Bobby, swallowing hard. God, she was adorable. Adorable and about as ready for an adult sexual relationship as a sixth grader.

"That's sweet," he said.

Milly's heart sank. Why, why had she bought the stupid bear with her in the first place? She didn't want to be "sweet." She wanted to be sexy and sophisticated and irresistible. No wonder he treated her like a kid if she still behaved like one.

"Couldn't you sleep either?" Thrusting the toy behind her back, she made her best attempt at a sultry pout.

"No." His voice was hoarse with desire, which thankfully she misinterpreted as a sore throat. "Jet lag, I guess."

"Me too," she sighed. "I came out to get these." She waved her pill bottle at him and hoped she wasn't staring too obviously at his bare chest, although she had a horrible feeling she might be. His "pajamas" consisted only of a pair of white boxer shorts. When he leaned back against the wall of the corridor, it was like looking at a living Calvin Klein advert.

In fact it wasn't jet lag keeping him awake. It was the temptation and frustration of knowing Milly was sleeping down the hall, alone. Haunted by his fantasies, he'd gotten up to try to walk things out of his system, only to find himself faced with the reality of her warm, sleepy, half-clothed body not two feet away from him. Fuck, he wanted her so bad he could scream.

It would be so easy to make a move, too. Too easy. She might be too inexperienced to see his desire, but there was no mistaking hers. Sometimes, like tonight, her longing for him was so strong, he could practically smell it. He knew that the second he pulled her into his arms, she'd reciprocate.

But it wasn't right. Not with Milly.

There were plenty of other girls he could get his rocks off with. With her it would be like taking candy from a baby, literally. He couldn't do it.

"Right, well," he said, clearing his throat nervously. "I'll, er . . . I'll let you get back to bed. Good night."

"Good night."

Crushed with disappointment, Milly slipped back into her room and climbed miserably beneath the covers. He hadn't even given her a good night kiss on the cheek. Surely that would have been normal good manners, wouldn't it? The way he'd scuttled off like a frightened spider, it was as if he couldn't wait to get away from her.

What was wrong with her?

Okay, so she wasn't Heidi Klum. But was she really so utterly invisible, so sexless as to warrant being ignored by a man who, by his own admission, had slept with more girls in one summer in Newmarket than P. Diddy got through in a year?

Too tired to cry, she gave herself up to the melatonin pills and at last drifted off into a deep, deep sleep at about three. But at six she'd been rudely awakened by Bobby hammering sergeant major–like on her door, and half an hour later found herself on horseback, heading for the hills. Still in an exhausted, melatonin-induced fog she could barely speak, let alone ride.

"It's pretty simple," Dylan explained to her as they set off. "Basically we ride up to the hills, make a big circle, and surround the cattle. Then, when we've got 'em all nice and close, we pen them in."

What he'd failed to mention was that these so-called hills were more like sheer cliff faces, covered in loose shingle on which even the most experienced horse would struggle to get a grip. They were also over-grown with briars and brambles, impenetrably thick and head high in places, that had already cut her arms and face to ribbons as she strove desperately to stay in the saddle. And as for surrounding the cattle, that was about as easy as trying to hold on to a slippery bar of soap in high seas. No sooner did she come within a hundred yards of a cow than it turned, doubled back, and bolted, darting around the treacherous ter-rain with no more difficulty than if it had been ambling along the race-track at Newmarket.

After four hours, their little team of wranglers had not even located half the missing animals, let alone corralled them, and Milly thought she must have lost half of her body weight in sweat through a combina-tion of exertion and abject, outright terror.

"Come on up!" yelled Bobby, from his vantage point some sixty feet above her on the top of the ridge. Though they were on the same team of wranglers, riding within yards of each other, he'd barely exchanged two words with her all morning. And when he had, they'd been barked commands rather than anything more personal. It was hard not to feel dispirited. "Try to move a little over to your left. Ground's firmer there."

Yeah, right, thought Milly bitterly. Like I can move anywhere! She only hoped her pony, as Bobby ludicrously insisted on calling the great lug of a quarter horse he'd given her, had a better idea of what he was doing than she did and that some instinct of self-preservation would get him to the top of the hill without falling over backward and tumbling hundreds of feet to what she imagined would be certain death for both of them.

Finally, she arrived at the top of the hill, exhausted, and trotted over to join him.

"Okay?" he asked brusquely.

Okay? She felt like screaming. No, I'm not fucking okay. Just look at me, for God's sake. I feel like I've been through the bloody Somme and back.

What she actually said was, "Fine, thanks. But you might have warned me. That slope is a death trap. Someone could kill themselves doing that."

"People have," he said nonchalantly.

"What, died?" said Milly, horrified.

"Sure," he said airily. "Not experienced riders like you, though. I wouldn't bring you up here if I didn't think you could handle it."

She supposed it was a compliment, but it was hardly very reassuring, especially as she'd almost lost her footing more than once this morning.

"The more you can work with your horse, really feel him and control him in this sort of terrain," said Bobby, "the better you'll be on the track, believe me. It's all part of the process."

Milly groaned. She already knew he was big on the whole "holistic training" vibe. The very first time he'd watched her ride at Newells, he'd talked about the importance of all-around proficiency, a total understanding of each horse's dynamics. Ever eager to please him, she'd paid lip service to the idea. But privately she struggled to see how taking a working horse mountaineering or chasing some bloody stubborn cow around the countryside was going to make her a better jockey, quarter horse or otherwise.

Hopefully her days would soon involve more race training and less corralling. This whole cowgirl thing looked a lot easier on *Bonanza*, that was for sure.

Bobby looked at his watch. "I have to get back down to the ranch in a minute," he said. "I have a meeting. But I want you to stay up here and make your way over to that holding pen over there. You see it? Above those cedars?"

She nodded weakly.

"Dylan should be there in about twenty minutes, once he's got those two heifers from the other side. He can show you where to go from there. In the meantime, if you come across any more cattle, just keep north of 'em, okay? Don't let any get past you."

And how, exactly, do you propose I stop them? thought Milly, as he thundered off down the hill. All the cows she'd seen so far had paid her about as much attention as a dead leaf blown across their path.

Happily, a few minutes later Dylan came cantering over the ridge to her rescue. "Where's Bobby?" he asked, his irrepressible cheerfulness lifting Milly's spirits a little despite herself. "He hasn't abandoned you already, has he?"

"'Fraid so," she panted, pulling her pony up beside him. "He had a meeting, apparently."

Looking at her, Dylan couldn't help but grin. Her hair was all over the place, a tangled mess escaping in every possible direction from its pink elastic band. She had scratches all over her arms and face, giant rings of sweat pooled beneath the arms of her T-shirt, and she was also glowing with sunburn across her nose and the top of her forehead. The tips of her ears were as red as raspberries.

"Told you you should have worn a hat," he teased her. "You do realize your nose could get a job as a stoplight?"

"Bog off," she said, embarrassed but giggling, hastily covering the offending protuberance with her hand. Bobby had offered her a cowboy hat this morning, but she'd refused it because she thought it looked dorky, and she wanted to be as sexy as possible whenever he was around. So much for that plan.

"What happened?" asked Dylan. "Did ya get in a fight with a thornbush?"

"Something like that." She smiled ruefully, reluctantly uncovering her nose. "I had no idea it would be so hard. It was all I could do to keep my saddle! Bobby kept telling me not to let any cows get past me, but it's hopeless. I've been scrambling up and down hills like an idiot all morning. I may as well have stayed in bed."

"I know how you feel," said Dylan, quietly admiring the way her breasts rose and fell beneath her T-shirt when she got all het up. "If it makes you feel any better, we've been getting nowhere on the other side either, and I've been doin' this a whole lot longer than you. Some days it's easy, some days it's hard. That's ranching."

Milly sighed. "Bobby says this will all help me when I start racing, that it's all good experience. But I don't see how it can be."

"Well." He smiled. "I wouldn't know about that. But Bobby knows his stuff when it comes to horses."

"Oh, I know he does," said Milly earnestly. "That's why I'm here. He's amazing."

There was no mistaking the awe and adoration in her voice—Dylan had heard the same reaction from countless other girls. Bobby might not have noticed how pretty his protégée was, but the kid was obviously seriously smitten with him.

"I wouldn't sweat it if I were you," he said kindly. "This meeting of Bobby's is with an investor from LA. With any luck you'll be training quarter horses in a few weeks and your career as a cowgirl'll be over. I wish I could be so lucky."

Milly raised an eyebrow. "I thought you loved ranching? Bobby's always told me you're amazing at it, that it's your whole life."

"It is my whole life," said Dylan with a shrug. "But that's not the same as lovin' it."

"What would you like to do?" asked Milly.

"I'd like to paint," he said wistfully. "But it's not going to happen."

"You never know," she said. "Only a few weeks ago I thought I'd never race or even ride again. But now here I am."

"Here you are." He smiled.

She was a sweetheart, this one. Even bruised and battered after her dreadful morning, there was a sort of disheveled charm about her that he could easily see himself falling for. But there wouldn't be any point. It was Bobby she wanted, not him.

It was always the same with girls. Next to Bobby, he didn't exist.

Wyatt intercepted Bobby as soon as he arrived in the yard.

"Where's the guy?" Bobby asked, dismounting and peeling off his leather chaps.

"He's in the office," said Wyatt, putting a restraining hand on his arm. "But listen, Bobby. Be careful. There's something about this fella I don't trust."

"Like what?" Pulling off his hat, Bobby ran his fingers quickly through his sweat-drenched hair.

"I don't know." Wyatt frowned. "It's hard to describe. He's just . . . slick."

"I can handle slick," said Bobby dismissively.

"Maybe so," said Wyatt patiently. "But take your time, all right? Get to know the guy a little bit before you commit to anything. You do have a tendency to get carried away sometimes."

"Says who?" Bobby bristled. "My father? Look." He made an effort to keep the irritation out of his voice. "I appreciate the concern. But I'm not a kid anymore, Wyatt. I can handle this guy. I know what I want."

Wyatt nodded respectfully and stepped back, letting him pass. There was no point pushing it any further. The irony was that Bobby was far more like Hank than he realized: bullheaded as hell. Hank had never been one to take advice and Highwood had suffered as a result. Bobby was the same but with an added element of youthful bravado that made him potentially even more uncontrollable.

Wyatt prayed that his sixth sense about Todd Cranborn was wrong. But watching Bobby stride confidently into the office, he had the same, sinking feeling of watching a lamb gamboling off to the slaughterhouse.

"Bobby?" Todd got to his feet, smiling and extending his hand in greeting as Bobby walked in. He'd forgotten quite how model handsome the boy was, not to mention tall. A lesser man might have felt intimidated by the glaring size discrepancy between them, but Todd had no such qualms. "How are you?" he said affably. "We met a few years ago in Florida, if you remember."

Bobby gave him the most perfunctory of handshakes and sat down on the desk, without bothering to invite his guest to have a seat.

"I don't, I'm afraid," he said tactlessly. "But I understand from my ranch manager that you were once in some sort of negotiations with my father?"

Cocky little shit, thought Todd. But his smile didn't waver. "That's right. Well, 'in negotiations' might be overstating it. I'm in property development, as you know. I always had an interest in your father's land, but it was pretty clear he was never going to sell to me, or anyone else for that matter."

Reaching into his jacket pocket, he pulled out his inhaler and took one long, deep breath. The dander from horses, dogs, and cattle was swirling all around the little box of a room, and he could feel his chest tightening and eyes beginning to redden, despite having dosed himself up to the eyeballs earlier with antihistamine. How anyone could choose to live out in the sticks like this was beyond him.

"Sorry," he explained, sneezing. "Allergies."

"What interested you about Highwood?" asked Bobby aggressively, ignoring Todd's evident discomfort. He'd had a grueling morning, after not much sleep, and Wyatt's pep talk just now had only worsened his mood. He was determined to show everyone that he was more than capable of being a tough negotiator. "The oil, I suppose?"

"Not at all," Todd lied, not missing a beat. "First of all, the place has never been properly surveyed. I know there's been a lot of chat about your grandfather striking oil here, but no one knows for sure how oil rich this land actually is, or whether it could sustain a long-term drilling operation."

Bobby listened, trying not to give himself away by looking surprised. He had never heard this theory before. He'd been brought up to believe that Highwood's oil was a fact: part blessing, part curse, but definitely there. Racking his brains, he thought he vaguely remembered his father telling him that the land *had* been surveyed, once, many decades ago. But perhaps it was a false memory? Perhaps Todd was right?

"Besides," Todd went on, sneezing again. "Oil isn't my business. I made my money doing one thing and doing it well. Just like your old man."

Bobby nodded. "I see. Well, that makes sense."

Wyatt could be such an old woman sometimes. Cranborn seemed perfectly straightforward and up-front to him.

"So your interest now, today, is . . . what?" he asked.

"Quarter horses," said Todd, deadpan.

"Really?" Bobby looked skeptically at his immaculately cut suit and manicured hands, still clasping the inhaler. To say he didn't look like a typical quarter horse enthusiast would be putting it mildly.

"Don't get me wrong," said Todd, suavely adjusting the knot on his Hermès silk tie. "I've no desire to be involved in the nitty-gritty of horse training. None whatsoever. That's your area. I'm looking on this purely as an investment."

For the next ten minutes he smoothly trotted out his newly acquired knowledge of the quarter horse world. As he'd expected, Bobby lapped it up.

First rule of salesmanship: Tell people what they want to hear.

"I don't claim to be an expert by any means," he concluded, wrapping up his spiel. "But I've looked at the numbers, and your performance record as a Thoroughbred trainer, and I have to say I'm excited about the opportunity here. There's no hidden agenda: You need a cash investor. I need a partner who understands quarter horses and the training business. It's as simple as that."

"Let's walk," said Bobby, opening the door onto the yard and letting a blast of warm air into the air-conditioned cool of the office. Todd followed him outside.

"You've been honest with me, Mr. Cranborn," he said, "so let me be honest with you in return. I'm interested."

"Good." Todd nodded sagely. "I hoped you might be."

"But there is one thing I need to be clear about from the beginning," said Bobby. "Highwood was left to me by my father as a traditional ranch, with traditional cowboys running cattle."

Ah, here we go, thought Todd. Right on cue. Nostalgic cowboy bullshit time.

"I have a number of men and their families depending on me to keep the place going as a ranch and make it work. Horses are my passion, and I'm convinced that's where Highwood's future lies. But I can't just wave a magic wand and turn the place into a quarter horse version of Eight Oaks overnight."

"Look, I know that," said Todd. Eight Oaks was the ultimate Thoroughbred horse farm, and every Kentucky owner's wet dream. "You gotta clean the garbage off your plot before you can build on it, right?"

"Right," said Bobby. "Exactly."

"Well, how 'bout this," said Todd as casually as if it were an idea that had just that minute popped into his head. "I'll underwrite your debt—all of it—in return for an equity partnership in the ranch."

"Oh, I don't know . . ." said Bobby doubtfully. He could hear Wyatt's words of yesterday evening ringing in his ears: "If he starts asking for equity, get the hell out."

"Hear me out," said Todd. "I'll also put up a hundred percent of the capital to set us up as a quarter horse training stables."

"A hundred percent?"

Todd nodded. "Uh-huh. Every penny."

Visions of the gorgeous stables he could build with unlimited funds swam before Bobby's eyes like dollar signs. Imagine! He could be living his dream at Highwood, with the bank off his back too, in a matter of weeks.

Suddenly he felt awash with confidence. Wyatt was a great ranch manager, but he knew nothing about business and even less about horse training and the spectacular money to be made at it.

"The core cattle business remains yours and yours alone," said Todd. "Profits from the horse business we split eighty twenty in my favor."

"Sixty forty," said Bobby.

"Seventy-five twenty five," countered Todd with a grin. "You're not putting in a cent, remember."

"I'm putting in my expertise," said Bobby, "and my time. I'll be the one pulling in the business and running it."

"Seventy thirty," said Todd, extending his hand for Bobby to shake. "Done."

Poor kid. There he was smiling like he'd beaten him down and gotten some sort of deal. When in fact, for a measly few hundred grand, he'd just bought himself an equity stake in a multimillion-dollar property *and* taken one big step closer to controlling the Cameron oil.

The kid was so naïve and so fucking full of himself, he didn't even realize what had happened. And though he had nothing on paper yet, Todd knew that an old school, my-word-is-my-bond cowboy like Bobby Cameron would rather die than renege on a deal he'd shaken hands on.

It was done. Mission accomplished.

Still simmering with inner triumph as Bobby walked him back to his car, he noticed a figure lumbering across the yard toward them, dragging his feet with weariness as if even the effort of walking were too much for him. Only when the poor creature came within a few feet of him did he realize it was not actually a man but a girl. A very young girl.

She had matted, sweaty hair, a shiny red face, and riding clothes so torn and dirty she looked like she'd been wearing them for weeks. Nevertheless, she was extremely pretty in an elfin sort of way, and her baize-green eyes and wide lips gave her an intoxicating, woman-child quality that even her disheveled state could not completely conceal. Todd had been anxious to get on his way, but suddenly he was more than happy to linger a little. He always made time for extremely pretty girls.

"Hello." He smiled down at her. "I don't believe we've met. I'm Todd."

"Oh. Hello," she said absently. "I'm Milly." The first thing he noticed was her English accent. The second was the way she looked straight through him, focusing all her attention on Bobby, whose body seemed to have tensed up all of a sudden, as though the girl's attention bothered him.

Highly competitive in everything, but especially when it came to women, Todd despised being ignored. This was the second time a girl he'd been attracted to had shown a blatant preference for the Cameron boy. It infuriated him.

"We're done," said Milly, looking up at Bobby like a Roman slave girl might look at the emperor. "Is it okay if I go inside and take a bath now?"

"I guess," he mumbled gracelessly. "Don't be too long though. We still have more work to do."

His tone was so curt, Todd wondered if the two of them had fallen out. Or if, more probably, the boy's aggression was a symptom of deeper feelings he was unwilling or unable to express. Certainly there was a sexual tension and discomfort in the air that was impossible to miss.

"Bobby and I are going to be going into partnership together. We're starting a quarter horse training stable here at Highwood," he said, making a second attempt to capture Milly's attention. This time he succeeded.

"Really?" Her eyes lit up. "That's fantastic! How soon will you start? Bobby brought me over here to train me, you see. I'm a jockey. Well," she corrected herself, "I'm training to be a jockey. But I'm much better over short distant sprints, so Bobby thought quarter horses would be perfect for me, because—"

"Milly, Mr. Cranborn's a busy man," Bobby interrupted her tersely. He'd noticed Todd looking at her, and he didn't like it. He wanted her gone. "He doesn't have time for a rundown of your career aspirations."

"Oh, that's okay," said Todd, who'd seen the way the girl's smile had folded in on itself like a house of cards at Bobby's admonition. "I don't mind at all. An Englishwoman racing quarter horses, huh? That's interesting."

Milly smiled at him gratefully and noticed for the first time that he was actually quite handsome—for an old man, obviously. She didn't know why Bobby was being so mean.

"I hope we'll talk more, next time I'm here," he said, ignoring Bobby's scowl of disapproval. "But right now I *do* have to get going." Pressing a button on his car key, he popped the driver's door open and climbed in. "I want to stop into Buellton on my way home," he said to Bobby. "And, if I can, talk to my attorney tonight about our venture. Have him draw up some initial paperwork."

"Sounds good," said Bobby, shaking his hand again through the window.

With a rocket-launcher roar, the Ferrari's engine rumbled into life and Todd executed a lightning three-point turn, sending dust flying everywhere. "I'll call you," he yelled to Bobby, making a telephone sign with his hand, and then, to her acute embarrassment, blew a kiss to Milly before speeding off down the drive.

"What did you go and do that for?" Bobby turned on her as soon as the car was out of sight. He knew he was being a jealous prick, but he couldn't help it.

"Do what?" said Milly, fighting back tears.

"Flirt with him," said Bobby.

"*What?*" Her eyes widened. If he weren't being so mean about it, it would be funny. As it was she felt sick. "I didn't flirt with him!" she said hotly. "Don't be so ridiculous. He's ancient. I would never—I could never—" Fear and stress were making her insides flip like pancakes. It was hard to get a coherent sentence out.

"Hmmm," mumbled Bobby. "Well, okay. But just remember, he's a business partner, not a friend. I'll be running all the training day-to-day, so you'll have no reason to cross paths with him again. None whatsoever."

"Fine," said Milly defiantly, running back into the house so as not to give him the satisfaction of seeing the hot tears of anger and shame rolling down her cheeks.

How could he accuse her and humiliate her like that in front of a stranger? What had she done to deserve it?

She knew it was wrong to expect life at Highwood to be perfect, especially on day one. And she knew the pressures he was under. But not even Rachel's bitchiness, or Jasper's cruelty, or her mother's constant nagging were as bad as the way Bobby just turned on her.

It was almost enough to make her wish she'd stayed in Newmarket.

And that was saying something.

CHAPTER THIRTEEN

Milly sat on the battered leather couch in the McDonaldses' family room with a horse blanket pulled over her knees and the local paper open in front of her, wiggling her toes in cozy contentment. It was a Sunday in November and the first afternoon she'd had completely off in almost two months. She intended to enjoy it.

From the moment Bobby had signed on the dotted line with Todd, the quarter horse enterprise had taken off with breakneck speed, and she soon found herself training almost full-time. Riding again was a joy, but she was still expected to pitch in with ranch work too, and the combination was utterly exhausting.

And then there were the emotional stresses too. Things with her and Bobby were still not great. Admittedly there'd been no more blowups like the one they'd had on her first day over Todd Cranborn. But the closeness they'd enjoyed in England seemed to have evaporated for good. In its place had grown a working relationship that was cordial but heartbreakingly distant.

There were moments when the façade slipped. When she won her first race, a tiny local event sponsored by the agricultural college in Santa Ynez, Bobby ran over and hugged her, and she could see from the way he looked at her that he was genuinely proud. But it was no more than a flicker of the warmth he used to shower her with in the old days. Generally, now that he was training her, he was very much her boss. And though she still fantasized about him constantly, she had gradually started to give up all serious hope of anything romantic happening between them.

The truth was that even if they had been closer, they were both so tired and so focused on their respective futures, there wouldn't have been much time for a relationship, anyway. Every second of Milly's days was accounted for, and if anything Bobby was even busier: trying to split himself three ways between training her, running the ranch, and building the new quarter horse business.

He'd made remarkable progress, though. Even Wyatt had to admit that. Stable blocks and a spanking new indoor school were erected within weeks, in a frenzy of efficiency never before seen at Highwood. Tara was dispatched to print up beautiful glossy brochures, aimed at tempting owners and syndicates away from more established training schools at Bonsall and Romoland. And Todd Cranborn, for all that Wyatt still distrusted him, had so far been as good as his word, pumping a seemingly never-ending stream of cash into the ranch's coffers and coming up with a debt-restructuring plan that had finally gotten the bank off their backs.

Things were definitely looking up.

"You're not still reading that, are you?"

Summer, just back from her ice hockey match, had flopped down in an armchair on the other side of the room. Of course, it wasn't enough for her to be stunning and a *Doogie Howser, M.D.* brainiac. She had to be a brilliant sportswoman too.

"Surely you've soaked up all the praise by now? It was only a local race, for God's sake. Hardly Los Alamitos."

Keeping her temper for once, Milly put the paper down. There was a review in the sports section about her performance at Santa Ynez— the journo had described her as a "British cowgirl," which she secretly thought was incredibly cool. Dylan had pointed it out to her this morning and been lovely and encouraging about it, as he always was. But Summer, equally typically, couldn't resist having a dig.

"Not that it's any of your business," said Milly. She had long ago given up trying to be nice to Summer. "But I was actually looking at the article on the Ballard Rodeo. Bobby's entered me for two races there next weekend."

Summer yawned pointedly. "Whoop-de-do. The Ballard Rodeo. Big wow."

"Well, actually, it is pretty big," Milly shot back. "There are some top-name competitors entering this year."

"Oh, I'm sure," said Summer, her voice dripping with sarcasm. "This is your ticket to the big time all right. Next stop Ruidoso Downs. Hollywood! The world!"

"Bite me." Milly picked up the paper again to block her royal bitchiness out. Summer's hostility was as baffling to her now as it had been the day she first arrived, but she'd given up trying to figure her out. If the girl wanted war, she could have it. After a lifetime of Rachel Delaney, Summer McDonald was a walk in the park.

"Hey, guys." Tara, bubbly as ever, bounced into the room bearing a package for Milly. From the beginning she'd refused to be drawn into Milly and Summer's battles, and she pretended not to notice the tension in the air now. "This came to the office," she said, handing Milly the parcel. "Looks like it's from your folks."

Brightening, Milly began tearing it open. She felt a bit guilty that she hadn't called home much, especially with her dad still recuperating and apparently quite weak. But she'd been so caught up in racing and training, she hadn't felt remotely homesick. Besides, by the time she got done with work it was usually the middle of the night in England and too late to call.

Whatever it was, it was bloody tightly wrapped. Gnawing at the tape with her teeth, she decided it felt like magazines and hoped it might be the back issues of the *Racing Post* and *Horse & Hound* she'd asked Cecil for two weeks ago. But it wasn't. As the brown paper finally fell away, she saw with disappointment that it was a copy of this month's *Tatler,* with a brief note from her mother attached.

"Mills. Thought you'd like to see this," it read. "Page 34. Missing you. Though must say Rachel has done a marvelous job taking care of me—feeling quite spoiled! Call soon. Kisses. Mummy."

Instantly Milly felt her blood pressure rising. In the first place, why did her mother need to be taken care of? Other people's mothers didn't. She could just imagine the "marvelous job" Rachel had been doing in her absence, worming her way into Linda's affections like the snake that she was. She'd never forget her fake concern the night of Cecil's stroke and how she'd muscled in on the family.

Evidently, that night had just been the tip of the iceberg.

"Good-looking guy," said Summer, walking over to the sofa and looking over Milly's shoulder as she flipped gloomily to page thirty-four. "Someone you know? An old boyfriend perhaps?"

Any crush that wasn't Bobby was a good crush as far as Summer was concerned.

"Hardly," said Milly frostily. "It's my brother. And that slapper standing behind him"—she jabbed a finger at Rachel, as if she could somehow hurt her through the page—"is his girlfriend. Worse luck."

The shot was of Jasper and Rachel at a society hunt ball—her mother's wet dream, basically. They both looked as smugly attractive as a pair of children's TV presenters with their straight, gleaming white teeth and revoltingly regular features. The caption underneath read: "British racing's star couple: Rachel Delaney and Jasper Lockwood Groves dazzle on the dance floor."

"I think she's gorgeous," said Summer truthfully.

"Yes, well, you would," said Milly. Despite herself she found her eyes wandering to the article below. It recounted Rachel's recent successes on the track in classically *Tatler*esque, sycophantic style. But even if you stripped away the bullshit, it was clear she was doing well. Since Milly left she'd had a win at Bath and two places at York. And it looked as though her photogenic relationship with man-about-town Jasper had helped her profile in the British media even more. According to the article, she'd gotten two sponsorship deals in the pipeline, one for Hacketts and another for a new lingerie label. What next? Sports Personality of the bloody Year?

Suddenly Milly's own win at the Santa Ynez races felt like very small fry indeed.

Just as she felt the last vestiges of her good mood evaporating, Bobby stuck his head around the door, looking stressed and distracted.

"Has anybody seen my suitcase?" he demanded. "The green one with the leather straps?"

All three girls looked up from the magazine.

"It's in the attic at the big house," said Tara.

"Are you sure?" He ran his hand through his hair. "I looked already but I couldn't see it."

"It's definitely there," she said calmly. "I'll go and check if you'd like."

"Why do you need it?" asked Milly. She wished she didn't care about his plans, but she couldn't seem to help it. "Are you going somewhere?"

"LA," he said, "for ten days. I'm going to meet some potential new clients with Todd."

"Ten days?" Milly inadvertently dropped the magazine on the floor. "But that means you'll be gone next weekend. What about the Ballard race? You said you'd be there."

Bobby sighed. He felt bad about letting her down, but it couldn't be helped. Clients weren't going to fall out of the sky, and Cranborn had a whole roster of people for him to see.

The last month had been tough for him too. He knew it hurt Milly when he kept his distance—but he didn't know what else to do. Working with her every day, and sharing a house at night, was utterly torturous. He felt like a recovering alcoholic forced to take a job at a distillery. His only hope of dealing with it was to somehow mentally disconnect.

Unfortunately, it was a lot easier to feign indifference than to actually feel it. He was hugely proud of the way Milly had come along as a rider, taking to short, quarter horse sprints like a duck to water, just as he'd been certain she would. But he hadn't bargained how stressful it would be, protecting her from the other side of the quarter horse racing world: Her fellow jockeys were almost exclusively men and a minimum of five years older than her. Most of them were cowboys or laborers by day, tough guys from the wrong side of the tracks who liked to play every bit as hard as they worked.

To say that Milly was an exciting novelty to them would be putting it mildly. After every race, swarms of men would come up to her, inviting her to after-race parties that Bobby knew from his own experience were only one small step above frat house orgies. Most race days he felt more like her minder than her trainer, beating admirers off with a stick and dragging her home before things got out of hand.

And the more he played the parent, the more she played the sullen teenager. A few weeks ago, desperate to get out of Highwood for a few hours, he'd accepted an invitation to the birthday party of another local jockey, Danny Marron, at a neighboring quarter horse stables.

"Why can't I come?" Milly had whined over and over as he was preparing to leave. "I know Danny."

"You've met him once," said Bobby. "You don't know him. Besides, you weren't invited."

This wasn't actually true. But Danny was a notorious party boy, and there was no way in hell Bobby was letting Milly loose at one of his parties. It'd be like throwing a baby rabbit into a room full of snakes.

"I'm not a child, you know," she yelled at him, losing her temper. "You've got no right to stop me having fun."

"While you live with me," said Bobby firmly, pulling on his boots, "I have every right. You're not coming, and that's final."

Overnight, it seemed, he'd gone from friend to father and from mentor to jailer. It was a role reversal he hated every bit as much as Milly did.

"Dylan'll take you to Ballard," he said now, watching the clouds of disappointment form over her face. "You can still race. But I have to go, sweetheart. It's business."

Secretly, he hoped the LA trip might involve a bit of pleasure too. Sean O'Flannagan was still in town, working for that creep Jimmy Price, and he'd promised to take him into West Hollywood for some action.

"It's a serious health risk, you know, celibacy," he insisted, when Bobby told him about his saintly restraint with Milly. "I knew a bloke once, back in Ireland. Hadn't had it for so long he dropped dead. Testosterone poisoning."

Bobby laughed. But talking to Sean made him realize just how stressed out he was. A little light female refreshment might be just what the doctor ordered.

"Remind me again," said Bobby, as Sean took another corner at stomach-churning speed. "How the fuck did you talk me into this?"

It was Thursday night, and they were heading out to spend the weekend at Jimmy Price's estate in Palos Verdes.

"Well," said Sean, tightly gripping the steering wheel of his beloved blue Porsche, "*you* said you needed to network with quarter horse people. So *I* said, in that case, you ought to talk to Jimmy. And *you* said—"

"I'd rather saw my own balls off with a rusty camping knife."

"Words to that effect, yes," admitted Sean. "But *I,* being the true friend that I am, told you to pull your head out of your arse and stop being such a stupid, stubborn bastard."

"And I was so drunk, I listened to you," said Bobby ruefully.

The last three days in LA had been a blast. Hanging out with Sean was as wild and crazy as ever. And business had also been booming. For a self-professed novice in the quarter horse world, Todd Cranborn was incredibly well connected. He'd already introduced Bobby to a slew of owners, many of whom seemed open to the idea of moving their horses up to Highwood, if the price was right. And though Todd wasn't someone Bobby would ever choose as a friend—he was too slick, too urban, and, though Bobby'd never admit as much to Wyatt, there *was* something innately shifty about him—as a partner he was all that he'd hoped for and more.

The only thing that still niggled him was how involved Todd seemed to want to be in the business. When they'd signed their deal, Bobby assumed he'd be more of a silent partner, the here's-your-check, don't-bother-me-till-we-turn-a-profit type. But he'd turned out to be the exact opposite, displaying an intense interest not just in the new stables but in all the financial and practical affairs of the ranch.

When Bobby mentioned the possibility of meeting Jimmy Price, Todd leaped on the idea with surprising enthusiasm.

"I can't believe you're even thinking about it," he said. "Of course we should go. Jimmy is to quarter horses what the Sultan of Brunei is to Thoroughbreds. You know that."

Bobby's protestations that he was also a nasty, wife-abandoning cocksucker who thought the planets revolved around him fell on deaf ears.

If Sean could get them invited, they were going. Period.

And so it was that, after an hour and a half of having his insides flipped over like pancakes while Sean tried to beat the land speed record, they finally drove through the electric gates of the Price estate.

The gates themselves were made of solid metal, and almost as thick as they were tall. It felt more like entering a bank vault than a home.

"What is this, Fort Knox?" asked Bobby.

Sean gave him a knowing look. "And then some. I've worked here almost two years and I still don't know the master code for the stable blocks. Jimmy's fanatical about privacy and security."

As they drew up to the front of the house, Bobby could see why. He'd visited a lot of beautiful homes, traveling around the world on his various training jobs. But Price's estate was something else.

The first thing he noticed was a thirty-foot fountain erupting like a cool, silver Vesuvius in the center of the vast, Tuscan-style forecourt. On either side of it, formal gardens stretched off into the distance as far as the eye could see. The house itself was built partly into the hill and loomed above them, at the top of a long, winding stone staircase. It was built of some sort of faded yellow stone that Bobby didn't recognize but which gave it the air of an old European château, and its aura of antiquity was further enhanced by the ivy and wisteria that wound their way around the eight-foot windows, dripping tendrils of foliage down the façade like streaky green mascara.

Certainly, it was nothing at all like the vulgar, LA McMansions he'd spent the week visiting with Todd. Jimmy Price might be an asshole, but he either had taste or the sense to hire an architect who did.

"What d'you reckon?" asked Sean, leaning over into the backseat and pulling out Bobby's suitcase for him. "D'you think your money-bags partner'll be impressed?"

"You can ask him yourself in a minute," said Bobby. A dark blue Ferrari Marinello with the giveaway license plate TC1 was already parked out front. "Looks like he's here already."

Bobby followed Sean as he bounded up the stone steps two at a time, and handed his hat to the liveried maid who let them in. He'd barely had a chance to take in the arabesque opulence of the deep blue, domed ceiling, when a brace of screeching two-year-olds came careening into the hallway, pedaling furiously on their tricycles across the slippery marble floor.

"Fuuuuuck!" Sean let out a yelp of pain as one of them ran straight over his foot. The child seemed blissfully unconcerned about the agony he'd just caused, glancing back only briefly before screeching off in the direction of the formal living room.

"Chase! Chance!" A harassed, very overweight girl came lumbering after them, patently out of breath and red faced from the chase. "Have you seen the kids?"

"Yeah," said Sean, pointing to the doorway through which the budding Schumachers had just disappeared. "One of them just maimed me for life, as it happens." He held up his foot for inspection. "Ran me over like a skunk, so he did, the little shit."

"Well, at least it was only you he ran over," said the girl, her face lighting up as she went to kiss him on the cheek. "Normally he does it to proper guests."

"Oh, thanks a million!" said Sean, grinning. "This is my friend Bobby, by the way. He's a proper guest. Bobby, meet Amy, the nicest thing about this place."

The girl took one look at Bobby and instantly blushed, like a clear glass filling up with tomato juice. He tried to remember the last time he'd seen anyone looking more awkward but decided it must have been a long time ago.

"Are you their nanny?" he asked, returning her shy smile with a beamer of his own. "Looks like you have your work cut out."

"Actually, no," she panted. She still hadn't gotten her breath back. "I'm their sister. For my sins."

Before she could explain any further, a truly stunning blonde emerged from the living room. She was wearing a floor-length, flesh-colored, slashed-to-the-crotch dress that had long since crossed the line from sexy to obscene. She teamed the outfit with a scowl at Amy that could have frozen blood.

"The kids are running wild in there," she barked. "Go and see to them before your father has a coronary."

"They don't listen to me," said Amy, exasperated. "I've been trying to get them up to bed for the last hour."

"Well, try harder," snapped the goddess. "If you weren't so goddamn fat they wouldn't be able to run rings around you like they do. Oh!" Belatedly she registered Sean and Bobby's presence. In an instant her features softened and the scowl was replaced by a broad, if fake, smile. "I didn't see you boys there. Hi."

Her accent was Southern and strong, giving the two-letter word a good three or four syllables: haaaaiiiii.

"Ah'm Candy Price," she drawled, gazing lasciviously at Bobby. "Jimmy's wife."

She reminded him of a cat, with narrow, slanting green eyes and cheekbones so pronounced they were like little shelves on either side of her face. A taller, younger, sluttier Michelle Pfeiffer.

"And you are?"

"Put him down, Candy, for God's sake," said Sean, kissing her on both cheeks. He obviously had a very relaxed relationship with his employer's family. "This is Bobby Cameron, a friend of mine."

"Ah!" she giggled coquettishly. "The cowboy. Ah've just been hearin' all about you."

"Really?" said Bobby.

"Uh-huh. From your business partner. It's a pleasure to meet you, Bobby."

"Likewise," he said, somewhat unconvincingly. It had been only a five-second exchange with Amy, but it was enough for him to have decided categorically whose side he was on. The second Mrs. Price was clearly a card-carrying bitch.

"I didn't know Jimmy'd married again," Bobby hissed in Sean's ear a few moments later, as the pair of them followed Candy's swaying backside into the living room.

"Five years ago," Sean whispered back. "But he's so private, a lot of people don't know. Even now that they've got kids."

"That's a little odd too," said Bobby. "She doesn't exactly seem the maternal type."

Sean rolled his eyes. "She's a horror," he said. "Gorgeous but a real wasp eater. And she makes poor Amy's life hell."

Walking into the Prices' reception room was like walking into the big barn at Highwood. Or a cathedral. Or some other, ludicrously outsized space. If it hadn't been for all the priceless antiques and overstuffed Ralph Lauren couches crammed into it, Bobby was pretty sure there would have been an echo.

The first thing he noticed, however, was Jimmy. He was leaning against a grand piano in the far corner, puffing away on his cigar and apparently chatting to Todd like the two of them were old friends.

"There you are!" He advanced upon Sean and Bobby, beaming jovially, his trademark cigar clamped between his teeth, just as it had been in Florida the last time Bobby met him. "My long lost vet. And if he hasn't brought the Lone Ranger along with him." He slapped Bobby hard across the back. "How ya doing, kiddo? I've just been talking to your partner here about your new business. Or should I say your 'pardner'? Uh? Howdy, pardner!"

Pleased as ever by his own joke, he laughed till the tears streamed down his face. Clearly, there was something about cowboys that Jimmy found hilarious.

Bobby smiled through gritted teeth, digging his nails into his palms so hard he almost drew blood. Biting back what he really felt like saying to this squat little toad of a man with his wealth and his power and his fat fucking cigar, he settled for "Hello, Mr. Price."

"I thought you said you had work in LA," he whispered to Todd, once their host had turned his attention to his beautiful wife for a few moments. "I wasn't expecting you till tomorrow."

"My calendar freed up," said Todd, with a what-of-it? shrug. "Thought I may as well get a jump on the traffic."

In reality, needless to say, he had his own reasons for wanting to ingratiate himself with Price, and they had nothing to do with quarter horses. He was still looking for investors in a sweet little deal to build four new apartment blocks in downtown LA. Jimmy was known to dabble in property if the deal was right, and he had a bank balance bigger than Croesus's. Weekend invitations to Palos Verdes were rarer than gold dust and potentially a good deal more valuable, if you knew how to exploit them—which Todd certainly did.

"Have you met my baby boys?" Jimmy had one toddler under each arm and waved them both at Bobby and Todd with all the grinning pride of a fisherman showing off a prize catch. On closer inspection, Bobby could see the boys looked incredibly like him: with their chubby arms and bright shocks of tufty ginger hair, all they needed was the cigar to look like bona fide Mini-Me's.

"This is Chase." Jimmy pointed to the howling child on the left, distinguishable from his brother only by a fine dribble of snot snaking its way down from his nose to his mouth. "And this is Chancellor." He indicated the snot-free baby. "We call him Chance, don't we, buddy?"

Pinching his son's cheek with paternal affection, he was instantly shot down with a heartfelt death stare from the boy.

Bobby found himself warming toward Chance.

"They have a lot of energy," said Jimmy with devastating understatement, setting the boys down and rolling his eyes indulgently as they tore off around the room, screaming like banshees. Unlike his wife, he seemed quite genuinely paternal, taking off after them with a smile on his face.

"Hey." As soon as he was out of earshot, Todd nudged Bobby in the ribs and nodded in Candy's direction. "Did you check out the wife already? Talk about a body!"

Candy was again having sharp words, this time with the hapless maid, who scurried out of the room afterward like a frightened mouse.

"Not my type," said Bobby coolly.

Todd felt his hackles rising. Who did the kid think he was, Brad fucking Pitt? Candy was every man's type.

"Oh, really?" he said. "Don't tell me. You prefer Tweedle Dita over there."

He gestured toward Amy, who had finally managed to grab both her brothers and was fighting a losing battle trying to drag them off for their bath.

"C'mon," said Bobby. "She seems like a sweet girl."

"Jesus Christ, are you kidding me?" Todd laughed nastily. "Look at her. She's a fucking dump truck."

Bobby winced. He was no saint, especially when it came to women. But he wasn't cruel. And this wasn't the first time he'd heard Todd being vindictive either. Over the past week, his partner had revealed a certain casual ruthlessness that made Bobby distinctly uneasy. Nothing dramatic had happened and they hadn't fallen out, at least not openly. But Wyatt's warnings about not rushing into partnership with a man he barely knew had started playing over and over in his head like an eerie, scratched record. Tonight he was finding them particularly hard to ignore.

At last a nanny arrived to relieve poor Amy of her wriggling charges, and Sean immediately thrust a stiff drink into her hand and pulled her over to a sofa for a chat. It would be dinner in a few minutes, and he wanted to give her a chance to unload on someone before they all sat down.

Meanwhile, Jimmy was talking real estate with Todd, with one fat arm wrapped proprietorially around his wife's waist. Bobby hovered in the background watching, trying to gauge the dynamic between them.

Candy stood almost a foot taller than her husband in her gold stilettos. She reminded him a bit of a sexed-up Snow White petting the fattest and gingeriest of the dwarves: Though some decades Jimmy's junior, there was nevertheless something almost maternal about the way she ran her fingers through his thinning hair. It was creepy. At the same time, she was clearly as happy to flirt with Todd as she had been with him out in the hallway a few moments ago. Jimmy seemed not to notice the way she giggled girlishly at all Todd's jokes and compliments, blatantly leading him on. He evidently felt secure in his wife's affections—more secure, Bobby suspected, than he had reason to be.

"Excuse me, ma'am." The maid was back, approaching her mistress with understandable timidity. "I don't mean to interrupt you. But dinner is served."

At dinner the talk was all of horses and the extortionate prices reached for some of the average-looking Thoroughbreds at the recent Kentucky auctions.

"I could buy six top-flight quarter horses for the price of that filly Magnier picked up last month," said Jimmy, treating the table to a view of his mouthful of semimasticated food as he held forth. "Tuberose or something, she was called. Sounds like a fucking scented candle. Of course"—he swallowed, washing the food down with a slug of red wine—"I have been known to spend a fair bit on Thoroughbreds myself."

"No shit," said Sean under his breath.

"But I'm making more money on my quarter horses," said Jimmy. "A lotta people find that hard to believe."

Bobby, who had Amy on his right, caught her stifling a yawn and grinned.

"You're not interested in horses?"

"Oh! Yes, of course I am," she mumbled automatically, blushing through a mouthful of mashed potato, before deciding that her father wasn't listening and admitting, "well, actually, no, I'm not. Thoroughbreds, quarter horses. It's all double Dutch to me, I'm afraid. When it's around you all the time, you just sort of switch off. But Daddy's completely obsessed."

"Some people say the same thing about me," said Bobby. "That I'm obsessed, I mean. Horses are my passion."

Amy laughed bitterly. "I very much doubt you compare to my father."

It was the first time he'd had a chance to take a good look at her. She could only have been a year or so younger than her stepmother, but the differences between the two women could not have been more marked. She was wearing a plain black linen shift dress that looked like a sack, teamed with a pair of too-chunky black heels that only emphasized the heaviness of her legs. Her hair was thin and blond—the very pale, borderline-albino variety—and she seemed to have inherited her father's red eyelashes, as well as his weight problems. Her features on the other hand—the short, straight nose, deep-set, soulful eyes, and perfect Cupid's bow lips—must have come from her mother. And though their beauty was all but lost in the fat, waxy roundness of her pale face, you could see that if she shed fifty pounds or so, she might actually be pretty.

"You see, it's not just the animals Daddy loves or the buzz of winning," she was saying, keeping her voice low so that Jimmy couldn't hear. "It's the whole social scene that goes with it. I call him a sceneoholic. Candy's the same. So was my mother, when she was younger."

Bobby shifted uncomfortably in his seat at this unexpected mention of the first Mrs. Price.

"Oh, please, don't worry," said Amy, clocking his reaction. "It's fine. I can talk about her now. It was a long time ago. Really."

"You know, my mom was a bit of a party girl too," he said. "Still is, in fact."

"Amy." Jimmy's voice boomed across the table. "Quit boring him, would you?"

Amy shrank back into silence, and Bobby's heart went out to her. It was like watching an ant getting sprayed with Raid—one moment she was animated and lively, the next she was shriveled away to nothing.

No prizes for guessing which of his kids Daddy loved best. And no wonder Candy was so dismissive of her stepdaughter: She obviously took her cues from Jimmy.

"He wants to talk horses, don't you, kid?" Before Bobby had a chance to answer, Todd jumped in.

"We're starting small at Highwood, but Bobby's reputation as a trainer is second to none, and we've got high hopes for the place. In terms of facilities, there's no one in mid-California to match us."

"Is that so?" said Jimmy. "And you say you're already training out there?"

"Only my own horses," said Bobby. "I have a young girl from England, a very promising jockey, who I'm working with right now."

Jimmy looked at Todd.

"Milly, right? The sexy one."

Bobby felt a lump rise in his throat and looked daggers at Todd. The sexy one? Was that how he thought of her?

"She's seventeen," he said icily. "She's a child."

"I'd like to meet her," said Jimmy, either ignoring his hostility or failing to register it. "I've been saying for years I'd like to find a really good girl jockey to promote. If she's good enough, and as hot as Todd says she is, she could make herself a small fortune in sponsorship deals. With the right backing, of course . . ."

Bobby ground his teeth together so hard it hurt. The idea of Milly being "backed" by Jimmy, or even meeting the man, made him feel sick to his stomach. And as for Todd's "interest" . . . they'd be having words about that later.

He told himself his feelings for Milly stemmed from protectiveness—but deep down he knew it was more than that. He was scared of losing her. With every day that passed, her incredible talent as a jockey became more and more evident. How long could it be before she outgrew little local races and wanted to spread her wings? Not long enough, that was for sure. She'd be off traveling the quarter horse circuit in no time, surrounded by sharks like Price and perhaps even worse. And he'd no longer be able to protect her.

Where the fuck did Todd get off, ogling her like some sort of pervert and putting ideas about her career into Price's head?

"Milly's nowhere near ready for a national career," he blurted out, more curtly than he'd intended. "And when she is, *I'll* be the one to manage her. She's interested in racing, not sponsorship deals."

Jimmy laughed.

"Don't kid yourself, Mr. Cameron," he said, relighting the stub of the cigar he never seemed to put down, not even while eating. "Everybody wants fame. Women especially."

"Well, Milly doesn't," growled Bobby. "And she's not a woman. She's a girl."

Todd said nothing, allowing the conversation to drift back into safer waters. But inside, his mind was racing.

Clearly, Bobby had the hots for Milly, and he had them bad. Interesting.

He hadn't yet figured out exactly how he might exploit this situation. But if he wanted to get his hands on that oil one day, he needed to start looking for chinks in the Cameron armor.

Perhaps, in the form of Miss Milly Lockwood Groves, he might have just found one?

CHAPTER FOURTEEN

November in Cambridgeshire had been as gray and dreary as ever. Duvet-thick layers of cloud had failed to take the edge off the biting Siberian wind as it sliced across the fens, ripping the last of the leaves from the trees and turning the rain into flying needles. Everywhere people shivered and grumbled under parkas and scarves, longing for spring or at least a break in the weather.

Rachel was used to it. She'd grown up riding in all conditions, but it still depressed her. So today, when a dazzling winter sun had finally deigned to make an appearance, and the clouds had given way to a thin, almost translucent-blue sky, she woke up in unusually good spirits.

Turning up the radio in the hundred-thousand-pound Mercedes convertible her parents had bought her for her eighteenth, she set off on the fifteen-mile journey to Newells. These days she stayed over there more days than not. But last night she'd finally cracked and decided she needed a break from Jasper and his constant whining. Ever since the disaster at Epsom his career had been on a steady downward slope, just as hers was skyrocketing into the big league. As a result his ego, fragile at the best of times, now needed almost constant massage and attention. Normally she was pretty good at it, listening patiently and without laughing to his ludicrous conspiracy theories about why he wasn't being picked for more races, dutifully praising him every time they made love, sticking to him like glue whenever they went out in public. But sometimes even she needed a quiet place where she could go and scream.

Still, she thought, as the sunlight streamed through the windscreen so brightly she had to squint to see the road ahead, it was all worth it. When Cecil had first decided to let Milly go to America to race, she was so furious she'd almost dumped Jasper then and there. After all, if the whole point of the relationship was to get under Milly's skin, then why continue with it, if she wasn't even going to be in the country?

But within a day or two she'd changed her mind. Milly's absence wasn't a setback, it was an opportunity. It left the way completely clear for her to win over the gullible Linda, who would no doubt be looking for a daughterly shoulder to cry on, what with Cecil still so weak. And though it was annoying that the little brat was being allowed to race at all, the fact that Milly had been banished to some obscure, cowboy sport on the other side of the Atlantic meant that she was no longer even a potential threat to Rachel's own ambition to become the most successful girl rider in England, an ambition that she was getting closer to realizing every day.

By the time Milly came back—if she ever did—she'd find she'd been well and truly usurped.

And in the meantime, as irksome as Jasper could be, there were other, additional benefits to dating him. Rachel's media value, she'd rapidly realized, was doubled by being part of a high-profile couple. Despite his career doldrums, Jasper was still in enough demand on the party circuit to be considered high profile. And then there was the sex. He might be a pathetic, vain, needy buffoon most of the time. But even Rachel had to give credit where credit was due: He was a lot better at fucking than he was at racing. Since they'd been together, he'd learned what worked for her and what didn't, to the point where she now regularly orgasmed two or even three times whenever they slept together, which even after five months was on a daily basis.

"Rachel, sweetheart. There you are!"

Linda, dressed in her gardening togs: pristine green cord trousers with matching green wellies and jumper, both of them printed with little pictures of trowels and forks—no outfit was complete, apparently, without a theme—came rushing out of the house to meet her as she pulled into the yard.

"Now, don't keep me in suspense. What's this marvelous news, hmmm?"

Rachel groaned inwardly. Bloody Mummy. She must have gotten on the blower the minute she left the house this morning. One of the major drawbacks of having to pretend to like Milly's family was that her parents had taken it as their cue to adopt Cecil and Linda as new best friends.

"Hello, Mrs. LG." She gave Linda a fixed smile of faux warmth before kissing her on both cheeks. "It's not that big a deal, actually."

"What isn't?" said Jasper. He was standing in the kitchen doorway, still in his pajama trousers, with a skintight cashmere and silk sweater sprayed onto his torso. Whenever possible he preferred to go topless so he could show off his rippling triceps and broad, hairless chest, but even he didn't fancy it with frost on the ground. The sweater was the next best thing.

"Julia called a few minutes ago," said Linda breathlessly. "Apparently, Rachel's had some thrilling news. But she will insist on being modest about it."

Rachel regarded her with silent disdain. She was like a child, or a puppy, painfully eager to please. No wonder J. was so ashamed of her.

The truth was, she did have news, news that she was certainly excited about. But something told her Jasper might not be quite so pleased. She'd wanted time to figure out the best way to break it to him. But now Hyacinth bloody Bucket had forced her hand.

"I'm not being modest," she said, slipping her arm around Jasper's waist as they all went inside. "But it's honestly no great shakes. Have, er . . . have you heard of a magazine called *Loaded*?"

Linda looked blank. Jasper pulled away from her as if he'd just been stung.

"Is it a shooting periodical?" Linda asked tentatively. She'd tried for years to get Cecil to agree to go shooting, thinking it would help them to mingle socially with the local aristocracy, but he'd never had the slightest interest. As a result, she was not au fait with the smart shooting and fishing mags. She did hope she hadn't just betrayed her ignorance in front of Rachel.

"No," said Rachel, trying to sound lighthearted in the face of Jasper's patent fury. "It's a lifestyle magazine. For men."

"Oh," said Linda, none the wiser. "I see."

"It's soft bloody porn, that's what it is!" Jasper exploded. "You're not doing it."

"Don't be silly, darling," said Rachel, lighting up a cigarette to steady her nerves. "Des thinks it'll be great for my image. You know, as a female jockey, making it in a man's world, that sort of thing?"

"Who's Des?" Linda was starting to feel out of her depth.

"My agent," said Rachel proudly. She loved saying the word "agent." It made her feel like a movie star.

"Des is out of his mind," barked Jasper. "It's bad enough you parading around in your undies for *Heaven Sent*." *Heaven Sent* was the lingerie firm that had recently signed Rachel as a model. "But no girlfriend of mine is going to strip off for some cheesy lads' mag, rolling around in foam or whatever the fuck it is they make you do."

Rachel pouted and forced the tears into her eyes. No way was she giving up a three-page feature in *Loaded* just because Mr. Insecurity was jealous. But at the same time, she couldn't afford to lose him. Not yet.

"Oh, now, come along. Don't cry," said Linda, putting her arm around Rachel and frowning at Jasper. She hated it when they rowed. Ever since they'd gotten together she'd spent many happy hours picturing the big society wedding, perhaps in *Hello!*, with Jasper looking handsome as could be at the altar and herself, mother of the groom, in what? A John Galliano suit, perhaps? Or something more conservative. Maybe a Stella McCartney?

But it wouldn't happen if J. kept throwing his weight around and upsetting the girl.

"Jasper, darling, I think you should apologize," she said sternly. "See how you've upset her."

"But, Mother," he yelled, exasperated. "It's *porn!*"

"What's porn? Oh, hello, Rachel." Cecil, just back from the first cover of the morning, had wandered in in search of a cup of tea. He still looked terribly thin, Rachel thought idly. And Linda had confided in her that ever since the stroke he'd been low on energy. Give or take a few nervy clients, who'd taken their business elsewhere, the stud had pretty much bounced back from the equine flu debacle. Even so, Cecil sorely missed Milly's free and valuable help around the yard, and it was clear that the day-to-day running of Newells was tiring him a lot more than it used to.

"*Loaded,*" said Jasper bitterly. "Rachel seems to think that getting her baps out in every WHSmith in the country is going to boost her career."

Linda gasped, and her voice dropped to a horrified whisper. "You wouldn't . . . I mean, it's not really . . ." she could hardly bring herself to say it, "*pornography?* Is it, Rachel?"

"No, no, no," said Cecil dismissively. "Of course it's not. Give over, J. You read *Loaded.* It's not exactly *Penthouse,* let's face it."

"Maybe," said Rachel quietly—she was still playing the wounded and demure card for all it was worth—"maybe we could do it together? Make it some sort of hot couple thing?"

"Well," Jasper mumbled grudgingly. "That would make it a *bit* better, I suppose."

Gotcha! thought Rachel. Honestly, if it weren't so pathetic it would be funny. He couldn't bear for her to have the limelight. But as soon as there was a chance of him being involved, he was backtracking faster than an Italian tank under enemy fire.

"Anyway," she sniffed, "we don't have to decide now."

Jasper pulled her onto his lap, and Linda breathed a sigh of relief. Milly's defection to America had been a blow to her social aspirations. But it was a blow greatly softened by the love blossoming between these two wonderful young people.

"Well," she said brightly. "I'd better get back to my gardening. Leave you two to, er . . . talk. Come on, Cecil."

"But I haven't had my tea yet," Cecil protested lamely.

"Never mind that," said his wife firmly. And taking him by the arm, she pulled him back outside into the cold blue sunshine of the day.

It was equally clear and bright a few days later in California for the opening of the Ballard Rodeo weekend.

Despite Summer's scathing remarks, Ballard was, in fact, a huge and eagerly anticipated event on the local calendar: a sort of hybrid county fair and serious racing fixture. For three days in late November, this tiny town—composed of a few Victorian cottages strung along a single-lane road, an old red schoolhouse, and two dilapidated but well-attended churches—was transformed into a bustling center of commerce, gambling, and raucous entertainment.

By nine A.M., horse trailers and trucks littered the roadside and had already filled up the three large fields loaned every year for the event by local farmers. Vendors from nearby Los Olivos and Santa Ynez, some even from as far afield as Santa Barbara or even Oxnard, had arrived hours earlier, ready to sell everything from fresh-grown fruit and vegetables to candles, soap, furniture, clothing, even ranching equipment to the families who flocked in the hundreds to the event. Some were serious racing fans. Others were more interested in the traditional cowboy events, such as roping and barrel racing, or the more lighthearted competitions, from cake baking to vegetable growing. There were beer stands for the moms and dads, a whole slew of games and attractions for the kids, and of course, the ubiquitous betting booths, ensuring that everybody was kept happy, busy, and, most important of all, spending.

Milly arrived with Dylan at nine fifteen, an hour and a half before she was due to race, and was blown away by the size and scale of it all.

"Holy shit." She whistled nervously through her teeth as Dylan pulled the trailer into their reserved competitor's spot close to the racetrack. "I've never seen so many people in one place in my life. I thought this was just a local thing."

"It is," he said, turning off the engine and unclicking his seat belt. "But 'local' in cowboy terms covers a lot o' ground. Last year they had twelve thousand here on the Saturday. I'd say it's more 'n that today."

"D'you think they've come to see Ben Devino?" asked Milly.

A winner at Los Alamitos earlier in the season, Devino was the local boy made good and an undoubted rising star in the quarter horse world—not least because, as well as being a terrific jockey, he had the looks of a young Robert Redford.

"I'm sure some of 'em have," said Dylan, smiling. "And maybe some of 'em have come to see you: Milly Lockwood Groves, the one and only English cowgirl!"

215

"Yeah, right." Milly giggled. "I don't think so, somehow." But she was grateful for his support all the same. What with Summer being such a bitch to her and Bobby away in LA for her big day, it was nice to have at least one friendly face around.

She knew it was petty and stupid, but ever since she'd seen that bloody *Tatler* picture of Jasper and Rachel, she'd been gripped by a feeling of inadequacy. Overnight she'd gone from enjoying the thrill of racing again and being quietly proud of her progress in a new and very different sport to feeling like an obscure failure. Rachel had sponsorship deals, for God's sake. She was riding topflight racehorses at tracks that everyone had heard of. Santa Ynez might as well be Mars for all it meant to people back home. It was depressing.

When Bobby talked about quarter horses, it all sounded so thrilling— network TV coverage, multimillion-dollar purses, speeds unrivaled anywhere else in the horse racing world. But she hadn't seen much of that so far. Even today's race, where she'd be competing against at least two nationally known riders, had a purse of only ten thousand dollars. And the only TV crews she'd seen so far were local.

"Let's see how His Majesty's doing, shall we?" said Dylan, lowering the back of the new aluminum trailer. Bought with Todd's money, it was a smart, ultramodern affair with a huge black "H" for Highwood embossed on the side. The joke was that the horses now traveled in much more comfort and style than the humans.

"Hello, lovely." Milly beamed, running up the ramp to pet Danny, one of the newest colts at Highwood but already one of her favorites. Reaching into her pocket, she held one of her dwindling supply of Polos under the horse's dry, rubbery lips—she'd been horrified to discover they didn't sell Polos in America—and grinned as Danny hoovered it up. "That's for energy," she said seriously, like a coach addressing his star player. "I want a hundred and ten percent out of you today, boy. Let's show Bobby what he's missing."

As with the other races she'd been to, the atmosphere at Ballard was far more casual than anything she'd seen in England, with competitors and spectators wandering around in a giant free-for-all. With so many people on horseback, it was hard at first to determine who *was* compet-

216

ing and who wasn't, but, thankfully, Dylan was on hand to guide her and Danny through the throng.

He led them over toward a long row of trestle tables where a group of men with clipboards were ticking off names on a list and handing out paper bibs printed with numbers to the various riders.

"I feel like I'm at a school sports day," said Milly as a green bib printed with the number four was pinned unceremoniously to her T-shirt. All the jockeys were in T-shirts and jeans, and only a couple of them, Milly included, had thought it necessary to wear a helmet. "It's not very professional, is it?"

"Well, sure it is," said Dylan. "Professional means you get paid, right? You win, you'll pick up ten thousand dollars. And I'll get five hundred."

"You will?" She looked perplexed.

"Sure. I bet on you," he said proudly. "Ten bucks at fifty to one."

"Fifty to one?" Milly spluttered. "Fifty to fucking one? Just exactly how shit do they think I am? There are only twelve runners, for God's sake. How can I be on at fifty to one?"

Ignoring her, Dylan ran through the important information again.

"The green bib means you're riding in the third race," he explained. "That's in about"—he looked at his watch—"fifteen minutes."

"Shit," said Milly, coming down from her indignation cloud with a bang. "Fifteen minutes? We'd better get over to the paddock then, no?"

There was, in fact, no paddock, just a rough stretch of grass beside the short, straight racetrack where the jockeys were chatting with one another like they didn't have a care in the world—some of them were even sipping beer. It was a far cry from the pre-race atmosphere at Newmarket, that was for sure. The early morning cold had evaporated already, replaced by a mid-morning sun that packed a strong enough punch to have people reaching for cold drinks and horses lathering up into foamy, excitable sweats.

Fleetingly, Milly wished Bobby were here to give her some last-minute words of advice or encouragement. But then she pulled herself together. She wasn't a child. She didn't need Bobby to hold her hand.

She could do this. She could do it on her own.

*   *   *

"What time did you say she was racing again?" Bobby asked Summer, desperately scrabbling around the kitchen table for his car keys. He'd put them down only a second ago but they seemed to have gone AWOL already.

"Jeez, Bobby, I don't know, okay?" she replied, unable to keep the irritation out of her voice. Her surprise and joy when he'd walked in the door five minutes ago, a day earlier than expected, soon turned to resentment when she realized it was Milly he had rushed home for. "I think Dylan said eleven, but I'm not sure. All I know is, they left an hour ago, and the Ballard traffic's always superbad. Just forget it and let me make you somethin' to eat. There's no way you're gonna make it in time."

"I'm not hungry," he snapped, flinging papers onto the floor as he searched in vain for his keys. "Goddamn it. Where are they?"

The trip out to Jimmy Price's had been a disaster. After dinner on the Thursday night, he'd tackled Todd about Milly, expecting him to back off. But instead he'd pushed the point even further.

"It's no good you trying to hold the girl back," he insisted. "Eventually she's gonna outgrow Highwood, and when she does, she'll need someone to back her."

"*I'll* back her," said Bobby furiously. "This has nothing to do with you."

"Sure it does," said Todd. "You signed a deal with me to run a training stables, remember? I don't want you flying around the country micromanaging this kid's career just because you've got the hots for her."

"I do not have the hots for her!"

"Besides," Todd pressed on, "are you seriously saying you can provide her with the support a guy like Jimmy can offer? The guy makes careers. He creates people outta nothing, throws hundreds of thousands of dollars, sometimes more, behind his riders. You can't do that for Milly."

This conversation had bothered Bobby so much, he barely slept a wink all night. Was he holding Milly back? Was that what he was doing? Was it inevitable that she'd leave him and move on to bigger and better things, as everyone seemed to think?

As a result he spent most of Friday in a foul mood. What little appetite he'd had for milking Jimmy as a contact had now completely dis-appeared, and the prospect of making fruitless small talk for another forty-eight hours rapidly began to seem unbearable.

He announced at dinner that he had a family emergency that de-manded his return to Highwood. It was an obvious lie, but no one questioned him. Before sunup this morning, he'd gotten a taxi back to LA where his truck was waiting and by seven thirty he was headed north on the still relatively empty 101.

As the miles shot by, he found himself plagued by horrible, worry-ing thoughts. When Todd had said all those things to him about Milly, he wanted to tell him to shut up, that he would damn well manage her career if he wanted to, that it was none of Todd's goddamn business what he did with his life or hers. But now the creeping realization dawned on him that it *was,* in fact, Todd's business. That having a part-ner meant more than getting the bank off your back and being able to train quarter horses. It also meant a loss of freedom, a loss of control.

He'd been so impatient to get started, to prove to everyone that he could do a better job of running Highwood than Hank, that he'd sold a share in his life, and the land he loved, to a man he barely knew. A man who, increasingly, he found he didn't much like.

He was far too proud to admit it. But Wyatt had been right all along.

Somehow he'd have to find a way out of his partnership with Todd. In the meantime, the last two days had been a wake-up call as far as Milly was concerned. The vultures were already circling. He'd have to keep a much, much closer eye on her from now on.

"Aha!" he said, catching sight of a glint of silver beneath a pile of open envelopes. "There you are."

Snatching up the keys, he was halfway out the door when the kitchen phone rang.

"Aren't you gonna answer that?" said Summer petulantly.

Bobby shrugged. "It's not my house." But seeing that she made no move to get it herself, he reluctantly doubled back and, giving her a dirty look, picked up the call.

"Highwood."

Summer watched in silence as his expression turned from annoyance, to shock, to something not far from panic. After a few "I see"s and "sure, of course"s he put down the receiver and stood there swaying, while all the blood drained from his face.

"Bobby?" She went over to him. "What is it? What's wrong?"

He stared at her blankly. "I have to get over to Ballard," he whispered. "Right now."

The fifteen minutes she spent waiting for her race to be called were the longest Milly could ever remember. Pacing Danny round and round in a slow circle, she tried to focus her energies inward, like Bobby had told her to, and not to pay attention to the gaggle of cowboys staring at her as though she'd just emerged from a UFO. But it was hard.

Unlike traditional racing, quarter horse events were short sprints along ramrod-straight tracks, over almost before they'd begun. Even so, the two warm-up races before the main event seemed to take an absolute age. With every minute that passed she felt her nerves fraying further till it was all she could do to hold on to her reins and breathe in and out.

At last, a laconic voice crackled out through the ancient speaker system, asking all entrants for the third and final race of the morning to make their way down to the starting line.

"Good luck," said Dylan, smiling up at her. "And for God's sake, relax a little, wouldya? It's a horse race, not an execution."

Everybody else certainly seemed relaxed enough, thought Milly. The slow trickle of cowboys making their leisurely way over to the track, handing their Stetsons, beer bottles, and any other paraphernalia to family and friends, all looked as unconcerned as if they were setting off on a family picnic.

Leaning forward in her saddle, she patted Danny's neck affectionately, and smiled as he whinnied in response. The love affair between the two of them was entirely mutual.

"You've got to help me, sweetheart," Milly murmured into his cashmere-soft ear. "Okay? Let's make this the last time anyone gives us odds of fifty to one."

The starting line they'd been summoned to turned out to be little more than a simple white crease of chalk, drawn by hand across the grass. (This thing was getting more like sports day by the minute.) Glancing to her left, Milly saw the godlike figure of Ben Devino on his beautiful buckskin colt, Domino. It was funny to think that this time last year she'd been mad about Robbie Pemberton. Now he seemed tiny and doll-like in comparison to the divinely brawny Ben. Like most quarter horse jockeys, Devino could have made a light lunch of Robbie Pemberton and still had room for dessert.

"Hi." Tipping his hat he smiled at her, reducing her already shaky stomach to pure liquid.

"Hi." Nervously, she smiled back. Bloody hell, he was fit, almost chiseled and brooding enough to give Bobby a run for his money. Almost.

Damn bloody Bobby. She knew she was being childish. Of course he had to work, and that came first. But she still wished he'd cared enough to rearrange a few things and be here for her today.

"On your marks, boys." The starter raised his pistol in the air, and Milly instinctively leaned forward to reassure Danny. In an instant all thoughts of Devino, Bobby, and every other man in the world vanished from her mind. All that existed was the five hundred yards of straight track stretching out in front of her.

A hush fell over the chattering crowds of spectators, lining the course on rough, tiered wooden benches. It seemed to Milly as though they all took one long, collective breath, before the crack of a single shot rang out through the silence, and they were off.

Bobby had drummed two key, unbreakable rules into her head in the last two months: to move back a little in her saddle for balance and to keep loose with her reins. As the gun went off, she forgot both of them, throwing her body so far forward she could almost feel the tips of Danny's ears against her belly and digging both heels into his flank for all she was worth. The result was that the surprised pony shot forward like a heat-seeking missile. Breaking sharply from post four, he surged straight into a half-length lead over Domino, the favorite. The only question now was could he hold it.

On such a short, straight track, with horses reaching speeds of over forty miles per hour, there was no time for the sort of tactical race planning Milly had learned in England. This was all about instinct. She really had no idea what she was doing. But whatever it was, it seemed to be working.

Dylan, watching her from a front row seat a few feet short of the finishing post, shook his head in wonder. He'd seen her in training and at the local race in Santa Ynez, so he already knew she was good. But today was like nothing he'd ever witnessed before. She rode like a woman possessed.

Whooping encouragement as the tight group of leaders came closer—there was so much dust it was hard to see who was where, but the top four were lengths ahead of the others—he was surprised to see Bobby, head down and scowling, pushing his way through disgruntled fellow spectators toward him.

"You been watching this?" he yelled through the din, once Bobby was within earshot. "Milly's been phenomenal. Aren't you supposed to be in LA, by the way?"

"Never mind that. I need to talk to you," Bobby shouted back. But his words were carried away by the roar of the crowd as sixteen hooves thundered past, hurtling toward the finish with all the speed and power of runaway trucks.

Through the frenzy, Bobby could see that Milly was in second place, behind Devino, but there was hardly a whisker in it. Her style was horrific—she was all over the place, leaning much too far forward, barely in control—but somehow she was managing to wrench every last ounce of power from Danny, who looked magnificent with his rippling, oversized hindquarters and long, thin neck, bounding forward like a giant hare.

In seconds it was over. Milly came tearing past the finishing post, one long pigtail of hair flying out behind her, apparently neck and neck with Ben Devino.

"Awesome!" Dylan punched the air. Then, turning excitedly to Bobby, "Did she win? If she won, I just made myself a ton o' money."

"She didn't win," said Bobby, deadpan.

He was already making his way down to the area of open grass where the jockeys were gathering for postrace congratulations or commiserations with family and friends. Jogging to keep up, it dawned on Dylan for the first time that something was seriously wrong.

"Hey, man," he said, resting a concerned hand on his friend's shoulder as they finally drew level. "What is it?"

"Bobby!" Milly's shriek of delight could be heard all around the showground. Leaping from the saddle, she sprinted over to where he and Dylan were standing and, throwing caution to the wind in her elation, launched herself into his arms.

"You came! I can't believe you came!"

"Milly . . ." he began, but her excitement overwhelmed him.

"How much did you see? Did you see the whole race?" she jabbered. "Omigod, Danny was amazing. Amazing! Ben Devino only beat us by, like, a foot or something. Ben Devino! And they had us on at fifty to one, did Dyl tell you? Can you believe the cheek of it, fifty to fucking one? Sorry," she said, misinterpreting Bobby's stony face. "'Scuse my language. But, honestly, don't you think that's ridiculous?"

"Milly," he said again. This time she heard him.

"Yes?" she giggled. "What? You look awfully serious, you know."

"I've got some bad news. I think you'd better sit down."

Clasping her hand, he pulled her down onto the now-empty bench. Milly felt a strange shiver of foreboding and found herself gripping his warm fingers tightly, like a child. It was weird, changing gears so suddenly from joy to apprehension—the emotional equivalent of someone cutting your elevator cable. She looked up at Dylan for elucidation, but he seemed as baffled as she was.

"What?" she said.

"It's your dad," said Bobby. "Your mom called the house an hour ago. He had another stroke, a massive one, in his sleep last night."

Milly put her hand over her mouth as she felt the vomit rising up into it.

"They rushed him to the hospital." Bobby gripped her hand tighter. "But his brain had been so severely damaged, there was nothing anyone could do. I'm so sorry, sweetheart. He died at eleven thirty this morning."

CHAPTER FIFTEEN

For Milly, it was the worst Christmas ever.

Plunged into unimaginable depths of grief as she struggled to come to terms with the loss of the father she adored, she longed to be able to turn to someone, anyone, for comfort. But Cecil had been the glue that held her family together. Without him, she, Linda, and Jasper rattled around Newells like three odd parts of a defunct machine. They had nothing to say to one another.

Oddly, the funeral itself was the easiest part. Bobby flew in for it, so Milly wouldn't feel alone, and Linda was able to temporarily keep her own tidal wave of loss at bay by hurling herself into the mammoth task of organizing everything. But as soon as it was over and the last of the guests had left, the gaping hole of silence left in the once happy, bustling household was even more deafening than before.

"I'll have to stay, at least till New Year," Milly told Bobby on the depressing drive to the airport two days after the funeral. Shivering in a bottle-green, skinny-rib sweater and cords two sizes too big for her, she looked gaunt and worn-out with stress. Between dealing with the horses, fielding the flood of condolence letters that Linda was too overwrought to look at, and trying to make sense of her own grief, she'd barely eaten in the last three days and it was starting to show.

"Take as much time as you need," he said kindly. "The real quarter horse season won't get going till the spring, anyway. You won't have missed much."

There was so much she wanted to say to him, so much she wanted to ask. It was only six months since he'd lost his own father, after all. He'd probably understand the maelstrom of emotions she was going through better than anybody.

And yet, somehow, the words always seemed to die on her lips. Deep down, she still felt close to him—closer than ever now, in a strange way, with her dad gone. But still the distance, the horrid formality that had grown up between them, refused to budge. Everything she said, or tried to say, sounded false. Forced. Wrong.

She wished he weren't going.

"Call me," she said lamely, as he heaved his case out of the trunk and stuck his head through the window to say good-bye. "And wish them all a happy Christmas back home. Especially Dylan."

"I will," he said, kissing the top of her head. She smelled of shampoo and horsehair. "And listen: Try not to let Rachel get under your skin, okay? This is about you and your family. Not her."

"Yeah, I know," she sighed. "I'll try."

But, boy, was it easier said than done.

As soon as she'd arrived back from California, Milly saw for herself just how successfully Rachel had replaced her at Newells. Her dad had been the only one who hadn't fallen for her bullshit. But with him out of the picture, Linda was more vulnerable than ever, and Rachel had wasted no time in capitalizing on her weakness, moving in for the kill with all the silent ruthlessness of a black widow spider.

Under the pretense of being helpful—"Really, Mrs. LG, you mustn't. Let me deal with the trustees; Jasper and I can take care of the banking for you. No, honestly, it's no trouble at all"—within days she'd established a grip on not only her mother's fragile heart but, more disturbingly, her financial affairs as well.

It worried Milly deeply. But the more she tried to warn Linda off, the more she seemed to alienate only herself.

"Honestly, Milly, I know you've always been a bit jealous of Rachel," said Linda the last time she'd broached the subject, to Milly's frank amazement. "But surely even you can make an effort to get over it now, for me? If it hadn't been for Rachel's help these past few days"—fumbling in her cardigan pocket for a handkerchief, she dabbed her eyes with it before blowing her nose loudly—"I don't think I could have coped at all. I really don't. And she's been a tower of strength for poor Jasper."

In the end there was nothing for it but to sit back and watch, while Rachel hijacked what should have been a subdued, private family Christmas. And the worst part was that she did it so well, covering her tracks, making sure she was nothing but sweetness and light whenever she spoke to Milly. It was infuriating.

On the evening after Boxing Day, Milly was upstairs in her room, desperately struggling to put the stud's accounts for the last month into some sort of order. Math had never been her strong suit, and the bewildering array of papers, contracts, checks, receipts, and invoices that lay scattered willy-nilly over her bedspread now might as well have been written backward in Hungarian for all the sense they made to her.

"Can I come in?" Linda knocked tentatively a couple of times before sticking her head around the door.

"Of course." Milly forced a smile, clearing a space in the sea of paperwork for her mother to sit down. "I'm not getting very far with this lot, anyway. God knows how Dad managed without an accountant."

Smoothing down her tweed skirt—ever since Linda had noticed Julia Delaney's fondness for tweed she'd tried to adopt something of a country theme in her own wardrobe—she sat down on the newly cleared corner of the bed and, to Milly's horror, started to cry.

"Oh, Mummy." Shoving the rest of the papers onto the floor, Milly clambered over the bed and put her arms around her. "Come on. Don't. You know how Daddy hated to see you upset."

"I know," Linda sniffed. "You're right. But it's so hard. Everything reminds me of him. Everything." Leaning over, she picked up a photograph of herself and Cecil with Milly at the last gymkhana she'd competed in before her accident. As usual, Milly was clasping a first place rosette and grinning from ear to ear, as was Cecil; while Linda looked awkward and out of place in a blue and green spotted shirt-waister and hat, both plainly far too dressy for the occasion.

"I need to get away," she said, her eyes brimming over with tears once again.

Gently, Milly took the picture from her and placed it back on the dresser. This was the first time since her dad's death that her mother had opened up to her. And though she hated herself for it, she couldn't help but be relieved that for once it was *her* Linda had turned to and not tower-of-strength Rachel.

"I think that's a great idea, Mummy," she said, smiling. "A change of scene will do you a world of good."

"Do you really think so, darling?" said Linda, visibly brightening. "Well, I must say, I'm terribly relieved. I thought you of all people wouldn't understand. I mean, I know it's your childhood home, so it's absolutely understandable you're fond of the place . . ."

Her brain was so addled from the accounts, it took a few moments for the import of what her mother was saying to sink through and hit home. But when it did, Milly found herself starting to shake. With an effort, she kept her voice level and calm.

"What are you talking about?"

"Newells," said Linda, perplexed. "What did you think I was talking about? It's just too full of memories for me, darling." She sighed. "I need to move on."

"You're not—" Milly was so choked, she found it hard to get the words out. "You're not seriously contemplating selling up?"

"Honestly, Milly, I don't see any other option," Linda mumbled. At least she had the decency to look shamefaced about it.

"Why not?" The suspicion in Milly's voice was rapidly morphing into open outrage. So much for their moment of mother-daughter bonding. "Dad's life insurance alone should mean you can comfortably afford to stay. Newells has been in the family for generations."

"Only three generations," said Linda defensively. Why did Milly always have to be so difficult about everything? "It's hardly a stately home. Besides, you know I haven't a clue about the stud business. I'd never be able to keep it going."

"But, Mummy, that's nonsense!" said Milly, jumping to her feet. "*I* know the business. I could stay here and run it."

Linda let out a tinkling laugh of derision. "Don't be silly, darling. You're not even eighteen till next month." She glanced meaningfully at the accounts now strewn across the bedroom floor. "I know you loved daddy's horses, but you haven't the first idea about running a business."

As this was undeniably true, Milly let it go. "So hire a manager," she said, right back on the offensive. "It isn't rocket science."

"Darling, I do wish you'd *listen* to me," Linda snapped. She simply hadn't the energy to argue the toss with Milly any longer. "I don't *want* a manager. I want a new start. A chance to get away from—" She swallowed hard, trying to repress the sadness that kept threatening to break loose and drown her. "A chance to get away from everything. I've never enjoyed the stud business. In fact, in all honesty, I'm not much of a horse person."

At last, she admits it, thought Milly bitterly. Better late than never.

"I'll be much better off in a nice little town house. Newells ought to belong to someone who loves horses as much as your father did. Someone who'll carry on his good work."

For the second time in ten minutes, Milly felt a gnawing sense of unease.

"Are you trying to tell me you've already sold the house?" Her voice was so quiet it was barely audible.

"Darling, the sooner these things are faced, the easier they are for everyone. It's what your father would have wanted."

"Who to?"

Linda developed a previously unknown fascination with her wedding ring, staring down at her hands and twisting it around and around on her finger like she was trying to tune in TV reception or pick up satellite messages from space.

"Who to?" Milly repeated, more loudly this time. "Who have you sold to, Mummy?"

"To me."

Rachel, smiling smugly, appeared in the doorway with Jasper standing protectively behind her. She could scarcely have been a less welcome sight if she'd been wearing a black hood and carrying a scythe.

"Your ma decided to sell the house and the stud to me," she trilled. "It's for the best."

"And since when do you have that kind of money?" asked Milly, clinging desperately to the hope that this must be some sort of sick joke.

"Well," said Rachel, tossing back her blond mane imperiously. "I'm not at all sure that's any of your business, Milly. But since you ask, I came into my trust on my eighteenth. I still have to clear all major purchases with the trustees, of course. But they all felt Newells was an excellent investment." She looked down at her fingernails, as if bored by the whole thing, before adding nastily, "even though, understandably, your poor father had rather let things slide this year—"

That, for Milly, was it. In that instant, all the years of enmity and frustration came exploding out of her like water through a shattered dam. Launching herself at Rachel with an almighty scream, she took her completely by surprise, rugby tackling her to the floor. Straddling her, she pinned her arms down to the carpet and proceeded to lift her head up by the hair, slamming it down repeatedly on the hard floor.

"You bitch!" she spat, emphasizing each word with a thud of Rachel's skull. "You fucking vicious, manipulative bitch!"

"Stop it!" Linda wailed hysterically, flapping her hands around uselessly like a broken windmill. "Milly, for God's sake!"

But Milly clearly had no intention of stopping, and in the end there was nothing for it but for Jasper to wade in and try to pry her off. By the time he succeeded, Rachel's face was already badly bruised and bloodied. Milly, still squirming and straining in his arms like a crazed animal, refused to be calmed.

"I swear to God," she yelled, "this is *not* the end, do you hear me? I'll get Newells back, and I'll make you pay for what you've done to my family if it's the last thing I do on this earth."

"Stop it, Mill," said Jasper weakly. "You're being ridiculous. Rachel's bought the house. She hasn't poisoned anyone."

"She has!" shrieked Milly. She knew she sounded hysterical, but she couldn't seem to stop herself. "She's poisoned all of you. But you're both too blind to see it."

"Milly!" said Linda, shocked. "Take that back."

"It's all right, Mrs. LG," said Rachel, through a mouthful of blood. Now that Milly's arms were finally pinned behind her back, she felt safe enough to speak. "I'm not offended, and you mustn't be either. We have to understand. She's grieving."

Linda looked at Rachel with tears of gratitude, as if to thank her for being so generous and forgiving. While Milly, wide-eyed with hatred, was practically foaming at the mouth at this show of see-through sympathy.

Rachel had played out this scene a thousand times in her mind's eye. But the reality was turning out to be more gratifying than anything she could have imagined.

As painful as it was now, her bruised face would heal. But what she'd taken from Milly—the hole she'd blown in her life—that could never be repaired. And they both knew it.

She had the career. She had Jasper. She had Linda. And now she had Newells.

And Milly? Milly had a return ticket to California.

The sooner she used it, the better.

Summer's Christmas, though not perhaps as miserable as Milly's, was also a pretty poor affair.

She knew it was wrong to feel happy about anybody's death, and she tried hard not to think that way about Milly's father. But she couldn't help but feel a tinge of relief that Milly wouldn't be spending Christmas at Highwood after all, hogging Bobby's and Dylan's attention and generally making herself objectionable.

Her relief soon dissipated, however, as Bobby increasingly spent the holiday mooching around the ranch like a bear with a sore head, alternately withdrawn and silent or strident and demanding as his moods shifted from bad to worse and back again.

"Try not to take it personal, honey," her dad said to her kindly on Christmas Eve, taking her aside after Bobby had flown off the handle at her for some perfectly innocuous joke. "He's got a lot on his mind, and none of it's to do with you. This is the first Christmas since the boss died, remember?"

In fact, Hank was not behind Bobby's bad mood—or only tangentially, anyway. If he thought of his father at all, it was as a constant, disapproving presence, a daily reminder of the mistakes he'd already made at Highwood and how he'd failed to live up to the Cameron name.

Bringing Todd in as a partner, he now recognized, had been a mistake. Not even his gorgeous new training stables could make up for the fact that he now had to ask someone else's permission before he did anything on his own ranch. At first, Todd had been reasonably quiet, but as time went on, he'd become more and more involved and more and more demanding by the day, making frequent visits to the property and throwing his weight around with the ranch hands in a way that put just about everybody's back up. He co-owned Highwood, and he wasn't about to let Bobby or anybody else forget it.

What Bobby ought to do, of course, was turn to Wyatt. To admit he'd made a mistake and try to figure out a way they could undo it, together. But he was far too proud and far too stubborn for that. Hank would never have shown such weakness—never in a blue moon—and neither would he. He'd gotten them into this mess and he'd get them out. Alone.

But the high road was a lonely and often depressing place to be. Having no one to share his troubles with (he couldn't talk to Dylan in case it got back to Wyatt, and Milly, even if she hadn't been in England, had problems enough of her own to deal with) he began to feel increasingly isolated. For years, all his life really, he'd dreamed of the day he would inherit Highwood and make it his own. But now that he was finally living the reality, he found himself more miserable and stressed than ever.

And underneath it all, the dull ache of his longing for Milly continued. She turned eighteen next month, which was something, but she was still terribly young. And now that Cecil was dead, the promise he'd made him to take care of his daughter seemed even more sacred. Almost like a dying wish. It made Milly even more forbidden to him than she had been before, a thought that did little to lift his battered spirits.

On New Year's Eve, desperate to lift himself out of his funk, he'd agreed to go to a party at a neighboring ranch with Dylan and the girls.

He'd expected to hate it. But after a few beers, to his surprise, he found himself loosening up, and soon he was actually enjoying himself.

"Wanna dance?" A buxom redhead in the tiniest pair of hot pants Bobby had ever seen—and he'd seen a few—swayed over to the bar where he and Dylan were standing and boldly grabbed him by the hand.

"Sure." He grinned. "Why not?"

The party was being held in a giant barn, a good half of which was set aside as a makeshift dance floor, complete with a huge, cheesy, seventies disco ball courtesy of Santa Ynez's only traveling DJ. It was packed, with couples bumping and grinding away to Prince's "Purple Rain" and singles propping up the bar (another makeshift affair of hay bales with an oilcloth hastily thrown over them, beside which were piled crate upon crate of Budweiser) hoping to find someone among the drunken throng to go home with, or at least to pair up with for that all-important midnight kiss.

"You don't remember me, do you?" said the girl, slipping her thigh between Bobby's legs and pulling his body closer into hers as "Get Off" started booming out of the speakers.

"No," he said, slipping one hand around her waist, then allowing it to wander idly downward to stroke her taut, muscular butt. "Should I?"

"Yeah." She laughed, arching her lower back in response to his touch. "You should! But then you always were an arrogant son of a bitch. I was in the year above you at Solvang High. Samantha Baker."

"Sammy." He smiled as the dim memory clicked into place. "Anthony's sister, right?"

"That's right," she said. "You remember my brother, but you don't remember me?"

Locking eyes with him, her head cocked, she moved her left hand around to the front and, sliding it between their tightly pressed bodies, stroked the outline of his dick through his jeans.

Bobby cleared his throat.

"Your brother and his friends liked to kick the shit out of me," he said, gripping her butt more tightly as he felt his dick start to harden. "That was memorable. But I won't be forgetting you again in a hurry. Sammy."

"Damn right you won't." She grinned, expertly opening his button fly one-handed and slipping her fingers inside. "Bobby."

Across the other side of the barn, Summer watched the two of them glued together like limpets and bit down on her lip so hard it bled.

"Ow. Shit," she said, grabbing a tissue from her purse and dabbing at her mouth.

"You okay?" said Tara, who was standing beside her, sipping a beer from which she'd been allowing her little sister the occasional illicit taste.

"Yeah," said Summer unconvincingly. "I'm fine."

"Don't let him get you down," said Tara, following her gaze to Bobby but misinterpreting her frown as one of sisterly rejection. "I know he's been tough work this vacation. But Dad's right, it's not really you he's mad at. Things'll get better."

"Look at that slut Sammy Baker." Summer couldn't hide her disgust. "She's all over him like a rash."

Tara shrugged and took another swig of Budweiser. "Who knows? Maybe that's just what he needs? At least he's smiling for once."

"It is not what he needs!" snapped Summer. And turning on her heel she stalked off, leaving her bewildered sister wondering what on earth she'd done to upset her.

Three hours later, Bobby sat bolt upright in bed and moaned. A naked Sammy, her long legs wrapped around his waist, arched her back so violently her head was practically touching the sheets and clamped her muscles even more deliciously tightly around his cock.

"Come on, you fucker," she panted. "Do it. Just do it!"

With both hands on her hips he pulled her down even harder onto him, driving into her so deeply that he half expected to see his dick boring out through her back on the other side like an electric drill.

"Jesus!" She laughed after they'd both come, collapsing off him onto the bed in a crumpled heap of satisfied exhaustion. "Did you just get out of prison or something? You fuck like you haven't had a woman in years."

Slumping back against the pillows beside her, Bobby stared up at the ceiling and wondered if he'd ever escape from the prison of his love for Milly. But then he looked over at Sammy and told himself firmly to stop being such a maudlin bastard. She'd just given him the fuck of his life. This was no time to be feeling sorry for himself.

"You're incredible," he said, leaning over and tracing a slow, lazy finger over her flat belly, still glistening with sweat. "That was . . . really good."

"You're funny," she said, reaching down and rifling through her purse for a cigarette, now that she'd gotten her breath back. " 'Really good'? Is that the best you can come up with?" He looked so crestfallen, she couldn't help but laugh again. "Don't worry, I'm only kidding," she said. "It wasn't your giant vocabulary that won me over. Let's just say we both had a majorly happy New Year and leave it at that?"

Suddenly, Bobby heard something clatter downstairs, like somebody fumbling with a door.

"What was that?"

"What?" Sammy inhaled deeply, blowing the smoke back out through her long, aquiline nose. "I didn't hear anything."

"That," said Bobby, leaping out of bed and picking up a heavy lamp from the dresser as the noise came back again, louder and more protracted this time.

"Shit," said Sammy, concerned now. Stubbing out her cigarette, she pulled the sheet up to her chin. "You think someone's breaking in? This house is so fucking creepy." She shivered.

"If they are," said Bobby, winding the lamp cord around his hand and opening the bedroom door, "they're gonna wish they hadn't."

Lifting the lamp above his head and letting out an almighty roar, he went thundering down the stairs, as naked and terrifying as a Zulu warrior.

A small figure, crouched in the shadows of the hallway with some sort of bag, saw him and screamed, at the same time reaching up for the light switch by the front door and turning it on.

"Milly!"

"Bobby!"

She clapped her hands over her eyes. Realizing belatedly that he was butt naked, he clapped *his* hands over his cock.

"What—what are you doing here?" he stammered. "I thought it was a burglar. You're supposed to be at home." Whipping the linen cloth off the hall table, he wrapped it sarong style around his hips. "It's okay," he said. "You can look now."

Tentatively, Milly brought her hands down from her face. He could see at once that she'd been crying.

"I don't have a home anymore," she said, her voice already faltering. "Mummy sold the farm."

"Oh, baby." He moved forward to comfort her. But she wasn't finished.

"To Rachel," she said, unable to hold back the tears any longer. "She's sold Newells to that bitch, and I couldn't—" She faltered, shaking her head at the horror of it, hands fluttering as she tried to get her breath. "I couldn't stay there . . . anymore. I needed someone to talk to." She looked up at him desperately, willing him to understand, to break the deadlock of distance between them, to take her in his arms and comfort her and tell her everything was going to be all right. "I needed you."

Oh God. He couldn't take it anymore. He didn't care if she was too young. He didn't care about his promise. He didn't care about anything. He had to have her. To hold her. Stepping forward with outstretched arms, his face full of the love he'd tried so hard to hide for so long, he suddenly froze. A sleepy female voice rang out from the top of the stairs behind him.

"Bobby? Is everything okay? You coming back to bed?"

Milly looked up the stairs and found herself face-to-face with the second naked person she'd seen in as many minutes. But this one was not only female but stunning, with a Victoria's Secret figure that she obviously wasn't remotely shy about showing off. She must have been fifteen feet away, but the unmistakable smell of sex hit Milly full in the face at once. She thought for one awful moment that she was going to be sick.

"Oh!" said the girl. She sounded more amused than surprised. "Hello. And who might you be?"

"This is Milly," said Bobby, his deadpan voice masking his inner desolation. "She lives here."

235

"She does?" said the girl. She seemed to be finding the situation funnier by the minute. "Well, I guess that makes you a naughty boy, Mr. Cameron. Doesn't it?"

"We're not together . . ." Milly stammered.

"It's nothing like that," snapped Bobby. Suddenly he hated Sammy with a passion. "Milly's training here. Her father is—was—a friend of mine."

"Hey." Sammy held up her hands in innocence. "None of my business. I'm just trying to get some sleep is all." She gave Bobby a knowing, lascivious wink. "It's been a tiring night."

"I should get to bed too," said Milly, holding herself together with a titanic effort. "It's been a long journey."

Bobby put his hand on her shoulder, but she jumped back as if he'd electrocuted her. "I'm sorry," he said, jerking his head back toward the top of the stairs, from where Sammy had now retreated back into the bedroom. "New Year's Eve, you know. We'll talk properly in the morning. About Rachel and stuff."

"Sure," said Milly. She smiled. But he knew he'd lost her. "You go back to bed."

Crawling under the covers of her own bed a few minutes later, she waited until she heard his bedroom door click shut and the house was completely silent.

Then, muffling her sobs with a pillow, she cried her heart out.

CHAPTER SIXTEEN

Milly spent the first three months of the year working harder than she'd ever done before.

Determined to put her heartache behind her and move forward, she made a vow to herself on New Year's Eve: She would not set foot in England again until she had enough money to buy Newells back and a foolproof plan for forcing Rachel to sell. Making it to the very top as a jockey had always been her ambition and her dream. But now it had become more than that. It had become a necessity. From now on, until the day that she held the keys to her father's house in her hands, she would live and breathe quarter horses. Everything else could go to hell.

"Everything else," specifically, meant both Bobby and her family. Having thrown in her lot with Rachel, Linda had become persona non grata with Milly. She steadfastly refused to take her calls at Highwood until, in the end, Linda gave up trying.

"You're making a mistake, you know," Bobby told her, after she'd forced him, reluctantly, to get rid of yet another call from home. "What happened happened. But she's still your mother. She loves you."

"Well, she's got a funny way of showing it," said Milly. She was sitting in the living room at the McDonalds', in jodhpurs as usual with one of Cecil's old T-shirts on top, hiding behind a British newspaper. But she turned it around now, flashing a half-page picture at Bobby of Linda arm in arm with Rachel and Jasper at some black-tie event or other. Even he had to admit the three of them looked very cozy. The shot must have hurt Milly.

"Anyway," Milly bristled, "I don't see you spending a lot of time on the phone to *your* mother."

"I don't refuse her calls," said Bobby reasonably.

"You would if she'd sold Highwood to your worst enemy," Milly shot back.

He relapsed into silence. He couldn't argue with that.

Since New Year's Eve things had been different between them for sure. But this time it was Milly who had changed, not him. He could see that she resented his well-meaning efforts to build bridges between her and Linda; that she interpreted all his mitigating arguments on her mother's behalf as a lack of support for her.

"Don't you get it?" she lashed out in exasperation the last time he tried explaining Linda's behavior. "She's betrayed everyone. Not just me but Daddy's memory too, and the horses. How could she sell to Rachel? How could she sell at all?"

In fact, Milly was wrong. Bobby did get it. He'd tried to shield her as best he could from the awful stories he heard from friends and contacts in England: Apparently Rachel had sold most of Cecil's stud stallions, and all the colts, including Radar and a number of others dear to Milly's heart, to a Middle Eastern sheikh well-known for his cruel treatment of horses who were past their prime. Her rationale—that she wanted to get rid of any animals potentially tainted by last summer's equine flu—had evidently been enough to pull the wool over Linda's eyes. But anyone with a shred of discernment could see that her real motivation was to rub still more salt into Milly's wounds.

But as much as he sympathized, Bobby couldn't give Milly the one form of comfort that she wanted. And as the weeks turned into months, her sadness and longing for him hardened into a protective shell of resentment that soon made it impossible for him to offer any sort of comfort at all. All the mental and emotional energy she'd expended on him so fruitlessly for the last nine months she now directed wholeheartedly toward her racing. And even though her career was making steady, measurable progress—between January and April, he entered her in seven California events, three of which she won—she began to complain loudly that he was neglecting her training, spending too much time traveling and locked in meetings with lawyers.

Though she didn't know it, he was actually devoting untold hours, not to mention all the cash he earned from training jobs, trying to figure out a way to legally extricate himself from his partnership agreement with Todd. Unfortunately, so far, all his efforts had been in vain.

It was the second Friday in April, and the Santa Ynez valley had been gripped for almost a week by a freak late spring cold spell. At dawn, a light frost was still clinging to the grass at Highwood, separating and stiffening each blade into tiny, white-green daggers. Later, as the frost thawed, a thick, cold, cloudlike mist descended over the pastures, snaking its way visibly around the trees and fences and clinging like a damp poultice to joints, both equine and human, already aching with the unaccustomed cold.

Milly, back from an early morning ride with Charlie Brown, Highwood's newest resident, wandered into the McDonalds' kitchen for a warming cup of coffee. Despite the cold it had been an exhilarating ride and she was in better spirits than she had been for days. The gorgeous red roan colt had a stride so powerful that even she had struggled to contain him as they galloped over the fields. She wondered how hard it would be to persuade Bobby to buy him from the Santa Barbara syndicate who owned him now, and made a mental note to ask him about it tonight, when he got back from his week-long training job in Montana.

"Wow," she said, bending down to smell the massive bunch of roses and freesias, still wrapped in their white satin bow, that were lying on the kitchen table. "Those are stunning. What a scent!"

"Beautiful, aren't they?" said Maggie, advancing upon them with a vase and a sharp knife. "Bobby sent them. For Summer."

Immediately Milly felt her good mood draining away like pus from an abscess. Summer had found out yesterday that she'd been accepted into Berkeley to study law. Naturally, the whole McDonald clan were overjoyed; as was Bobby, who made sure he phoned the day her results came through, so he heard the good news within minutes of the rest of them.

Milly had watched Summer walk away from that call with a smile on her face like she'd just won the lottery. When she saw the flowers, she was going to go ape shit.

Milly tried not to feel jealous, but it was hard, it really was. Okay, so coming first in a stakes race at Los Alamitos might not be the same as getting into Berkeley. But it would have been nice if Bobby had at least bothered to call to see how she'd done.

Dylan, bless him, had made a bit of a fuss over her. But with Summer's news coming the very next day, her moment of glory had been painfully short-lived.

Even if she hadn't hated the girl like poison, it would still have hurt, watching Summer's family, especially Wyatt, rallying around and showering her with praise and love. The whole thing made Milly miss her own father more than ever. Just looking at the flowers she felt a cattle-prod jolt of homesickness, bitterness, and grief. They didn't even smell good anymore.

"Are you okay, honey?" asked Maggie, noticing the change in her expression with some alarm. "You wanna sit down?"

"No," said Milly. "I mean, no thanks. I'm okay. I think I just need a little air."

Back out in the yard, a welcomed crisp, cool breeze blew the loose strands of hair out of her eyes and she felt her head clearing.

As always when she felt low, she had an overwhelming urge to be with her horses. Today, specifically, it was Danny she needed. Crossing the yard, she made a beeline for his stall.

"Hello." She grinned, opening the door to find herself being practically nuzzled to death by her ever-affectionate favorite. "Aren't you a sweetheart?"

"Thanks," a laconic voice drawled from somewhere behind her. "It has been said before. But it's always nice to hear."

"Jesus." Spinning around, she flicked on the light, almost jumping out of her skin. Todd Cranborn was standing in the far corner of the stable. Dressed in a dark gray woolen suit and silk tie, his black businessman's brogues gleaming like polished jet against the straw at his feet, he looked about as out of place as Donald Rumsfeld at an antiwar rally. "You scared the life out of me. What are you doing here?"

"Well, now, that's not very welcoming, is it?" He smiled. "Not what one would expect from"—he pulled a square of newspaper out of his pocket and began carefully unfolding it, before reading aloud—"what does it say here? 'Solvang's hottest new lady jockey'?"

Milly blushed. "Yeah, well, that's the local rag, isn't it?" she mumbled. "What else have they got to write about?"

"Record crowds at The Alameda quarter horse races last Friday cheered on the English rose," Todd continued. "They love you out here, don't they?"

Milly's color went from red to purple. She looked dreadfully tomboyish in those dirty riding pants and that baggy old top, with her hair scraped back like a schoolgirl's. But even the scarecrow couture couldn't hide her stunning figure. And there was something endearing about her awkwardness, all the blushing and mumbling, that he found weirdly sexy.

"Relax," he said smoothly. "I don't bite. I was in the vicinity looking at my housing development, as it happens. Thought I'd stop by and check out my investment while I'm here."

He laid a nervous hand on Danny's back and the horse's ears shot instantly backward. "I'm afraid I don't have your way with horses," Todd said, reaching for his inhaler and taking a deep drag of antihistamine. "D'you mind if we continue this conversation outside?"

"Oh, no," said Milly, composing herself. "Of course not. If you'd like to come over to the big house I'll make you some tea. It's a bit cold to be standing outside, don't you think?"

"Yeah," said Todd, taking off his suit jacket and, despite her protests, draping it over her shoulders. "I do. And tea sounds great, thanks."

Ten minutes later, they were ensconced in the pantry next to the wood-burning stove, sipping the last of the PG Tips that Milly had brought back with her from England.

"Seriously, I've been following your form, you know," said Todd. "That win in Los Alamitos was a real landmark—very impressive."

"Thanks." Milly beamed. Warmed by the tea and the unexpected compliment, she was starting to feel a lot better. "I hope Bobby will think so."

"Why wouldn't he?" asked Todd casually. Loosening his tie, he could already feel his eyes and skin starting to burn. Even indoors Highwood was an allergy sufferer's nightmare, with no chair or couch free from animal hair of one sort or another.

"I don't know," sighed Milly. "Sometimes he just doesn't seem interested anymore, you know? Unless it's about Summer, or ranch business, he doesn't want to know." The bitterness in her voice was unmistakable. "But I don't really care. I got ten percent of the prize money for that race." She jutted her chin out proudly. "Not much, I know, but it's a start."

It was funny. She didn't really know Todd very well—had only met him twice, in fact, since he and Bobby became partners—but there was something about him today, the way he listened, and seemed genuinely interested in her life and her career, that made Milly want to open up to him. It was the same feeling she'd had with Bobby when he first came to Newells. Like finding a kindred spirit. Soon she was pouring her heart out about Cecil's death, her feud with Rachel, and her desperation to somehow get her home back before Rachel destroyed it completely.

"That's terrible." Todd furrowed his brow in a good imitation of genuine concern once she'd finished. "This girl, Rachel. She's well known in Britain, you say?"

Getting up, Milly left the room for a few moments, returning with February's copy of *Loaded* magazine.

"That's her," she said, pointing contemptuously to the cover. Under the title "What a Ride!" a filthy-looking blonde was crouched on all fours, naked but for an infinitesimal sliver of metallic material at her crotch, a riding hat, and skintight patent leather riding boots. She was overmade-up and, judging by the plastic-smooth look of her thighs, had been airbrushed to within an inch of her life. But there was no denying she was sexy.

Sensing that any sort of positive reaction on his part would go down like a sack of shit, however, he wrinkled his nose in distaste. "She looks like a hooker," he said. "I find it hard to believe she's taken seriously as a sportswoman with poses like that."

"You'd think so, wouldn't you?" said Milly, shoving the magazine under a cushion and sitting on it. "But somehow, she is. 'The finest horsewoman to be seen in England since Lucinda Green,' that's what they call her in that stupid bloody wank mag. Sorry," she said, blushing again at her own bad language.

"Oh, please," said Todd, "don't mind me."

"And now she reckons she's a bloody business genius as well," Milly ranted on. "I mean, what on earth does she know about running a stud farm? I'll tell you. Fuck all, that's what."

So, thought Todd, assessing the situation. She felt tired, vulnerable, overworked, and ignored. She was alive with resentment and hatred for this other English girl who'd fucked her over and who seemed to be hitting the big time back home while she was stuck racing for peanuts in Butt-Fuck County, Nowheresville, California. And meanwhile, Bobby Cameron was back to his arrogant, self-absorbed best, doing a good impression of someone who didn't give a shit about her problems.

If that wasn't a situation ripe for exploitation, then his name wasn't Todd Cranborn.

Gaining Milly's trust clearly wasn't going to be a problem. All she wanted to do was talk, and he was more than happy to listen. Sooner or later she was bound to spill something, some nugget of information that he could use against Bobby to get his hands on that wasted oil. And in the meantime, he could enjoy the challenge of trying to seduce her. Not only did he find her combination of sexiness, ambition, and innocence a turn-on but he knew Bobby did too. Stealing Milly from right under Cameron's nose was going to make his enjoyment of her all the sweeter.

"Look," he said, leaning forward enthusiastically with his hands on his knees. "I don't mean to stick my nose in. But you look like you could do with a little fun. Are you done here for the day?"

"Well, yeah." Milly shrugged. "I guess so. I mean, I have to turn the horses out into the lower pasture . . ."

"One of the hands can do that," said Todd imperiously. "When was the last time you got dressed up and went out?"

"God," said Milly, shaking her head and trying to think. "I don't know. A long time ago, I suppose. Things have been so busy around here."

To be fair, Dylan and Tara had invited her into town for dinner a couple of times last week, while Bobby was away. But she'd been so exhausted from training and racing it was all she could do not to nod off at the table.

Todd showing up like this was bizarre and completely unexpected. But seeing as he *had* shown up and been so nice and offered to take her out . . . why not? He was Bobby's partner, after all, and so nominally her boss. She ought to get to know him. Besides, it was the weekend, and she deserved a break.

"When were you last in LA?" he asked.

"LA? Never," she said simply. "Well, I've landed at the airport. Twice. But I guess that doesn't really count."

"Never?" Todd feigned surprise. "You've been here for six months and Bobby's never taken you to LA? Jeez. No wonder you're climbing the walls."

She'd never thought of it like that before. But, come to think of it, Bobby *had* always left her behind when he went to the city or, indeed, anywhere fun. Suddenly, she started to feel quite taken for granted.

"Come with me." Leaping to his feet, Todd grabbed her hand and pulled her toward the stairs.

"What are you doing?" she said with a giggle, breaking into a jog to try to keep up with him. For a short man, he was surprisingly strong. She felt like a puppet having its strings pulled too hard as he yanked her along.

"Where's your bedroom?" he demanded.

Milly's eyes widened. Oh, shit. He wasn't going to try anything, was he?

"Don't worry," he said, grinning as he caught the look. "I'm not going to ravish you. I'm going to help you pack."

"Pack?"

"That's right," said Todd. "I'm taking you to LA for the weekend. And I'm not taking no for an answer."

CHAPTER SEVENTEEN

When Bobby arrived home that evening, he was already in a foul mood. Not only had his flight been delayed, but when he'd finally gotten on the damn plane he'd found himself sitting next to a Texan woman with verbal diarrhea and perfume strong enough to stun a bull at twenty paces. The combination had left him with a splitting headache that the crawling Friday night traffic on the freeway had done nothing to dissipate.

All he wanted was a hot bath, a double shot of bourbon, and his bed. But as he turned his truck wearily into the drive, the first thing he saw was Domino and Charlie Brown, his two most valuable quarter horses, still out in the paddock and without so much as a blanket between them.

"Where the hell is Milly?" he snapped, bursting into the McDonalds' living room as soon as he'd dumped his cases. "She's left the horses out and it's freezing out there."

The whole family was in the living room, glued to *American Idol*. It was a few seconds before any of them even heard the question.

"Oh, hi, you're back," said Dylan eventually. "How'd it go?"

"Fine," said Bobby, trying not to lose his temper. "But where's Milly?"

"Not here," said Summer, smiling up at him from the couch. She'd washed her hair and changed into her tightest, sexiest pair of jeans for his return, but as usual her gorgeousness seemed to be passing him by.

"What do you mean, 'not here'?" He frowned. "Where'd she go?"

"To LA," said Dylan, finally tearing himself away from the TV to talk to him properly. "Todd Cranborn invited her down there for the weekend."

Bobby felt like he'd been punched in the stomach.

"Todd was here?" he said. "Why? He knew I was away. What possible business could he have . . ." The words died on his lips as his mind flashed back to that awful dinner at Jimmy Price's mansion and the comments Todd had made about Milly. It was *her* he'd come to see. He'd deliberately waited till Bobby was in Montana so he could make his move.

Dylan shrugged. "No idea. But Milly looked really happy to be going. You shouldn't be too hard on her about the horses. She's been working like a dog since you've been gone, you know."

Seething with rage—at Todd for being so conniving, Milly for being so naïve, and himself for being so fucking stupid—he stormed into the kitchen and picked up the phone. But after pacing up and down with it in his hands for a few minutes, he finally slammed it back into its cradle.

Who was he going to call? Todd? Milly? And what would he say if he got hold of them? "How dare you take a weekend off?" He'd sound like an even bigger fool than he felt, not to mention a controlling, jealous prick. There was nothing he could do. Nothing.

"Hey."

Spinning around, he saw Summer standing in the doorway. Even in bare feet and jeans, her legs looked endless and her newly washed hair shimmered in the dusky half-light like a blond halo. Guys would be all over her like a rash when she got to Berkeley, he thought protectively.

"Hey." He smiled, trying to cheer up for her sake. "You look very pretty. So how about a hug from the college girl? Or are you too smart and sophisticated for that now?"

"Never." She grinned. Slipping into his open arms, she pressed her body against his, closing her eyes and breathing in the warm man smell of his chest. God, she wanted him.

With one hand on the back of her head, Bobby, still lost in unpleasant thoughts about Milly and Todd, began stroking the soft, silky curtain of her hair. It was quite unconscious on his part. But for Summer, it was heart-stopping.

First, he'd sent her flowers—a *very* un-Bobby thing to do, even after a major achievement like Berkeley. Then he'd called her "pretty" for the first time in her life, ever, and *then* he'd hugged her—no, he'd actually *asked* her to hug *him*, another Bobby first. And now he was stroking her hair, brushing his fingers softly over her neck like a lover.

All she wanted to do was reach up and kiss him. But even now, with all these new and wonderful signals, she didn't dare. Instead, she merely wrapped her own arm around his waist and pulled him closer, allowing her hand to rest tantalizingly on the belt loops of his jeans.

Milly was gone. For one weekend at least, she had him all to herself. She intended to make the most of it.

Milly adored LA.

Everything about the place, even the drive down from Highwood with Todd, was exciting. She loved the way that he drove: fast, very fast, but with the confidence and self-assuredness of a really good driver. It was the same way her father used to drive, although with Cecil she had never experienced the same rush of bright sunshine on her face and wind in her hair, or the incredible, shimmering azure beauty of the ocean as they sped down Pacific Coast Highway, so close that at times she almost felt that the foamy white spray from the waves might splash across their windscreen.

She remembered how full of hope and anticipation she'd been with Bobby last year when she'd first arrived in America, making the drive the other way. Highwood was supposed to open up a perfect new chapter in her life. But instead the months that followed had brought nothing but grief and loss. Months later, she could see that her hopes of winning Bobby's love had been little more than a foolish, childish crush.

But it didn't even matter anymore. What was one more disappointment after everything that had happened? All that mattered now was her racing and getting Newells back.

Still, it felt wonderful to be able to get away from it all, even if it was only for a weekend. Finally, as the canyons and hills gave way to highrises and megamalls, she found herself switching off the voices in her head. For the first time since before her father died, she was actually having fun.

By the time they turned in to Bel Air's east gate just before lunch and began snaking up into the hills, past an endless stream of multimillion-dollar mansions, their electric gates protecting long, grandiose driveways and their perfectly tended yards overflowing with blossoms of every possible color, she was just about ready to pee her pants with excitement.

"Wow," she said, as the road twisted back down to Stone Canyon and past the famous Bel-Air Hotel. "How much money do these people have? These homes, these cars. It's unbelievable."

"Yeah," said Todd with a practiced air of nonchalance. "It's a nice part of town."

She remembered Dylan and Bobby both telling her how much they despised LA. How had Bobby put it again? "It paralyzes people, then sucks the good out of 'em, like a spider with a fly." Looking around these picture-perfect streets, with their sprinklers and their white picket fences and their all-around American dreaminess, she found it hard to fathom what on earth he could have been talking about.

"Bloody hell," she said, when they finally pulled into the ornate, wrought-iron gates that marked the entrance to Todd's own property. It was low built, Spanish, and in better, more muted taste than most of the over-the-top piles they'd just driven by; although it was every bit as huge, sprawling over a full three acres of flat, manicured gardens with a view over the golf course and out to the ocean beyond that was nothing short of spectacular. "You're seriously rich, aren't you?"

He laughed, gratified. He liked to have his success admired. But he liked Milly's naïveté even more. She was so young, she still hadn't learned to edit herself and had a habit of blurting out everything that popped into her head, a habit that should make her easy to manipulate, both in bed and out of it. Push the right buttons and with any luck she'd be spouting everything she knew about Bobby Cameron's business affairs like a leaky sieve before you could say "exploitation."

Of course, he didn't know for sure that Bobby had an Achilles' heel. But his gut feeling told him he did and that Milly could lead him straight to it. Either way, with all that oil at stake, he intended to find out.

"Come on in," he said, lifting her overnight bag out of the trunk.

"I'll show you to your room, and then we can go down into town. How does lunch and shopping in Beverly Hills sound?"

"Amazing." Milly beamed, but then just as suddenly her face fell.

"What's up?" said Todd.

"All my winnings are going straight into my Newells fund," she announced with endearing gravity. "I can't afford to go shopping. And I don't have anything smart to wear for lunch either."

"Relax." He smiled. "This weekend is my treat. All you have to do"—he opened the front door for her with a flourish—"is enjoy yourself."

If Bel Air had overwhelmed her, her eyes were on stalks when they got down to Beverly Hills and Todd swept into the cobbled forecourt of the Peninsula, slipping the gray-suited valet a twenty to keep the car parked and ready for them out front.

"I feel like Julia Roberts in *Pretty Woman*," Milly whispered, as they sat down to a lunch of chilled lobster tails and fresh truffle risotto, which she wolfed down unashamedly. She hadn't eaten since her six A.M. breakfast at the ranch and was absolutely famished. "Look at all these women. They make me feel like a bag lady."

Her bare face and jeans and T-shirt combo did indeed stand in marked contrast to the immaculately coiffed, couture-clad elegance of the Hollywood wives surrounding them. Todd, who had changed out of his suit at home into a pale blue polo shirt and chinos, looked across the table at her appraisingly.

"Hmmm," he said. "Yes. You could do with a bit of smartening up."

Milly blushed. It was true, of course, but she had expected him out of politeness to contradict her and tell her she looked fine. Perhaps months spent living among cowboys, who for all their faults were without doubt the most polite men on earth, had left her with unrealistic expectations?

Putting down her knife and fork, she found her appetite had suddenly vanished.

"Don't look so crestfallen," said Todd. Reaching across the table, he gave her hand a quick, reassuring squeeze. "I have something in mind. A plan." He smiled. "But you're going to have to trust me. Put yourself completely in my hands. Do you trust me, Milly?"

"Of course." She laughed nervously. He did ask very odd questions sometimes. "Why wouldn't I trust you?"

"Good." He grinned. "Then eat up, there's a good girl. We've got a busy afternoon ahead of us."

As soon as lunch was over and the check was paid, he drove the three blocks to Rodeo Drive, making a few brisk, monosyllabic calls on his cell phone on the way.

"Excellent," he said, hanging up as he squeezed his gleaming midnight-blue Ferrari with effortless precision into a tiny, metered parking space. "They can fit you in. Follow me."

For the second time that day, Milly allowed herself to be taken by the hand and dragged, this time into Jennifer's Beauty Salon.

"'Allo, dahlink," the crone behind the reception desk rasped at Todd, desperately trying to contort her surgery-ravaged features into a smile and directing the resulting grimace toward him. "Ees zees the young lady?"

She looked at Milly as though she had just crawled out from under a rock. Panicked suddenly, Milly wished that she could run and crawl back under it. The woman looked like something out of *The Rocky Horror Picture Show.*

"Yes, this is Milly," said Todd. "She wants everything done: brows, lashes, nails, full wax. We have Mimi's at five thirty, so I'll be back for her at quarter after five."

The crone looked at her watch and shook her head, clicking her tongue and staring at Milly like a plumber despairing at the state of an ancient, broken-down boiler.

"Only two hours?" she said regretfully. "Ees not long."

"Katinka, you're a genius," said Todd, leaning forward and planting a kiss on her powder-encrusted cheek. "I know you can do it, my darling."

Milly watched as the old woman's face flushed with pleasure at this endearment. Eeeeugh! Did she fancy him? Todd was old, but this creature was old enough to be his mother, if not his grandmother. Rank!

"For you, dahlink, I try my best."

The grimace again.

"You're not leaving me here?" Milly clutched at Todd's arm in terror as he headed for the door. She remembered the last time she'd been subjected to beauty treatments, the day of her coming-out ball in London. How horrific that had been! And something told her that this vile drag queen of a woman was planning something a lot more hard-core than just a blow-dry and a manicure.

"Don't be silly," he said, prying himself free from her grip. "I have work to do. You'll be fine. Have fun, and I'll see you around five."

He returned two hours later to find a scowling, still slightly blotchy Milly waiting for him by the front desk.

"That was fucking agony," she complained, while he silently handed over his black AmEx to the busty nineteen-year-old who had taken over from the crone on reception. "I look like one of those spooky hairless dogs people carry around in baskets."

"No you don't," he said firmly. "You look a lot better."

He was right. Though her skin was still inflamed from her facial and all the waxing, her previously natural, bushy, Brooke Shields brows were now neatly arched and trimmed and her newly dyed black eyelashes gave a brilliant definition to the green of her eyes. When he took her hand, the skin of her palms felt smooth, with only tiny bumps where before there had been fully fledged calluses formed by long hours tugging on lead ropes and reins. And her broken, chewed child's nails had been rounded, buffed, and polished in a natural, coral pink. A distinct improvement.

Their next stop was the hairdressers, where Todd had to physically restrain her from bolting out of the chair when he began discussing drastic cuts with Mimi, one of LA's most sought after stylists.

"Oh, no, no, you're not touching my hair. A trim, but that's it," she insisted. "I love my hair long. It's the one really pretty thing about me."

"Rubbish," said Todd. "It's too young for you that length. And it hides your face. You said you trusted me, didn't you?"

"Well, yes," she stammered. "But I didn't mean—"

"Well, trust me then." The way he said it, it was not a request. "It needs cutting."

To Milly's horror, Mimi the Merciless appeared to agree with him. Soon the two of them were running their hands through her hair and discussing the options as though she weren't even present.

She left the salon with hair three shades darker, cut in a series of short, feathered layers, the longest of which clung to her neck like curling tendrils of chocolate ivy, just skimming the very tops of her shoulders.

All the way back to Bel Air, she gazed at herself in the vanity mirror above the passenger seat, pulling at her new, choppy wisps with her fingers and running her hands over her newly shaped brows. This morning she'd been riding Charlie Brown, looking forward to another ordinary, dull weekend at the ranch. Not even the prospect of Bobby coming home had filled her with much excitement or enthusiasm. But now, here she was, driving around Los Angeles with Todd Cranborn, of all people, looking and feeling like a completely different person.

"Do you like it?" he asked, pulling off Beverly Glen onto Sunset as the impressive façade of Bel Air's east gate hoved once again into view.

"Yeah," she said. "I think so." Her hands were still in her hair. She couldn't seem to stop touching it. "It's very . . . different."

"It's better," he said. "Sexier."

She glanced across at him. His eyes were still on the road and there was nothing flirtatious or suggestive in any of his gestures or movements. Obviously, the compliment was meant to be just that—a compliment—and not a come-on.

Even so, she couldn't help feeling a tiny flutter of gratification that he thought she looked sexy. Back home, Rachel had always been the sexy one. At Highwood it was Summer. She, Milly, had always been "pretty" or "natural looking," or, worst of all, "cute." Nobody ever called her sexy.

As for Bobby, these days he barely even registered that she was female, let alone attractive.

But Todd saw her differently.

He made her see herself differently.

It was a nice feeling.

"Thanks for doing all this for me," she said, tearing herself away from the mirror at last and flipping the visor shut. "I really had an incredible day today."

Reaching over, he lightly rested a hand on her knee.

"You're welcome, my dear," he said. "Like I said, you deserved it."

They had dinner that night with a large group of his friends at Katana, the ultratrendy sushi mecca looming above Sunset in West Hollywood.

At first Milly resisted wearing the flesh-colored silk slip dress Todd had bought her that afternoon while she was being preened and plucked at Jennifer's, insisting it was far too girlie and lacy and she'd be much more comfy in her old jeans. But when she saw what the other girls were wearing she was glad she'd given in. Dolled up to the nines in Gucci and Marc Jacobs, their rail-thin, bronzed bodies ornamented by large, unashamedly fake breasts and diamonds the size of hazelnuts glinting at their necks, ears, and wrists, they reminded her of the Fashion-Model Barbie her mum had bought her for her ninth birthday (instead of the Show-jumping Barbie she really wanted—typical Linda).

The men were more casual, most of them in jeans, with untucked shirts unbuttoned very low. Privately, Milly thought they all looked a bit cheesy, especially the ones who insisted on keeping their sunglasses on indoors. But she soon found she was too busy trying to negotiate her chopsticks or nodding knowingly when asked if she preferred yellowtail or ahi tuna to pay them much attention.

"What did you think?" Todd asked her when they finally got home, turning the lights on in the kitchen while Milly perched on the countertop, kicking her shoes off and rubbing her aching feet. "A little different from Solvang, huh?"

She yawned and nodded, still with one eye on the reflection of her incredible new hair in the dark window. It *was* different from Solvang. So different, it was hard to take it all in. Todd, his house, his glamorous friends, the fancy food, her new clothes, her hair. She felt as though she'd been sucked up into some crazy whirlwind and then spat back out, like Dorothy, into a weird and wonderful new world.

"Tired?"

"Mmm," she sighed. "I had fun though. Bobby's been away so much, traveling and such, so it's been kinda lonely at Highwood recently."

"Really?" Todd asked casually. He sensed the conversation might be about to take an interesting turn.

"To be honest, even when he is home he's like a bear with a sore head," said Milly. "This break was just what I needed."

"What's been eating him?" Pouring two mugs of decaf from the coffeepot, he handed one to her. "Money problems?"

"That's part of it, I think," said Milly. "Although we have a bunch of new clients at the stables, and he seems to have a lot of work on, so I don't quite get what the problem is. But now everyone's talking about all these lawsuits in Wyoming. So that's been stressing him out even more."

"What lawsuits?"

"Oh, God, I don't really understand much about it." She sounded thoroughly bored with the subject already. "Something about gas companies forcing cowboys off their land. To get the methane. Or something. It hasn't happened much in California, but everyone in the valley's worried about it."

"Is that so?" said Todd, concealing his excitement only with an effort. This might be just the break he was looking for. "Well, I'm sure it'll all work out."

Yawning, Milly covered her gaping mouth with her hand. Putting down his coffee cup, Todd walked over and slipped both hands around her waist, gently lifting her off the countertop and setting her down on the floor. It was only a small gesture, but it was unexpectedly intimate, especially as it left her no choice but to look directly up into his eyes when he spoke to her.

"In the meantime," he said, withdrawing his hands with some reluctance but keeping his gaze fixed on hers. "You need to stop worrying about everybody else's problems and get yourself a good night's sleep."

As soon as she was safely tucked up in bed, in one of the guest suites at the far end of the house, Todd hurried into his study and picked up the phone.

"Jack?"

The lawyer's voice was slurred and sleepy on the other end of the line.

"Todd? Is that you? Jeez, what time is it?"

"Never mind what time it is," said Todd impatiently. "I may have a lead on Highwood. I need you to find out everything you can about suits between Wyoming cowboys and oil and gas companies."

"Wyoming?" said the lawyer groggily. "Er . . . sure, okay. When do you need it by?"

"Tomorrow morning," said Todd, and hung up.

Milly woke the next morning to blinding sunshine streaming into her bedroom through the open blinds.

"Wakey wakey." Todd threw open her windows to let a cool blast of honeysuckle-scented air into the room and Milly instinctively pulled the covers farther up around herself. He might have knocked. Thank heavens she'd worn pajamas.

"It's nine fifteen already," he said, rubbing his hands together briskly, "which means you have half an hour to be up, dressed, and outta here."

"Out . . . where?" she mumbled, still bleary with sleep.

"It's your lucky day." He grinned. "We're going riding."

The Mandeville Canyon Equestrian Center was the closest place Milly could imagine to heaven on earth.

Just a couple of miles north of Sunset in Brentwood, a wealthy residential suburb of LA, lay this vast, quasi-rural property with lush green paddocks, a natural stream, and what appeared to be hundreds of acres of hilly, woodland paths. At the foot of the canyon was a yard, immaculately swept and surrounded by a white picket fence, inside which a horseshoe of pristine, traditional wooden stables housed more beautiful horses than she had ever seen in one place, even at Newells.

Only the two towering, perfectly symmetrical palms at the front gates, the dazzling sunshine, and the bland, blond good looks of all the grooms told you that this was indeed LA and not a horse farm in rural Kentucky.

"Todd Cranborn. What a surprise!" A strikingly beautiful girl, who stood out from the rest of the grooms by being the only visible brunette, came forward to greet them. She was wearing cut-off denim shorts and a white shirt tied loosely beneath her breasts to reveal a glint of bright-red bikini top. "It's not like you to visit us in person. And who is this?" She smiled at Milly.

"Milly Lockwood Groves, meet Chloe Colgan." The two girls shook hands. "Milly's training at my new stables out in Santa Ynez," Todd explained. "She's just starting out as a quarter horse jockey."

"My" new stables? Bobby would have hit the roof if he'd heard that, thought Milly, although she supposed it was technically true, or at least half true.

"Is that so?" said Chloe, raising a skeptical eyebrow at Todd. As one of his many casual exes, she found it hard to believe his relationship with this very pretty, very young-looking girl was of a purely business nature. Or if it was, that it would stay that way for long. Nor did Milly look much like any quarter horse jockey she'd ever seen. "So what brings you both out here? Did you want to see Demon?"

Todd sneezed loudly and reached into his jacket pocket for his inhaler, taking a long puff before replying.

"Please," he said. "Demon is a rather beautiful colt I recently inherited," he explained to Milly, adding, by way of elaboration, "Poker game. I won him off a local breeder. The guy loved gambling but he was short of two essentials—talent and money—so in the end he gave me the horse."

"How terrible!" said Milly, shocked. Despite having grown up on a profitable stud farm, she was far too emotionally attached to horses to ever see them as commercial commodities, let alone something that could be won and lost at cards.

"I was gonna sell him," said Todd, failing to register her indignation, "at the yearling sales in San Mateo. But Chloe here reckoned he had promise and I should hold on to him. I wanted to see if you agree."

For a moment Milly forgot to be horrified and flushed with pleasure at the idea that someone as worldly wise as Todd would seek out *her* advice. She was used to being treated like a child by her parents and then by Bobby. It was nice to be taken seriously for once.

Todd turned back to Chloe. "I have another friend dropping by in about half an hour," he said, glancing at his watch. "I hope that's okay. He's going to take a look at Milly out on the track."

"Sure, no problem," said Chloe, smiling at Milly. "I'll saddle Demon up right now and you can take him for a test drive. How does that sound?"

"What friend?" Milly started to ask Todd. But Chloe was already hurrying her off toward the stables. In any case as soon as she laid eyes on Demon, all thoughts of the mystery visitor fell straight out of her head.

"He's a beauty, isn't he?" said Chloe, slipping a bridle over his sleek, bay head with its smattering of white markings.

"No kidding." Milly nuzzled up against the soft skin of his nostrils. The horse had pretty, wide-set eyes like Bambi, framed by long, fluttering lashes, but his musculature was anything but delicate. He looked like an equine version of Mike Tyson with Marilyn Monroe's face stuck on top. "Bobby would go crazy for this horse."

"Bobby Cameron? The cowboy?" Chloe's eyes lit up. "So it's true then? He's the one Todd's gone into business with? I've heard he's a genius as a trainer and drop-dead gorgeous with it. Has he been training you?"

"Yes. When he has the time, that is," said Milly bitterly. "Recently I've barely seen him, he's been traveling so much."

She found that even thinking about Bobby was enough to take the edge off her good mood and decided to drop the subject.

"Here." Relieving a second, buxom groom of Demon's saddle, she settled it gently onto his broad back. "I can do that." Then, leaning into the horse's ear, she whispered, "Let's see if you're as divine to ride as you are to look at, eh boy?"

Jimmy Price rolled a mouthful of the finest Cuban cigar smoke across his taste buds before expelling it into the pure, canyon air. "Remind me," he drawled at Todd. "What the hell am I doing here?"

The two of them were sitting on hard, uncomfortable plastic chairs in the open air, preparing to watch Milly race Demon along the practice quarter horse track. The kid was gonna have to be something else to distract Jimmy from the numbness in his ass, that was for sure. For many years now, Price's rear end was used to being comfortably cushioned in seats of the squashy, luxurious, chairman-of-the-board variety. As a result, his discomfort-tolerance levels were legendarily low.

"Just watch," said Todd. "You won't be disappointed, I promise you."

He was right. Watching Milly erupt out of the starting gate was like looking at a long dormant volcano bursting back into life. She was so tiny, and the horse was so huge and barrel-chested, but somehow she seemed not only to control him but to push him to a speed Jimmy wouldn't have believed possible. It was a long time since he'd seen anyone ride with such total abandon. Just looking at her made his heart pound with excitement and his mind race with the seemingly limitless possibilities of what he could do with a jockey like that if he got his hands on her.

"I'll admit it," he said, shaking his fat head in admiration. "I'm impressed. She's fucking good."

"And," said Todd, "she's marketable too. You haven't seen her face close up yet, but she's cute as hell. And bored out of her tiny mind up at that ranch."

"Hmm," grunted Jimmy. "She could do with losing a few pounds if she wants to race for me." It wouldn't do to show too much enthusiasm.

"Not a problem," said Todd, although privately he thought Price was smoking dope. Milly was already tiny. "I can whip her into shape within a week. She's very"—he smiled to himself as he searched for the right word—"malleable."

Right on cue, Milly turned and waved at him from the track, grinning from ear to ear.

Todd waved back, beckoning her over.

"Milly," he said, holding out his hand to help her dismount as Chloe ran over to take Demon. "This is Jimmy Price. Jimmy, may I introduce the new quarter horse sensation, Miss Milly Lockwood Groves."

Still flushed and sweating from her ride, she was too taken aback at first to say anything. Price was one of the best known racehorse owners in the world. She'd grown up hearing his name from her father and other people in Newmarket; although not until she met Bobby did she realize that he was also a big name in quarter horse racing.

She also knew that Bobby hated the man with a passion, although the reasons he'd given for this had always struck her as rather vague. Except for the bit about his first wife, she now remembered, and how she'd killed herself after he'd left her. That really was awful. . . .

"Pleased to meet you." Her internal monologue was interrupted when she realized he was not only talking to her but gripping her hand and pumping it so violently she felt like a slot machine that had accidentally swallowed his money. "Todd tells me you're serious about racing quarter horses."

"Oh, I am," she said, regaining her composure instantly. "Deadly serious. I need to make more money. A lot more money, actually," she added.

Jimmy laughed. "A girl after my own heart. Well, we'll have to see what we can do about that, young lady."

If she hadn't heard so much bad stuff about him from Bobby, Milly would probably have thought him quite a jolly, jovial figure—a sort of fat, cigar-smoking Father Christmas type. He was certainly polite and friendly, not to mention flatteringly interested in her own so-called career.

"Excuse me," said Todd, checking the number on his cell phone as it started buzzing. "I'll have to leave you both to it for a moment, if you don't mind."

As neither of them so much as glanced in his direction, he assumed they didn't mind and, stepping back a few paces, turned his attention to his caller.

"What's up, Jack?"

It was his lawyer, returning his call of late last night.

"Okay," he said. "Wyoming. I think what you're referring to is the Powder River basin methane reserves."

Taking Todd's silence as his cue to continue, he went on.

"Basically there's a bunch of failing cowboy ranches out there with tons of methane sitting beneath the surface. Under Wyoming law, the cowboys only own the surface land, not the natural resources beneath."

"Who owns them?" said Todd.

"The government. Sort of. Put it this way, the government can grant mining rights to oil and gas companies, who get to drill up the land and keep all the profits, whether the landowners like it or not. Which mostly, as you can imagine, they don't."

"Hmmm." Todd's mind was whirring. "I see. And the lawsuits?"

"Well, the cowboys don't have a leg to stand on legally," said Jack. "But they've been giving it their best shot anyway, trying to stall the gas companies. They can force 'em to do a bunch of soil reports, vegetation studies, and shit like that, which all takes time and money. Couple of 'em even got restraining orders to keep the gas men off their land. They were overturned eventually, but delays are costly."

"I'll bet they are," said Todd. He'd been through similar legal wrangles with some of his housing developments and knew what a pain in the ass they could be.

"Some of the gas companies have been making cash arrangements with the landowners, just to avoid the legal hassles," said Jack. "But officially, they don't have to pay these guys a red cent. If gas is found and they get the state permits, they can go right on in and take it."

California law, he went on to explain, was a little more complicated. But all the big oil and gas companies—Chevron, Devon Energy, Seneca—were looking for ways to pull the same stunt along the West Coast.

"Thanks, Jack," said Todd, unclipping his earpiece. "I'll get back to you."

Well, well, well. No wonder Bobby was worried. Highwood, with all her legendary oil, must be California's biggest sitting duck. And he wouldn't have known a thing about it if it hadn't been for Milly.

Glancing across, he saw she was laughing and joking with Price, her earlier gaucheness apparently gone. That new haircut he'd gotten her really made the most of her elfin features and that beautiful, wide mouth. He found himself getting hard as he thought about just how much he'd like to see those pale pink lips of hers wrapped around his dick.

The way Bobby talked about her, it was like she was a child or the

Virgin Mary or both. But from where Todd was standing, she was definitely all woman.

He hadn't entirely figured out what his next move should be, or how he should use this fascinating new nugget of information about Highwood. But now that Milly had proved herself such an effective, albeit an unwitting, mole, it was more important than ever for him to get her firmly on his side. Somehow he had to drive a permanent wedge between her and Bobby.

Suddenly Jimmy Price was starting to look more and more wedge shaped by the second.

"How are we doing over here?" He smiled his most honest, disingenuous smile at both of them.

"Mr. Price has just offered to sponsor me!" said Milly excitedly, hopping from foot to foot.

"Please," Jimmy said, "you're making me feel old. It's Jimmy, okay?"

"Sorry. Jimmy," mumbled Milly. She was making no attempt to conceal how ecstatic she was—clearly negotiation was not one of her strong points. They'd have to work on that. "But, Todd, isn't it amazing? He says I can train five days a week at Palace Verdy—"

"Pal-*os* Ver-*des*," corrected Todd, not unkindly.

"Yeah, there, and that you can stable Demon there—if you want to, that is, obviously. And he's going to promote me in the papers, kind of like Rachel, but different—"

"What did you have in mind?" Todd asked Jimmy, interrupting the ceaseless flow of Milly's excited chatter to force a word in edgeways.

"I'm not sure exactly," said Jimmy, "but something along the lines of the 'British cowgirl' press she's already started getting. 'English rose among the hillbilly thorns'—that sort of thing. Of course, it'll all be dependent on building her track record. But it sounds to me like your friend Mr. Cameron's been holding her back on that front too."

Todd nodded sagely. The more he could get other people to criticize Bobby, so he didn't have to, the better.

"My trainer, Gillian Sanders, will be putting her through fifty-hour weeks with some of the best American quarter horses on the planet," boasted Jimmy. "If she can't make it with that sort of support, she'll never make it."

"Oh, I'll make it Mr. P— Jimmy," Milly piped up. "I promise you that."

A picture of herself returning home to Newmarket as a world-renowned quarter horse star, weighed down by trophies, leaped unbidden into her mind. She imagined Rachel, her own career having mysteriously crashed and burned, dragging her suitcases miserably down Newells's drive like a refugee—only fatter and with cellulite and spots—while she, Milly, gloriously reclaimed her home in front of a cheering crowd led by a humbled Linda, who finally admitted she'd been wrong about Rachel all along.

In the past, when Milly'd had this fantasy, it always involved her being married to Bobby. But today, for some reason, she seemed to have skipped that part. Today it was all about her, and her alone.

It was only in the car, on the way back to Bel Air with Todd, that reality began, belatedly, to reassert itself.

"I'll have to leave Highwood, won't I?" she said suddenly, apparently out of nowhere, as they turned onto Bellagio.

"Well, sure," said Todd, not taking his eyes off the road. "Is that a problem?"

"Bobby might think so." She sighed. "I mean, I doubt he'd miss *me*, as such," she said sadly. "But you know he hates Jimmy."

"Oh, now, I'm sure that's not true," lied Todd. "They barely know each other. Besides, Bobby cares about you, right? He wouldn't begrudge you a once-in-a-lifetime career opportunity like this. Would he?"

One thing he *had* decided was that it wouldn't pay to start bad-mouthing Bobby just yet—not directly, anyway. Better to leave things be and let the cowboy screw things up for himself with Milly. Give him enough rope and all that.

"I don't know," said Milly. "He might. I think he wants to keep training me himself. But the problem is, he never has enough time."

"Exactly!" said Todd. "In all honesty, you'd be doing him a favor. He has a training stables to run, not to mention a struggling ranch, plus all his overseas work. With Jimmy, you'd be racing and training full-time. And I'm talking serious races: Los Alamitos, Bay Meadows. Maybe next year, the Triple Crown. Who knows?"

Milly's heart thumped. The Triple Crown was the ultimate prize in quarter horse racing. Run in New Mexico, it consisted of the Ruidoso Derby in June, the Rainbow Futurity in July, and the All American Futurity on Labor Day. To compete in any one of those races, even to get to the trials, was the stuff of dreams as far as she was concerned.

Todd was right. She'd be doing Bobby a favor, setting him free from a relationship that, for whatever reason, was no longer working for either of them.

"Can I borrow your phone?" she asked.

He looked at her quizzically.

"I'm going to tell Bobby what's happened. No time like the present, right?"

"Right," he said, grinning. He was starting to like this girl more and more. "Just one small point though. Where are you going to stay while you're training?"

"Oh." Milly's face fell. "I sort of assumed . . . I mean, not for the long term obviously . . . but I sort of thought . . ."

"You could stay with me?" Todd finished for her. "Relax." He laughed. "I'm only kidding. You're more than welcome. I'd be happy to have you."

Summer only heard a few, screamed fragments of the conversation.

"No, I don't care what he said. . . . Put him on the line . . . MILLY, put Cranborn on the FUCKING line!"

Bobby had taken the call in the McDonalds' kitchen. Summer was in her bedroom directly above, supposedly studying but in reality, of course, hanging on every word of the drama unfolding beneath her with her ear pressed hard to the floorboards. Even without the additional decibels, she'd have been able to piece together the thrust of what was being said: Milly had been offered and apparently (oh joy of joys!) accepted an offer to race for an owner in LA; some guy called Jimmy who Bobby seemed to think of as the devil incarnate. And he seemed to be blaming Todd for what had happened.

263

At one point, she thought gleefully, Milly must have actually hung up on him, because she could hear him mumbling obscenities as he punched out the digits of another number before the roaring started again: "Don't you DARE put the goddamn phone down on me," he yelled. "Yes, you are . . . you ARE a child! Put him on the line, Milly, I mean it."

Things carried on in this vein for a few more, utterly unproductive minutes, before eventually the shouting stopped and she could hear the phone being replaced and the kitchen door slammed as Bobby stormed out into the yard. Moving from floor to window, she looked out to see him striding over toward the stables, his fists still clenched in fury.

It was a spur-of-the-moment thing. Slipping out of her Abercrombie sweatpants, she pulled a burgundy sweater dress on over her head. It was an old one of her mother's from the sixties, and she'd always loved it, but it was rarely cool enough to wear it at Highwood. Today, though, she reckoned she could just about get away with it. Pulling the elastic band out of her newly washed hair, she tipped her head upside down and ruffled it with her fingers to give it some body, before flicking it back and hurriedly applying some blusher to her cheeks and a swipe of Vaseline over her lips and eyelashes. Finally, she pulled on her favorite pair of black leather boots and ran down the stairs and out into the cold afternoon air after him.

When she caught up with him he was out in the small office he used exclusively for quarter horse work, desultorily throwing a miniature basketball toward a hoop pinned to the back of the door.

"Oh, hey, sweetheart," he said, when he saw her come in. "Sorry about that. Did I put you off your schoolwork?"

You put me off my schoolwork just by breathing! she wanted to yell at him.

"No" was what she actually said. "You seemed upset, that's all. I wanted . . . I thought . . ." Come on, Summer. Don't lose your nerve. Not now. "I thought you could maybe use some company."

Her heart was pounding so loudly she was sure he must be able to hear it. But she forced herself to walk over to the desk where he was sitting and perch on the end of it. She had one hand on his shoulder and the other resting on the bare, brown skin of her own thigh, just inches below his face.

"I knew Milly would let you down in the end," she whispered, moving her fingers from his shoulder to the back of his neck, which she started to caress gently. "She doesn't love you, you know. She doesn't love you like I do."

Clasping tighter to his neck, she brought her face down level with his and pressed her soft, trembling lips to his own.

For a second, Bobby kissed her back. She was so beautiful, after all, and so sensual and desiring and . . . there. At that moment it would have been the easiest thing in the world to make love to her, to lose himself in the glorious softness of that body, of those lips. To forget Milly, and Todd, and block out all the images of the two of them together that he'd been sitting here trying and failing to expunge from his sick, fevered imagination.

But then he got a grip on himself. This was Summer, for Christ's sake. Little Summer McDonald!

"Don't," he said, pushing her away firmly.

"Why not?" Bending forward she kissed him again.

The wool of her dress was soft as a baby's blanket, and he couldn't help but notice the way it skimmed the top of her thighs, like the red woolen trim on a Christmas stocking. He couldn't remember the last time he'd seen her in a dress, let alone one as sexy as this. It took every ounce of his willpower not to rip it off her right then and there and do exactly what she appeared to want him to.

"Don't you want me?"

"Shit, Summer," he said, wishing to God he didn't feel so aroused. He'd never, ever thought of her as anything other than Dylan's kid sister—picturing her naked was *so* not part of the deal. "I . . . yes, of course I do. Of course I want you," he admitted. "But we can't."

"Why can't we?" Pushing away his restraining hand, she eased herself off the desk and down into his lap, burrowing her face in his shoulders and sliding both hands up under his shirt. "You want me. I want you. Why can't we?"

"Aaaagh!" Leaping to his feet, he picked her up with both hands and put her forcibly back onto the desk, jumping away from her as if she were a rattlesnake. "Because!" he yelled. "Because we can't, okay? Because you're Wyatt's daughter and Dylan's sister. You're Summer, for Christ's sake. Jesus. No."

Her eyes welled up with tears of shame and hurt.

"But you sent me flowers," she said desperately. "And today, when we hugged, you were . . . different."

"How?" Bobby looked horrified. "How was I different? I wasn't different."

"You stroked my hair!"

"I was being affectionate! Hell, Summer, I care about you. You're like a sister to me."

"Bullshit!" she sobbed. The humiliation was more than she could bear. "You're just using that as an excuse. It's because of Milly, isn't it? That's why you don't want me. You're in love with her."

"That's crazy," said Bobby. But he was aware how unconvincing he sounded, even to himself. "No, that's not it. That's not it at all. Milly and I . . . it's complicated," he finished lamely.

"No, it isn't," said Summer. With nothing left to lose, she could at least get everything off her chest. "It's not complicated at all. It's simple. You want her, and you can't have her, and now maybe somebody else is gonna have her and it's driving you out of your mind."

He looked miserably down at his feet. She was going to make one hell of a lawyer someday with closing arguments like that. And there he was thinking he'd done a great job of hiding his feelings. Summer'd seen right through him from day one.

"I feel for you, Bobby, I really do," she said, tears streaming down her face as she headed for the door. "Believe me. I know what it's like to love someone who doesn't love you back."

After she'd gone, he moved back over to the desk and sank back down into his chair with his head in his hands.

What a mess.

What a total fucking mess.

CHAPTER EIGHTEEN

Amy Price adjusted the sun umbrella above her lounge chair and tugged hard at her bikini top, stretching the pale blue fabric that was cutting painfully into her breasts. A red line—part sunburn, part pressure from the too-tight elastic—was already forming at the top of her cleavage, and two unpleasant rolls of pinkish flesh were spilling out above it, like sausages protruding from a bun.

Turning over onto her stomach, she opened her book of Donne sonnets. Something of an amateur poet herself—her dream was to one day be published—she tried to lose herself once again in the beautiful language, blocking out her baby brothers' splashing and shrieking in the pool behind her.

Usually she hated sunbathing. But she'd recently read in *Marie Claire* that a tan could make you look as much as ten pounds lighter, so when Candy offered to watch the twins herself for an hour in an unheard-of display of maternal affection, she'd seized her chance.

Sweating and uncomfortable, she was already starting to wish she'd opted for a decent fake tan instead—although knowing her luck it would probably have turned out streaky and orange and awful. Closing her eyes she tried to imagine herself, somewhat improbably, being sun kissed and slim for the family's annual trip to New York in September. Not that Garth would notice her, even if she were.

Garth Mavers, a chiseled playboy from Martha's Vineyard, was her father's latest protégé on the Thoroughbred circuit and Amy's hopeless obsession. A talented jockey, he was even more accomplished as a womanizer and was utterly ruthless in both pursuits. He'd slept with Amy a couple of times last season, when he'd come to California hoping to insinuate himself with her wealthy, powerful father, and she'd fallen for him hard. But as soon as Jimmy hired him, of course, he dropped her like a stone. The last thing he needed was Price's clinging lump of a daughter around his neck, with a line of LA's long-limbed lovelies already forming at his door.

Amy, needless to say, was devastated by his defection, though she tried her level best not to show it. She'd just reached a point where she was able to hear his name mentioned in conversation without having to run off to the restroom and cry when, a month or so ago, hideous rumors reached her that he was secretly engaged to a supermodel.

In her heart, she knew there was no chance for her with Garth, with or without the supermodel fiancée. And yet despite all the stern talkings-to she had been giving herself—he didn't love her, he never had, he'd just used her like all the others—the thought that she would see him again in September, when he rode at Aqueduct for her father, made her heart flutter with hope and excitement.

Squirting another dollop of sunscreen into her hand—it was only SPF six, but she figured she wouldn't get any color at all if she went much higher—she slathered it onto her roasting shoulders and tried, once again, to relax.

If only she had a place of her own. Somewhere where screaming children and nightmare stepmothers didn't exist, or could at least be switched off like a bad episode of *Jerry Springer.*

But at the age of twenty-four, she had never lived away from home. Jimmy, embarrassed by her weight problem and lacking the sensitivity to know how to talk about it, not only neglected her shamefully but showed a consistent, casual cruelty toward her that made all the staff at Palos Verdes wince. But despite it all, Amy loved him. Despite his behavior, despite his bitch of a wife, despite his blatant favoritism toward his baby sons, he was all the family she had. One day, she was sure, the fantasy world he had built for himself around the vicious, gold-digging Candy (Jimmy was convinced his wife loved him and was faithful and wouldn't hear a word said against her) would come crashing down around his ears. And when it did she, Amy, would be there to pick up the pieces.

In the meantime, her life in the gilded prison of Palos Verdes was a deeply lonely one. Donny, her real brother (Candy's evil IVF spawn would never be true brothers to her), had never forgiven Jimmy for their mother's death. He moved to Manhattan the day he graduated college, and since then rarely called, and never visited. He made no secret of the fact that he considered Amy to be betraying their mom's memory by living under the same roof as Candy, and he flatly refused to understand her loyalty to their bastard father. Though she tried to brush it off, Donny's abandonment hurt Amy dreadfully.

Every now and then, when life at home became unbearable, she would venture out into the LA social scene, but inevitably she got her fingers burned, and/or her heart broken. Constantly seeking the love and affection she had been starved of growing up, she embarked on a string of disastrous affairs with handsome young actors who were only interested in her money—why else would they be dating a fat girl in a city full of some of the best-looking women in the world?—or playboy jockeys like Garth. Each time she was used or abandoned by one of these chancers, she would retreat to Palos Verdes to lick her wounds like an injured animal, taking comfort in the one thing that had been a constant in her life since her early teens: food.

Over the years Amy had tried every diet, exercise program, and psychotherapy under the sun to try to shed the pounds. But in the end, none of them had worked. Even her beloved poetry hadn't helped. Her need for the comfort and security that chocolate gave her overrode everything else. She had long ago accepted that she was destined to be a big girl and that there was really nothing much she could do about it.

"You're burning."

She looked up to see Sean standing over her, his short, stocky body casting a shadow over her reddening back.

"Shit. Am I?" She sat up, blushing, and hastily covered herself with a towel. Like everyone else at Palos Verdes she thought her father's head vet was utterly gorgeous. But unlike most good-looking men she knew, he was also a sweetheart: kind, funny, never dismissive of people simply because they were poor or fat or in some other way less than perfect. He'd become quite a friend since he moved onto the estate last year, one of the few people she could relax and be herself with.

"What are you doing up here?" she teased him. "Shouldn't you have your arm thrust up a horse's backside somewhere?"

"Now, now." He grinned. "Enough of your dirty talk, Miss Price. I come with orders from on high. Your father wants to see her majesty over there. Pronto."

He nodded toward Candy, whose discarded orange bikini top lay by the side of the pool, so tiny it would barely have covered one of Amy's nipples. Standing topless and waist deep in water like an Amazonian goddess, she was trying and failing to keep control of her sons.

"Looks like they're trying to drown her," said Sean.

"Good luck to them," said Amy with feeling.

Chase and Chance, both ensconced in more orange, inflatable devices than the Michelin man and covered with so much white sunblock they looked like they were preparing to swim the Atlantic, were happily splashing as much water as they could onto their mother's carefully pinned-up bird's nest of gleaming blond hair. She looked far from happy.

"Amy. *Amy!*"

Christ, thought Sean, what a voice. Fury had transformed her sexy, Southern drawl to a harpylike screech that could strip paint off the walls.

"Don't just lie there sunning yourself like a beached whale. Come help me with your brothers."

"You stay where you are," said Sean firmly. "Don't jump every time she says jump. I'll do it."

Striding over to the pool, he lifted both boys effortlessly out of the water, one under each arm. Much as he despised Candy, he couldn't help but admire the view of her pert, apple-round breasts as she rose, dripping, to greet him, reveling in her nakedness like a young Bo Derek.

"Thanks," she said, looking him right in the eye and making no effort to look for a towel. The sexy drawl was back with a vengeance now. "You're an angel."

Eeeeugh! And you're the devil, thought Amy, staring enviously at her stepmother's smooth, slender thighs, unsullied by even a hint of cellulite. She knew it was shallow and pathetic, but she did wish that her own thighs didn't look quite so much like two vats of porridge squeezed into plastic wrap.

Still, she mustn't envy Candy. She refused to. The woman was everything she despised.

"Jimmy wants you," said Sean, dropping the screaming, wriggling boys down into their poolside playpen. They both needed a good old-fashioned clip round the ear if you asked him. "He's in his study. Something about arrangements for New York, I think."

"Hmmm." Candy looked supremely bored but wrapped herself in a peach silk kimono anyway and prepared to go inside. "Well. If his lordship's calling, ah guess ah'd better go." She pouted.

Jimmy was the perfect sugar daddy in many ways—indulgent, generous, unsuspecting. But he did have a thing about not being kept waiting. Besides, a half hour in her children's company had more than exhausted her earlier rush of maternal enthusiasm.

Once she'd gone, Sean reached into his back pocket and, pulling out a small white envelope, handed it to Amy.

"This came for you, by the way," he said. "It was under a bunch of flyers and crap in the office. I almost threw it away."

"Thanks," she said, examining the hand-written address and the New York postmark stamped in the top right corner. For one brief, crazy moment her hopes soared that it might be from Garth, but she soon got a grip on herself. Why on earth would Garth be writing to her now?

Shoving it under her pile of clothes—she'd open it later, after Sean had gone, just in case it *was* something personal—she smiled up at him.

"You know we've got guests tonight," she said. "That guy Todd, your buddy Bobby's friend. It's the third time he's been here in a month."

"Yeah, I heard," said Sean skeptically. "I don't think Bobby likes him much, actually. Neither do I, as it goes. He's a smarmy bastard, don't you think?"

Amy giggled. "Maybe. I don't really know him. Anyway, he's bringing some girl with him apparently, a quarter horse jockey that Daddy wants to promote. Jilly or something, I think her name was."

"Noooo!" said Sean, putting two and two together. "Not Milly? The girl Bobby brought over from England?"

"That's it," said Amy. "Milly, yes. She's English."

"Holy shit." Sean shook his head. "I wonder if Bobby knows she's coming here? And with his partner too . . . that's gratitude for you. After everything he's done for that girl."

"What do you mean?"

"Well, no offense to you, angel, but Bobby's not the biggest fan of your old man."

"Oh," said Amy, "I see."

"And my guess is that Milly must know that. It's a shame. Bobby's nuts about her, so he is. He's been a changed man since he met her, and not for the better."

"Well, all I know is that Daddy saw her ride last weekend and says she's phenomenal," said Amy. "I wouldn't want to hurt Bobby, but I hope she does train here. It'll be nice to have another girl around."

"Hmmm," said Sean. "We'll see. At least I'll finally get to see what all the fuss is about."

Walking up the stone steps to the Price mansion later that evening, her newly darkened hair contrasting dramatically with the shimmering silver sliver of a cocktail dress Todd had bought her as a congratulations present, Milly could feel the adrenaline coursing through her veins like electricity through a wire.

Normally, she'd have been nervous at the prospect of spending an evening with a new sponsor, especially one as awesomely powerful and major league as Jimmy Price. But her conversation with Bobby two days ago had left her so angry—who the hell did he think he was, anyway, ordering her around like a bloody sergeant major—that she was still wound up now and ready to take on just about anyone.

She'd expected mixed feelings from him. Hoped, though she dared not admit it, that he'd feel sadness at the prospect of her moving out of Highwood, mingled with pride that her career was at last taking off. Secretly, she'd imagined that by moving away and striking out on her own, she might finally prove to him that she was in fact an adult and a woman and not the untouchable, innocent little girl he seemed to see her as.

But instead of pride and affection, what she'd gotten was pure indignant rage. Not only had he accused her, quite unfairly, of betrayal and ingratitude toward him. But he'd implied that Todd was somehow using her and that, far from being mature, she was actually being naïve.

The hypocrisy was breathtaking. It was fine for him to obsess endlessly about Highwood, neglecting everything, including their friendship and her training, in his increasingly desperate attempts to get the entire ranch both profitable and back under his sole control. But when it came to *her* trying to earn the money to buy back Newells, he was dismissive almost to the point of ridicule.

"Have you any idea how much that stud was worth?" he'd snapped derisively on the phone. "You know nothing about the value of money, Milly, nothing. Do you really think you can earn enough from race winnings to buy the place back? It'll take you a lifetime."

Well, she'd show him. He could hate Todd and Jimmy as much as he liked. He could even hate her if he wanted to. She was, she told herself defiantly, if not entirely truthfully, past caring. She was going to make it as a quarter horse star. And she was going to get Newells back too, with or without his support.

In a way his anger, and his unreasonableness, had made the whole thing easier, incinerating whatever guilt she might have been feeling and replacing it with a steely resolve. It was almost liberating, to finally be able to feel something for him other than hopeless, unrequited love. She nursed her resentment deliberately now, as she followed Todd into Jimmy Price's lair.

Relinquishing her coat in the same marble hallway where Bobby had stood with Todd only a few months earlier, she found herself being led into a dining room so exquisite she couldn't help but gasp. Lit entirely by candles, their flames flickering into a million refracted shards of light that ricocheted off the crystal and silverware like silver bullets, the table looked as though it had been spread for Titania's banquet. Wine glowed rich red in glass decanters capped with burnished silver tops, and bowls overflowing with fruit made elaborate centerpieces, surrounded by squat, square onyx vases crammed with white roses.

"Ah, at last. Come in, my dear. Come in."

Jimmy sat at the head of the table, very much the king of his own castle. The aura of power and authority around him was even more palpable than it had been at Mandeville Canyon, despite his almost clownlike features: the shock of ginger hair, the eyes sunken into his fleshy face like wizened chestnuts pressed into dough, the arms apparently composed of rolls of fat stuck together like a line of raw Sunday joints pressed end to end. For some reason Milly hadn't focused on his physical ugliness at the weekend. But this evening it was thrown into even sharper relief by the beautiful girl sitting next to him, who she assumed must be his wife.

"Sorry we're late," said Todd, looking anything but sorry as he flashed a confident smile to the table at large. "Traffic."

"Forget about it," said Jimmy. Without getting up, he extended a hand in greeting toward Milly, who shook it firmly. "You've missed the appetizer, but you're right on time for the main event. Please, sit down. The both of yous."

She looked briefly at Todd for direction, and he gestured toward the empty chair at Jimmy's left. He, meanwhile, took a seat between Candy and a terribly overweight girl in a truly awful lobster-pink caftan, who Milly recognized from Bobby's description as the sweet but put-upon Amy. Her dress seemed designed to draw attention not only to her size but to the shiny pinkish sunburn that was spread all over her face, culminating in the peeling red tip of her nose.

Instinctively, Milly smiled at her, and was immediately rewarded by a beaming grin in return.

Amy, in fact, had more reasons to be happy than Milly or anyone else suspected. Her letter from New York wasn't from Garth, but it was the next best thing: a note from a small but respected publishing house expressing interest in her poetry! Of course, they hadn't actually *said* that they would print the poems she'd sent in—not in so many words, anyway. But they had asked to meet with her when she was next in New York. That alone was enough to put a smile on her face that not even the thought of a formal dinner with her father could completely extinguish.

"Let me introduce you," said Jimmy, putting one arm around Milly's shoulder while waving the other magnanimously around the table. "Everyone, this is Milly Lockwood Groves. She's gonna be training here and, I hope, riding for me next season."

Milly flushed with pleasure. Hearing him say it again made it even more real and wonderful.

"And Todd Cranborn," he added, "who most of you already know."

Milly noticed that Candy shot Todd a knowing glance, and that he returned it with a flirtatious wink. For some reason this annoyed her intensely. For the last day and a half she'd gotten used to being the sole object of his attention, and having some melon-breasted tart swan in and steal it pissed her off more than it ought to. She couldn't think why it didn't bug the crap out of Jimmy, too, but it didn't seem to.

"This is Candy," he said proudly, unperturbed by the mini-seduction going on opposite him. "My *very* lovely wife."

"Hiiiiiii," rasped the blonde, tearing her attention reluctantly away from Todd for a split second and giving Milly the sort of imperious look that incredibly beautiful women always give to lesser mortals—a sort of patronizing, Rachel Delaneyesque sneer.

Witch.

"And this is Amy," Jimmy went on. "My daughter."

He couldn't have sounded less enthusiastic if he'd been introducing a wart on his foot. Poor girl. Milly watched her blush miserably, and her heart went out to her. How could Jimmy be so warm and friendly to her, a complete stranger, and so harsh to his own flesh and blood?

"Hi," she said, trying to think of something kind to say that wouldn't be an outright lie and eventually opting for, "I love your earrings."

"Thanks," said Amy, genuinely grateful. "They're new." Milly, she'd decided, was quite lovely.

"This," said Jimmy, gesturing toward the small, darkly good-looking man directly opposite her, "is Sean O'Flannagan. Sean takes care of all my quarter horses."

"Oh. Hi," said Milly brightly. "Sean. You're Bobby's friend, right? He's told me so much about you. Although I expect I got the edited version," she joked.

"Likewise," mumbled Sean, with a look that could only be described as withering. The smile died on Milly's lips. "Charmed, I'm sure," he added sarcastically.

That was odd. Why was he being so hostile?

Before she had a chance to think of any sort of comeback, or to probe him any further, Jimmy was demanding her attention and introducing her to his trainer, Gill, a butch, dour-looking woman in her fifties. She had closely cropped gray hair and wore a man's riding jacket, but unlike most trainers Milly knew, she at least was polite, giving her a brief but friendly nod of acknowledgment.

"And last but not least," said Jimmy, smiling to the man on Milly's immediate left, "I'd like you to meet Brad Gaisford. What Brad doesn't know about PR ain't worth knowing."

"Actually I'm, er, I'm more of an image consultant than a PR guy," said Brad pretentiously. "Some people call what I do holistic PR, but that's not really me. I'm all about image generation."

"Oh," said Milly blankly. "Right."

"Hey, Brad," said Todd from across the table, talking to him as though he were an old high school buddy rather than a man he'd just met. "Whaddaya think of Milly's accent? Great, isn't it?"

"Hell, yeah." Brad nodded. "Dig the accent. Dig the name. She's vibing on Austin Powers, man. Exactly what we've been looking for."

Milly frowned. He was a nerdy-looking guy, Brad. Probably around forty but trying to dress younger in combat pants and a too-tight long-sleeved cotton T-shirt that he obviously believed showed off his pecs to some sort of advantage. With his rimless glasses and weak little beard, he reminded her of a middle-aged version of the Fonz. What sort of man still used the word "dig," for God's sake? And as for "vibing"—she hadn't heard anything quite so tragic since Justin Timberlake started trying to sound black. It was cringeworthy.

"I've decided to use Brad to handle all your press and promotion," said Jimmy, in between stuffing vast hunks of oil-drenched bread into his blubbery, wet-lipped mouth.

Why? Milly wanted to ask, but she thought better of it. Instead she simply stared at his mouth and tried to imagine it locked in a kiss with the beautiful Candy. It was tough.

"Todd and I discussed it this afternoon," Jimmy went on.

"Oh, you did?" Milly looked at Todd quizzically. He hadn't mentioned anything to her.

"Uh-huh," said Jimmy. "You're a talented rider, but that's not gonna be enough on its own. Image. That's what we need to work on. That's what's gonna be key."

"Key," echoed Brad, nodding sycophantically. "Absolutely key."

"Well," said Milly, setting about her newly arrived plate of lamb shank and green beans with unashamed gusto, "I don't really care about image, to be honest with you, Mr. Price. I just want to race. And win. And make a lot of money."

"Unfortunately, my dear," said Brad with a patronizing smirk, "Jimmy's right. You can't have one without the other—money without image, that is. This is America."

"Let me guess," said Sean, who was making equally light work of his own lamb as well as knocking back the cabernet at an impressive pace. "You're going to work this English-cowgirl angle." He raised one eyebrow mockingly at Brad. "Very original."

"It's not about originality," Brad hissed. Evidently there was no love lost between those two. "Although as a matter of fact I think it *is* quite original."

"So do I," said Todd. He remembered the surly little Irish fucker from the last time he was here with Bobby and he was starting to get bored with his negativity.

"It's about marketability. The accent, the look." Brad pointed at Milly like a farmer might point at his prize heifer. "We can sell that. With Jimmy's media clout behind her, we can sell it for a goddamn fortune."

"Maybe," said Sean, who didn't doubt it for a second. He knew firsthand how many doors the Price name could open. "But it's a bit tacky, don't you think?" He was talking directly to Milly now. "After everything Bobby Cameron's done for you, I'm surprised you'd want to cheapen the old Western traditions that mean so much to him with some gimmicky PR stunt."

"I don't . . ." she blustered. "I mean, this wouldn't be about Bobby." Suddenly, she felt out of her depth. Was he right? Would Bobby see all this as a slap in the face?

"We're all getting ahead of ourselves," said Jimmy, deftly diffusing the situation. He didn't know why Sean was so bent out of shape, but he didn't want his new jockey and his brilliant vet coming to blows on day one. "The first priority is to get Milly known on the national quarter horse circuit. Everything else comes later."

"Will you be living here?" asked Amy timidly from across the table. She'd barely spoken a word all evening and was obviously anxious not to draw more attention to herself than absolutely necessary.

"No," said Todd dismissively. "She'll train here, nine to six, five days a week whenever she's not competing. Right, Jimmy?"

Jimmy nodded. "That's right."

"But she'll be living with me."

Milly sat silent through this exchange, turning from one to the other like a dog watching a tennis match. She was starting to feel like she didn't exist. Todd and Jimmy hadn't bothered to consult her on any of this, after all. They'd just steamed ahead, making plans for *her* life.

Still, she could hardly complain. At the end of the day they were offering her everything she'd ever wanted.

Everything but Bobby Cameron.

But after everything that had happened in the last few days, she was finally coming to accept that Bobby was the one dream she was never going to make come true.

Shivering in his pickup truck outside the gates of Todd's Bel Air mansion, Bobby tried desperately to stay awake.

Maybe Dylan was right? Maybe he shouldn't have come?

But no, fuck it, why shouldn't he? Was he just going to roll over and let that bastard Cranborn take Milly away from him? Let him corrupt her and hurt her, push her into a cutthroat world she wasn't ready for and then drop her like a stone the minute he'd gotten what he wanted?

And that was the other thing. What was it, exactly, that Todd wanted? Was it Highwood? He definitely had a hidden agenda there, Bobby was sure of it, although so far he'd been unable to prove a thing. Or was it Milly herself that he was after?

Obviously he wanted her. That much had been clear since that awful night at Jimmy's last year, the weekend Cecil died. But again, he had the strong feeling that there was more than straightforward lust at stake here. Where, for example, did Price fit into all this? Why would Todd go out of his way to bring Milly and Jimmy together? It was almost as if the guy had a personal vendetta against him, although why or how that could be, he had no idea.

Maybe Dyl was right, and he was just being paranoid. Certainly the pressure he'd been under, inheriting Highwood, starting the quarter horse stables, and trying to keep a lid on his feelings for Milly, was starting to take a physical and emotional toll. Maybe he *was* imagining things.

But he couldn't shake the feeling that he was living his life behind smoked glass—that everything was not quite what it seemed—and that somehow Todd Cranborn held the key to it all.

And then, of course, there was Summer. He still hadn't begun to figure out what he was going to do about that situation. On the drive down, the only distraction he'd had from the Milly-Todd nightmare was trying to think of all the signals he must have missed. When had these feelings started? He shuddered at the thought that he might, unwittingly, have encouraged her in some way.

Not that she wasn't beautiful. And sexy. He was ashamed to admit it but part of him, a big part, would have loved to fuck her, to screw Milly out of his system for good and all.

But one thing all the girls he'd slept with had in common was that he'd never truly loved any of them. And that wasn't the case with Summer. He loved her. Not in the same way he loved Milly, perhaps, but it was love nonetheless. Quite apart from the furor it would cause at the ranch, an affair with her could only complicate his life. And lord only knew he didn't need any more complication right now.

By one A.M., despite himself, his head was lolling back against the headrest and he was drifting off into a fitful sleep. Only the sudden glare of Ferrari headlights sweeping across his face was enough to jolt him back into consciousness.

"Bobby?"

Todd had wound down the window and was smiling that maddening, self-satisfied smile: a smile that had started to haunt Bobby's nightmares.

"This is a surprise. Please, come on in."

Bobby could see Milly slumped forward in the passenger seat. At least, he thought it was Milly. What the fuck had happened to her hair?

Before he had time to look more closely, Todd revved up his engine with an almighty roar and surged through the gates, leaving him no option but to restart his truck and follow. By the time he'd parked and eased his stiff legs out onto the forecourt, Todd had already opened the front door and disabled the alarm and was ushering Milly inside.

"Why haven't you returned my calls?" Pushing past Todd, Bobby grabbed her roughly by the shoulders and spun her around to face him. In her short, shimmering silver dress she looked like a will-o'-the-wisp, ethereal and otherworldly.

She swayed a little unsteadily on her high heels and tried to focus. God, he was so, so beautiful, even when he shouted at her. The urge to reach up and stroke his thick blond hair, to fling herself into his arms, was powerfully strong, even now. But she mustn't, she knew she mustn't. If she didn't stand her ground now, she'd never get her career off the starting blocks. And he wouldn't respect her either, not in the long run, or ever see her as an adult if she kept backing down and giving into him.

"I've been out to dinner," she said, defiantly. "In Palos Verdes. With big bad Jimmy Price."

"You're drunk," said Bobby harshly, as she lost her footing again and ricocheted off the doorframe into him. For a split second he held her. Feeling the downy hairs on her arms brushing like silk against his skin, he could have wept with longing.

"No, I'm not," she said, pulling away. "I had a few drinks, that's all. To celebrate."

"Yes, I can see you've been celebrating," he said viciously. "You even went out in your underwear and dyed your hair for the occasion."

"Oh, shut up!" yelled Milly. "My hair looks lovely. You know it does."

"It looks tacky as hell," he spat. He knew he was being an asshole but he couldn't seem to stop himself. "You had beautiful hair before. Your father would be horrified and you know it."

"You leave Daddy out of it!" she sobbed. The tears that had already started welling up in her eyes spilled over now, and she crumpled like a rag doll. It was true that Cecil had loved her long hair even more than she did, although she hadn't thought about that till Bobby said it. "Just because your father hated you, don't you dare make assumptions about mine."

"I suggest you both calm down," said Todd coolly. "Why don't you take a seat in the living room, Bobby, and I'll have someone fetch you a drink?"

"No thanks," snarled Bobby. "One of us needs to stay sober. Look at the state she's in." He pointed at Milly. "She's under twenty-one, you know. And don't tell me you hadn't been drinking too, before you climbed into that death trap of a car and drove her home."

"If anyone's car's a death trap," said Todd, casting a disdainful glance over his shoulder at Bobby's ancient truck, "I don't think it's mine."

Closing the front door behind him, he strode into the living room and took a seat on the couch. Milly, looking utterly shell-shocked, followed.

"So. Tell me." Todd opened his arms expansively. "What exactly is your problem, Bobby? You can hardly expect me to believe that you drove all the way down here because you were worried Milly might have had a drink. I don't think even you could be *that* overprotective."

"Never mind me," said Bobby. "What's *your* problem?"

"I don't know what you mean." Todd looked bemused.

"Sure you do," snarled Bobby. "Let's start at the beginning. What were you doing at the ranch last weekend? You knew I was away."

"Yeees," said Todd, like a teacher explaining something mind-bendingly simple to a small child. "I knew you were away. But I had some business in Buellton, so I thought I'd stop by and see how things were going."

"Bullshit. You were spying!" Bobby started pacing furiously in front of the fireplace. "I'm not blind, although it appears I may have been stupid for ever trusting you in the first place. You've been all over the valley, asking questions, poking your nose into my business—"

"*Our* business," Todd corrected him. "I have a stake in Highwood too now, remember? I have a right to know these things."

"What things?" said Bobby. "What the hell are you grubbing around in the dirt for? What are you hoping to find?"

"Nothing. Jesus, what's with the paranoia? I'm a businessman. I like to stay informed about my investments. If you were a little older and wiser, kid, you'd realize that that's not so unusual. We're not all fly-by-the-seat-of-our-pants cowboys, you know."

But Bobby was done arguing the point. Leaning down, he grabbed Todd by the collar and picked him up one-handed. For one brief, gratifying moment he saw a flicker of real, physical fear in Todd's eyes as he pulled back his other arm, ready to punch.

"Don't patronize me, you two-faced son of a bitch," he said. "You knew my feelings about Jimmy. You deliberately waited till I was out of town to bring Milly down to meet him. And now you think you can wave some sponsorship deal in her face and it's all done and dusted? Well, it's not going to happen, do you hear me?"

To Todd's enormous relief, he released him at this point and turned his attention back to Milly, grabbing her forcefully by the wrist.

"She's coming back to the ranch with me."

"Don't you think," said Todd, straightening his tie and attempting to get both his dignity and his breath back, "that that should be her decision? She's not a child, after all."

"Oh yes she is," said Bobby. "And what's more, she's a child in my care. Go get your things," he ordered, shoving Milly toward the door.

That was the last straw. What with Jimmy and Todd and the awful Brad debating her future without so much as a by-your-leave, and now Bobby doing his heavy-handed Lord Capulet routine, she'd had enough of being pushed around for one day.

"You know what, Bobby?" she said, wrenching herself free of his grip. "You're not my fucking father. So stop acting like it."

The juxtaposition of the sexy, adult dress and haircut with the smudged makeup and childishly jutting, defiant chin was heartbreaking. She looked like a kid who'd raided her mom's closet. He wanted to protect her so much, to make her see what he could see—that Todd was a ruthless, predatory shark. That he'd hurt her. But he realized miserably that everything he'd said and done tonight had only made him look more and more like a jealous, selfish idiot.

"I know I'm not your father," he said, finally lowering his voice. "But I promised Cecil I'd take care of you—"

"For God's sake," said Milly. "When are you gonna get past it? Todd's right. I'm not a child. You may want me to be, but I'm not. Whatever you think about him, Jimmy's offered me an amazing chance."

"Oh. So it's 'Jimmy' now, is it?" said Bobby churlishly.

"I'll be riding some of the best quarter horses in the country," said Milly, ignoring him, "entering serious races, statewide and beyond. He's even talking about Ruidoso Downs next year."

"He's trying to flatter you," said Bobby, not thinking how insensitive he must sound. "You're nowhere near that standard."

"Oh, really?" Milly was furious. "Well, *he* seems to think I am. He wants to promote me too, give me this whole new image."

"Oh, I'll just bet he does!" Bobby shook his head. Try as he might, he couldn't seem to keep a lid on his anger for more than thirty seconds. "You have no idea, do you? You're so fucking naïve."

"*I* don't have any idea?" Milly laughed. She was properly angry now. "What about you? You're too blind to recognize your own motives. You're jealous!"

"That's ridiculous," said Bobby.

"You are," Milly insisted. "You don't want me to succeed. You want to keep me as your little pet project, your little child slave up at the ranch forever."

"Now you're being melodramatic," he snapped.

Todd, meanwhile, was sitting back on the couch, enjoying the show. Happily, Bobby was shooting himself in the foot very nicely without any additional help from him. All that repressed cowboy pride—he couldn't help but push the girl away. Things couldn't have gone better if he'd scripted tonight's proceedings himself.

"Look," said Bobby, "I'll make it simple for you: Jimmy Price hurts people. I'm not going to let him hurt you. He may have great horses, but the guy's evil."

"Evil?" she hit back at him. "*Now* who's being melodramatic? Anyway"—tossing back her hair, she sat down on the couch beside Todd and, very deliberately, put her hand in his—"I don't care what you say. I'm not going back to Highwood with you. Not now, not tomorrow, not ever. I've been given a chance and I'm taking it. If you really cared about me like you say you do, you'd understand that."

For a moment she thought she saw something—fear, remorse, desperation even—register in his eyes. But then it was gone, a grille of self-protective impassivity descending in its place. Classic Bobby.

"Fine," he said. "That's just fine. You stay here if that's what you want. But don't come running to me when it all falls apart. When you've grown up enough to realize that this guy's using you." He jabbed a finger at Todd.

"Using me?" Milly looked genuinely bewildered. "How? For what?"

"To get to me. To Highwood," said Bobby. "It's the ranch he cares about, Milly, not you."

"You know, this really is getting a little crazy," said Todd, still maintaining a façade of affability. "No one's trying to get to anyone. All I wanted was to help Milly out. There's nothing in it for me. The last thing I wanted to do was to come between the two of you."

"Save it," said Bobby, holding up his hand. "You might be able to fool a teenager who doesn't know any better . . ." Milly's face flushed with renewed indignation. "But you don't fool me. I want you out of the business and off my land."

"Now, come along, Bobby." Todd chuckled. "It's not quite as simple as that, as you well know. I've made an investment in Highwood. And that gives me certain legal rights—"

Before he knew what was happening, he found himself being grabbed for the second time, but now Bobby wasn't fooling. Within seconds

Todd was gasping for breath, panicking as he stared up at two hazel eyes narrowed into slits of liquid hatred.

"Set foot on my ranch again," Bobby whispered, "and I swear to God, I'll kill you. Is that simple enough for you, Mr. Cranborn?"

Todd nodded helplessly. Hurling him unceremoniously down onto the floor, Bobby stormed out the front door, slamming it behind him with an almighty bang.

It took a full minute for Todd to regain his composure sufficiently to try to get to his feet.

"You okay?" he asked Milly.

"Me? I'm fine," she said. "It's you I'm worried about." But he could see she was shaking like a leaf in her flimsy dress. Any residual drunkenness had been shocked out of her system, and she looked white-faced sober, tearstained, and definitely very far from okay.

"Come here," he said. Dragging himself back up onto the couch, he pulled her toward him.

Instantly he felt her taut body start to relax. Up close like this, her youth was almost palpable, like a living, physical presence. He'd slept with plenty of much younger women, including quite a few teenagers. But there was a world of difference between the hard-nosed nineteen-year-olds of Hollywood, with their surgically sculpted bodies and knowing sexuality, and this fragile little English girl, all softness and innocence and trembling emotion. Bobby was right about her naïveté—and, boy, was it a turn-on.

His brush with death seemed to have made Todd even hornier than usual. Aware of Milly's full, pert breasts pushing up against his chest, he felt his cock start to harden.

Milly felt it too, and for a second she pulled away, frightened.

She'd pictured losing her virginity a thousand times. In her fantasies it was always Bobby's face above hers, bursting with a longing and desire as passionate and all-consuming as her own. She'd imagined the tenderness with which he would make love to her, wary at first, then more assured as he felt her need, pulling him body and soul ever deeper inside her. . . .

But these were childish dreams. Hazy images, hijacked from romantic novels and the cheesy daytime soaps she'd watched as a child.

Before her now was the adult reality: Todd, a grown man, his dick pressing like iron against her thigh, his breath heavy with a lust that was anything but tender.

Dim memories of a poem—or was it a prayer she'd learned at school?—floated back to her. Something about "putting away childish things."

Tonight she'd told Bobby that she wasn't a child. Now was the time to prove it.

Reaching down, she tentatively began stroking the outline of his erection through his cotton pants. He groaned, then leaned forward, kissing her greedily on the mouth as his hands groped for the zipper at her neck. Finding it, he undid her dress so fast, she barely had time to blink. Underneath she wore no bra, just a simple pair of white cotton panties with cute yellow daisies all over them.

"Sorry." She blushed. "Not very sexy, are they?"

"*Au contraire*," said Todd, slipping his hot hand under the fabric and running his fingers through the silky pubic hair beneath. "I love the little girl look."

He hadn't planned to seduce her tonight. He'd imagined it would take weeks to win her trust, maybe longer. He had Bobby to thank for propelling her into his arms and, he fervently hoped, onto his dick so soon.

Milly heard herself gasp and felt a rush of pleasure engulf her as he began gently rubbing her clitoris with his left hand, simultaneously easing himself out of his pants with his right. Glancing down, she caught the briefest of glimpses of his dick, so big and hot and alive it looked like a separate creature, rather than a part of his body.

"Don't worry." Todd grinned, seeing her eyes widen. "I won't hurt you."

This turned out to be a lie. With one sharp, violent thrust he pushed himself inside her, making her cry out with pain. It felt like someone trying to drive an express train into a hose.

"Shhhh, shhhh, it's okay," he murmured into her hair as she bit down hard on his shoulder.

"You said it wouldn't hurt!" Her face was so indignant, he couldn't help but laugh. Relieved that the worst was over, Milly soon found she was laughing too.

"It won't anymore," he said. "I promise. See?"

Slowly he began to move, rocking back and forth inside her, and she closed her eyes, losing herself in all the new, delicious sensations consuming her from the inside out. After a few minutes, she could feel her climax building. Instinctively, she tightened her grip around the back of his neck. Her legs began flailing wildly, seemingly beyond her control. It was like drowning, except . . . wonderful. She wanted to drown him with her.

With one deep, full-throated groan he pulled out of her, shooting hot, white liquid over her stomach as he did so. Mesmerized, like she'd just seen a magic trick for the first time, Milly reached down and touched it while Todd got to his feet and started pulling his pants back up.

"Tomorrow," he announced firmly, "you're going on the pill. And I don't want any arguments. I almost didn't make that."

Milly wasn't about to argue. She merely nodded vaguely.

Tomorrow.

What did she care about tomorrow?

All she could think about was today. The day she became a woman. The day that everything changed.

Tomorrow could take care of itself.

CHAPTER NINETEEN

"Easy now. Easy."

Milly stroked Demon's neck gently as they waited at the starting gate, and wished he would stop shivering. He wasn't well, poor baby.

It was July, and they were at Santa Rosa, one of the premier quarter horse tracks in California, about to take part in a trial for next month's big stakes race. Sean, never her biggest fan at the best of times, had torn a strip off her this morning for going ahead with it. "I'm telling you, that horse isn't right," he insisted angrily as, with the help of two grooms, she'd loaded Demon into the trailer. "He should be resting."

Privately, Milly knew he was right. Though Sean was always having a pop at her for something or other (he'd somehow gotten it into his head that she'd betrayed Bobby by riding for Jimmy—a nice line in hypocrisy, given that he himself was the man's head vet!—and by "shacking up," as he put it, with Todd), this time he had every right to be angry. For almost two weeks Demon had been struggling with his breathing in the punishing summer heat. Only yesterday he'd started spontaneously bleeding at the nose after she took him out for a breez-ing—a long ride through the open Palos Verdes countryside—and she had to bring him back to the stables early to cool down and rest.

But having run a whole battery of tests last night and come up with nothing, Jimmy was adamant he was race fit and should go to Santa Rosa as planned. There was really very little that Milly, as the jockey, could do about it.

"He's fine," she told Sean defensively. "The tests were clear." But though she wouldn't let him know it, she was worried. After Easy's death, she'd vowed never to get close to a horse again. But over the past two months, the horse Jimmy had bought from Todd specifically for Milly's training had won her over completely with his dopey eyes, incurable competitiveness, and the cute barrel-chested waddle that made him look more like a cart horse than a racehorse. She loved him madly and would rather die than see him hurt.

Sometimes it was hard to believe she'd been riding for Jimmy for only ten weeks. It felt more like ten years, so completely had her life changed.

Her learning curve at Palos Verdes had been not so much a curve as a perpendicular cliff face. Gill Sanders, Jimmy's quarter horse trainer, turned out to be a tougher taskmistress even than Bobby, which was quite an accolade. After one intensive week of grueling workouts in the indoor school, she'd started Milly and Demon on practice three-hundred-yard sprints. Soon she had them entering trials at all the big-name California tracks—Ferndale, Alameda, Fairplex Park, Los Alamitos—for serious stakes races like the Gold Rush Derby and the Miss Princess Handicap. As the weeks rolled by and they got to know each other better, their form improved consistently, with Milly winning trial after trial, often with increasingly impressive margins over much more experienced riders.

It was all a very long way from the Ballard Rodeo. Thanks to Gill, she gained more race experience in her first five weeks at Palos Verdes than she had at Highwood in six whole months. She and Demon became inseparable.

But there was a downside.

Not everyone involved in quarter horse racing, it appeared, was as laid-back and gentlemanly about the sport as the cowboys from Santa Ynez. The camaraderie Milly had been so struck by at Ballard simply didn't exist in LA, or anywhere else where jockeys, trainers, and owners were competing against one another for big bucks. Sexism was also rife in the sport.

"We haven't had a decent female jockey in quarter horse riding since Tami Purcell retired in 2000," Jimmy reminded her at one of the trials, after a competing rider had elbowed her dangerously hard in the ribs, and the offense had gone unpunished. "There's still a lot of resistance to the idea. But you have to try to look beyond all that."

Milly nodded earnestly, rubbing her bruised side.

"Don't get me wrong," Jimmy went on. "Tami was a great rider: fifty-five stakes wins, including the All American, and you can't argue with that. But she didn't have what you have: the looks, the youth, the accent, the image. She was never branded correctly."

"Correct branding," Milly was beginning to learn, meant a round of PR commitments every bit as grueling and time-consuming as her training and racing schedules. But despite a chronic lack of free time and being in an almost permanent state of exhaustion, deep down she felt happier than at any time since her father's death. After all those months yearning hopelessly after Bobby, coming to LA was like a rebirth. Even more important, she felt she was at long last making progress in her career—progress toward getting Rachel out of Newells before she destroyed the stud and her father's legacy completely.

Stroking Demon gently between the ears, she tightened her reins and readjusted her position in the saddle as they came under starters orders. Thankfully, it was a slightly cooler day today, and his earlier shivers seemed to be dying down.

In any case, there was nothing she could do now but focus on the race ahead. Luckily, Demon seemed to feel the same way. The instant the gates came up he rocketed forward, looking for all the world like a horse in peak condition. Within a few short seconds, they'd pulled to the front of the pack.

"Good lad," Milly yelled encouragingly into the wind. "Just a little longer, Deems, and it'll all be over. You can do it."

The crowd wasn't huge, a couple of hundred at best, but it was enough to bring out the natural showman in Demon. Under the weather or not, he was more competitive than any other horse Milly had ever ridden, Thoroughbred or quarter, and reveled quite unashamedly in the attention and applause. The moment they crossed the finish line—first place, again, for the second time that week—he tossed back his head and started showing off, kicking excitedly with his hind quarters in what was becoming his trademark victory dance, to the delight of the spectators.

Looking up, Milly saw Gill dashing over toward them. She looked uncharacteristically upbeat in a bright-yellow-plaid golf sweater and striped pants. Normally she eschewed any color that didn't fall comfortably between the ranges of charcoal and swamp, so she was obviously in celebratory mood.

"That was fine," she said, panting as she pulled up alongside them. "Good job."

"Really?" Milly grinned. A "fine" from Gill roughly translated to a "fucking fantastic" from anybody else. "Good job" was almost unheard-of.

"Definitely. You made very good time," she said, patting Demon on the neck. "I can't see how you won't get through with that."

"I hope you're right," said Milly nervously. "There are still two trials to go though." Dismounting, she looked around, scanning the sea of congratulatory faces swarming around them. "Is Todd here, d'you know?" she asked as casually as she could manage.

"No idea," said Gill, who was already totally focused on Demon, covering him with a blanket and beckoning one of Jimmy's junior vets to come check on his temperature. "Haven't seen him."

Milly bit her lip and fought back a ridiculous urge to cry. Goddamn it. He promised he'd be here. Now she'd have to ask Amy for a lift home—again.

Since the night she lost her virginity to him back in April, Todd had become the center of Milly's world. The change was gradual at first and began in practical ways. Living in his house meant she had to fit in with his timetable and habits from the start. As a nondriver in LA, she was even more beholden to him than she might otherwise have been—or at least to Miguel, his relentlessly chipper Mexican driver, who took her back and forth to Palos Verdes every day for training.

Milly soon discovered that Bel Air, though glamorous, was incredibly isolated. There were no shops, no coffeehouses, no neighborhood at all. Everybody hid behind their big electric gates, peering at one another with binoculars and trying to figure out how much everybody else's real estate was worth. It was the kind of area where you could live on a street for thirty years and never meet your next-door neighbor, as Todd had told her proudly, without a hint of irony.

Even if there had been anywhere to go, the streets were so wholly designed around the car that there weren't even sidewalks, so she'd still have been trapped. At least at Highwood she'd been able to walk or ride into Solvang and get a newspaper and a coffee when the mood took her. Now she needed Todd's help just to leave the property.

The whole thing was such a rigmarole, she ended up spending more and more time at home. Cut off from her family and friends in England, and now estranged from Bobby too, there was a huge hole in her life, and no one but Todd to fill it. It wasn't long before the relationship had swallowed her whole.

With Bobby, it was like everything had happened in slow motion. Or, rather, nothing had happened but over a very long time, allowing her frustration to build to a boiling point. Being with Todd was like taking the lid off a pressure cooker. It was not so much a release as an explosion.

She'd never imagined herself being with an older man before. But now that she was, it felt like the most natural thing in the world. Under Todd's practiced tutelage, she took to sex like a duck to water, basking in the confidence that his desire gave her. She was no longer little Milly, Cecil Lockwood Groves's horse-mad kid, or Bobby Cameron's charity case. She was a strong, sexual woman, with a rich, handsome older lover. Instead of any of the tall, sophisticated LA models he could have had, Todd had picked *her*. For Milly, that was the biggest aphrodisiac of all.

Soon she not only accepted his control but delighted in it. Having lost her father and her home in a few short months, and seen her world turned completely upside down, it was lovely to be with someone who made all the decisions. It made her feel safe.

So when Todd bought her a fabulous new wardrobe but insisted on personally picking out every single item in it, she didn't complain. Nor did she object when he devised a strict diet plan for her—Jimmy had decreed she must lose a few pounds to give her more competitive edge in the saddle—and then hired a full-time eating counselor to follow her around and make sure she stuck to it.

The downside, of course, was that she'd effectively handed him all the cards in the relationship from day one. And he didn't hesitate to play them, making sure he kept her in a permanent state of insecurity as to his motives and affections. He was always flirting with other girls, and made no effort to hide it. Often he would return home in the small hours from some party or other, without even bothering to concoct an excuse. Milly would fly into a tearful rage—but he could always placate her by taking her to bed.

Todd had been delighted to discover that Milly's latent sexuality, once unleashed, was a far stronger, more animal thing than he'd expected. Her lack of sexual inhibition was almost total, an openness that also extended to her emotions. Playing hard to get was evidently not in Milly's repertoire.

"Hey." Amy, car keys in hand, floated over, dressed in a huge, shapeless pink shirt and matching pants. She looked like a cross between the Pillsbury dough girl and a giant raspberry, but Milly couldn't have been more pleased to see her. "What's wrong? Oh, don't tell me." She frowned. "He didn't show up, did he?"

Milly shook her head and tried not to look as miserable as she felt. "He probably had a crisis at work."

"Yeah," said Amy sarcastically. "Sure."

The two girls had become firm friends ever since Milly started riding for Jimmy. Milly was a valuable ally for Amy, sticking up for her whenever Candy's bullying got too much. In return, Amy provided Milly with unconditional adoration and a permanent shoulder to cry on, patiently listening for hours while she ranted on about Rachel Delaney, getting Newells back, her awful brother and mother back in England, and her rift with Bobby Cameron.

The only bone of contention between the two of them was Todd. Amy couldn't stand him and couldn't understand how someone as gorgeous and talented as Milly could allow herself to be controlled by such a womanizing jerk.

"I can give you a lift home if you like," she said, deciding to drop the subject of Todd's no-show. Milly looked miserable enough without her rubbing it in.

"To Bel Air?" said Milly. "But it's miles out of your way."

Amy shrugged. "I'm hardly in a rush to get home. Candy's got two of her girlfriends over tonight. The longer I can spare myself the bitches of Eastwick, the better."

Milly giggled. No matter how annoying Todd was being, Amy never failed to make her see the funny side of things.

She smiled naughtily. "I was so pissed at her this morning for dumping the boys on me again, I took the Porsche." Candy's pink Porsche—the Barbie-mobile as it was known to all the grooms and staff at Palos Verdes—was her pride and joy. She'd hit the roof when she found out Amy had swiped it. "Don't tell me you're gonna pass up a ride in that?"

"Give me two minutes to change and I'll be right there," said Milly, trying to push images of Todd in bed with some nameless bimbo out of her mind.

"Forget it. Just come like that," said Amy. "I'll be Barbie, and you can be Ken."

Milly laughed, linking arms with her friend. "All right then," she said. "After you."

Six thousand miles away, Jasper wiped his clammy palms on his trouser leg for the second time in five minutes and wished his hands would stop sweating.

He was sitting alone at the virtually empty bar upstairs at the Electric in Notting Hill, waiting for Ali Dhaktoub to come back from the gents and wondering what on earth had possessed him to agree to this meeting in the first place.

It had all started innocently enough a few weeks ago. (Innocence was a relative concept, after all, and what Rachel didn't know wouldn't hurt her. Or, more importantly, him.) Amelia Kelton, the pretty daughter of a local trainer who he'd been screwing on and off for the past three weeks, had offered to introduce him to a friend of hers, a race-horse owner and the son of a billionaire Arab oil magnate. Ali, she thought, could be a potential employer for Jasper. And God knew those were thin enough on the ground at the moment.

The truth was he was desperate to revive his fortunes as a jockey for a number of reasons, chief among them being his disillusionment with Rachel and their so-called partnership. When she'd first floated the idea of buying the stud, he'd been all for it. Not only would it involve his receiving an immediate injection of cash—his mother would officially get the money, of course, but tapping Linda for a few thousand here and there had never been an issue—but he would also be guaranteed involvement in the business on his own terms, while simultaneously squeezing Milly out. Or so he thought.

In fact, Rachel had been stubbornly resistant to all his input from day one. It was almost as if she didn't value his opinion, despite the fact it was patently obvious that what she herself knew about running a stud farm could fit comfortably on the back of a stamp. She'd already made a huge mistake, selling off some of Cecil's most consistently high-earning sires and overspending on new, untried animals.

And it wasn't just at Newells where he was being sidelined. Rachel's success both as jockey and as a media star in her own right seemed to grow exponentially by the week. Right now she was still making noises about her commitment to promoting them as a couple. But with his own career in free-fall, he had a hideous, creeping feeling that the writing was already on the wall for the Rachel and Jasper show.

His paranoia probably wasn't helped by the increasing amounts of coke he was taking. Since Cecil's death, his open-ended line of credit at Bank of Linda, combined with the oodles of free time he had on his hands, made it easier than ever for him to indulge all his vices with free rein. Casual sex with girls like Amelia soothed his vanity and gave him a brief illusion of power in his relationship with Rachel. But the reality was that his life was slipping out of his control, and he knew it. He had to do something, anything, to make his own money and be his own man.

And that, he hoped, was where Ali Dhaktoub came in.

When they first met at Nam Long in South Kensington, a popular hangout among London's young, spoiled rich, Jasper had dismissed Ali as just another Arab cokehead dilettante, playing at horse racing with his daddy's money but with no serious interest in the sport and still less in employing *him*, a low-ranked jockey of minimal experience who he didn't know from Adam.

But as the cocktails began to flow, and he listened to Ali talk, he swiftly revised this opinion. True, the guy knew nothing about horses. But he did understand gambling—and coercion—and the subtle balance of risk and reward involved in both. All of a sudden, he was speaking Jasper's language.

What Ali wanted him to do was to stop his horses. To deliberately lose races on firm favorites, dead certs where he should have won.

It was match fixing. In a nutshell, fraud. If he was caught, he would be stripped of his license to race, fined, and quite possibly imprisoned. If he wasn't, he stood to make a potentially huge amount of money.

In Nam Long, it had all sounded exciting and dangerous, a thrill. The Dhaktoubs operated in a shadowy, gray world where the lines between legitimate and illegal business were murky and vague, a world very far removed from his father's upright and honest business practices and those of his English, establishment clients. But now, three weeks later, in the sober afternoon of a deserted London club, all the vagueness of that earlier, drunken conversation had been stripped away and the thrill replaced with a gut-gnawing fear as the specifics of what he was being asked to do hit home.

He was probably committing a crime of some sort just by having this conversation with Ali, he thought, feeling a cold sweat of fear forming all over his body.

On the other hand, if he weren't caught, he'd be earning far more than he could ever hope to make as a legitimate jockey. More than Robbie Pemberton and Dettori and Jakey Forster, riders who he had grudgingly come to accept he would never be able to rival on the track. More than Milly, who he'd heard from various sources had dumped the cowboy and been talent spotted by Jimmy Price, of all people. Much to his fury, she actually appeared to be making a bit of a name for herself in America.

And, most important of all, more than Rachel.

"So. You have considered my proposal?"

Ali came sauntering back from the men's room, grinning. With his slicked-back black hair, dark skin, and open-necked white shirt, he reminded Jasper of a pirate. All he needed was the cutlass between his teeth.

It bothered him that this guy his own age should so effortlessly assume the upper hand in their negotiations. But the reality was, Dhaktoub held all the cards, and they both knew it.

"Like I say, Ali, I really don't know," he said, playing for time. "It's a lot to take in."

"Is it?" Ali looked nonplussed. "It seems quite simple to me. I need somebody to stop General's Boy at Bath in a fortnight's time. It's only a small meeting, but it would be a perfect opportunity to get you started quietly. If we were racing him to win we'd use Pemberton, but my father has a rotating group of jockeys, so it won't arouse suspicion to slip you in."

"I see," said Jasper, looking green. He still wasn't sure he had the stomach for this lark.

"You take the race. You lose," Ali went on. "Twenty thousand cash, plus commission if you bring him in fourth and look convincing. It's money for nothing, my friend."

Jasper thought about it. The blow to his ego at the suggestion that he was good enough to lose races but not to win them was softened greatly by the prospect of twenty thousand quid cash in hand and the possibility of even richer pickings to come.

And what could go wrong, really? As far as his mother and Rachel and everyone in Newmarket were concerned, he'd be riding legitimately for the Dhaktoubs, and he'd just happen to lose. It wouldn't be the first time. . . .

"I need some more time," he said, draining the last of his scotch on the rocks. "A week. To think it over. You're asking me to risk my career here, Ali. I have to be sure."

Ali frowned and gave him a look that might have meant "what career?"

"You have two days," he said, reaching into his back pocket and pulling out a crisp wad of notes, which he left on the bar beside their empty drinks. Clearly, men as rich as Ali didn't bother with trivialities like bills and change. "If you don't want the job by Thursday, I'll find someone else who does. You've got my numbers."

He swaggered out of the bar without a backward glance. No hand-shake, no good-bye, no nothing. For a moment Jasper felt annoyed. Who the hell did this fellow think he was, some slave wallah from Abu Dhabi?

But he let it go. What did it matter, after all, what Ali did or didn't think about him? Pocketing two of the ten-pound notes on the bar be-fore the barmaid saw him, he slipped off his stool, and followed his soon-to-be employer out into the drizzly London evening.

CHAPTER TWENTY

Dylan McDonald stood in Carol Bentley's small, whitewashed gallery in Los Olivos, shifting his weight nervously from foot to foot.

"She's been a long time, hasn't she?"

Summer smiled and squeezed his hand reassuringly. "Not really," she said. "She's appraising it. That's her job."

She'd practically had to drag him out here today, but she was determined to show the local art dealer his finished portrait of Wyatt. Summer was no artist herself, but she knew when something was really, seriously good. Dylan had captured their dad's spirit perfectly, whatever he might say to the contrary. But it was no good her telling him that. He needed to hear it from Carol.

"Yeah, but she's taking forever," he said, biting his nails as he worked himself into an ever deepening frenzy of self-doubt. "I mean, either she likes it or she doesn't, right?"

It was a horrible thing to think, but in a way Summer was glad Dyl was being so nervous and needy this morning. It gave her something to focus on other than her own problems for a change. Plus, dragging him into town gave her the perfect excuse to get off the ranch. Bobby had a friend, Sean, arriving from LA for the weekend. The thought of having to be sociable and chatty with some stranger, and make small talk around Bobby for hours on end, filled her with a deep, creeping dread that made her palms sweat and her head throb with anxiety. If it couldn't be avoided, at least it could be delayed for a couple of hours.

Ever since her disastrous, failed pass at him in April, the weekend that Milly had gone off with Todd Cranborn, the tension between her and Bobby had been unbearable. They were polite to each other of course, and as far as she knew, no one else at Highwood had the slightest inkling that anything had happened at all. But *she* knew it, and *he* knew it, and that was quite enough to make her burn up with shame and mortification whenever she was around him, which was basically every single day. Only the prospect of starting at Berkeley had kept her going. But the weeks till her departure stretched ahead like years. Even making it through this weekend with Sean whatever-his-name-was seemed an insurmountable task from where she was standing.

"Do you have any more like this?" Carol emerged from the back studio smiling, cradling Dylan's portrait in her arms. "Portraits, I mean."

Dylan nodded. "A couple, ma'am. I do more landscapes, really. But I have one or two."

"He has plenty," said Summer firmly. Now was not the time for false modesty. "Willy, Mike, most of the hands up at the ranch—"

"Some of those are just sketches," corrected Dylan hastily.

"Well, I'll take whatever you've got." Carol smiled. "Sketches, finished pieces, I really don't care. If they're anything close to this in standard, they'll be perfect for the Santa Barbara gallery."

Dylan frowned and rubbed his temples. Carol looked perplexed.

"What's the matter?" she asked. "You do want to sell them, don't you?"

"Sure he does," said Summer, kicking her brother on the ankles. "Right?"

"What about Dad, though," he whispered, pulling her aside for a moment and out of the dealer's earshot. "You know how he feels about my art. Won't he hit the roof?"

She gave him a look that was somewhere between exasperation and compassion. "He might," she admitted. "Yeah, you know what, he might. But come on, Dylan. At some point you gotta make your own decisions about your own life. She wants your pictures." She pointed back at Carol, who was watching their fevered little aside with interest. "Are you really gonna let that go?"

Seeing the boy was still wavering, Carol decided it wouldn't hurt to weigh in. "I haven't seen work of this standard for a very long time," she said. "It's different, but I think it could be very commercial. You could sell your existing work, build up a reputation, and then look to do commissions. This sort of traditional portraiture is a dying art, you know."

Dylan took a deep breath.

Fuck it.

Bobby was training racehorses at Highwood, Summer was about to go to college. Even Milly was off following her dream, becoming a quarter horse star down in LA. Why should he, Dylan, be the only sucker still sacrificing *his* dreams to live up to some mythical, idealized vision of Highwood that didn't even exist other than in his father's mind? Even if it did exist, it was Wyatt's dream, not his.

"All right, Ms. Bentley," he said, nodding slowly. "All right. I'll do it. I'll give you the rest of my stuff."

Back at the ranch, Bobby dumped Sean's case in his room, the spare room at the big house that had once been Milly's, and dragged him straight out to look at the stables.

"Not bad," said Sean, with an appreciative whistle, as they came to the end of a handsome row of stone stalls and continued to the indoor school. He'd been meaning to visit Highwood for a while—Milly turning up at Palos Verdes had only heightened his curiosity about the place—but Jimmy very rarely gave him a whole weekend off and he hadn't had a chance till now. "How many animals d'you have here?"

"Twenty-two liveried with us full-time," said Bobby proudly, "and another six stabled locally that I train here. Four are my own."

"Ah. A trainer and an owner, eh?" Sean looked suitably impressed. "And are they just yours or Cranborn's too?"

Bobby's face instantly darkened and he jammed his hands deep into his jacket pockets.

"Do we have to talk about that fucker?"

"Sure, no, of course we don't," said Sean, swiftly changing the subject. "I was only wondering where things stood. You know I can't stand the sloimy little shit any more than you can."

Bobby hadn't spoken to Todd, or Milly, since that awful night in

Bel Air back in April. He'd expected her to call him the next day and try to make up. She was always the one to make the first move when they fell out. She knew how stubborn he was.

But this time, it hadn't happened. It took a few days before he finally realized she expected *him* to call. But by then enough time had passed to make it awkward, and he didn't know what to say or where to begin.

Soon afterward, to his utter horror, he heard from a number of people in LA that she and Todd had become what Wyatt would have called "an item." Distraught, he did what he always used to do as a child when he felt powerless—like when his mother took up with some unsuitable hippie asshole or other and turned his life upside down for the umpteenth time: He stuck his head in the sand and tried not to think about it.

But even now, months later, he still sometimes found himself waking in a cold sweat in the middle of the night, haunted by an image of Milly being pawed by that decrepit, perverted bastard. It made him feel physically ill.

Nor did it help that Milly was rapidly becoming one of the most recognizable faces in quarter horse racing, at least in California. Although she'd yet to win a major stakes race, with the awesome Price media machine like an unstoppable force behind her, her image seemed to prosper regardless. Advertising campaigns for Boot Barn and a handful of other cowboy-related companies had helped promote her faster than her racing career could keep up and would no doubt soon be followed by bigger, national sponsorship deals.

Not that she was doing badly on the racing front. Some sort of masochistic urge compelled Bobby to keep track of her results, and they were undeniably impressive. If she kept up her current form she and Demon were bound to be entered in all the Californian majors next season. From there she'd have a shot at a national career and the distance between them, already huge, would become a gaping, unbridgeable chasm.

Leading the way back across the yard toward the big house, he pulled his jacket tighter around him. Despite being noon in mid-August, there was a cool breeze blowing down from the hills behind them and he was glad of the warmth the battered old leather provided.

Sean followed him inside and along the hallway to the living room. After helping himself to a large bourbon from a tray on the sideboard he sank down on one of the couches. The room had been very little used since Hank's death—Bobby spent almost all his free time over at the McDonalds'—and it showed. The decor was cold and drab to the point of sterility, all heavy dark wood furniture and gloomily ticking clocks. There wasn't so much as a rug or curtains to warm the place up, and a thin layer of dust coated everything from the ugly low coffee table to the battered parquet floor.

"No offense," said Sean, plumping up the cushion behind him and sending a cloud of dust billowing up toward the ceiling in the process, "but don't you find it a bit depressing here?"

Bobby shrugged. "Not really." He didn't want to talk about his father's taste in interior design, or lack of it. He wanted to know what was going on with Todd. The fact that they were not speaking, though a relief in many ways, had its disadvantages. The chief one being that he now had even less of an idea what his so-called partner might be planning with regard to Highwood. Clearly it was too much to hope that he'd simply forgotten about the place. The longer he heard nothing, the more nervous he became.

"Is he still around much? At Palos Verdes?" he asked.

"Cranborn?" said Sean. "Yeah. Like a bad smell. Supposedly he's there to see Milly, but most of the time he's either locked away talking business with Jimmy or sniffing around his missus like a dog with a hard-on. You remember Candy, right?"

Bobby's upper lip curled like he'd just caught a whiff of rotting meat.

"Beach ball Barbie? How could I forget?"

"But as to what he's up to, mate, I haven't a clue," said Sean, taking another sip of the deliciously smooth bourbon. At least old Hank provided that comfort for his guests. "Jimmy never talks business with me, other than the horses, of course. I'm down at the stables all day."

"And Milly?" said Bobby in as casual a tone as he could muster. "You must see her all the time, right? Has she let anything slip?"

"No."

It was horrible listening to Bobby talk about Milly, watching the light of hope click on in his eyes, despite everything. Poor bastard. He insisted he was over her, but it didn't take Freud to figure out he was talking out of his arse.

Sean, who had never been in love himself, made a mental note never to try it.

"We're not exactly bosom buddies, Milly and I," he said. "And even if we were, I don't think she knows anything about lover boy's business dealings. She's pretty well besotted with him as far as I can tell, but he keeps his distance."

"What do you mean?" asked Bobby.

"You know," said Sean. "He gives her the runaround, doesn't he? Other girls, parties, keeping her hanging, all of that. He knows Jimmy's got her working all hours, so she can't keep tabs on him. Training, racing, more and more PR—she's turning into a one-woman industry these days."

Bobby's face fell still further.

"I'd be surprised if Todd confides in her," Sean finished hurriedly. "That's all I'm saying."

He was racking his brains, trying desperately to think of any news from LA that might comfort Bobby even marginally, when he was distracted by the entrance of a Christie Brinkley circa 1984 lookalike.

"Lunch is ready," the vision announced, tossing her hair back out of her eyes with the same sort of casual flick the girls in the shampoo commercials used. He noticed that, although she addressed herself to Bobby, she seemed reluctant to look him in the eye and that he seemed equally awkward in her presence, replying in little more than a mumble.

"Really?" He looked at his watch. "It's only twelve thirty."

"I know." The girl shrugged. "Dyl and I only just got back from town, but Mom says we all have to eat now."

"I'm Sean." As soon as he'd recovered the power of speech he was on his feet, grabbing her hand and kissing it enthusiastically before Bobby had had a chance to introduce him. "Sean O'Flannagan. My God, is it a pleasure to meet you."

Summer laughed. "Summer McDonald," she said, adding politely, though completely untruthfully, "I've heard a lot about you from Bobby."

Sean looked panic-stricken.

"All lies, every word of it," he said, slipping his arm around her waist in a semiprotective, semiflirtatious manner. "You can't believe what this fella tells you."

"Don't worry," said Summer with a knowing look at Bobby that he pretended to ignore. "I don't."

A few minutes later, once she'd disappeared to the office to fetch Tara, the two boys made their way over to the McDonalds' alone.

"Is there something going on between you two?" asked Sean.

"Going on? Of course not," said Bobby, rather more tersely than he'd meant to. "What makes you say that?"

"Oh, nothing," said Sean, recognizing a land mine when he trod on one. "You just seemed a bit distant, that's all."

"Summer's like a sister to me," said Bobby.

"Roight." Sean nodded. "Sure. I can see that."

"She's only eighteen, she's much too good for you, and you can't have her," Bobby added for good measure.

"Roight," said Sean again, failing to suppress a big grin. "Gotcha."

It was two weeks after Sean's weekend trip out to Highwood, and Milly was standing in front of the mirror in Amy Price's dressing room trying on outfits she'd brought over from Bel Air. Todd was taking her to a party at the Playboy mansion tonight, something she'd been in a thorough state of overexcitement about for weeks—although the shine had been slightly rubbed off this morning when she learned that Sean, now her sworn enemy at Palos Verdes, was also invited.

"I mean, why?" she moaned, pouting despondently at her reflection in the antique French mirror. The backless emerald-green dress that Todd bought her only last month, a guilt present for his having failed to turn up at Santa Rosa, was already far too big for her, thanks to the strict, low-carb diet Jimmy insisted she follow. It hung shapelessly from her bony shoulders now, making her look like a cast member from *Les Misérables* who'd fallen into a vat of glitter, or a Vegas showgirl with severe malnutrition. "Why does he have to come? He's such a total pain in the arse. And why do I look so bloody hideous in everything?"

"You're crazy," said Amy, chomping her way through a big bowl of pistachios on the bed while dispensing her sage style advice, and ignoring the jibe about Sean. Personally, she liked him, although she could see why Milly didn't. "You always look beautiful. All you need to do is pin it in a little with a brooch or something. What I wouldn't give to have your figure."

Though they were as different as chalk and cheese, Amy and Milly had become like the sisters they had both wished for growing up. As the only jockey training full-time at Palos Verdes—Jimmy's other racing stars, Garth Mavers and Michael Shaw on the Thoroughbred circuit and the quarter horse jockey Ricky Crawford, put in occasional appearances when their hectic race schedules allowed—Milly was pretty lonely most of the time, with nothing but the unspoken envy of the grooms and Sean's outright hostility for company down at the stables. Amy's friendly face and constantly chirpy, bubbly spirit had been a godsend.

For Amy, Milly was a breath of fresh air. Confident, talented, beautiful—in short, everything that she herself was not—Milly was nonetheless down-to-earth and never treated her like a second-class citizen the way that other pretty girls did. Better still, she was funny. Her bitchily brilliant impressions of Candy frequently reduced Amy to tears of mirth, and the two of them spent many happy hours between Milly's training sessions, giggling together about the absurdities of LA life and the racing world.

Only two subjects were taboo between them: Bobby (because Amy thought he was gorgeous and romantic beyond belief and that Milly was crazy to have left Highwood and fallen out with him) and Todd (because Milly clearly still thought the sun shone out of his ass, while Amy considered him pond scum of the lowest order).

Today though, unusually, both conversational minefields had come up at once. Milly thought she'd overheard Todd on the phone a few nights ago talking about Highwood's oil rights and had made the mistake of challenging him about it.

"All I did was ask what was going on," she complained to Amy, hoping no doubt for some sisterly support. "But he absolutely bit my head off. He said I'm always cross-examining him about Bobby and the ranch, which is completely bloody ridiculous. We never talk about Bobby. Never."

"What do you think is going on?" said Amy. She knew from Sean that Bobby suspected Todd was up to something at Highwood but that he didn't know exactly what. "Is he after the oil, do you think?"

"Todd? Oh no." Milly shook her head vigorously. "Definitely not. There's a clause in their contract about not drilling up the land. I remember Wyatt forcing Bobby to put it in."

"Good for Wyatt," said Amy. She had never met any of the McDonalds, but Milly and Sean's vivid descriptions made them feel like old friends. She could picture Wyatt now, struggling to rein in the headstrong Bobby and protect him from sharks like Cranborn.

"Anyway, Todd wouldn't do a thing like that. I know he doesn't like Bobby very much but . . . no. No, he would never do that."

Amy wasn't sure whether it was she Milly was trying to convince or herself. Either way, it didn't seem to be working.

"You think the gold earrings then? Or the blue?" asked Milly, changing the subject. She'd settled at last for a pale-gold, flapper-style dress that made her look marginally less gaunt than the others. She wouldn't mind the thinness if it weren't for the fact that her tits seemed to have completely vaporized, and half the girls at the party tonight were sure to have breasts that weighed more than her entire body. Every time she and Todd went out in LA, there was some bottle blonde or other flinging her beach-ball mammaries at him like trophies. It made Milly's blood boil.

"I think the blue," said Amy firmly.

No one had ever asked her advice on matters of beauty or style before, and she was absurdly gratified that someone as beautiful as Milly should be seeking *her* opinion. Just being around Milly seemed to make her more confident.

If only she could bring her to New York next month as a magic talisman for when she met the publishers and, perhaps, saw Garth again. But she knew Milly's race schedule wouldn't permit it. And in any case, Amy hadn't told her, or indeed anyone, about the interest in her poems. It seemed too much like tempting fate.

"Milly!" A cacophony of horn tooting started up beneath Amy's window. Heaving herself up from the bed, she got up to have a look. Todd was standing in the graveled forecourt, pointedly looking at his watch in between beeps and yelling Milly's name bad temperedly. Amy was gratified to see that from directly above he had a small but distinct bald spot forming. Hopefully it would soon grow into a full tonsure, which would serve him right, the vain so-and-so.

It took a lot to make Amy really dislike someone, but Todd Cranborn had achieved the feat in record time. If it had just been his rudeness to her, the sneering looks and endless stream of barbed comments about her weight, she might have found it in her heart to forgive him. But the way he lorded it over Milly, bossing her around and playing on her insecurities, especially with other girls, made her stomach churn. As did the patently sycophantic, self-serving way he hung around her father, scavenging for scraps from the Price table like the bloodsucker he was.

But as always, Milly's face lit up like a beacon as soon as she heard his voice.

"Hi!" she yelled, waving at him brightly and choosing to ignore the testy scowl she received in return. "I wasn't expecting you to pick me up. Why don't you come up to Amy's room. We're just finishing up."

"I'll pass, thanks," he said, checking his watch for the fourth time. "We're kinda pushed for time, you know, baby."

If Amy disliked Todd, the feeling was entirely mutual. As far as he was concerned a woman's primary duty was to be thin and beautiful— and if they couldn't manage that, then they should be quiet and useful. Amy Price was none of these things, which rendered her existence wholly pointless. He had no idea what Milly saw in the fat slug.

"I'd better go," said Milly apologetically, slipping the dress off over her head and pulling her jeans back on. "He hates it when I keep him waiting."

"Well, we couldn't have that, could we?" said Amy archly, but immediately regretted it when she saw Milly's crestfallen face. "Look, sorry. Just, make sure you have a good time tonight, all right? And don't let Sean or"—she edited herself—"or anyone else get you down."

"I won't," said Milly, scooping up an armful of clothes and shoes and heading for the door. "And have a good night yourself."

Yeah, thought Amy. Right. Just me, Candy, and Dad. It'll be a ball.

But she didn't care. This time in three weeks she'd be in New York, with Garth. Beside that, nothing else mattered.

Milly couldn't remember whether she'd actually seen pictures of Shangri-la, LA's fabled Playboy mansion, before or whether her imagination in this instance was just amazingly accurate.

Either way, as Todd nudged the Ferrari forward and announced their names to the infamous talking rock intercom, a faux granite boulder set to one side of the huge, wrought-iron gates, and they swung open obligingly to let them through, the scene that unfolded in front of her was almost exactly as she had pictured it—like a cross between the Garden of Eden and a *Benny Hill* set.

"Wow," she said, fiddling yet again with her tit tape to make sure her dress wasn't about to come unglued. "It's amazing, isn't it?"

But Todd, already busy waving and smiling to gaggles of girls as they drove by, wasn't listening. He'd been to the mansion so many times, nothing here amazed him anymore.

Originally built in the twenties for the heir to a Broadway department store fortune, the Gothic house had been comprehensively Heff-ed in the mid-seventies, its gardens transformed into a kitsch shrine to sex and hedonism. Amid the undeniable beauty of the six-acre grounds— rolling hills sat side by side with mini-Tolkienian forests; an aviary; and, of course, the notorious grotto—seminaked women and besuited middle-aged men strolled past signs reading CAUTION—PLAYMATES AT PLAY.

"How often do they do these parties?" Milly hissed in Todd's ear, trying to get his attention as he handed their keys to an improbably proportioned valet girl. The gold flapper dress that had earlier seemed passably sexy now made her feel more flat chested and androgynous than ever. She should have gone for something vampy and red and solid enough for her to shove a padded bra underneath. "Oh, my God. Did you see that?"

A woman who must have been seventy if she was a day wandered past the valet parking in the direction of the grotto, wearing nothing but a silver lamé bikini. Above a body draped in folds of crepey skin, which spilled over the shiny fabric of her outfit, shaking slightly as she teetered along, sat a spooky doll's face: smooth, almost waxy white skin; orange, drawn-on eyebrows; and fake lashes that looked like they'd been glued on in 1957 and left there ever since.

"Heff might be sexist, but he's definitely not ageist," said Todd, laughing at Milly's horror-struck expression. There was nothing unusual about seeing decrepit former starlets at these events. In a funny way, he'd always thought they rather added to the whole debauched, Hieronymus Bosch atmosphere.

"And try not to look quite so much like Dorothy in Munchkinland, would you? You're going to see a lot worse than that tonight, believe me."

He was right. If the grounds were what she had expected, nothing could have prepared her for the bizarre, circuslike melee of freaks and fashionistas, bunnies and businessmen, gathered on the mansion lawns. To the left of her, two suits were calmly conducting business, tapping figures into their Palm Pilots as they sipped their mineral water, while to her right a completely topless teenager escorted what looked like, but Milly could only pray was not, her grandfather to one of the hot tubs where a mini orgy was already in full swing.

But most disconcerting of all was how many people, and in particular how many girls, seemed to know Todd.

One after another, women came bouncing up to him—she was starting to see why people called them bunnies—flinging their arms around him like he'd just gotten back from years at sea and whispering in his ear right in front of her, as though she didn't exist.

In Newmarket, or even up in Solvang, people at a party would have asked her where she was from or what she did. Even if they'd never heard of quarter horses, most people would be interested in the fact that she was a jockey—especially now that she'd finally started to become successful.

But here, no one asked you what you did. No one asked you anything, in fact, unless you were a recognizable actor, a billionaire, or prepared to cart your bare breasts around in front of you in a wheelbarrow.

"What the fuck was her problem?" she said, finally losing it when a drop-dead gorgeous Latina called Mia, who'd been all over Todd like a rash, suddenly spotted someone richer across the lawns and zoomed off like the Road Runner.

"What do you mean?" He shrugged. "It's a party. The girls are paid to make people feel welcome."

"Well, she didn't make me feel very welcome," fumed Milly. "Honestly, these bloody bimbos look right through me. Don't they realize we're together?"

"Relax." Smiling, Todd pulled her to him and ran a leisurely finger around the nape of her neck, making her hairs stand on end. It was so ridiculously easy to make her jealous, although he still derived a satisfying rush of power from the experience.

Rather to his surprise, he still found her very physically attractive, despite the fact that they'd now been together five months, a personal best for him. Even after the thrill of stealing her from Bobby had worn off, he still found her combination of innocence and eagerness to please, particularly in bed, a phenomenal turn-on.

"Why don't you get yourself another drink?" he said, pulling away from her and wandering off yet again. "Go mingle. I'll catch up with you a bit later."

"Mingle?" Milly yelled furiously after his retreating back. "How am I supposed to mingle with these half-wits? I don't know anyone. Todd!" But he'd already been sucked into a group of giggling girls. Trying to pry him out would be as impossible as it was humiliating.

"Lost control of him already, have you?"

Milly spun around, the beaded tassels of her flapper dress swinging behind her. She'd have recognized that mocking Irish accent anywhere.

"Dear, oh dear. That's *not* a good sign."

"Sean," she said caustically. "What a nice surprise."

Always a thorn in her side, since his recent trip to Highwood he'd been particularly unbearable, waxing lyrical about the place and the people, as if he knew them better than she did. Her nuclear fallout with Bobby meant she hadn't spoken to anyone at the ranch, not even Dylan, since the day she left. But she still had an immense, proprietorial fondness for the place. It bugged the crap out of her to have to hear Highwood news from Sean self-righteous O'Flannagan, of all people.

Sean, for his part, was happier than usual to have run into Milly. At least winding her up would provide a welcome break in the tedium of the night's proceedings.

No one could accuse him of not loving a good party or of failing to see the charm in crowds of seminaked women. But he'd been to a few of these Playboy bashes now, and they always depressed him. There was something so forced about the smiles, so wooden and rehearsed about the girls' come-ons, that left him with a bitter taste in the mouth. It ought to have been erotic, but somehow it just wasn't.

It didn't help that he couldn't seem to get Summer McDonald out of his mind. He'd failed woefully to make any progress with her whatsoever during the rest of his stay at Highwood, though God knows he'd tried: every line, every technique, from shoulder to cry on to laugh-their-knickers-off jester. Nothing had worked. She continued treating him with the same polite detachment, then disappeared off to the library on his last morning without so much as a good-bye. He was obviously losing his touch.

"Don't you have some plastic tits you should be burying your face in?" asked Milly, trying to look past him for Todd, only to find he had now completely disappeared from view behind a throng of bimbettes.

"I did," Sean said drily, "but your boyfriend seems to be borrowing them just now."

Milly glowered at him.

"I understand he's a regular at the mansion?"

"You should know," Milly shot back, not missing a beat.

"Or perhaps I'm leaping to conclusions?" said Sean. "Perhaps you were the one invited tonight, and he just tagged along? I mean, your latest Boot Barn ad wouldn't be out of place on the Playboy Channel, would it? Tell me, how *do* they airbrush in cleavage? I've always wanted to know."

"Fuck off," snapped Milly. She'd never understood what Bobby and Amy and everyone else seemed to see in Sean. He'd never been anything less than poisonous to her.

Stopping a passing bunny girl, she replaced her empty flute of champagne with a full one and took a big gulp, sending bubbles rushing unpleasantly up her nose and making her eyes water.

"You're just jealous because I have a career that's actually going somewhere," she said, forcing a smile. "And you're going to spend your life elbow deep in a horse's arse."

"Jealous? Of you?" Sean laughed. "Not in this lifetime, sweetheart." He looked pointedly over at Todd, who now had a redhead on one arm and a Grace Jones lookalike on the other, and was throwing his head back in laughter like he hadn't a care in the world. "You do realize he's out to screw Bobby, don't you?"

Here we go again, thought Milly.

"I mean, I know you're not the sharpest tool in the box," said Sean, "but you do get that, right? Your boyfriend's a fockin' user and the whole of LA knows it."

Turning on her heel, Milly strutted off toward the house, locking herself in the safety of the ladies' room. Ever since their row over Highwood the other day, she'd had a niggling suspicion that perhaps Todd did have some ulterior motive for starting a relationship with her. She'd convinced herself she was being paranoid. But hearing Sean put her fears into words plunged her back into a flood of doubt.

Fumbling in her gold clutch for her powder, she fumed silently as she retouched her makeup. Fucking Sean. Who the hell was he to take the moral high ground with her, slagging off her Boot Barn commercial, or with Todd for that matter? Everyone knew he'd shagged every woman with a heartbeat—and probably a few without—within a fifty-mile radius of Palos Verdes. Even Bobby, who liked the guy, always used to describe him as a hopeless womanizer.

Even so, his comment about Todd bothered her more than she wanted to admit.

Was he using her, to get at Bobby? And, if so, how? And why? On one level, it all seemed so far-fetched. But on another, it felt worryingly plausible. Certainly he wasn't behaving much like a devoted boyfriend this evening, flirting with those awful girls right under her nose. It was all most confusing.

Her face repaired, she emerged into a candlelit corridor and paused to get her bearings. She appeared to have stumbled into a sort of shrine to Marilyn Monroe, who according to the memorabilia smothering the walls was the first ever Playmate. Through glass double doors to her left she saw Todd deep in conversation, this time, mercifully, with a man. She was just about to walk over and join him when she was accosted herself by a strikingly handsome guy.

He looked to be in his early thirties and was smiling so broadly his teeth seemed to glow in the dark, which was mildly off-putting. Even so, he was still exactly the sort of chiseled, Cary Grant type that she'd hoped might come and chat her up right where Todd could see them.

After all, two could play the flirtation game.

"I'm Johnny Haworth," the Adonis introduced himself. "Aren't you the girl from that sportswear commercial? The cowboy rider girl?"

"That's right." Milly beamed, immensely gratified to have been recognized. She only wished Sean were around to see it, but annoyingly he seemed to have slunk off. "I'm Milly Lockwood Groves. Pleased to meet you."

She spoke just loud enough for Todd to catch her voice and felt a small surge of triumph as, out of the corner of her eye, she saw him making his excuses to his companion and heading over toward them.

Ha! So he *was* jealous!

But her smile faded as, moments later, he greeted her new admirer with a familiar smile. Was there no one here he didn't know? "Hey, Johnny," he said warmly. "How's business?"

"Pretty good." The Adonis nodded, looking straight past Milly now and giving Todd his full attention. "The AACS just ranked me number one on the West Coast for breasts and eye lifts. In fact, I was about to give this young lady—Jilly, wasn't it?—my card. In case she wanted to consider a little augmentation, you know?"

Reaching into his jacket pocket, he pulled out a business card and thrust it into Milly's hand. It read: DR. J. HAWORTH, M.D., COSMETIC SURGEON.

So much for making Todd jealous. The guy didn't want to chat her up. He wanted to carve her up! She didn't think she'd ever felt so humiliated.

"It's Milly," she said frostily. "Milly, with an 'M,' okay? And I'm perfectly happy with my body, thank you very much."

Johnny looked down at her flat, bony chest and for a moment an unspoken "really?" hung in the air between them.

"I'm a professional jockey," she snapped. "We don't come with built-in air bags."

"Hey, fair enough," he said, throwing his arms wide in a gesture of innocence, like a footballer admitting a foul. "It never hurts to ask, right? Hey, Adrianna! Wait up?"

He scuttled off into the more voluptuous arms of what was probably one of his satisfied clients, leaving Todd and Milly alone.

"That was a great line." Todd laughed. "Air bags—I like that."

"Really," said Milly angrily.

She'd wanted to play it cool, but what with Sean's insinuations earlier and now this awful doctor shaming her so publicly, all pretense at sangfroid went out the window.

"Well, air bags are obviously your thing, aren't they? You've been ogling every bloody pair of knockers in here for the past hour."

Todd loved the way she looked when she was angry, the way her lower lip shot out in an almighty pout and she wrinkled up her nose. Sometimes she really was eighteen going on eight.

"I don't know why you even bothered to bring me here in the first place," she sulked, "if all you're going to do is dump me at the bar like a piece of left fucking luggage while you go off on the prowl!"

Putting one warm hand on the back of her neck, he pulled her toward him.

"Poor little Milly," he purred. "We have been feeling sorry for ourselves, haven't we?"

She knew she should pull away. Keep her anger going. Teach him a lesson for once. But it was so reassuring to have him hold her, after all her insecurity before, she couldn't do it. All it took was the faint smell of his aftershave and the soft warmth of his fingers pressing gently into the back of her neck and already her knees were weakening with desire. She wished she didn't want him so much, but it was hopeless. Closing her eyes, she leaned into his stocky, boxer's chest and inhaled the scent of him.

"If you must know," he said, growing hard himself as he felt her tiny, needy body pressed hard and insistent against him, "I haven't been 'on the prowl,' as you so poetically put it. I've actually been doing a little business on your behalf."

"What sort of business?" she mumbled.

"Well, no promises," he said, his breath tickling the top of her ear. "But I think I may have landed you a *Playboy* spread."

Milly leaped back from him in horror. "You *what? Playboy?*" Her voice was rising. "Have you lost your mind? You want me to strip for *Playboy?*"

"Sure." Todd looked nonplussed. "Why not? You're trying to raise your profile, aren't you?"

"Why not?" Milly was incredulous. "Erm, well how about because I'm a sportswoman, not a porn star? Rachel Delaney might be happy to mince around in a bra and a bit of spray paint, but I'm not. Besides," she ended on a rather more practical note, "Jimmy'll hate the idea."

"No, he won't," said Todd. "He'll love it. And it just so happens they have a special sports issue coming out next month. Kinda weird that Brad Gaisford missed it, actually. Most of the editorial's already shot, but they always have room for late additions, if they're hot enough." He gave her a knowing smile. "If Jimmy wants your name out there, this'll do it. Screw fucking Boot Barn."

She was torn. On the one hand it was awful, tacky beyond words. Her mother would have a heart attack—not that Milly particularly cared what Linda thought since she'd sold out to Rachel, but still. And then there was the ribbing she'd get from the grooms at Palos Verdes and all the other chauvinist pigs on the quarter horse circuit. It was bad enough being the only female competitor at 99 percent of races, but a *Playboy* spread? She might as well just hand them her head on a platter. Sean would have a field day.

But, on the other hand, it *would* mean overnight notoriety. The modest taste of fame she'd experienced so far had been more enjoyable than she'd thought it would be—more than it probably ought to be, but who cared? Why shouldn't she be the center of attention for once?

"Look." Todd took her hands in his and pulled her close again, despite her protestations. "You wanna buy your farm back from Rachel, don't you?"

"Of course," she admitted grudgingly. "You know I do. But naked pictures . . ."

"It's not just the money," he whispered. "I'd like you to do it. For me. I think it'd be sexy as hell."

Milly could feel her resolve crumbing. It wasn't just that she wanted to please him, although she did. But she was scared too. She knew that if she pushed him away tonight, there were a hundred blondes lining up to take her place. This evening's party felt ominously like a bad trip to Christmas Future.

"I'll think about it," she said, standing up on tiptoes to kiss him on the lips.

"Good." He smiled the satisfied smile of the victor. "Now let's get out of here. I want to get you into bed."

CHAPTER TWENTY-ONE

Rachel Delaney sat in the bathroom of her father's Knightsbridge flat, waiting for her top coat of hot-pink nail polish to dry while flicking through the new issue of *Playboy*.

"Fuck," she said, biting down on her lower lip in fury as she flipped through the pages and saw that no less than four had been devoted to Milly as the "English Cowgirl." "How the fuck did she get that?"

One of the most infuriating things about Milly Lockwood Groves—and there were many—was the way she kept popping back up no matter how many times you flattened her. She was like that bloody girl in *Austin Powers,* the one that wouldn't die even after she'd been hurled from a seven-story building and riddled with machine-gun bullets. One minute she'd sailed off to America with that twat Bobby Cameron, destined for a life of lassoing or whatever the fuck obscure cowboy sport she'd gone there to do. And the next she was all over the press as American racing's Next Big Thing, with her gorgeous, millionaire boyfriend and her scrawny little body plastered across *Playboy.*

It was ridiculous. She might have a new haircut and have perfected a pout, but she was still Milly Lockwood Groves. She still brayed in the forest. *And* she had no tits.

If that was what Jimmy Price's sponsorship did for you, it was high time Rachel met the man. Des Leach could bloody well pull his finger out of his arse and set her up some meetings in America.

Leaning forward to blow gently on her toenails, she reflected on how bored she was in England, anyway. True, she'd had a good summer season, by far her best to date, with a win in the Ascot Ladies Diamond Stakes, and she was now well known enough to have her picture in *Heat,* the ultimate litmus test for British celebrity. Although as often as not she was still pictured with Jasper as one half of "Racing's answer to Posh and Becks," which infuriated her. What had he ever done to deserve the attention, other than been linked to her?

But despite her success, an inordinate amount of her time and money were being sucked into Newells. It was starting to depress her. When she'd bought the place from Linda, she'd thought she'd landed a bargain. But running a stud turned out to be a lot harder than it looked, and Newells was hemorrhaging money at an alarming rate.

A few weeks ago she'd finally hired an experienced manager to take over the day-to-day running of the business for an exorbitant salary. He told her point-blank that selling off so many of Cecil's stallions had been a mistake, which did little to improve her mood. She might have hurt Milly, but she'd done so at a great cost to herself, and the bills only seemed to be rising.

Too proud to ask for help from her father, she might almost have turned to Jasper. Presumably even he must have picked up something about stud management by osmosis growing up at Newells. But he seemed to have gone completely off the rails recently. For one thing he was throwing money around like water. She assumed he was stinging Linda for it, but even by his mother's legendarily indulgent standards, this was a lot of cash. And most of it was going straight up his nose.

Her thoughts were disturbed by somebody buzzing repeatedly on the doorbell below.

"Fuck," she muttered, flinging the magazine to one side and smudging her little toe in her haste to get to the entry phone. "Yes, all right, all right, I'm coming."

All she could see on the fuzzy black-and-white monitor was a hunched male figure, wrapped up tight in a raincoat and with a cap pulled down over his face.

"Who is it?" she snapped. "If you're selling tea towels, we don't need any, so just bugger off, all right?"

"It's me," Jasper's voice came crackling over the intercom. He was panting and clearly out of breath. "Open the door, Rach, for fuck's sake."

Buzzing him up, she left the flat door open so he could get in and hopped back to the bathroom to redo her ruined nail. When he appeared in the doorway a few minutes later, she got the shock of her life.

"Oh, my God," she gasped. "What happened?"

His face had been so badly beaten he was almost unrecognizable. Big, spreading plum-blue bruises covered his cheeks and jaw, and trickles of blood had dried beneath his smashed nostrils and split lower lip, like badly smudged makeup. The flesh around his right eye was so swollen that the eye itself was now no more than a tiny slit; and with his left eye he looked around him nervously, as if expecting his assailant to jump out at any moment from Rachel's bathroom cabinet.

"I need a brandy." He was still shaking as he dumped his overnight bag unceremoniously on the floor. "Have you got any?"

"In the drinks cabinet in the drawing room," she said, taking his hand. She was feeling more warmly disposed toward him than usual since he had whisked her off to St. Tropez last week for a surprise mini-break. Watching his tanned, rippling torso as he'd strolled around the deck of their rented yacht glued to his cell phone, arranging no-expense-spared parties at Les Caves for which he invariably picked up the tab, she'd felt the first stirrings of genuine attraction for him. There was nothing quite like money to add to a man's sex appeal and give him instant spray-on confidence.

Not that he looked remotely confident now, shivering like a *Titanic* survivor as she sat him down on the sofa and quickly fetched his drink. Her father appeared to be out of brandy, but figuring any spirit would probably do, she poured a good four fingers of her mother's Grand Marnier into a tumbler and handed that to him instead.

Jasper took one big gulp and coughed at the strength of it, before sinking back weakly into the sofa. Slowly, the warm liquid began to work its magic.

"We need to get you to hospital, you know," said Rachel eventually, once his breathing had slowed to something approaching normal. His battered face looked even worse in the bright drawing room light than it had in the bathroom.

"No," he said, getting agitated again. "No. I can't."

"Why not?"

320

And piece by piece, the whole sorry tale began to emerge. He had been on his way to King's Cross to catch the Newmarket train when, yards from the entrance to the tube, a big lump of a man had accosted him, claiming to be a friend of Ali Dhaktoub's. Before he had a chance to say anything, he found himself being bundled into a van, in the back of which were two more thugs, one white, one black, who had proceeded to beat the living shit out of him. At some point he must have lost consciousness, because the next thing he knew he was waking up in a pile of boxes at the back of a warehouse in East London. That must have been about two hours ago—the time it had taken him to get his bearings and walk back across town to Rachel's flat—and now here he was.

"I fought back, of course," he assured her, between comforting sips of the Grand Marnier. "Gave them a run for their money."

In fact he'd whimpered like a baby and begged for mercy from the moment the van doors were opened. But Rachel didn't need to know that.

"Problem was there were three of them and one of me. I didn't stand a chance."

"But . . . I don't understand," she said slowly. "Why would Ali Dhaktoub's friends want to beat you up? It doesn't make sense."

Looking up, Jasper caught sight of his battered face in the mirror above Sir Michael's Regency fireplace and groaned. He was vain enough to care more about losing his looks than the throbbing pain in his face and ribs. The bruises would heal, but his nose looked well and truly broken. What if it never set back into its former straight, handsome line? He'd end up looking like some battered linebacker! Dear God, it didn't bear thinking about.

He tried to pout but, finding his lips were too swollen, let out a melodramatic wail instead.

"Well," said Rachel firmly, "you can explain it all to me at the police station. If you won't go to the hospital then at least we can report the incident."

"You don't understand, Rach." He shook his head. "I can't go to the police."

Draining the rest of his Grand Marnier for courage, he decided to come clean with her. He was in over his head and he had to talk to someone.

Once he'd gotten over his initial nerves, he soon discovered that stopping horses for cash was in fact laughably easy. Unfortunately, as his income shot up, so did his expenditure. Women were an expensive habit, as was coke—and it wasn't long before greed got the better of him and he started using his inside info to place bets on his own online account. Ali had strictly forbidden personal bets, for the sensible reason that they drew unnecessary attention to their scam. The odd little indiscretion here or there he might have forgiven. But Jasper's recent wagers had been enormous. Hence today's "personal warning."

For a few moments Rachel was stunned. Not only that she'd somehow managed to miss all this but that Jasper had had the foresight and daring to try such a thing in the first place.

"Probably a silly question," she said eventually, "but it is illegal, isn't it?"

"Abducting people and beating them up?" snarled Jasper. "Yes, of course it's illegal." He scowled at his reflection again. "Do you think my nose could be reset?"

"No, not that," said Rachel tetchily. "I mean you, placing all those bets."

"Well, yes, technically," said Jasper. "But it's damned difficult to prove. And there's a lot of money in it, if you've got the balls. How do you think I've been paying for all the holidays and the Porsche and that ruby pendant I bought you?"

Rachel's mind was working overtime. The truth was, she neither knew nor cared how he'd paid for them until now, although with hindsight she supposed it *was* rather odd that his racing career had been going one way while his bank balance went the other. Certainly this new, daring, rich Jasper who dabbled with dark criminal forces was a lot more interesting and exciting a boyfriend than the old dull and lazy version. But she had to be careful. Enjoying his money was one thing, but she couldn't afford to let her own image get tarnished if somehow he got caught.

"What are you going to do now?" she asked him. "D'you think . . . I mean, will Ali still want you to work for him?"

"Probably." Jasper nodded with an involuntary shiver. "I'm too far in to go back now."

This was true. And even if it hadn't been, he didn't see much of an alternative to going back to work other than playing it straight, facing up to his lack of talent as a jockey, and crawling back home to Linda, none of which was an option.

"Is there anything I can do?" murmured Rachel, already lost in a fantasy of herself as a gorgeous gangster's moll, loyally watching Jasper battling it out with gangs of East End thugs in order to keep her in illicit furs and jewels.

"Well, first of all," he sighed, relieved that she seemed to be taking it all so well, "I need a decent cover story for my mother. Something to distract her from the bruises, stop her asking too many questions."

Rachel's eyes lit up. Dashing back into the bathroom, she retrieved the *Playboy* and handed it to him.

"Page twenty-two," she said triumphantly. "If that doesn't distract your ma, nothing will."

"Jeeeeeeeesus!" said Jasper, the pain in his face momentarily forgotten as he stared, stunned, at his sister's pictures. The last time he'd seen Milly was right after their dad's funeral. She was barely recognizable as the same girl, and not just because she was naked. Rachel might not want to admit it, but she looked good. Damned good.

"After all the fuss she made about my *Loaded* shots, too." Rachel pouted. "What do you think?"

"I think," he said slowly, still unable to tear his eyes away from the pictures, "that for once in her life my little sister might actually have done me a favor. Mummy's going to hit the roof. And you"—he kissed her, wincing at the stinging in his lips—"are a bloody genius."

In New York for his annual end-of-summer trip, Jimmy Price was in a foul mood.

The city had awoken to a beautiful September morning. Bright rays of sunshine broke through the few solitary clouds, as clear and tangible as strands of copper, and the lingering fall blossoms on the trees outside the Four Seasons were still bursting forth in a candy-cane riot of pink and white, as if unwilling to admit that the long hot summer was finally over.

But Jimmy was oblivious to the beauty surrounding him.

Thanks to yesterday's unexpected rise in interest rates, he'd woken up to find his share price had fallen by 5 percent overnight, and spent the first two hours of his day on the phone, trying to reassure worried investors. He really ought to fly back to California and sort things out in person. But he'd been looking forward to this New York trip for months and was damned if he was going to miss today's racing.

"Can I get you anything, sir? More toast?"

The waiter was unobtrusively polite, a mascot for the impeccable service that kept Jimmy coming back to the Four Seasons when he could so easily have bought and furnished a permanent town house in the city. Candy was always on at him to get them a place in New York. But Jimmy liked hotels. They were efficient and impersonal, rather like him.

"No thanks," he said, not glancing up from the *New York Times*'s sports pages. "Just some fresh coffee. Very hot."

Ever since he bought his first horse, Lost and Found, over a decade ago he'd become addicted to racing, to the degree that numerous members of his board complained frequently and vociferously about the amount of time he spent at the track. It was hard to pinpoint exactly what it was—the exhilaration of winning, of course, was always a high; but he loved the social side of horse racing too, the kudos that being a successful owner brought him in the sort of smart, old-money circles where being a billionaire press baron didn't necessarily cut it. Owning racehorses legitimized his wealth. It socially laundered and gentrified it. Plus, it provided a unique escape from the pressures and problems in the rest of his life.

After his first wife killed herself, he'd started coming to the track to forget and block out his guilt, pouring all his emotional energy into his horses—Thoroughbreds first, and later American quarter horses. As the years passed, and the hideous train wreck of his first marriage faded to a faint memory, he kept coming. Now it was the rush of being envied that gave him the biggest thrill. Walking into a stadium or a party with the radiantly beautiful Candy on his arm, knowing that every other owner wanted her: It was a buzz beyond anything he'd experienced in his business life.

If it hadn't been for Amy, he might have succeeded in blocking out the past altogether. But every time he looked at his daughter's overweight, unhappy face, he saw her mother staring back at him. Her very existence was like a reproach, a daily reminder of all the mistakes he'd made, all the damage he'd done that could never be undone. Some days he could barely bring himself to look at her.

He wouldn't have let her tag along to New York if Candy hadn't insisted that they needed her help with the boys. Yet another nanny had quit a few days ago—the fifth this year—so if they wanted Chase and Chance with them, it was Amy or nothing.

If only she could have been a little more like Milly. Disciplined, focused, and ambitious far beyond his expectations, Milly had moved mountains to lose her extra saddle weight and had already proved herself totally committed to her training as well as to building her commercial value with the media. He could have used a daughter like that.

Though it wasn't to his personal taste, the *Playboy* shoot had been one hell of a coup so early in her career. He was proud of her—although, of course, it was Todd Cranborn he really had to thank for that.

Todd had also turned out to be a pleasant surprise. Most of these property guys were all piss and wind, but Cranborn had already gotten him in on the ground floor of two very interesting real estate propositions—one of which, a deal to build a bunch of condos out in Orlando, he was seriously considering financing in its entirety.

Unfortunately, dabbling in real estate was small fry in comparison to the grim prognosis for Price Media, Inc.'s stock price. Fucking bank rates. Why hadn't his economists seen this coming? What the fuck was he paying those bozos for anyway?

Spearing the last morsel of crispy bacon dripping with egg yolk onto his fork, he gazed out of the window at the bright sunshine of the morning and frowned.

The share price free fall wasn't the only thing bringing him down this morning. Last night he'd embarrassingly lost his erection halfway through making love to Candy. She'd seemed unfazed by it at the time, rolling over and falling back to sleep as though nothing had happened. But he fervently hoped this lapse didn't mark the beginning of the end for his virility. Most of his contemporaries, he knew, now relied heavily on Viagra to keep their much younger second or third wives satisfied. But due to an inherited heart condition, he was unable to resort to the magic blue pill. It worried him.

Losing his wife was the worst thing Jimmy could possibly imagine. Worse even than losing his company or, God forbid, his horses. In his eyes, Candy was the pinnacle of womanhood. Marrying her had been his finest single achievement, payback for all those girls who'd rejected him in college when he was just a nerdy, ginger-haired kid without two bucks to rub together.

Buffy, his first wife, had loved him back then. Back when he'd had nothing. But she'd never made him feel as confident, as fucking triumphant and elated, as Candy did.

She'd be upstairs in their suite right now, he reflected. Showering, most probably. The thought of his wife's naked, dripping, soap-covered body made his dick start to harden.

"Great," he mumbled bitterly, dabbing at the corners of his mouth with a napkin and waving to his server for the check. "That's just great, buddy. A fat lot of use you are to me now."

In fact it was Amy, not Candy, who was still in the shower.

The twins had been driving her insane since daybreak, shrieking the place down, demanding their mother, and generally wreaking havoc. Their favorite trick was to run amok among the priceless Japanese vases and early American sculptures in the Presidential Suite, no doubt chosen by some childless, gay interior designer who'd be horrified to see his objets d'art being used as makeshift footballs.

Candy, as usual, was no help at all. She'd spent the last hour and a half locked in the bathroom, adding the finishing touches to her already flawless makeup. She wanted to look perfect, if not better, when they got to the track, knowing every eye would be on her.

Amy longed to start getting ready herself. Today she would finally see Garth again, for the first time in almost a year. She hadn't slept a wink all night for thinking about it. But, unfortunately, not even *SpongeBob SquarePants,* usually a fail-safe pacifier, had calmed the boys down this morning, and she'd had to wait till they burned themselves out and fell asleep on the couch before she could at last make a dash to the bathroom.

Sitting on the stone ledge of the enormous power shower, she let the blasting jets of hot water soothe her, rinsing away shampoo suds along with all the aches in her muscles. She was so tired, all she wanted to do was crawl back into bed and sleep.

Yesterday had been a terrible day. Her long-anticipated meeting with the publisher in midtown was a crushing disappointment. They said they liked her poems, but it soon became clear that their real interest was in getting her to pen some sort of exposé of her father.

"How did it feel to lose your mother in your teens and in such a cruel way?" the hard-faced, hair-sprayed harridan from nonfiction had asked her, reaching out and placing her emaciated, crone's hand on Amy's knee, presumably in an attempt at sympathy.

I mean, what sort of a person did they think she was?

She would never betray her dad like that, in print or otherwise. Never.

Grabbing the loofah, she began scrubbing at her butt and thighs—she'd read somewhere that scrubbing was good for the circulation and reduced cellulite—gently at first, but then harder and harder, until big red welts began to appear on her flesh. Somewhat to her own surprise, she found herself starting to cry.

Sometimes she wanted to rub herself out. Just scrape off all the fat and fear and failure and start again.

She must have been crazy, thinking anyone would actually want to buy her poems. Why would they? As for getting Garth to love her again—as if he ever had in the first place—that was even crazier. With a body like hers she couldn't hope to attract any man, let alone one as beautiful and talented as he was.

If only Milly were here to talk to. Milly was forever telling her she was lovely and worth a million Garths and that if people couldn't see past a little extra weight it was their problem.

Easy to say when you had a *Playboy*-perfect body yourself, of course.

Wiping away her tears, she made an effort to pull herself together. Milly was her friend. She must *not* be envious. It was far too mean-spirited.

She'd just have to do the best she could to smarten herself up before the twins woke up. After that, whatever happened with Garth would be in the lap of the gods.

They were late arriving at the Aqueduct, plunging Jimmy into an even more toxic mood as they filed en famille into his private box. He was still grumbling about the terrible Queens traffic as he took his seat next to Candy.

"Honey, do you mind if ah run to the restroom?" she asked, interrupting another rant. Immaculate in a demure white Armani skirt and blue silk shirt, she smelled of Rive Gauche and rose oil, and he could feel her silken blond hair brushing the side of his cheek as she leaned close to speak to him. Fuck, she was beautiful.

"Sure." He smiled at her indulgently. "Just don't be long, okay? The next race should be a good one. And you know how I like to show you off."

"Awww, baby." Getting up from her seat, she planted a kiss in the middle of his carefully blow-dried and lacquered ginger bouffant. "My little Jiminy Cricket. Course I won't be long."

Eeeugh, thought Amy. Somebody pass me a bucket.

Chase and Chance had finally stopped crying and were munching their way through peanut butter and jelly sandwiches beside her, excited to be out watching the "hosees." It had taken so long to get them ready, she'd had next to no time to dress herself. In the end she'd grabbed the nearest thing at hand: a shapeless cream linen dress, which did her absolutely no favors, and flat pumps. Her pale blond hair still hung damp and limp to her shoulders—there'd been no time to dry it, let alone style it—and the bronzer and mascara she'd hurriedly applied before running out the door failed to hide the telltale traces of exhaustion on her face.

"Is that the best you could do?" Jimmy observed viciously, as she got into the limo. "You could've at least dried your hair. It's embarrassing."

Biting back her tears—streaky mascara would be adding insult to injury at this point—Amy felt the last vestiges of self-esteem crumbling.

Why did he have to be so cruel?

"You know what, Dad?" she said now, lumbering to her feet at the back of the box a few minutes after Candy's exit. "I think I need the restroom too."

Against her better judgment, she planned to take a walk down to the paddock in the hope of seeing Garth. In her mind's eye she pictured herself accidentally-on-purpose bumping into him and delivering her carefully prepared, nonchalant line about what a surprise it was to run into him before the race.

"Now?" said Jimmy testily. "What about the boys?"

"Oh, they're fine for a minute," she insisted. "Anyway, I need to pee. I won't be long."

Before he could raise any further objections she slipped out and hurried down through the stands toward the paddock. Garth, unfortunately, was nowhere to be seen.

Damn it. If she had to wait till after the race, he'd be surrounded by people and she'd never get a chance to speak to him alone.

Looking around, she saw the large, trampled, muddy area to the left of the stands and behind the winners' enclosure that served as a makeshift parking lot for competitors' trailers. It was closed to the public, cordoned off with a sagging line of rope and manned by a couple of racecourse officials. But they all knew Amy was Jimmy Price's daughter and cheerily waved her through.

Hitching her dress up above the worst of the mud, she picked her way through the trailers, ignoring the curious looks and sniggers from other jockeys and trainers as she passed. If anyone stopped her she would simply say she was lost and looking for the ladies' room. No one needed to know she'd been searching for Garth like a lost puppy.

She was on the point of giving up and heading back to the box— Jimmy would go ape shit if she left the twins alone for too long—when she suddenly stopped dead in her tracks.

For there, not ten feet in front of her, was Garth.

Sitting on one of those portable, folding chairs behind one of her father's horse trailers, he had his breeches around his ankles and was being straddled by an enthusiastically moaning Candy, whose white Armani skirt was pushed up around her hips as she bucked and arched on top of him.

"Oh, Garth! Garth!" she panted, as the taut, toned globes of her pantyless buttocks slapped down audibly and rhythmically against the tops of his thighs. "Harder! C'mon, baby."

Amy stood transfixed. Bizarrely, all she seemed able to think about in that instant was that her stepmother sounded just as bossy and demanding during sex as she did normally.

If it hadn't been Garth, she'd probably have laughed. The whole scene was so sordid and ridiculous. But it was Garth—her Garth, the Garth who she remembered making love to *her* last summer as if it were yesterday. The expression of selfish urgency and concentration he wore on his face now as he tried to make himself come was hideously, grotesquely familiar.

Then suddenly, with no warning, he opened his eyes and looked right at her. Amy's stomach lurched.

She could feel her knees shaking and hoped she wasn't going to sink ignominiously into the sodden ground, but the feeling of faintness wouldn't go away. Pain, embarrassment, and shock welled up simultaneously within her till her vision blurred and her head began to throb.

This couldn't be happening. It couldn't.

Candy could have any man she wanted.

Why did the heartless bitch have to pick Garth?

Now she was looking right at him, waiting for a look of guilty surprise to register on his face. She had, after all, caught him in flagrante with her father's wife. Surely that concept must worry him just a little?

But instead, without breaking the rhythm of his thrusts for so much as a second, he smiled at her.

The bastard actually smiled.

The next thing Amy knew she was running, blinded by sobs, back through the maze of trailers and out into the crowds thronging around the paddock, preparing to place their bets. Dabbing her eyes and gulping big, deep breaths of air into her lungs, she willed herself to get a grip.

She couldn't just collapse. She had to get back to the kids.

"Where the hell have you been?" Before she had a second to compose herself, she looked up to see her dad yelling down at her, leaning over the edge of the box. "That must have been the longest piss in history."

A few people around her tittered, but she didn't care. Holding it together somehow, she climbed back up through the stands, taking her seat as quietly and unobtrusively as she could. Chase and Chance, bored now that the novelty of the horses was wearing off, immediately began clambering all over her, smothering her dress in sticky, peanut butter handprints. Half an hour ago she'd have cared—another outfit ruined. Now, she almost welcomed the distraction.

"Did you see Candy down there?" asked Jimmy tersely.

"Sorry?"

"Jeez. Candy. In the fuckin' ladies'. Was she there?" he repeated.

"No," said Amy, blushing scarlet at the lie. "She wasn't. I guess she must have tried a different restroom. Looking for a shorter line or something."

Right on cue, the door to the box opened and Candy sauntered in.

Her blond mane of hair, that minutes ago had been flowing long and loose around her shoulders, was now pinned up once again in a neat chignon and her eyes were covered with huge, Jackie-O sunglasses.

Guilt concealers, thought Amy bitterly.

"Sorry ah took so long," she drawled, slipping back into her seat next to Jimmy without so much as a glance in Amy's direction.

Perhaps she didn't know she'd been spotted? Amy had assumed Garth would have told her, but maybe he hadn't?

"Never mind," said Jimmy. "You're here now." Reaching over, he took her hand—the same hand that had just been wrapped like a vise around Garth's cock—and pressed it to his lips.

Amy felt the bile rising up in her throat.

"Sorry," she said, staggering out of her seat. "I'm really not feeling well. I think I need some air."

Jimmy frowned. "What's eating her?"

"Who knows?" said Candy, snuggling in closer to him. "Lovesick, ah expect. You know what a crush she has on Garth. Forget about it."

"Don't you worry," he said, running his hand proprietorially up the inside of her thigh. "I intend to."

CHAPTER TWENTY-TWO

October proved to be an exhausting month for Milly. As Todd predicted, her appearance in *Playboy* catapulted her into the public eye far more effectively than her racing could ever have done, and her promotional work quadrupled overnight. Not since Liz Hurley showed up at Hugh Grant's premiere in a couple of safety pins had one picture made such a difference to a girl's career. Suddenly it wasn't just Western-wear companies queuing up to sponsor her. Everyone from potato chip manufacturers to perfumiers to cell phone giants began beating a path to Brad Gaisford's door. And it wasn't just Milly herself that these endorsements helped put on the map. Interest in the whole sport of quarter horse racing climbed to an all-time high. Local cable channels now found themselves competing with the likes of ESPN for TV rights to races that two years ago could barely raise a half-decent local audience. Times were changing in the sport, and there was a tangible smell of money in the air.

At first Milly felt giddy with excitement, being at the epicenter of it all. With a string of valuable endorsements under her belt and her track record going from strength to strength, she had a lot to celebrate. Her schedule left her no time to dwell on her insecurities over Todd, or any other troubling thoughts, such as how her mother had reacted to the pictures, or what terrible things Rachel might be doing at Newells.

But it wasn't long before a sort of jaded exhaustion kicked in. She was still putting in good times, but she knew she could have done better if she weren't permanently being pulled in a million different directions. Plus a lot of the work she was doing, though well paid, was cheesy as hell; the sort of tacky interpretation of cowboy culture that used to send Bobby off into stratospheric rages. She couldn't help but feel a little guilty to be part of it.

As for Todd, she'd barely seen him in weeks. Staggering home in the small hours most nights she'd collapse into bed beside him, too shattered even to think about sex, and then have to dash off to the stables or for business meetings with Brad at the crack of dawn. Todd never complained. He was a workaholic himself, after all. But Milly couldn't help but fret that her long absences must be leaving a hole in his life and his bed that a string of LA whores were falling over themselves to fill.

She was also worried about Demon. Still dogged by health problems, the last thing he needed was to be overraced. But despite her protestations, Jimmy and Brad kept entering him for all the biggest meetings, insisting that the horse and Milly were branded as a team now and that the crowds turned out for both of them.

It was weird, to have success arrive so quickly and effortlessly, only to find herself less in control of her own life than she had been before.

A month after his return from New York, Jimmy threw a party at Koi in Milly's honor, to celebrate her landing a much-coveted endorsement deal with T-Mobile. There were hundreds of sportsmen and -women in far better known fields who would have given their right arm for such a deal—Garth Mavers was positively fuming about it, apparently—so for a little known, foreign rider like Milly to pull it off was quite a coup.

But after another long day, yukking it up at Koi with a bunch of Jimmy's cronies and T-Mobile execs was the last thing Milly felt like doing. Especially with an important race tomorrow at Fresno. Her attendance wasn't optional, and at least it would provide a chance for her to chat to Amy properly, something she hadn't been able to do since the Prices got back from New York. She felt bad about that actually, as Amy was obviously very down. But it couldn't be helped.

"I think a toast is in order." Jimmy smiled at the assembled guests, grasping his beer glass with a fat, clammy paw and raising it high. "To Milly, our very own English cowgirl."

"To Milly!" An assenting murmur rumbled around the bar.

Shifting uneasily on her bar stool, Milly tried to look happy and suitably humble—not an easy look in the outfit Brad had picked out for the occasion and insisted that she wear: a dramatic red Badgley Mischka dress, backless and slashed to the tops of the thighs, and a borrowed Fred Leighton diamond pendant that wouldn't have looked out of place at the Oscars.

The paparazzi, who'd shown up in force half an hour ago, after a tip-off from Brad, were thrilled with her over-the-top look. Stepping out of the Ferrari with Todd, she brought La Cienega to a virtual stand-still, posing for picture after picture with her new crystal-encrusted, customized cell phone clearly visible in every shot.

That part, she had to admit, was fun. But as soon as she got inside she felt like an overdressed idiot. Everyone else was in jeans, even Candy, who looked sick-makingly stunning in a simple silver Chloe top. Todd wasted no time rushing over to say hello to her, which plunged Milly into even deeper gloom.

Spearing a raw sea urchin with a toothpick, she plunged it angrily into some soy sauce, then put it in her mouth, instantly regretting it as a horrible salty ooze seeped out over her taste buds.

Naturally it was right at that moment that Sean came over to corner her.

"Enjoying yourself?" he asked, since it was quite obvious she wasn't.

Trying not to vomit, Milly spat the offending mollusk into a paper napkin and took two huge gulps of Diet Coke before replying.

"No," she said honestly, staring at Candy's lissome brown back. "Not really."

Following her gaze, Sean saw Candy whispering in Todd's ear, and Todd throwing his head back with laughter. God, the man was a wanker. Whatever Milly's faults (and as far as he was concerned there were many), she deserved better than having to put up with a smug cunt like Cranborn for a boyfriend.

"Ignore him," he said. "He's only doing it to wind you up."

Milly looked at him, amazed. It was the first time Sean had ever said anything remotely nice to her. She had no idea how to react.

"Do you think so?" she said doubtfully.

"Sure. Besides, you're getting your fair share of attention in that little number." He glanced at her utterly inappropriate red dress, which was indeed drawing stares from all around the restaurant, and smiled. Despite herself, Milly smiled back.

"Look," he said, taking advantage of this unexpected thawing in relations to make a serious point. "I've been meaning to talk to you actually. I'm worried about Amy."

"Oh, me too." Milly nodded fervently. "Have you spoken to her? I was hoping I'd see her tonight, but she doesn't seem to be around."

"I think she's been making herself sick," said Sean. "She's losing weight like crazy. My guess is it's something to do with Garth Mavers."

"He's such a fucking prick, that guy," said Milly with feeling.

"He is," agreed Sean. "And a little bird told me he's been using his fucking prick to service the wicked stepmother over there." He nodded toward Candy. "Five'll get you ten that's why our little Amy's been sobbing her heart out."

"Really?" said Milly. She knew she ought to be concerned for poor Amy. But she couldn't help but feel a smidgen of relief for herself. If Garth was screwing Mrs. Price, it stood to reason that Todd wasn't.

"She needs you, you know," said Sean, as if reading her mind. "Amy. She's always been a good friend to you. But now that she needs support herself, you're never around."

"Yes, I am." Milly instantly bristled. What was it that made Sean think he had the right to preach to her? And since when was her and Amy's friendship any of his business? "I've just been crazy busy since the whole *Playboy* thing. You know what it's like. There's never enough time in the day."

Sean shrugged.

"Whatever," he said, downing the rest of his drink with a last, meaningful look at Todd. "But, if you ask me, I'd say you have an uncanny knack of making time for all the wrong people."

The next morning dawned crisp and clear over the Fresno district fair. By ten A.M., when Milly arrived, it was sunny enough to warrant the giant sunglasses that obscured the best part of her face and protected her from prying eyes as much as from the intense, crystalline blue sky.

Having ridden competitively since she was four years old, Milly rarely suffered from pre-race jitters, but today she felt jumpier than a bird in a cattery. This was her first race since becoming T-Mobile's "English Cowgirl," and she knew every eye would be on her. She might have felt better if she'd gotten a good night's sleep. But her conversation with Sean at last night's party, about Candy and Garth's affair and her not being a good friend to Amy, kept coming back to her. She'd lain awake for hours, next to a drunkenly snoring Todd, alternating between anger at Sean for sticking his nose in and disappointment in herself, because deep down she knew he was right.

She'd hoped to drive up to Palos Verdes early this morning, check on Demon before he got loaded into the trailer, and, hopefully, see Amy. Maybe if they drove to the track together it would give them a chance to catch up?

Unfortunately, her new sponsors had other ideas. A car had arrived at six to whisk her off to a radio interview for KCRW, where some imbecilic DJ had proceeded to ask her a bunch of fatuous questions about ranching and whether she preferred rounding up cattle to horse racing. Then, after a snatched breakfast at Dunkin' Donuts, where she managed to scald her tongue on coffee that she'd helpfully succeeded in sweetening with salt, it was straight to the racecourse for three solid hours of glad-handing in the corporate hospitality tent.

Not only had she not seen Amy, or Demon, all morning but Todd had flaked on her yet again. He'd sworn faithfully this morning that he'd be at the track by eleven. But at one o'clock, when she was at last allowed to go change into her silks, there was still no sign of him, or even any message on her cell phone.

"Asshole," she muttered under her breath as she climbed up onto the scales. All the smiling and nodding she'd been doing had left her with an aching jaw and a neck as weak as a strand of overcooked spaghetti.

But as soon as she saw Demon, his tail swishing happily in eagerness for the race ahead and all the attention he was going to get, her heart lifted. Vaulting onto his back, Milly walked him over to the paddock, patting his neck and talking to him constantly. Sadly, even there, with minutes to go before the race, she wasn't to be allowed any peace. She could have coped with the press photographers. They were easy enough to tune out. But Reuben Goldstein, the pushy little nerd with fishy breath and a striking profusion of nose hair who some lunatic at T-Mobile had assigned as her PR guy, refused to leave her side, running after her and Demon like a shadow.

"What you gotta remember," he was telling her in his whiny, reed-thin voice, jogging to keep up as she tried repeatedly to trot away from him, "is to always be camera ready. In layman's terms, that means smile and know your lines—you're thrilled to be representing the T-3000, blah, blah, blah. . . . Got it?"

"Sure, Reuben." Looking around for any excuse to escape, she was overjoyed to catch sight of Amy making her way over from the stands. "I'm sorry, but you'll have to excuse me," she said. "That's a friend of mine." And, nudging Demon into a canter, she rode off, leaving him mid-sentence.

"Making your escape from Captain Charisma, I see?" said Amy.

Milly grinned. "Yeah. He's a nightmare."

Sean was right. Amy had lost an astonishing amount of weight. Today she was in jeans and a blue shirt, nothing particularly exciting, but for the first time ever Milly could see her waist. Unfortunately, she also looked terribly pale and drawn. And despite her attempts to put on a cheerful front, her eyes were clearly puffy and red from a very recent bout of crying.

"But, look, never mind Reuben," said Milly. "What's been going on with you? I've hardly seen you since— Oh, hang on a sec."

A group of teenage boys, egging one another on with nudges and shoves, came up to her with disposable cameras and autograph books, begging for pictures.

"You're the *Playboy* girl, right?" asked the boldest, blushing like a stoplight.

"Among other things," said Milly.

Amy stood back and watched the way her face lit up at the attention. She really was loving it. Needless to say, none of the boys gave *her* a second glance.

She tried not to feel resentful. But it was hard. Before *Playboy*, Milly had been her constant companion. Now she was never, but never, around. Whatever her protestations to the contrary it was clear she reveled in her newfound fame. She justified it by telling herself, and anyone else who'd listen, that all she wanted was to raise enough money to buy back her family home. But more and more that was starting to look like an excuse, a front to allow her to bask in the limelight to her heart's content.

She'd changed in other ways too, all too often egged on by Todd. Two weeks ago she'd pulled a no-show at Amy's birthday dinner, when he offered at the last minute to take her with him to some industry bash in Century City.

"You understand, don't you?" she said the next day, calling with a belated and halfhearted apology. "He's been working so hard recently, I didn't want to let him down."

Of course not, thought Amy. But letting me down—that's not a problem, is it?

It was always the same story. Whenever there was a chance that the press might show up at an event, Milly hurtled off like an iron filing toward a magnet. In LA speak, this was known as doing a BBD (bigger, better deal), something the old Milly would have abhorred. But these days she made Paris Hilton look camera shy.

"Sorry." Turning away from the boys at last she beamed at Amy. "What were you saying?"

"Nothing," said Amy quietly. "I wasn't saying anything. I never got the chance."

"Oh." Milly looked nonplussed. "Sorry. Oh, come on, don't be mad at me. Tell me what's wrong?"

Amy longed to tell her. She longed to unburden herself about New York, about Garth and that cheating whore Candy, about the look he'd given her like she was nothing, or worse than nothing, like she was a laughingstock. About the publishers only being interested in a tell-all about her father. About how weird it was to feel so fat and ugly and yet, at the same time, invisible. At least the combined misery of these two events had finally prompted her to lose some weight. But not even that silver lining could stop it hurting or take away her need to confide in someone.

Months ago that someone would have been Milly. But she was so caught up in her own world now, it was impossible. She wouldn't have understood.

"I'm not mad. And nothing's wrong," she lied. "I'm a little tired, that's all. The twins have been worse than usual this week."

Both girls turned to look as a stream of riders started moving past them toward the gates.

"Looks like that's your cue," said Amy.

"Yeah," said Milly. Their conversation hadn't exactly been the bonding session she'd hoped for, but there was no time to dwell on it now. Her nerves were back with a vengeance, so much so that she was almost relieved now that Todd hadn't made it in time. She already felt under more performance pressure than she could bear.

A few minutes later, Amy had joined Sean front and center in the grandstand, next to an anxious-looking Gill. Jimmy had had to fly up to Canada on urgent business this morning, so for once he wasn't there to cheer on his protégée. But a record-breaking crowd *had* turned out to see the *Playmate* rider in action.

"D'you want my coat?" said Sean, not waiting for an answer as he slipped off his leather jacket and wrapped it around Amy's shoulders. "It's getting cool in this breeze. You're shivering like mad."

"I'm okay," she said. "I'm nervous for Milly, that's all." Despite her recent self-absorption, the real Milly was still in there somewhere. Amy wasn't ready to give up on her just yet. "I really want her to do well out there."

"I know you do," said Sean, squeezing her hand. "The funny thing is, so do I."

The rest of his words were drowned out as, with a great roar, the crowd leaped to its feet. Sixteen quarter horses shot out of the gates—

Milly and Demon were slap bang in the middle of the pack—and were almost immediately lost in a cloud of dust.

"Nice start," muttered Gill under her breath. She must have X-ray vision, thought Amy, who couldn't make out a thing through the dust and who had to rely on the announcer's voice telling her that after breaking from post three, Milly had quickly opened up a half-length lead over Dash with Ease.

"Look. There she is!" said Sean, pointing out a tiny hunched figure at the front of the pack a few seconds later. "See her?"

"Yes. Yes!" said Amy, hopping up and down excitedly. "I see her. If she can just hold that lead . . ."

But at around a hundred and fifty yards out, something suddenly happened. The crowd groaned as one, but the visibility was so bad, it was hard to see what the commotion was about. All Amy was aware of were equine legs flailing in the air and jockeys looking anxiously back over their shoulders as they rode on.

"What is it?" she asked, turning to Sean. "Did you see?"

"It's Demon," he said, already vaulting over the barrier onto the turf below. "He's down."

Sitting on the hard ground of the track, her head pounding as though millions of little men with hammers and anvils had magically materialized inside her skull, Milly struggled to reorient herself. By the time she'd begun to make sense of her surroundings the race was already over. Some of the other riders were cantering back toward her, joining the growing crowd of race officials, paramedics, and Looky Loos who already seemed to have appeared out of nowhere.

"I'm pleased to tell ya that Milly Lockwood Groves is sitting up, folks," the commentator's voice rang out over the loudspeaker. "Looks like she's okay. But we do ask you to please keep back from the trackside so the veterinarians and paramedics can do their jobs."

Scanning the strange sea of faces, Milly searched vainly for anyone familiar and was immensely relieved to see Sean, head down like an angry bullock, forcing his way through the throng.

"You okay?" he asked, when he finally reached her.

She nodded weakly. He didn't think he'd ever seen her look so vulnerable. Tears of bewilderment and shock were streaming down her face.

"What happened?" he asked gently. "You seemed to be going great."

"I don't know," she sobbed. "One minute we were ahead and the next . . ."

She looked across at Demon, who was still lying immobile on the ground only a few yards from where she'd been thrown. His chest was heaving with alarming speed, and he was wheezing like a pair of broken bellows. When he saw Sean, his watery eyes widened in what could have been recognition but could just as easily have been fear or pain. A slow, steady trickle of blood was pouring from his flared nostril onto the grass.

"Please, don't try and move, miss." One of the paramedics laid a hand on Milly's shoulder as she staggered woozily to her feet. But she brushed him aside, stumbling blindly over to where Demon lay.

Please God, let him be okay. Just let him be okay.

Kneeling at his side, Sean was already loading up a shot of Dormosedan to calm him enough to be examined. She could hear the track vet filling him in on what happened.

"It was awful," he was saying. "I saw the whole thing. Blood was flying out of his nose, then his foreleg just kinda crumpled underneath him. Like snappin' a match," he added, cracking his knuckles for emphasis. Sean winced. "Poor fella went straight down."

Milly heard a noise coming out of her mouth that was part scream, part primal, grief-laden moan. She shouldn't have raced him. Why hadn't she stood up to Brad and Jimmy? Why hadn't she protected him?

An announcement echoed around the grandstands that Dash with Ease was the official winner, but nobody seemed in celebratory mood. All eyes remained firmly glued to the drama unfolding on the track.

Soon it was not just eyes but cameras too. It was always sad when a horse was seriously injured, but Demon being so young made it all the more poignant—and newsworthy. But of course, the real story was that it had happened to Milly, and during her first major, nationally televised race too.

Who knew quarter horse racing had so much drama? ESPN was certainly getting its money's worth.

While Milly was distracted talking to Sean, banks of TV cameras seemed to have emerged spontaneously from the earth like the hounds of hell. Within seconds they'd surrounded her, forming a threatening, intrusive wall between her and Demon's prone, shuddering body.

The yelled questions came one after the other, like machine-gun fire.

"Milly, are you hurt?"

"Did somebody bump you?"

"Is Demon gonna make it? What have they told you?"

"Milly! Look up! Over here, sweetheart."

"Christ," said Sean, shaking his head as an overwhelmed race steward struggled to push back the baying media. "Can't you do something? Get those fockers out of my face? This animal's terrified enough as it is."

Finally, after what felt like an eternity, reinforcements arrived, led by Gill, who managed with some difficulty to convince Milly to leave the vets to it and come inside.

"You're not helping him by staying out here, you know," she said gently. "The sooner you leave, the sooner the TV crews will back off. It's you they're interested in, not Demon."

She was right, of course. Brushing aside the army of track doctors and jittery insurance agents who kept trying to convince her to go to the local hospital, Milly let Gill take her into the relative privacy of the clubhouse. Relative because the place was swarming with T-Mobile execs, led by an excited-looking Reuben.

"Any news?" Milly sounded desperate.

"Not yet," he said, stepping forward to remove a smudge of dirt from her cheekbone with his handkerchief. "But in the meantime, let's talk about how we present this."

Milly looked blank. "What do you mean? Present what?"

Reuben gave her the same look an impatient teacher might give a retarded student.

"The story," he sighed, exasperated. "We have to take control of the story. Present you in the best possible light. I'm sorry if that sounds callous, but it's my job."

Milly was so dumbfounded that at first she said nothing. Didn't he realize that Demon was fighting for his life out there?

Misreading her silence as acquiescence, Reuben went on.

"The main thing is to keep it real. To let people see what you're feeling. That way, if he makes it, the fans can feel the joy and relief right along with you. And if he doesn't—"

The shrill, insistent ring of Gill's cell phone cut him off before he could finish, leaving Milly no time to arrange the words "yourself," "fuck," and "go" into a coherent sentence.

"Hello?" Gill picked up. Milly and Reuben both stared wordlessly as she turned her back on them, cradling the receiver tightly against her ear so she could hear better.

"Uh-huh." She nodded, after what felt like an interminable silence. "Okay, yeah. I'll tell her."

When she turned back around, her face told Milly everything she needed to know.

"He's dead, isn't he?"

"I'm sorry," said Gill, the tears brimming in her own eyes. "But, yes. That was Sean. There was nothing more he could do."

The next three hours were a complete blur. Milly remembered sleep-walking through a couple of TV interviews and was dimly aware of an endless series of camera flashbulbs and microphones being thrust in her face before Todd finally arrived and took her back to Jimmy's trailer.

"It's my fault!" she sobbed, flinging herself into his arms. "I should never have raced him today. I pushed him too hard."

"Nonsense," said Todd, wishing she wouldn't use one of his best Gucci jackets as a handkerchief. "He was a racehorse, darling, not a pet. And it was Jimmy's decision to run him, not yours. These things happen. You mustn't beat yourself up."

It was hardly the comforting response Milly had been hoping for. Suddenly she remembered the way that Bobby had comforted her after Easy died—the warmth and the love and the understanding that they'd shared. Unlike Todd, Bobby knew what it was to love an animal. He knew the pain she was going through.

For the first time in many long months, Milly found herself wanting to talk to him. But after all this time, and with the feud between him and Todd running hotter than ever, her bridges back to Highwood were well and truly burned.

"Knock, knock. Can I come in?" Amy's kindly face appeared around the trailer door.

Milly's eyes welled up with tears of gratitude. She didn't think she'd ever been so pleased to see anyone.

But before she could speak, Todd took control. "Thank you, Amy, but she's fine," he said. One hand was already on the door, ready to shut her out. "What she needs is a hot bath and bed. I'm going to take her home and see that she gets both."

"Mill?" Refusing to be fobbed off, Amy pushed her head further into the room and raised a questioning eyebrow at her friend. "Are you sure? There's nothing that you need? Even just to talk?"

For a second, Milly wavered. She would have loved to talk to Amy. To say sorry for the way she was before, for not listening, and to pour her guilty heart out about Demon. Amy might not be a horse lover, but she was the most instinctively sympathetic and kind person Milly had ever met. But one look at Todd's impatient face changed her mind. He'd always hated Amy, for reasons Milly had never fully understood. Asking her in now would only cause a row between them. And she didn't have the mental strength to deal with that, not now.

Todd might not be the warmest and cuddliest of boyfriends. But right now he was all she had.

"Yeah," she said. "I'm sure. Thanks. Todd's taking care of me."

"See?" said Todd briskly. And with that he slammed the door in Amy's face.

CHAPTER TWENTY-THREE

Bobby spent the afternoon of Christmas Eve at Hank's grave.

It was oddly quiet in Solvang. Those still on a last-minute present dash had all gone to the big malls in Santa Barbara, where they could stock up at the same chains—Gap, Brookstone, and the Discovery Store—and buy the same sweaters, gadgets, and toys as the rest of America. Everyone else, it seemed, was indoors, cooking, eating, or watching *It's a Wonderful Life* on TV. Main Street was all but deserted, and once Bobby turned onto the Alisal road toward the cemetery he found himself completely alone.

Laying down the small bunch of flowers he'd brought with him, he used his hands to sweep away the leaves that had built up at the base of the headstone.

HANK CAMERON. COWBOY. 1918–2003.

That was all it said. No "Loving husband and father" or "Much missed" like the other memorials. Just plain, curt, and to the point. In death, as in life, Hank didn't like to give much away.

Squatting down on his haunches, Bobby tried to say a prayer or at least to dredge up a clear mental picture of the father he'd spent most of his childhood trying and failing to please. But it was no good. His mind kept racing back to all the subjects he'd rather forget—like the ongoing, uneasy stalemate with Todd; the awkwardness that wouldn't go away with Summer; and of course, Milly.

Her *Playboy* pictures had been a knife in the heart. It was three months now since Dyl had taken his life in his hands and shown him the magazine, but to Bobby it felt like yesterday.

Spread over four pages, under the heading "Ride 'em, Cowgirl!" were a series of naked images of Milly, all of them Western themed and all of them now seared on his consciousness forever like cattle brands. The first shot showed her lying back on a horse, her head resting against its mane as she gazed at the camera, tiny breasts jutting upward like walnut whips on top of her now-superskinny frame. Others were less modest. In one, she was kneeling on a hay bale, wearing nothing but a ten-gallon hat and a string of pearls, her neatly trimmed dark bush not only visible but very much front and center.

To this day he struggled to get his head around what had made her do it. Sure, there was the money. But there were other ways to earn a dollar. The Milly he knew wouldn't have dreamed of prostituting herself like that.

But maybe that was the point: She wasn't the Milly he knew. Not anymore. The innocent, freckle-faced kid he'd brought over from England was gone forever. And all because of the devil incarnate himself—Todd fucking Cranborn.

Running his hands over the roughness of his dad's headstone, he let out a short, bitter laugh. He'd been so full of himself when the old man died. So convinced that he had the answers to Highwood's problems; that with a stroke of the pen, he could drag the ranch into the modern world and everything would work out fine.

What he'd actually done, of course, was to open the door to the biggest Trojan horse of all time. Todd had already stolen Milly. Surely it could be only a matter of time before he found a way to take Highwood too? Bobby had seen it happen in Wyoming: families who'd owned land for six generations or more being forced out to make way for oil and gas companies. As the ranch's sole owner, he'd at least have been in a position to defend her legally if an oil company launched an attack. Now, with Todd as his legal partner, he couldn't even do that.

Hank must be spinning like a top down there.

Even if, by some miracle, there was no takeover bid, Highwood was still in trouble. Bobby had refused to accept a cent from Todd since Milly's defection, which provided some small comfort for his battered pride but none whatsoever for his bank balance. The quarter horse business was barely breaking even, and the beef cattle continued to lose money hand over fist.

Reluctantly, he'd reached a decision last month to close down the stables—quarter horses were a dream he could no longer afford. He'd have to go back to the Thoroughbred circuit in January. It broke his heart to leave Highwood at her most vulnerable. But without Todd, they needed cash, and a training tour was the only way he knew how to make it.

Scrambling back to his feet, he brushed the dirt off of his jeans and, thrusting his hands deep in his pockets against the winter wind, turned back toward the road.

"I know I've let you down, Dad," he said with one last lingering look at Hank's grave. "I've let everyone down. But I swear to you, on my honor as a Cameron, I'm gonna fix this. Whatever it takes. I'm gonna fix it."

Back at Highwood, Summer was busy hanging Christmas cards on a long piece of string that stretched the length of the McDonalds' living room. She loved Christmas. Everything about it—fumbling through old boxes for the dog-eared decorations she and Tara and Dylan had made in kindergarten; helping her dad set up the live Nativity in the old barn; pigging out on her mom's incredible pecan pie and cinnamon rum toddies, a Maggie McDonald specialty. Whatever else might be going wrong in her life, Christmas at home never failed to lift her spirits.

Balanced precariously on a kitchen chair, she put the rude Santa card that Sean had sent her next to a boring religious card from her old school principal, smiling again as she read Sean's inscription:

"Darling Summer. LONGING to fill your stocking. Happy Christmas from your not-so-secret admirer, S xoxo"

Though she couldn't return his ardor, she did love Sean for making her laugh. He'd become a regular e-mail buddy since they'd met in the summer, brightening up her first semester at Berkeley with a string of outrageous, utterly unbelievable stories, usually featuring himself in various heroic situations. The notes were silly, but they made a welcome change from her dry-as-dust law books as well as from her gloomy, obsessive thoughts about Bobby.

Climbing down from the chair, she walked over to the living room window and looked out across the yard. Though not yet four, it was already getting dark, but she could make out the shadowy figures of Bobby and her brother talking, before Dylan turned back toward the house and Bobby struck off in the direction of the stables. They were empty now—the last of the quarter horses had gone last week—but he still spent a lot of time up there. It was where he went to think.

"I love you," she whispered, tracing the outline of his silhouette against the glass with her finger. "I could make you happy."

"Make who happy?"

She jumped out of her skin as Dylan came in behind her.

"Nothing. No one," she said, blushing furiously. "I was just daydreaming."

"Oh." He gave her a big, dopey grin. "Right."

"What are you looking so pleased about?" she asked. "You look like you just won the lottery."

"Me?" Flopping down on the couch, he helped himself to a huge handful of sugared almonds from the bowl on the coffee table.

"Yeah, you," Summer laughed, making him scooch over so she could sit beside him. In her oldest pair of cords, a tight turtleneck sweater with holes in it, and her hair scraped back in a ponytail, she looked terribly young, with that same eagerness to share his secrets that she'd always had as a child. "You're obviously bustin' to tell me," she said. "So come on, spill it. What's the word?"

"Okay," said Dyl, clasping her hands excitedly. "But it's still a secret, okay, so you can't tell anyone. Especially not Dad."

"Sure, sure," she said impatiently. "My lips are sealed."

Dylan took a deep breath. "The Gagosian Gallery in New York contacted Carol Bentley yesterday. They want to do an exhibition of my stuff."

"Oh my God!" Summer screamed, leaping to her feet. "The Gagosian? Holy *shit*, Dyl! That's huge."

"Shhhhh," he said, pulling her back down onto the couch. Her pride in him was really touching, but he desperately did *not* want to have to tell his father, at least not till after Christmas, when hopefully he'd have figured out a way to soften the blow that he was planning to give up ranching for good. "It's a secret, remember? I haven't even told Tara. Only you and Bobby know."

"Okay, okay, but when?" she whispered. "When are you going to be there? Oh, Dyl, just imagine! They'll probably throw you a party and write articles about you in *The New Yorker*, and—"

He laughed. "Let's not get carried away. And I don't know for sure when it would be. Probably not till the summer. But it's pretty cool, though, right?"

"Pretty cool?" Summer felt her eyes welling up with tears. She'd been so emotional lately it was scary. "It's incredible. And once they get used to the idea of you being an artist, Mom and Dad'll be thrilled for you too. I know they will."

Dylan wished he could share her confidence.

"I hope so," he said. "I really do."

Just then, the doorbell rang. They both raced to answer it first, pushing and elbowing each other out of the way like a couple of kids. Dylan was the winner, pulling open the door to reveal a diminutive female figure so swaddled in coats and scarves and fur that at first he didn't recognize her.

"Merry Christmas!" said the bundle. "Surprised to see me, sweet cakes?"

"Diana?" Only as the layers peeled off did he at last recognize Bobby's mother. "Is that really you?"

"It is!" She beamed at him disarmingly. "And don't look so shocked, Dylan. I can't have changed that much since the old boy's funeral."

"Sure you have," said Dylan. He adored Bobby's mother. As kids, he and his sisters had always considered her wildly exotic and bohemian, and she was scarcely less so now. "You look younger than ever."

"Flattery, my dear, will get you everywhere." Diana grinned, hugging him. "Now where's that reprobate son of mine?"

Up at the deserted stables, Bobby sat on a hay bale with his head in his hands, staring down at his boots despondently.

He had to cheer up. Moping around like this wasn't any good. It wasn't going to help Highwood, or get rid of Todd Cranborn, or bring Milly back.

He was jolted out of his reverie by the sounds of two cars pulling up outside the barn—Town Cars, if the smooth, deep rumble of the engines was anything to go by. Sure enough, when he stuck his head around the door, two sleek black Lincolns had parked just a few feet down the hill, like a gleaming pair of black panthers. Their suited occupants were already picking their way over the bumpy ground in his direction.

"Mr. Cameron?" asked the first suit, extending a black-gloved hand in Bobby's direction.

"That's me," he said. Though he towered over them in his cowboy boots, something about the three men in front of him felt menacing. "Who's asking?"

"I'm Paul Reeves, and these are my colleagues, Charlie Hill and Ted Burrows. We're from Comarco."

Bobby's eyes narrowed and his heart began pounding. "Comarco oil?" he asked, unnecessarily. There was only one Comarco, a Texas conglomerate so giant that even the most backwoodsy hick had heard of it.

"Exactly," said the suit. "We're here at the invitation of your partner, Mr. Cranborn." Reaching into the inside pocket of his long cashmere coat, he pulled out a bundle of folded legal paperwork. "He's asked us to look into your oil reserves. See how we can best utilize the natural resources."

"All right, Mr. Reeves," said Bobby with a thin smile. Taking the papers from him, he made a brief show of examining them before ripping them, slowly and deliberately, into small pieces and throwing them to the wind. "Let's get one thing straight. Highwood is my property. My family's property. And it'll be a cold day in hell before I let you, or anyone, dig her up for oil."

The suit looked unperturbed. "That's a little childish, isn't it?" he said with a smile that was almost a sneer. "Ripping that up doesn't change the legal position one iota. Ted, here, is a lawyer. He can explain everything to you. But, in layman's terms, the oil beneath your land does not necessarily belong to you."

"I'm well aware of that," snapped Bobby. He knew he shouldn't lose his cool, but it was impossible, watching the scene he'd dreaded and dreamed about for so many months playing out in front of him word for word. "But this is still private property. You need permission to access it, which I deny."

He took a step toward his opponent, who instinctively took a step back, almost losing his footing on the muddy slope as he did so.

"I understand that," he said. "But your partner, Mr. Cranborn—"

"Fuck Cranborn," roared Bobby. "And fuck you." He was now nose to nose with the suit, who was looking a lot less smug all of a sudden. "Get the hell off of my property before I do something I won't regret for a minute."

"Bobby?" Wyatt had heard the raised voices and came running up the hill, followed by Dylan and . . . was that his mom behind them? "What's going on?"

"Nothing," snarled Bobby, looking menacingly at the three Comarco agents. "These guys were just leavin'. Weren't you, fellas?"

Climbing back into the safety of their Town Cars, Reeves wound down his window and spoke to Wyatt as he turned the key in the ignition.

"If you've got any sense, you'll talk to him," he said, nodding toward Bobby. "We have a legal right of access. We'll fight him through the courts for it if we need to. But those kind of legal battles aren't cheap. And our pockets are a lot deeper than yours."

That wouldn't be hard, thought Wyatt as he watched them drive off. He knew teenagers with more disposable income than Bobby had handy right now.

He reached out and tried to put a comforting hand on Bobby's arm, but he shrugged it off.

"Just leave me alone, Wyatt," he said, fighting back tears. He should have punched that Comarco fucker's lights out while he'd had the chance. "All of you. Leave me alone."

The church service on Christmas morning was unspeakably awkward. Bobby was there in body—with his world collapsing around his ears, maintaining the old Highwood traditions seemed more important than ever—but his mind was obviously elsewhere.

He completely ignored Diana, which she seemed not to mind, although all the McDonalds were in agonies about it.

"He's had a lot on his mind recently," Maggie explained lamely. "I'm sure it's not personal."

"Of course, it's personal," said Diana. "He's pissed at me for not being around more and for showing up unannounced. But that's okay. We've always been different like that. I'm more of a free spirit. And he's *sooo* much like his father, though he'll never admit it."

She was right about one thing: Bobby was annoyed about her turning up unannounced. It was all too reminiscent of his horrible early childhood: the "spontaneous" changes of plan that had uprooted and unsettled his existence and ripped away his security more times than he cared to remember.

"It's Christmas, Mom, for God's sake," he hissed at her before they went into lunch, once she'd finally challenged him about what was wrong. "People make plans. You can't just show up and expect to get fed and looked after at the drop of a hat. It's not fair to Maggie and Wyatt. Not to mention me."

It was a relief when, after Maggie's delicious lunch, he was finally able to sneak off to the ranch office and be alone. He wanted a chance to look through the legal files again. He and Wyatt had already gotten together a veritable library of information on the Wyoming cases, what tactics had worked and what hadn't, as well as reams of information on the complicated California state law on land disputes.

But after an hour spent chin deep in reports, he'd gotten precisely nowhere and was actually pleased when Summer knocked on the door, bearing a plate with a hefty slab of pecan pie on it and a mug of mulled wine.

"Figured you could use some brain food," she said, setting them down on the desk. She'd changed into the new cream, low-cut sweater that Tara'd given her this morning that showed just the barest hint of bronzed cleavage. Without thinking, Bobby caught himself admiring it, looking hastily away when she caught the direction of his gaze.

"It suits you," he said. "That sweater."

"Thanks." She wished a simple glance and a compliment from him wouldn't fill her with so much hope and desire. But she'd learned her lesson from last time. If anyone made a move on anyone now, it would have to be him. She wasn't about to make a fool of herself a second time.

"Any joy?" She glanced at the stack of papers in front of him.

"Uh-uh." He shook his head. "I have no idea what to do. If there's a way out of this, I don't see it."

"Come on," she said firmly. "That's not the Bobby Cameron I know. Where's your fighting spirit? We'll take them to court, of course. Get an interim injunction against them while we get our case together."

"You make it sound so easy," he said.

"Well, it's not rocket science." She shrugged, with all the confidence of a future Harvard Law student. "Todd defrauded you. He tricked you into signing away half the ranch."

"I wish that were true," said Bobby. "But I can't blame anyone but myself for this mess and that's God's honest truth. What hurts most . . ." He cleared his throat, and when he looked up she could see with horror that there were tears in his eyes. "I know this is stupid. But what hurts most right now is the fact that Milly must have known he was planning this. I mean, she lives with the guy, right? She knew he was gonna stab me in the back with these oil guys, and yet she never said a word."

"Oh, Bobby." Forgetting her earlier scruples, Summer sat down on his lap and wrapped her arms around him. In that moment, all she wanted was to comfort him. To let him know that none of them blamed him. That it was okay to make mistakes, okay not to be perfect. And that though Milly might have let him down, she, and everyone else on the ranch, would always be there for him.

Hugging her back, he suddenly felt acutely aware of the warmth of her body, gift-wrapped in the soft cream wool and pressed so tightly against him. He could smell the shampoo in her hair and the faint lingering scent of some lemony, citrus-based perfume at the base of her neck.

It was so long—ridiculously long—since he'd had a woman, or

even felt aroused. Whether it was Summer's undeniable sexiness or her compassion or just the pressure and stress of the last few months that simply needed to be released, he found he could no longer hold himself back. Slipping his hand around the back of her neck, he pulled her head down and kissed her, a long, passionate kiss that seemed to go on for minutes.

"I'm sorry," he said gruffly, finally pulling away, the desire in his voice strong.

"Don't be," she whispered, her soft, powder-pink lips already parted in anticipation of the next kiss. "I'm not."

He leaned in and kissed her again, harder this time, slipping his hands up under her sweater onto her bare back, which she arched in response, kissing him back with all the passion of an unrequited love finally unleashed.

"Whoa there, kids!" Diana appeared in the doorway. She looked surprisingly shocked.

Instinctively, Summer leaped up off Bobby's lap like a surprised rattlesnake and started straightening her hair and clothes.

"Diana. We didn't see you there," she stammered guiltily.

"So I see."

Summer expected her to smile—normally Diana would be the last person to get on her moral high horse about sexual things, and they'd only been kissing, anyway. But she looked resolutely serious.

"I actually came to talk to Bobby. Would you mind giving us a few minutes?"

"Sure." She glanced at Bobby, who was blushing himself but managed to flash her a brief, reassuring smile. "No problem. I'll, er . . . I'll go help Mom clear up in the kitchen."

Diana waited for her to go, then started pacing nervously up and down the small office like a general considering his battle plans.

"What do you want, Ma?" asked Bobby. He loved his mother, but he was still pissed at her for imposing herself on the McDonalds the way she had. And, as usual, her timing was terrible.

"How long has it been going on?"

"What?" he asked testily.

"Don't give me 'what'!" she snapped. "You and Summer, of course. How long have you been lovers?"

"Jesus." He shook his head in disbelief. "Unbelievable. Coming from you, I gotta say, Mom, that takes the cake. *You* disapprove of *my* love life? Is that what you're saying?"

"How long?" Diana was practically shouting now.

"Not that it's any of your goddamned business," Bobby said, annoyed. "But we're not 'lovers,' as you so quaintly put it. That kiss—what you saw—that was the first time."

"Thank God," said Diana, sinking weakly down into a chair. Her normally rosy face had gone white as a sheet. For the first time, Bobby realized that she actually looked quite ill.

"What's wrong, Mom?" he said, his tone softening. "Is something the matter?"

Diana nodded miserably.

"There's something I have to tell you," she said. "Something I probably should have told you a long time ago."

A few minutes later, it was Bobby's turn to look ill.

It couldn't be true.

It couldn't.

"You're wrong," he said, shaking his head. He'd felt so sick when she told him, they'd had to move outside into the cool evening air, and he was leaning against the outside wall of the stables now as he spoke to her. "You have to be wrong."

Diana came and leaned beside him.

"Bobby, honey, I wish I were."

She wanted so badly to comfort him, but she didn't know how. In one fell swoop she'd robbed him of the few shards of truth and certainty he'd clung to all his life, revealing them as smoke and mirrors. No wonder he didn't want to believe it.

"I truly wish I were. But you needed to know, before things had a chance to"—she struggled to find the right words—"to go any further between you. What I saw today. That *is* all that happened, right?"

"Yes." He nodded furiously. "Yes. I mean, there's been some sexual tension between us before." He felt nauseous now, just talking about it. "But nothing serious. We're not in love or anything."

"Honey, speak for yourself," said Diana. "I saw the way Summer looked at you just now. You're blind if you can't see how crazy in love with you that girl is. It's a problem."

"No, it's not," he said. "I mean, *she's* not. In love with me. At least, I'm pretty sure she's not. Oh, God." He put his head in his hands again. "Is she?"

"Whether she is or not, it doesn't matter," said Diana. "What matters is that Hank was her father. You two can never be together. Never. And she must never know. You have to promise me, Bobby."

"Of course I promise. You think I want to hurt her?" he said, tearing at his hair in exasperation. "But how do *you* know, Mom. I mean, are you sure?"

"A hundred percent," said Diana. "I'm sorry, Bobby. But there's absolutely no doubt."

Briefly, she filled him in on the history. Although he only seemed able to process fragments of her words: "Mistake . . . both regretted it . . . Maggie and Wyatt . . . going through some tough times back then . . ." It was enough to paint a horribly vivid picture: Hank betraying his best, his only true friend in the most appalling way imaginable.

"What I can't get my head around is Maggie," Bobby kept repeating.

"She was depressed," Diana explained. "And I don't just mean a bit down. She was clinically depressed after Tara was born. And Wyatt was working crazy long days."

"For Dad," said Bobby bitterly.

"I think it's hard for you to appreciate how lonely and isolated Maggie was," said Diana. "Hank was there. Sometimes it really is as simple as that."

"But Summer doesn't look anything like him," reasoned Bobby, clutching at straws. "She looks like Tara. And Maggie."

"She has a lot of her mother in her," conceded Diana. "But she's the only one of those kids with blond hair. And look at her eyes, Bobby."

Bobby felt his stomach give an involuntary lurch. He *had* looked at her eyes, only minutes ago, although now it felt like hours, even days since their kiss.

They were hazel. Just like his.

"Her paternity was never at issue," said Diana. "Maggie admitted the affair to Wyatt before she even knew she was pregnant. There was no doubt Hank was the father. She and Wyatt, like I say, they were going through a low patch. They hadn't shared a bed in months."

"And what?" said Bobby. "Wyatt just forgave them both?"

He sounded angry, and he was. True, he hadn't loved Hank, or even liked him much. But he had at least respected him. As a child, his father had had an authority that seemed almost godlike. And, boy, was he ever self-righteous about other people's sins and failings, especially Bobby's.

Till now, he'd genuinely believed that when his father had judged him, he did it with some degree of moral authority. But to find out Hank had been creeping around behind Wyatt's back—that he'd fathered *two* illegitimate children, and done his level best to wash his hands of both of them—it took away every last shred of decency, every good and noble thing that Bobby had ever believed about him.

"They were supposed to be friends, for God's sake."

"They *were* friends," said Diana with a shrug. "I know it might seem strange to you, looking back on it now. But the way Wyatt saw it, Hank and Maggie were both sorry. It was a mistake. And they were the two people he loved most in the world. Plus, of course, there was the child to consider."

"Summer." Bobby's eyes glazed over. "Wyatt brought her up as his own daughter."

"Wyatt's a good man. As far as he was concerned, she was his own daughter. She still is," said Diana firmly. "Hank had no interest in being a dad. You should know that better than anyone. You were five at the time and he'd only laid eyes on you twice. Both times under duress, I might add."

For the first time, Bobby had a vision of how hard it must have been for his mother, bringing him up alone in those godawful hippie communes. She'd made her mistakes, sure, but she was only a kid herself. Hank should have done better by her. He should have done better by all of them.

All this time, he'd been beating himself up about Highwood, scared of letting his father down, of not living up to the legend. But now it was brought home to him, in the cruelest, most horrible way, that that was all Hank's so-called heroism was: a legend. A story that people needed to believe about a distant, noble cowboy, fighting the good fight to keep the old ways alive.

But the truth was very different. Hank wasn't a giant among men. He was weak and selfish and thoughtless. If anyone was the heroic cowboy, it was Wyatt. But, of course, he didn't have the great Cameron name.

"Summer has no idea?" he whispered, breaking the long silence between them. "She never guessed?"

Diana shook her head. "Why should she?"

Pushing off the wall, he paced a few feet into the darkness, thinking.

"You do promise not to say anything, Bobby?" said Diana anxiously.

"I have to say something," he said. "I mean, not about Dad. But she's gonna wonder why I'm not interested anymore. After . . . you know."

"Oh, come on," said Diana. "You said yourself it was only a kiss. Just tell her you see her as a sister and it wouldn't work."

"I tried that before."

"Well, try it again." Diana was firm. "Besides, it's true, isn't it? It's not Summer you're in love with."

"What do you mean?" said Bobby. "I'm single, Mom. I'm not in love with anyone."

"Whatever you say, sweetheart," said Diana, raising a skeptical eyebrow. "Whatever you say."

CHAPTER TWENTY-FOUR

Rachel sat with her feet curled up beneath her on the beige suede sofa, flicking contentedly through a fat pile of press clippings about herself. It was April, her fourth month in America and her second riding for Randy Kravitz—probably the most successful racehorse owner in the U.S. after Jimmy Price, although, unlike his great rival, Randy was purely a Thoroughbred man. So far the gamble to move to the States seemed to be paying off in spades.

Relaxing in her palatial rented apartment in Palm Beach, only a few minutes' drive from Kravitz's training facility, she was currently sitting with Des, her agent, trying to figure out which of the many magazine spreads she'd been offered to go for next.

"What about *W*?" she asked wistfully. "I've always loved their style. And they have the best photographers, much more edgy than those boring Testino, *Vanity Fair* shots with everyone in ball gowns."

"Oi've told you," said Des with a sigh. "It's no good pickin' a publication out o' the blue, just 'cos you like 'em. We've got to target your audience, 'aven't we?"

"Which is?" Rachel asked frostily.

"Sports mags, gossip rags, and the papers. Back home, we'd go for the Sundays." He pronounced the word "Sun-dees," which set Rachel's teeth on edge. "Here, it's a bit tougher to pitch. But basically racing fans, horny blokes, and girls who are interested in the 'ole soap opera, you-versus-Milly fing."

Rachel yawned. Des was annoying at the best of times but never more so than when he was right. Much as she might like to play the fashion maven, it was the story of her feud with Milly that had really captured the popular imagination and kick-started her debut season in American racing.

With Milly's T-Mobile ads now everywhere—billboards, TV, even in movie theaters (Rachel had had to sit through one of the ghastly things while waiting to watch *Bridget Jones 2* the other day), Milly was clearly the bigger star and much more widely known in America than she was. But Rachel had no intention of playing Ashlee Simpson to her Jessica. At least not for long.

Her first coup was to land Kravitz as a backer. Soon after that, as both her looks and talent began to get her noticed by the racing press, she accidentally let slip a few rumors to diarists and gossip columnists about her and Milly's lifelong feud, spicing it up with juicy tidbits about how quarter horse racing's darling was no longer speaking to her family after her *Playboy* pictures and how she, Rachel, was in a long-term relationship with Milly's brother. Who also happened to be handily photogenic.

As a story it had everything—two beautiful, foreign girls, brunette versus blond, skinny versus curvy, both talented, both ambitious, both trying to make it in America, riding for famous rival owners. The family drama angle only added to the *Dynasty*-esque fabulousness of it all. It was like Paris versus Nicole, but with sporting talent thrown in. What wasn't to love?

At first, much to Rachel's disappointment, Milly had risen above the fray, boringly refusing to comment on her personal life. But after Rachel implied in *Elle* that her *Playboy* spread had been a betrayal of Cecil's memory, the gloves were well and truly off. Milly responded with a long interview in *Vanity Fair,* spelling out how Rachel had "stolen" her family home and strongly hinting that she was guilty of abusing her horses. She was none too complimentary about Jasper either, or her mother.

Suffice it to say, it was a long time since stuffy old horse racing had been quite this interesting.

"Did you call your trustees back?" asked Des, putting aside the clippings for a moment.

"God, you sound like my bloody father," moaned Rachel. "Yes, I did, okay? I left another message."

After six straight months of losses, she'd finally bitten the bullet and put Newells back on the market. The three-million-pound price tag was a bit optimistic. But even if she cut her losses and took two point five, it'd be worth it just to have the millstone off her neck.

She hadn't mentioned anything to Jasper yet. Though still nominally together—it suited her purposes to keep him around as an extra in the feud story—he was stuck in England racing for Ali and she hadn't actually seen him for over a month. When they spoke on the phone, he was increasingly out of it. His coke habit was now completely out of control. Chances were he wouldn't give two shits about Newells and what she did with it, but the drugs made him horribly unpredictable, and she preferred not to raise the issue with him till it was a fait accompli.

"Well, let me speak to 'em when they call back, will you?" said Des. "It's about time they pulled their bloody finger out and found you a buyer. Then you can focus on really important stuff, like the Belmont."

Rachel sat up excitedly. "Has Randy said anything to you? Has he confirmed it?" she asked eagerly. The prospect of riding in the most important race in America in her very first season was tantalizingly close. Kravitz had hinted a couple of times that he was considering her for the June fixture but had yet to make a firm offer. If he did, it would be a feather in her cap to outshine anything that Milly had done to date. There was no quarter horse race even remotely as prestigious as the Belmont.

"Not yet," said Des, leisurely cracking his knuckles and dazzling her with a fistful of chunky gold and diamond rings as he did so. He'd always had a worrying penchant for jewelry, but since coming to America he seemed to have pimped up his style still further. "But don't worry. He will. I'm on the case."

Rachel didn't worry. He might be an annoying, slimy little weasel of a man, but Des had more than proved his worth as an agent.

If he said he'd get her in the Belmont, he would.

He hadn't let her down yet.

Back in Bel Air, Todd leaned out of the side of the bed and reached down for the little bag of coke he had hidden there, along with a fat rubber dildo and a tube of strawberry flavored K-Y.

"Stay right there," he said.

The girl, naked and on all fours on top of his rumpled sheets, did as she was told. Moments later he reemerged from under the bed with the drugs in one hand and the K-Y in the other.

"Now arch your back a little more. Perfect."

While she repositioned herself, he sprinkled a line of white powder across the raised arc of her ass, then reached around to grab her tits as he snorted it off her sweat-dampened skin. Man, did that feel good.

Wiping his nose with the back of his hand, he licked up the remnants greedily before slipping his cock back inside her, picking up where he'd left off a few moments earlier.

The girl's name was Natasha Oakley. Known to the tabloids as an up-and-coming Hollywood starlet and teen horror heroine, she was also known to all the wealthy male players in LA as a total coke whore. Later, Todd would have to share some of his drugs with her—that was the deal—but it was a small price to pay for two hours with her incredible, tight, twenty-one-year-old body. Last time, he'd made her snort her share of the precious white powder off his balls. For a dominance freak like Todd, it didn't come much hornier than that.

Life, he reflected as he pounded away at Natasha, was pretty fucking good right now. Business was the best it had ever been. After almost a year of careful wooing, he'd finally gotten Jimmy Price to invest in a huge commercial property deal in Florida which, if all went according to plan, could catapult him into a whole new league of personal wealth. On top of that, he'd sold his development in Buellton a month ago for a vast profit. And then, of course, there was Highwood.

After months of legal wrangling, the Santa Barbara District Court judge had granted Comarco an interim order last week, allowing them twenty-one days of exploratory searches on the property. It was a huge blow for Bobby's case, which must in any case be costing him a small fortune. With any luck, the legal costs alone would soon force the boy out of the game. Then, at last, the advantageous, personal deal Todd had struck with the oil company would start bearing fruit.

The most miraculous thing was that Milly had not yet gotten wind of his little coup vis-à-vis the cowboy, although he was going to have to tell her soon, perhaps even tonight. Though Milly hadn't spoken to him in a year now, Todd suspected that deep down she still had a soft spot for him. She'd probably be tiresomely outraged on his behalf when he filled her in on events. It was an argument he wasn't looking forward to, particularly as he was already starting to feel a bit bored by the relationship.

He'd stayed with Milly so far because the sex was still good, her lifestyle gave him plenty of opportunity to play around on the side, and her growing fame had opened doors for him, as her boyfriend, that no amount of money could open. Though he would never admit it, secretly Todd loved being invited to celebrity parties and award ceremonies. He particularly enjoyed being "papped" when leaving restaurants, even if it was Milly who made the pictures valuable rather than him.

On the other hand, ever since Demon died she'd become a terrible wet blanket. More emotional and needy than ever, she seemed to cry over nothing, and there was no doubt that her racing form had been steadily declining since Christmas. Even worse, ever since Rachel Delaney had turned up and started making waves in the press, the stress had caused her to lose a frightening amount of weight. He was all for skinny girls, but these days Milly's breasts were practically concave. No one wanted to fuck a bag of jutting bones.

Feeling his orgasm start to build, he quickly glanced at the Franck Muller watch lying faceup on the bedside table. Fuck. Six thirty. He'd better wrap this up and get Natasha out of here. He was meeting Milly for a romantic dinner at the Ivy at eight and would need a good long shower before then, not to mention changing the sheets.

Grabbing hold of Natasha's hair, he rammed himself even deeper into her, watching her drug-glazed eyes in the bedroom mirror as he came.

"Here," he said, throwing a fresh bag of coke down on the bed as he withdrew and walked straight into the bathroom, without even a backward glance. "Take it and get out. I'm in a rush."

"Come on!" yelled Milly, leaning hard on the horn of her vintage T-Bird convertible. She'd passed her test only a month ago, but she was already a classic, bad-tempered LA commuter. "Move!"

She was late, she'd had an awful, awful day, and now to top it all off, an accident on the 5 had turned the freeway into a parking lot.

This morning she'd had her third disappointing result of the month at a stakes race, coming fifth in a field she really ought to have dominated. The week before had been the first round of qualifiers for the All American. She'd gotten through, but with a margin so embarrassingly narrow she'd been given a bollocking by both Jimmy and her T-Mobile sponsors and told to pull her socks up or else. Somehow she doubted they'd consider today's performance "pulling her socks up."

At first she'd put her plummeting results down to Cally, officially California Boy, the new horse Jimmy had had her riding since Demon died. They just didn't seem to have clicked as a team. But as an excuse, she was aware, it was already wearing thin. Other jockeys had gotten excellent times out of him this season at out-of-state courses like Remington Park and Prairie Meadows. It was more likely that other things—all the stress with Rachel, and her ever-growing insecurity about Todd, for example—were affecting her form.

She wished she weren't still so obsessed with Todd. But, somehow, the more she saw him flirting and the more she feared losing him, the more desperate she felt to hold on to him. Since she'd grown apart from Amy, he was also now the only person she had to talk to, although she could tell that her moaning about Rachel bored him, and she tried not to do it too much.

Then, as if today's disaster weren't bad enough, she'd read in her new copy of the English *Racing Post* that Rachel had put Newells up for sale. Having to read about it in the paper was awful but not half as awful as the price tag. Three million pounds! Was it really worth that much? She'd had no idea. Suddenly her dream of earning enough to buy the place back looked more ridiculously distant than ever.

Yes, she was earning good money—although for how much longer remained an issue, especially if her times did not improve. But she realized now she hadn't saved nearly enough. Todd was always encouraging her to spend. The car had been his idea, as had three quarters of her wardrobe, but she was the one who paid for them. His idea of "taking her shopping" was to hit the most expensive boutiques on Robertson, pick out far more dresses than she either wanted or needed, then sting her for the bill. But she was so desperate to please him and to hold his interest in the face of so much female competition, she found herself going along with it.

Finally, almost forty minutes late, she pulled up outside the restaurant. She was so sweaty she had had to unstick her white trousers from the backs of her legs before handing the key to the valet and scrabbling in her purse for some Tylenol to relieve her throbbing headache.

"At last," said Todd, as she fought her way to the table through crowds of waiting diners, two of whom stopped her for autographs. "What the hell happened?"

"Sorry, sorry, sorry," she said, grabbing his hand and covering it in conciliatory kisses as she sat down. She saw that he'd already finished his appetizer and had a good crack at the bread basket, crumbs from which now littered the pretty red-and-white gingham tablecloth. "A truck turned over on the freeway and it took forever. I'd have called but there wasn't any cell reception."

"Hmmm," said Todd, pouring the rest of his beer from the bottle into his glass. He was pissed—thanks to her lateness he'd had to miss out on an extra hour's sex with Natasha—but on the other hand it suited him to have her on the back foot this evening. Hopefully it would help to tone down her reaction to the Highwood news.

Dipping the last morsel of bread into a saucer of olive oil, he changed the subject.

"How was the race?"

"Bad," said Milly, pouring herself a glass of water and gulping it down along with a third Tylenol. She looked thinner and more drawn than ever. "We came fifth. Jimmy doesn't know yet, but he'll hit the roof when he finds out. And guess what else I found out today?"

"I don't like guessing games," said Todd, making no attempt not to stare as a six-foot, miniskirted redhead shimmied past their table and quite blatantly winked at him. "Tell me or don't tell me."

"Newells is on the market," said Milly despondently. She knew he wasn't interested, but she had to tell someone. "For three mill, if you can believe that. After all that guff Rachel fed Mummy about being the best person to take over Dad's legacy, she's run the stud into the ground and now she's bloody selling the place."

"I can't keep up," said Todd, waving to a waiter to come and take their order. "I thought you wanted her out of Newells."

"I do," said Milly. "But not like this. I mean, what's going to happen to the rest of the horses? Maybe the new owner will close the stud altogether? Turn the stables into holiday cottages or something awful. . . ." Her face clouded over as the limitless possibilities, all of them bad, loomed into mental view.

"Well," said Todd, deciding to take advantage of her evident distraction to break the bad news. "I've had a good day, as it happens, businesswise. I've been talking to a Texas company—Comarco, you've probably heard of them—about a profit share in Highwood's oil rights. We've been having a few legal problems, but we've just heard we *will* be allowed to begin exploration this month. So that's good news."

It took a moment for the import of what he was saying to sink in.

"You mean . . ." she asked slowly, "you're going to dig the ranch up for oil?"

"That's right," said Todd, sipping his beer unconcerned. "It's about time someone did."

"But you can't," said Milly, aghast.

"Why not?"

"Because . . ." She shook her head, as if trying to loosen the right words from her vocabulary. "Because you can't. What about Bobby? That land has been in his family for six generations. He'd rather die than—"

"Please." Todd held up his hand to interrupt her. "Spare me the Cameron family speech. I'm sick of it. I took Highwood for the same reasons you British once took India. Because I was tired of seeing her potential wasted. And because I could. I don't owe Bobby Cameron anything. Anyway, whose side are you on? His or mine?"

That was the killer question, of course. Whose side *was* she on? Right now she felt like she was on Bobby's, but she dared not say that to Todd. Besides, she thought sadly, Bobby probably wouldn't thank her for her support anyway. There was no point sticking her neck out over nothing.

"Yours, of course," she lied. "But I still don't approve. Anyway, wasn't there a clause in your agreement saying you couldn't drill for oil?"

"There was indeed," he said. "But unfortunately for your friend Mr. Cameron, private contracts are superseded by the strictures of federal land law. Oddly enough," he added cruelly, "it was you who first put me onto it."

"Me?" said Milly, horrified. "How?"

"You told me about those cases in Wyoming with the gas companies, remember? The ones that Bobby was so worried about. Turns out, he was right to be worried. His only mistake was not to strike a deal with the oil companies himself, before I did. I suppose he figured I didn't know anything about it. Which I didn't, till you clued me in."

Milly felt sick. True, they didn't speak anymore, and true, Bobby had been such a jerk to her last year he'd as good as propelled her into Todd's arms. But she would never do anything to hurt or betray him. She couldn't believe that some throwaway comment she'd made so long ago could possibly have led to this.

"Please." She looked at Todd imploringly. "Please. Don't go ahead with it. For me. I'd never have said anything if I'd known, you know I wouldn't."

"No can do, I'm afraid, sweetheart," he said. "It's purely a business decision. But there are other parties involved now. I can't just pull out unilaterally, even if I wanted to."

"But—"

"Look." Moving his chair around to her side of the table, he wrapped his arm around her and kissed her on the cheek. It was the most tenderness he'd shown her in weeks and, despite everything, she felt herself melting with love and relief. "The only reason Bobby hasn't done this himself is stupid, stubborn pride. It's ridiculous, sitting on all that wealth the way he is and doing nothing about it. If I hadn't moved in on the oil, believe me, someone else would have."

Milly wavered. She so, so wanted to believe him.

"It would mean a lot to me to know you were behind me on this." Todd allowed his left hand to fall over her breast and brush lightly against the nipple.

"I feel bad for Bobby," she said, guilt now fighting with desire inside her. "That's all. It doesn't mean I don't love you."

Later that night, after a long and frankly exhausting lovemaking session, she lay awake beside a sleeping Todd, staring at the ceiling.

The more she thought about it, the more terrible she felt. It wasn't until they'd gotten home after dinner that it occurred to her what Bobby must be thinking: that she'd known about this all along and hadn't bothered to call and warn him or do anything to try to stop it.

By seven A.M., having barely slept a wink all night, she could bear it no longer. Creeping down to the kitchen, she picked up the cordless phone and punched out Highwood's number. It had been a year, but she still knew it by heart.

She was just about to hang up when, after seven rings, she suddenly remembered how early it was. But just then a female voice picked up.

"Hello?"

"Tara?"

"Yes. Who's speaking?"

Milly's heart was pounding so violently she almost hung up. But she'd come this far. She might as well guts it out.

"It's me. Milly," she said. The silence on the other end was deafening. "Listen, I just called to talk to Bobby and explain. He has to understand, I had no idea about Comarco, about what Todd's been doing. Last night was the first I heard about it. Honestly."

"Hold on." The line went quiet, and she could hear muffled voices talking in the background. Tara had obviously put her hand over the mouthpiece so she could fill the rest of the family in. Milly had forgotten that seven A.M. counted as a late weekday breakfast at the ranch and they were all up already. Then the voices went quiet and she heard the two distinct clicks of a different phone being picked up while the first receiver went down. Someone was taking the call in private.

"Bobby?"

Silence.

"Bobby? Is that you?"

"No." Summer's voice sounded more hostile than ever. "He doesn't want to talk to you. Ever. None of us do."

And she hung up, leaving Milly holding the phone in shocked, profoundly miserable silence.

CHAPTER TWENTY-FIVE

A month after Summer's curt phone dismissal of Milly, Rachel sat in the lobby of the Mondrian on Sunset Boulevard, picking nervously at the bowl of rice crackers in front of her and waiting for Jimmy Price to show up.

She didn't even like rice crackers. They always got stuck to your teeth. But she was so wound up, she couldn't seem to stop eating them.

Des, God bless him, had somehow managed to swing her a meeting with Price, as well as sewing up her ride in next month's Belmont. The timing couldn't have been more perfect. With her Belmont selection secure—she'd be riding the famous Never Better for Randy Kravitz— she had a much stronger hand to play with Jimmy. He was famously competitive and, she hoped, would enjoy nothing better than to "steal" his rival's hot new jockey. Although getting him to sever his links with Milly might be more of a challenge.

Pulling out a silver Links makeup mirror from her purse she made a sneaky check for rice-cracker pieces stuck in her teeth, but luckily all was well. Even her barely there lipstick, carefully applied this morning to give her the natural, sensual look, was still in place. In fact, if she did say so herself, she looked pretty damn hot. She just hoped Price appreciated the effort she'd made, not just to look fabulous but to fly all the way over from Florida for one measly lunch meeting.

"He'll see you, but it has to be in LA," Des had explained patiently when she started to bitch about it. "Between his business commitments and the start of the quarter horse season, he won't leave California right now."

"But are you sure he's really interested?" Rachel pressed him. "I mean, I don't want to drag my ass all the way out there for nothing. What if he sticks with Milly?"

"He won't," said Des confidently. "Not in the long term. Milly's been screwing up royally since the end of last season. She totally tanked in the Derby and the Rainbow." Rachel's eyes glazed over. Quarter horse race names meant nothing to her. "And," Des said, switching back to familiar ground, "she's been flaking on her promotional commitments too. Word is T-Mobile are starting to get itchy feet, and Jimmy's had it up to here with her bullshit. If she doesn't pull something major out of the bag at the All American, she's finished. Trust me. You'll never have a better window to squeeze her out."

"Fine," Rachel said gracelessly. "I just hope you're right. Jimmy might think he's the biggest thing since sliced bread, but I hope he realizes I don't appreciate having my time wasted."

Now that she was actually here, though, her fighting talk had deserted her and, after waiting twenty long, awkward minutes, she was starting to panic that perhaps he wouldn't show after all. But at long last she saw a fat, distracted little man waddling across the lobby. Stopping in front of her, he extended his hand in greeting.

"Rachel." He gave her a brisk, businesslike smile. "Sorry I'm late. Shall we eat?"

Price was so obsessively private, there were almost no pictures of him in the press, so she'd had to rely on Des's description. Luckily, it was pretty good. Even so, in her mind's eye she'd pictured him as having more stature, more presence, some sort of aura to reflect the vast power he undoubtedly wielded both in racing and in the media. The rather bad-tempered, ginger-haired dwarf leading the way to their table was, physically speaking anyway, a crushing disappointment.

The all-white, starkly minimalist restaurant was full, mostly with thirty-something industry types: record execs, producers and the like who glanced up and leered appreciatively as Rachel sashayed by in her coffee-colored pencil skirt and cream silk blouse. LA women were gorgeous, but few of them bothered to change out of their pink Juicy tracksuits for lunch, even in a restaurant as upmarket as this one. A well-dressed woman in West Hollywood was as rare as a stripper at a bar mitzvah, and Rachel drew an equivalent amount of attention.

"So." Jimmy sat down and immediately ordered caprese salads for both of them. "I hear you're confirmed for the Belmont. You must be pleased."

So he'd already heard, had he? That was definitely a good start.

"I am," she said. "It's an honor, really. And Never Better is such an incredible horse."

"Randy must have a lot of faith in you."

"Yes," she said, treading warily. "I suppose he does. Rather like you having so much faith in Milly."

Jimmy smiled. He knew she was casting a line out over the water, but he was happy enough to bite. After all, it was no secret that he was becoming disillusioned with his British protégée. He wouldn't be having this conversation otherwise.

"My feeling," he said, shoveling lumps of bread into his mouth while he spoke, "which Milly has always known, I might add, is that no one's any better than their last race. My guess is Randy's the same. He's giving you a shot at the Belmont. But if you fuck it up, I doubt you'll find him quite so supportive in future."

Rachel shrugged. "That's okay," she said arrogantly. "I'm not going to fuck it up."

"Tell me," said Jimmy. "What is it about her that you hate so much?"

He was already intrigued by this cocky, sexy girl and her well-publicized rivalry with Milly. Ironically, Rachel's confidence reminded him more than a little of the old Milly—the kid he'd been so impressed with until her spectacular meltdown of recent months. It was sad really, but he wasn't a charity. He liked his horses to win.

Before Rachel could answer, their salads arrived. Jimmy promptly drowned his in a sea of olive oil, while Rachel lightly doused hers with balsamic vinegar. She'd gained weight since moving to the States, thanks to a combination of her natural greed and the enormous helpings of absolutely everything, but she was trying to turn the tide.

"I wouldn't say I hate her, exactly," she said, playing for time.

Jimmy speared a dripping slab of cheese with his fork and stuffed it noisily into his mouth, waiting for her to elaborate. "We have a history, that's all."

"So I've been reading," he said. "Look, I'll be honest with you. What I'm interested in is promoting a big female racing star. Someone with the ambition and the commitment to stay the course. I thought I'd found that in Milly. But these last few months"—he shrugged—"I'm not so sure."

Rachel's eyes lit up like Christmas lights. That was all the go-ahead she needed.

"If it's ambition and commitment you want, Mr. Price, I'm your woman."

Leaning forward slowly and deliberately, she pressed her elbows together to afford him a better view of her delectable cleavage. Usually this was a fail-safe tactic with any man that wasn't a blood relative.

With Jimmy, however, it turned out to be a mistake.

"Let's get one thing clear, young lady," he said, not bothering to keep his voice down. "I'm a happily married man. I'm immune to that shit, so don't even try it. All right?"

Rachel blushed so violently she thought her cheeks might burst into flames at the table. Not since Bobby Cameron had anyone rejected her advances so completely, and at least Bobby was good-looking. To be slapped down by this horrid, fat little man was mortifying.

"Right now the jury's out on Milly," Jimmy continued, ignoring her rising color. "She may yet come good. But in the meantime"—he paused for dramatic effect—"I'm happy to explore some options with you."

Swallowing her pride, Rachel answered him. "What sort of options?"

"I don't know yet," he said. "Let's see how you do at the Belmont and have another chat after that."

"I don't know," she said churlishly. "I may have a number of offers on the table after the Belmont. Or I may choose to stay with Kravitz."

"Your call," said Jimmy, looking supremely unconcerned. Rachel had hardly touched her salad. But as he'd finished his, he didn't hesitate to flag the waiter down and ask for the check anyway. "Your agent has my number. If it makes sense to meet in June, then he can call me. I'll be in New York that whole week."

Inside, Rachel seethed quietly. What a rude, dismissive little shit! If it had been anybody else she'd have told him to stick it.

But she checked herself. This was Jimmy Price, after all, the man who held Milly Lockwood Groves's future in the palm of his fat, clammy hand. If proving herself at the Belmont was what she had to do to steal him from Milly, she'd do it.

"Fine." Getting to her feet she shook his hand with what was left of her dignity. "We'll talk again then."

Candy Price threw her head back against the pillow and moaned.

"Oh, my God, that's so good," she panted. "Don't stop, baby. Please don't stop."

Grabbing her around the waist as he bucked harder and harder inside her, Todd smiled. He had no intention of stopping. He'd waited for this moment a long, long time.

Ever since the night he first came to Palos Verdes with Bobby, in fact, he'd had the hots for Candy. But it wasn't until a few weeks ago that he realized the feeling was mutual.

He'd come to see Jimmy about the Orlando deal but arrived at the house to discover there'd been problems with the great man's G4 in San Francisco and he wouldn't be home for some hours. Candy had insisted he stay for dinner—not that he needed much persuading. They ate alone by the pool, where she flirted outrageously with him, at one point leaning over him in nothing but a microscopic gold bikini and heels and spoon-feeding him ice cream. That was an image he wouldn't forget in a hurry.

If it had been up to him they'd have fucked there and then. But Candy felt nervous in case one of the servants saw them or, heaven forbid, Jimmy got home earlier than expected.

"You surprise me, Mrs. Price," Todd had said, his lips so close to hers they were almost brushing and she could feel his breath on her face. "I'd put you down as a danger lover."

"Oh, believe me," Candy drawled, "I am. But these things are all the sweeter if you have to wait just a little for 'em, don't you think?"

He'd driven home that night so frustrated he could have strangled somebody, but made do with banging the life out of Milly instead. Still, Candy's promised delights remained very much on his mind. But first days, and then weeks rolled by and still he heard nothing from her. He was starting to think she must have chickened out and changed her mind. And then last night, out of the blue, she called to say that Jimmy would be tied up in meetings all day, and that she should be able to make up some excuse and sneak out to see him.

"All you have to do is get rid of Milly."

"Not a problem," Todd said, barely able to contain his excitement. It was a long time since he'd felt this fired up about a woman. "She's racing tomorrow, then in the afternoon she's shooting some new commercial in the Valley. She won't be back till very, very late."

Just when he'd thought he couldn't possibly want her any more, Candy showed up at his door at ten this morning in a berry-red trench coat and matching knee-high boots with nothing but some flesh-colored La Perla panties underneath. And she hadn't disappointed once he got her into bed either. Not only did she have the perfect body but she knew exactly what to do with it. It was quite a change from Milly's wide-eyed innocence.

"Mmmmmm," she groaned, closing her eyes in unashamed pleasure. "You're so fucking big."

"You do say the nicest things," he murmured, burying his face between her perfectly round breasts. He took his hat off to her surgeon. Some of those guys were little better than butchers, but Candy's body was a work of art.

They both jumped when her cell phone rang.

"Leave it," said Todd, pinning her arms back as she tried to reach down under the bed for her purse.

"Ah will," she said, wriggling free. "I'm gonna turn it off."

Retrieving the shrill, vibrating phone, she saw "Jimmy cell" flashing on the screen and, giggling, showed it to Todd.

"You're sure you don't want me to answer?" she teased him.

Snatching it from her, he hit the off button and flung the thing on the floor. "Just tell him you were otherwise engaged," he said, spreading her legs roughly and launching himself back inside her like a Scud missile. "I'm sure he'll understand."

Pulling into the driveway at Bel Air, Milly punched in the familiar code feeling more cheerful than she had in many days.

After weeks of disappointing times, she'd finally pulled it out of the bag at the Humboldt County Fair and beaten a decent field of runners, including Ramon Esteves on the awesome Pitchers Prince, to take first place. It wasn't enough to dig her out of the shit, but it was a start, and the first time that she and Cally had properly clicked, which was an achievement in itself. He was a good horse, really. It wasn't his fault he wasn't Demon.

After the race her day had gotten even better. Brad called and told her the director of today's commercial had called in sick, so they were going to have to reschedule. For the first time in . . . could it really be five months? she was going to have an afternoon off.

It was a bright, clear day, and as the gates swung open she saw the spectacular panorama of Century City, with downtown beyond, spread out before her like a futuristic mirage. It was weird how you could see a view that striking every single day and yet barely register it at all. But that was how it felt to Milly—like she was looking at it for the first time.

She was surprised to see both Todd's cars, the midnight blue Ferrari and the new silver Aston Martin Vanquish he'd had delivered last week, parked out front. He usually hit the gym at around this time, but she guessed he must have taken a rain check. Maybe—miracle of miracles—they would actually get to spend some quality time together.

Fumbling in her purse, she pulled out her key and let herself in. Downstairs everything sounded eerily quiet.

"Todd?" she called into the emptiness.

Nothing. Dropping her purse on the floor, she stuck her head around the study door, but it was empty. Maybe he was upstairs?

As she climbed, it suddenly hit her how physically tired she was.

Her limbs ached like hell. The race must have taken it out of her more than she thought. Boy, would it be nice to turn her phone off, collapse on the bed, and sleep for as long as she wanted.

"Babe?" she called again. Approaching the bedroom door, her pace slowed.

Was that voices she heard?

At first the noise was faint. It could have been anything. But as she got closer it became more and more distinct. It *was* voices, no doubt about it. A man's and a woman's.

And not just any man and woman.

She'd have recognized that whiny, Southern twang anywhere.

"Ahhhhh!" Todd, red in the face and sweating, naked except for a pair of white tennis socks, was on top of the bed, fucking Candy Price with such total abandon that he clearly had no idea they'd been discovered.

Candy was also oblivious at first, throwing her head back and forth melodramatically so her long blond hair flew everywhere, like a heavy metal rocker. Actually, what she most reminded Milly of was an Afghan hound bitch called Lucy they'd had at Newells when she was little. She was a lovely dog, but she did have a habit of tossing her head around in irritation whenever she had fleas, rather like Candy was doing now.

In shock, and not knowing what else to do, Milly cleared her throat loudly.

Candy was the first to look up. As soon as she saw Milly, she screamed and, unplugging herself from Todd's cock, dived under the sheet like a mouse that'd just seen a snake.

Todd, typically, was more composed.

"What are you doing here?" he said, pulling on his boxer shorts and smoothing down his disheveled hair. "I thought you were shooting in the Valley."

"It got canceled," Milly said numbly. It took a few seconds for her to clear her head enough to start to feel angry. "Anyway, what do you mean what am *I* doing here? I live here. What the fuck is *she* doing here?"

She pointed to the white, human-shaped lump whimpering under the covers.

"I'd have said that was pretty obvious," Todd said callously. "Wouldn't you?"

Milly's heart was beating so fast, it was hard at first to know what she was feeling. On the one hand, she'd suspected him of cheating for so long, it was hardly a surprise to finally see it. On the other hand, it still hurt.

She realized now, with searing clarity, that he'd never really loved her. Not properly. And that deep down, beneath all her insecurity and fear of losing him, she'd known it all along. But even in her wildest nightmares, she had never considered that Candy would be the one to replace her. How could she have been so stupid, so blind?

"How long?" she began. "I mean, how long have you two— Oh for God's sake, do get out from under there," she snapped at Candy. "You look completely ridiculous."

Like a naughty schoolgirl, Candy emerged, blushing, or at any rate red in the face. It might just have been sexual exertion.

"You won't tell Jimmy, or Amy, will you?" she pleaded, her drawl even whinier than usual. "Please, *please* don't say anything. It'd break his heart, Milly. He loves me, he truly does."

Unbelievable! Did neither of them have a shred of shame?

"I know he loves you," Milly said harshly. "Maybe you should have thought about that before you started playing hide the salami in *my* boyfriend's bed?"

Her flippancy was a defense mechanism. It was either that or break down on the floor howling, and she wasn't about to give either of them that satisfaction.

"Let's try to talk about this like rational adults, shall we?" said Todd.

"Oh, fuck off," said Milly. Even now, when he'd been caught red-handed, he still wanted to be the one in control. But she was through being patronized. "There's nothing to talk about. I'm leaving."

She was halfway downstairs by the time he caught up with her.

"Where are you going to go? You've nowhere to stay," he said, laying a restraining hand on her arm.

"Sweet of you to worry," she said sarcastically, "but I'll figure something out."

In fact, she realized sadly, he had a point. Other than Amy, she hadn't a single friend in LA she could turn to, and staying at Palos Verdes clearly wasn't an option—unless she fancied bumping into Candy over breakfast tomorrow morning. It'd have to be a hotel.

"Just as long as you're not planning on shooting your mouth off to Jimmy," said Todd. His tone left her in no doubt that he meant the remark as a threat.

"Oh?" Milly smiled defiantly, refusing to be cowed. "And what makes you think I won't pick up the phone to him the second I drive out of here?"

"Do, and you'll regret it," said Todd menacingly.

"Not as much as you will," said Milly. Even in the midst of her pain and humiliation, it felt good to finally stand up to him. "Bobby was right," she said. "You are a user. You betrayed him, and me, and now Jimmy. What's he ever done to you?"

"I wouldn't waste your tears on Price," said Todd. "In case you hadn't picked up on it, rumor is he's about to drop you like a stone. You know who he's been lunching with today?"

Milly glared at him silently.

"Your good friend Rachel Delaney."

"Bullshit," said Milly. "You're lying."

Todd shrugged. "Ask Candy if you don't believe me. I can assure you, your loyalty to Jimmy is entirely misplaced. Then again, you never were the most astute judge of character. Were you, my darling?"

But Milly wasn't listening. Every word that came out of the man's mouth was poison. She knew that now.

Grabbing her purse, she bolted out of the door and into her car, almost pranging Todd's precious Vanquish in her desperate rush to get away. She was crying, but they were tears of anger and shame more than sadness. She'd wanted to succeed so badly: to get Newells back, yes, but also for her own sake. The fame and the money and the lifestyle Todd gave her—in their own way they were all drugs, drugs that had hurt not only her but so many people she loved.

Because of them, she'd pushed her darling Demon so hard, she'd killed him. She could never forgive herself for that. Then there was Bobby, and Todd's betrayal over Highwood, that she'd been too blind to see and too foolish to stop. She'd let Todd cut her off from good friends, like Amy, and made decisions purely out of a fear of losing him, like agreeing to the *Playboy* shoot. It might have launched her career, but it had also been the final nail in the coffin for her relationship with her family, not to mention a gross betrayal of the cowboy culture of decency and family that Bobby had welcomed her into, only to have it all thrown back in his face.

Pulling out of the gates, she brushed her tears away with her sleeve and headed down the hill toward Sunset.

Some words of her dad's drifted back to her—"It's always darkest before the dawn," he used to say.

Milly hoped he was right. Because from where she was sitting right now, things looked very dark indeed.

CHAPTER TWENTY-SIX

It was the hottest, muggiest June Manhattan had seen in a decade.

Tired, irritable drivers leaned out of their car windows on Lexington desperate for a little breeze to ease the stifling heat of the traffic jams. Mothers dragged their children into stores, just to enjoy the air-conditioning for a few minutes, and every lunch break Central Park filled up with businessmen desperate for a chance to shed their jackets, ties, and even socks and shoes before the furnacelike air overwhelmed them.

Amy Price was one of the very few people actually enjoying the weather. Like everyone else in the racing world, her family spent the week before the Belmont in New York. Most years she dreaded it: being dragged from one dreadful, superficial party to the next, knowing she was bound to be the only heavy woman there and that Jimmy wouldn't hesitate to hide his embarrassment of her by cracking fat jokes at her expense.

But this year, everything was different. She was, for the first time in her adult life, thin. Not skinny, as such, but the sort of weight that meant she could wear a short skirt in hot weather without being stared at as a freak. Yesterday, she'd even managed to sneak a couple of hours off from babysitting duty and gone to Victoria's Secret to buy a new "Very Sexy" bra and some matching, seriously tiny panties—something that six months ago she wouldn't have believed possible.

It was the way Garth had looked at her last year when she'd caught him with Candy that started the change. She no longer just wanted to lose weight—she needed to. She needed to prove to all the Garths out there, but more important to herself, that she could do it. And weirdly, having made the decision, it wasn't even that hard. The first thirty pounds had pretty much melted away as soon as she cut back on the carbs. After that, it was harder work—she had to exercise for one thing, which was a giant pain in the ass. But the results were so tangible and gratifying, it was easy to stay motivated. Indeed, after a while it almost became addictive.

And it wasn't just physically that she'd changed. Tapping into her willpower had given her strength in other areas too. She was writing again—it would take more than one cynical New York publisher to crush her hopes—and learning to take her own advice and be her own coach, instead of relying on others to validate her and give her confidence. At first, when Milly had effectively dropped her as a friend to run around town with Todd having her picture taken, it had hurt Amy deeply. But over time, she came to see this as Milly's problem rather than her own.

Thankfully, things were now back on track between them. Having finally dumped Todd last month (she still hadn't told Amy why she left him or what had made her see the light, but who really cared? The main thing was he was gone, and good riddance) Milly had moved into one of the staff apartments over the stables in Palos Verdes. The first thing she did was come to Amy and apologize.

"You were right," she said, perching her bony butt on the end of Amy's bed, like she used to in the old days. "I was being selfish. And blind. He really is an asshole, isn't he?"

"The biggest," said Amy.

"I know I've been a cow and I don't deserve it. But I could really use a friend right now." It was so long since Milly had had a sympathetic ear, that once she started pouring out her troubles, she couldn't seem to stop. "It's not just Todd, you see," she gabbled. "My sponsors are on my case day and night about my weight and my race times, I still haven't saved anywhere near enough to get Newells back, and what I have saved I'm trying to give to Bobby—to fight this case with Todd, about the oil, you know—but anyway, he won't take it, the stupid, stubborn—"

"Milly."

"And now your father's even talking about having Rachel ride for him, I mean, Jesus! And there's no way he'll want to sponsor both of us, is there? I have to raise my game before Ruidoso Downs, I know I do, but it's so hard to focus when I'm stressed out all the time. Did I tell you Rachel's put Newells back on the market?"

"Milly." Sliding along the bed next to her, Amy hugged her tight, wincing inside at how horribly thin she'd grown. "For heaven's sake shut up."

But her smile told Milly she was forgiven, and soon both girls were laughing and hugging each other and sharing confidences just like old times.

Even so, Amy was worried for her friend. It seemed cruel that now that her own life had turned a corner and she could finally look with hope to the future, Milly should be so suddenly, desperately unhappy. She talked a good game about being over Todd. But Amy could tell she was lonely and that, whatever the bastard had done, it had hurt her pretty badly. Not being able to make things up to Bobby Cameron—last week Milly's face had lit up when a letter arrived for her from High-wood, only for her to open it to find it was her check returned without so much as a note of acknowledgment—plunged her into an even deeper spiral of regret and despair. No wonder her riding was suffering.

Still, thought Amy, she mustn't waste her precious week in New York worrying about Milly the whole time. Jimmy had made it clear that as long as she kept Chase and Chance out of their mother's hair, she was free to do as she liked on the trip—which meant a delicious week of culture, galleries, museums, and poetry readings stretched gloriously ahead of her. She intended to enjoy it.

Today she was off to the Gagosian, a gallery she'd wanted to check out for years. Stepping into the lobby at last, after a long struggle to get the twins' double-width stroller through the swinging doors, she felt a luxurious breeze of cold, conditioned air blasting her hot, sweaty face.

Thankfully, the boys appeared to have sunk into some sort of humidity-induced stupor, too exhausted to do anything other than suck lethargically on their lollipops in between naps. Despite all the battering and clanging as she'd wheeled them inside, both remained sound asleep now. She hoped they'd stay that way long enough for her to take in at least some of the exhibition in peace.

"There's a new show starting today," the receptionist informed her cheerfully. "Young Western Artists. It's free," she added, handing Amy a leaflet with a list of the painters featured. "But if you want to make a contribution to the gallery there's a box by the elevator."

"Thanks."

More out of politeness than anything else Amy started idly scanning the list. To her amazement she immediately recognized one name: Dylan McDonald.

It might not be the same Dylan, of course: the dark, handsome cowboy with a passion for portraiture that Milly had told her about. Bobby's best friend, the one who'd taught her to drive cattle. But the leaflet said he was from Santa Ynez, so there had to be a good chance it was him.

Wheeling the twins across the hall, Amy thrust a five-dollar bill into the donation box and stepped into the waiting elevator. A small group of people were already inside and sighed ungraciously as they were forced to make room for the stroller, one woman muttering "Kids that age, totally inappropriate," as the doors closed.

Emerging a few seconds later on the second floor, Amy headed for the bench at the far side of the room and sat down. Once she'd taken the weight off her feet for a minute she would search the various canvases for Dylan's work.

"Mind if I join you?"

Startled, she looked up into the smiling face of a divine being. Well, he was either that or a hallucination—real men didn't come that sexy. He was well built—not tall, but with the sort of chest and shoulders that made Desperate Dan look puny. And he had the most gorgeous hair, thick and curly, and playful blue eyes that somehow managed to twinkle even though they were practically closed into slits when he smiled, something he obviously did a lot if the fans of lines at his temples were anything to go by. She felt her throat go dry.

"No," she stammered. "Please. Go ahead. I was just . . ." He was so mesmerizing, she found herself unable to finish the sentence.

"Takin' a load off?" he offered.

"Ha-ha-ha!" she laughed nervously. Then, realizing this was not a joke, or even mildly funny, blushed and mumbled, "Exactly, yes. Exactly right."

Fuuuuck.

She hadn't expected to meet anyone today, so she'd made a point of running all the way from the hotel, convinced that all the sweat pouring off her would translate into at least two more pounds lost when she jumped on the scales tonight. But now—Murphy's law, of course—she'd bumped into, without question, the single most lovely man *in the world*—smelling like a trucker's armpit. Why? Why did these things always have to happen to her?

Luckily, unlike 90 percent of the good-looking guys Amy knew, this one appeared to be kind as well as handsome. He'd gallantly pretended not to notice when she'd gazed at him like an openmouthed retard, which was really awfully sweet of him.

"You an artist yourself or just an art lover?" he asked.

Help! He was making conversation with her. If only he'd stop smiling, she might be able to breathe.

Come on, Amy, get a grip. Say something. Anything.

"Er, no. No, no, not an artist. I'm a poet, actually. Sort of," she blurted, blushing bubble-gum pink as she heard the words tumbling out of her mouth.

"Really?"

He sounded genuinely interested, impressed even.

No, not really, she felt like screaming. What on earth had she said that for? She'd never even had anything published, for God's sake, and here she was claiming to be a poet!

She'd better change the subject before he had a chance to probe her any further.

"I'm interested in one of the artists here," she said. "Dylan McDonald. Do you know his work?"

"I should." The beauty laughed, tossing back his dark curls and revealing two rows of straight, even white teeth. Amy felt the panic rising within her. Had she unwittingly said something even more foolish? "That's me."

"*You're* Dylan McDonald?" She gasped.

"Last time I checked," he said. "But, you know, I think you must have me mixed up with someone else. This is my first exhibition. I'm not really a professional artist, you see, at least not yet. So I seriously doubt whether you've heard of me or my work."

"No, no, I have," said Amy excitedly. "I have, absolutely. Milly . . . You're the . . . cattle drives. I met Bobby. . . . Palos Verdes."

He nodded slowly. Her fragmented word association was difficult to follow, but he was starting to get the gist.

"What's your name?" he asked, once she'd stopped long enough to draw breath.

"*My* name?" She grinned inanely. "Oh, my *name*. Yes. I see. Amy. My name is Amy."

"Amy . . . ?" He raised a questioning eyebrow.

"Hmmm? Oh, sorry." It suddenly dawned on her what he was asking. "Price. I'm Amy Price. You've probably heard of my father, Jimmy."

Dylan did a double take. Bobby had described Jimmy's daughter as hugely overweight. But this girl was, if not exactly slim, then certainly no more than pleasantly plump. With her smooth, pale skin and shy, searching eyes she reminded him of a newborn calf: tentative, awkward, but in her own way quite beautiful.

"So you? Jimmy? Wow." Now it was his turn to be inarticulate.

It took them about fifteen minutes to untangle the whys and wherefores: what they were both doing in New York, what had brought Amy to the gallery, how long each of them were staying, before the conversation inevitably turned to Milly.

"How is she?" asked Dylan. Unlike Summer and Bobby, he had never blamed Milly for the current nightmarish situation with Comarco at Highwood. She might be many things, but he couldn't think her spiteful, or Machiavellian enough to sabotage her old friends so deliberately. Cranborn must have duped her the same way he duped Bobby. Those two had more in common than either of them wanted to admit.

"Not great," said Amy. "She feels awful about what happened at Highwood."

"It's still happening," said Dylan, shaking his head sadly. "The lawsuit's ongoing, and those assholes are all over the ranch like vermin. That's part of the reason I'm here. Figured if I could sell some pictures, maybe I could contribute a little bit to the legal fund, you know? If we lose the case, my family'll lose their home, their livelihood. Everything."

He had no idea why he was telling her all this. They'd only just met. But something about her made him want to open up.

"She really didn't know, you know," said Amy. "Milly, I mean. About Comarco and what Todd was up to. She wants to put things right more than anything. Do you think Bobby . . . ?"

Dylan shook his head. "Not right now. You gotta remember, even before all this Comarco bullshit, Milly was riding high with that whole 'English cowgirl' thing. The naked pictures." He blushed. "That really hurt Bobby. He felt she was making fun of our way of life, our heritage, exploiting it in the worst possible way. I guess it's hard to understand if you're not from a cowboy family."

"Not really," said Amy. "I understand. Milly can be very insensitive sometimes."

"Yeah." Dylan smiled. "Bobby too."

They fell silent then, both wanting to prolong the encounter but neither of them able to think of anything sensible to say. In the end they were interrupted by Chance who, after a long yawn, started whining for Amy to get him a drink.

"I guess I ought to be getting back." She sighed.

"Oh." Dylan looked crestfallen. "Really?"

"I'm afraid so," she said, glancing over at her increasingly fractious brothers. The cool air of the gallery seemed to have revived them, worse luck.

"Well, look, we should keep in touch, right?" Scrawling his e-mail address on the back of one of Carol Bentley's business cards, Dylan handed it to her. "I'd love to read some of your poems one day."

"Oh. Sure," said Amy, grinning from ear to ear like the Cheshire cat. It was the first time a man had ever given her his number unprompted—never mind a man as wonderful as Dylan. "Definitely."

Ten minutes later, she was skipping through the West Village, oblivious to the boys squabbling, and clutching Carol's business card to her chest like a talisman. She felt awash with a happiness so strong she could barely describe it, let alone control it. Ignoring the cynical stares of passing New Yorkers, she found herself laughing out loud and doing little pirouettes of joy all the way back to the hotel.

"We should keep in touch!" She repeated the words over and over, trying to conjure up the image of his face as he'd said them. "I'm Dylan McDonald. Let's keep in touch!"

For the first time in her life, she was properly, head-over-heels in love. With Garth she'd been obsessed. But this was different. It felt right in a way that things with Garth never had.

"Please," she prayed silently. "Please, please, God. I'll do anything you want. I'll be sweet to the boys and Candy, I'll go to church. Anything. Just please, let him like me back."

The day of the Belmont dawned fine and bright with only a light breeze rustling the trees in leafy Elmont.

By midmorning, a hundred thousand people would have descended on this sleepy suburb, famed only for its spectacular racetrack, Belmont Park, to witness the final and, many felt, most exciting of the Triple Crown races. This year the Derby and the Preakness had been won by two different colts, so in one sense the pressure was off. But on the other hand, the field was unusually wide open, which added an extra frisson of possibility for newcomers like Rachel.

If ever she was going to make an impression on Jimmy Price, this was her shot.

Thankfully, she'd slept well last night—not least because she'd been bored to death at dinner by Randy Kravitz's wife, who'd insisted on giving her the most long-winded history lesson about the Belmont Stakes.

"Not many people realize it," she droned, "but when August Belmont started the race, it was run in the Bronx. The Bronx! Can you imagine? Back in the 1860s?"

Rachel yawned. She couldn't imagine.

By the end of the night she was armed with more statistics about

Belmont Park than any rational human being ought to know. It was a 430-acre plot, had the world's largest grandstand, was the largest dirt racecourse anywhere in the world, and was, as Mrs. Kravitz must have reminded her a minimum of six times, "the greatest jewel of American racing."

Fucking snore. As if she gave a shit.

But even Rachel had to admit there was a certain energy about the Belmont that was different from anything she'd experienced in England. For anyone serious about Thoroughbred racing—owners, trainers, and jockeys—it was the pinnacle of their year. Owners fantasized about their jockeys lifting the coveted silver bowl, with its figure of Fenian, an early Belmont champion, adorning the lid. Jockeys imagined themselves as the next Eddie Arcaro or Bill Shoemaker, legends who'd won this most taxing and prestigious of races six and five times respectively.

"Of course, the one for you to beat is Julie Krone," Mrs. Kravitz told Rachel over coffee. "Randy knew Julie *very* well. She was the first woman to win. 1993 I think it was. Colonial Affair."

But by then, Rachel had switched off.

She knew exactly who she had to beat. And it wasn't Julie fucking Krone.

Unlike Rachel, Bobby had had a terrible night.

He was staying in some dive of a motel on the outskirts of town—anything to save a bit more money—but this was one economy he soon came to regret. Not only was the bed rock hard, with sheets made of some awful synthetic material that seemed specially designed to keep him drowning in his own sweat, but a broken faucet in the bathroom had dripped all night long like some kind of Chinese water torture, even after he'd painstakingly stuffed it with a rolled-up washcloth. By the time the first rays of dawn made their way through the grimy window above the bed, his eyes were so red he looked like one of those cartoon characters whose eyeballs shatter with exhaustion along the bloodshot fault lines, clinking into a million pieces on the floor. And if it were possible, he felt even worse.

Sipping grimly at a double-strength Starbucks coffee on his way to the track, he reflected again just how important today's race would be. If Thunderbird did well, he would at least be able to feel slightly less guilty about the risk he'd taken buying him. And if he didn't? Well, Bobby wasn't going to think about that.

With every penny he earned going into the legal fund to fight Todd and Comarco, there was nothing left for the cattle business, and the ranch he'd left at the start of the year when he began his training tour was on the brink of collapse. A few weeks ago, he'd even had to let go two hands who'd grown up at Highwood and whose fathers had worked for the Camerons for more than three generations. It was heartbreaking.

Wyatt had offered to break the news for him, but Bobby wouldn't hear of it, insisting on flying home to tell the men in person.

"I may not be much of a boss," he said, his guilt making him sound angry, "but I sure as hell don't need another man to do my dirty work for me. Call me a fool if you want to, Wyatt. But I'm no coward."

With Highwood on the brink of disaster, going in on a three-man syndicate with Barty Llewellyn on a colt he'd never even seen looked more than a little reckless. But Bobby's instincts told him it was a chance worth taking. Barty wasn't a man given to melodramatic displays of excitement, but when it came to Thunderbird he was like a kid at Christmas.

"Trust me," he'd said, in that one memorably breathless phone call six months ago, right after Comarco showed up. "If you don't get your ass on a flight to Kentucky and see this horse right now, today, you're gonna regret it for the rest of your life."

Bobby knew then that the gray colt would be something special. And so he turned out to be: flighty, unpredictable, but bullet fast when the mood took him. His only regret was that Barty got to be the one who trained him. Not that Llewellyn wasn't one of the best in the business, but Bobby would have dearly loved to spend more time with the horse himself. Still, it wasn't to be. With training jobs scheduled back to back all over the world to pay the attorney's fees, his travel schedule for the first six months of the year had been torturous. He'd had to content himself with hearing about the triumphs of Thunderbird's debut season secondhand. Even so, with every phone call from Barty reporting another win or success at another major trial, his spirits lifted. It was sad to say it, but at the moment Thunderbird's early promise was about the only positive, hopeful thing in his life.

He ought really to be in Ireland today, in the middle of a lucrative two-week training job. But he couldn't bring himself to miss out on seeing Thunderbird's first Belmont. Some things were still worth being irresponsible for.

Parking his rented Chevy in one of the reserved trainers' spaces, he marched across Belmont Park's famous grassy backyard, oblivious to the lush landscaping—towering oak and sycamore trees, and the two distinctive infield lakes—that earned the track its reputation for beauty.

"There you are." Barty, normally as calm as a Zen master on race days, sounded unusually anxious. "I thought you were gonna be here by ten? Damian's already on his way down to the weighing room."

"Sorry," said Bobby, rubbing his eyes, partly out of tiredness and partly in response to Barty's deep purple-and-pink-striped blazer. "I had a rough night. That's, er, quite a jacket you're wearing."

"Thanks," said Barty without irony. "It's lucky. It's the clothing equivalent of feng shui."

Fag shui, more like it, thought Bobby, but he didn't say anything. Llewellyn's dress sense had always been a law unto itself, and racetracks across America would be duller places without it.

Just then a brunette in skintight white jodhpurs and shiny black boots sauntered past, giggling over her shoulder as she caught him gazing appreciatively at her shrink-wrapped ass.

"Jesus, don't you ever quit with that?" Barty shook his head. "This is no time to be focusing on your dick, kid."

"I know that," said Bobby, tiredness making him snippier than he meant to be. Actually, his libido had been in hibernation for so long, he'd rather surprised himself by noticing the girl at all. Normally, training tours were open season as far as fucking around was concerned. Often it was only the thought of the girls that made being away from Highwood bearable. But this time, he simply hadn't had the energy.

Whether it was that the girls weren't as hot as usual or the financial stress that made him tired all the time or the thoughts of Milly—confused, angry, desperate thoughts that wouldn't go away no matter how hard he tried to shut them out—he didn't know. But whatever it was, his "batting average," as Sean used to call it, was at an all-time low.

"Look, sorry," he said. He didn't want to fall out with Barty, especially not today. "I slept like crap last night. I think I'm just feeling tense, you know?"

Barty nodded. He hadn't gotten a lot of rest himself.

"Why don't you go take a look at him? He's over there." He nodded toward a big silver trailer almost abutting the paddock. Thunderbird stood serenely on the grass in front, being rubbed down by two of Barty's grooms. "Happy as a clam, by the look of him."

Grinning, Bobby set off in that direction, only to find himself almost knocked off his feet by a girl in full silks, a jockey, coming the other way.

"For fuck's sake, look where you're going!" she hissed, despite the fact it was quite clearly she who had run into him.

The British accent instantly caught his attention.

"Rachel?" His surprise was genuine. Though he'd read some of her interviews slagging off Milly and was vaguely aware she was in the States and riding for Kravitz, he had no idea she was entered today.

"Oh. It's you," she said, with as little enthusiasm as it was possible to inject into only three words. Like Bobby, Rachel never forgot a slight. His rejection of her at Mittlingsford might have been two years ago, but it was seared into her memory banks for all eternity. "What are you doing here? Shouldn't you be running after cattle or mending fences or . . . whatever it is you do?"

Wow. He'd forgotten quite what a poisonous little madam she was.

"Actually, I have a horse running today. Thunderbird. Damian Farley's riding for us."

"Don't know him," she said dismissively, as though all the top U.S. jockeys were her personal friends and anyone not known to her was by definition an insignificant nobody. "Anyway"—she smiled maliciously—"I'm surprised you have time to spare for racing nowadays."

"What do you mean?"

"Well, perhaps I'm wrong." She fluttered her eyelashes innocently. "But didn't I hear that you were losing your family farm or something? I'm sure I did."

"I'm not losing anything," said Bobby through gritted teeth.

"No? I thought Milly's boyfriend—well, her ex-boyfriend, you know, the good-looking one—I thought he'd taken the place over? That must have been *terribly* tough for you. You know, Milly sleeping with the enemy, as it were."

She gave another tinkling little laugh. If she hadn't been a woman, Bobby would have hit her.

"It reminded me of something you once said to me, actually. At Milly's play. Do you remember?" Bobby looked at her blankly. "Something about only liking women you could trust. Wasn't that it?"

Each word was like an arrow twisting in his heart, but he wasn't about to give Rachel the satisfaction of showing it.

"Looks like you picked the wrong girl, as far as trust goes. Wouldn't you say?"

"What I'd say," he said, forcing a smile, "is that Milly had one thing dead right. You are a bitch. And you are quite fucking tragically obsessed with her. Why is that, by the way?"

Showing none of his self-control, Rachel exploded in righteous fury like a boiled-over teakettle.

"I am *not* obsessed with her! She wishes," Rachel spat.

"Oh, come on," said Bobby, who was starting to enjoy turning the tables. "Don't tell me you're dating that tool Jasper because you actually like him. Even you have more taste than that."

She spluttered but couldn't quite bring herself to contradict him on that point.

"That was purely to get at Milly," said Bobby. "As was buying Newells."

"I'm selling it now," Rachel said, for want of anything better to say.

"And starting this whole war of words in the press," said Bobby, ignoring her. "If that's not obsession, I don't know what is."

He had no idea why he was sticking up for Milly. After the way she'd let him down, and then having the brass balls to try to send him a goddamn check. As if he'd ever touch a penny of her English cowgirl, T-Mobile money. But Rachel's self-satisfied, mean-spirited needling was just too much for him.

"Luckily," she said, belatedly regaining her composure, "there are very few things less important to me than your opinion, Bobby. Now if you'll excuse me"—she turned on her heel, deliberately flicking her blond comet's tail of hair into his face as she did so—"I'm late for the weighing room."

Two hours later, Candy Price was up in her VIP seat, staring at her husband and wondering exactly how much longer she could bear to share his bed.

"Come on, Garth, you lazy son of a bitch!" Jimmy roared at the top of his lungs. "Move your fuckin' ass!"

Candy smiled. She remembered saying something very similar to Garth herself, at another New York racetrack only last year. Boy, did that seem like a long time ago now. She couldn't think what she'd ever seen in that idiotic peacock Mavers. Other than the fact that he wasn't Jimmy, of course.

Watching her husband's fat face grow redder and redder with each rising decibel, and the ugly purple veins at his temple begin to throb, she felt sure it couldn't be *very* wrong to hope for a heart attack. She'd given him five of the best years of her life, after all. Was a massive, instantly fatal coronary too much to ask in return?

It was only since she'd started seeing Todd that Candy had begun to find her marriage genuinely unbearable. Normally she had no trouble closing her eyes and thinking of her inheritance when Jimmy started pawing her—but not now. She'd had lovers before, of course, scores of them. But she'd never pined for any of them the way she did for Todd. She knew it was obsessive and impulsive and foolish, but she simply didn't care. Not since her teens had she felt so recklessly, hopelessly besotted. She wanted him, constantly, and Todd gave her every reason to believe that the feeling was mutual.

Soon, she feared, Jimmy was bound to start to suspect something.

Only a few nights ago he'd caught her crying after a surreptitious phone call to LA. (She was missing Todd so much on this trip, it was agony.) Anyway, she managed to think on her feet and told him she was missing the boys, which he seemed to buy. Unfortunately his response had been to "comfort" her—the same way all men had wanted to comfort her since her breasts started growing at fourteen. But she'd found his attentions so unbearable she had to feign a migraine and push him off.

It was almost getting to the point where she hoped he *would* find out and put them all out of their misery. Almost, but not quite. Losing her Learjet lifestyle and all the perks of being Mrs. Price was a huge price to pay. She had to be sure, a hundred, a thousand percent sure, that Todd would go the distance if she gave it all up for him. And right now, she wasn't.

In the meantime, she lived in constant fear of Milly spilling the beans to Amy or Jimmy or anyone at Palos Verdes. So far though, for reasons Candy couldn't fathom, Milly hadn't said a word. Maybe she was enjoying making her sweat? Or maybe, as Todd suspected, she had some sort of misplaced sense of honor or loyalty to Jimmy that held her back. Either way, having the ax hanging over her day after day was more than even Candy's nerves of steel could easily take. The sooner Jimmy dropped Milly and picked some other project to focus on— perhaps this girl Rachel?—the better.

"And it's still Best of Friends leading from Mommy's Boy," the commentator announced, "followed by Thunderbird, Guts and Glory, and Never Better coming up on the outside."

"Would you look at that!" Jimmy screamed, mistaking his wife for someone who cared. "That's Kravitz's horse in fifth, and he's fucking closing too. That British broad is riding the pants off Garth. I swear to God, I gotta fire that guy."

"Well, why don't you, then?" said Candy, bored stiff by the whole thing. "Sack him, and Milly, and hire Kravitz's girl instead. She can obviously ride, and she's more than pretty enough to promote."

"You know what?" Jimmy beamed at her. "You're right, as usual."

The best thing about Candy was that she wasn't just a pretty face. She got him, really got him, in a way that his first wife never had. He'd been thinking exactly the same thing himself, about hiring Rachel. Uncanny.

"Holy crap!" Along with the rest of the crowd, he leaped to his feet as Best of Friends, the favorite, inexplicably pulled up short within fifty yards of the finish line. Within the space of a few seconds, he was passed by no fewer than four horses. Suddenly it was a wide open race again.

"And it's Mommy's Boy," shrieked the announcer, whipping the crowd into a deafening frenzy of cheers. "Mommy's Boy from Never Better with Thunderbird closing, Mommy's Boy from Never Better . . . My goodness it's close between these three! And it's Mommy's Boy! Thurston Morton on Mommy's Boy takes the Belmont."

"God*damn* it!" said Jimmy, petulantly hurling his race card onto the floor. Garth Mavers had ridden like an amateur from the start.

"And surely it must be a photo finish for second place," the voice went on, "between Never Better, ridden by Miss Rachel Delaney, and the surprise star of this season, Thunderbird. What a brilliant performance from Damian Farley this afternoon on the little gray."

Jimmy clenched his teeth. He was tired of being disappointed. Be it quarter horses or Thoroughbreds, he raced to win. And his horses hadn't been winning, not for a good long time.

For months he'd been willing Milly to come good. But every time she suffered a setback in her personal life—first it was Demon dying, now the breakup with Cranborn—it seemed to knock all the competitive stuffing out of her. Real stars were made of sterner, steelier stuff. Like Rachel.

"I tell you." He turned to his wife. "If Milly doesn't pull off something pretty fucking spectacular at the All American, she's out."

"None too soon, if you ask me," said Candy. "You're much too soft, you know, Jimmy. You shouldn't let people take advantage of you."

He smiled. Garth may have just lost him the biggest race of the season. But he still had the most beautiful, loving, supportive wife in the world.

CHAPTER TWENTY-SEVEN

Linda Lockwood Groves flashed her member's badge at the steward and was waved forward, her natty new Range Rover Vogue directed toward the members-only parking spots directly behind the grandstand.

She'd driven up to York last night, to watch Jasper ride in the two thirty. It was July, but nobody seemed to have told the weather. The thin, gray drizzle that had settled over central Yorkshire late last night had at last stopped, but it remained gloomy overhead and dank underfoot, and the car park was still half empty as a result.

Cecil had always rather liked this sort of weather, Linda remembered sadly. It used to make him go all gooey and romantic. How many times had she heard him wax lyrical about the rain-drenched gloss on the landscape or the smell of the dry stone walls that reminded him of his childhood?

She'd never shared his love of the rain. But she had loved him with all her heart, and she still missed him terribly. So much had gone wrong in the last year, she was more in need of his advice and comfort than ever. Milly doing those awful *Playboy* pictures and turning her back on her family, Jasper never coming home and behaving more and more erratically. Even Rachel, who'd seemed like such a tower of strength and support in the beginning, had let her down, disappearing off to America without so much as a postcard and then saying all those hurtful things about Milly in the papers. It was all very strange, especially when one considered that she was still supposedly Jasper's girlfriend—although how the two of them kept things going at such a distance, Linda had no idea.

The final shock had come a couple of weeks ago. Bored one afternoon, she'd taken a stroll into town. (She often found herself at a loose end since her move into Newmarket. At the time she'd been thrilled at the prospect of leaving all the hassle of Newells behind and moving to a town house. No more early-morning starts to turn out ponies or check on grain deliveries, no blasted cockerel shrieking outside her bedroom window at all hours of the night. It was supposed to have been bliss. But the truth was, with Cecil gone and both the children away, she actually missed the old routines and found her new life in town crushingly lonely.)

Wandering aimlessly down the high street, she'd suddenly stopped in her tracks. A huge, full-color photograph of Newells was plastered all over the window of Jackson Stops & Staff. The little minx had gone and put it up for sale—and for a whacking great profit, mark you—without so much as a phone call to warn her! It was all most upsetting.

When she'd tackled Jasper about it on his last trip home, he'd claimed to be as in the dark as she was.

"There's no point asking me, Ma." He pouted, holding up a purple silk tie next to his new pale blue Thomas Pink shirt, trying to decide whether it worked or was a bit too news-readery. "If Rach condescends to call me at all these days I consider myself lucky. She's far too high and mighty to ask for my advice, let alone my permission."

Linda didn't understand it at all. Rachel had been so considerate, such a treasure when Cecil died. She couldn't imagine what had happened.

Still, she mustn't dwell on it. Making her way precariously across the muddy ground toward the clubhouse, she fixed a smile to her face and tried not to think about her ruined Patrick Cox mules, or how out of place she felt at the races without Cecil. Today was Jasper's day. That was the important thing. Even if all the other women in his life let him down, she, his mother, would be there for him.

Down in the jockeys' changing room, Jasper made sure nobody was looking before taking another furtive peek inside the envelope. Few things gave him more satisfaction than the feel of note after note of ready cash brushing against his fingertips, and this time Ali had been more than usually generous. Twenty thousand pounds—all in fifties. It was more than he'd ever been bunged on a single race before.

He needed it, too. He still owed money for his share in the yacht he'd chartered with some mates last month in Sardinia, not to mention five grand to his coke dealer.

What a great fucking party Sardinia had been. For all his moaning about Rachel leaving him in the lurch and his pathological, obsessional envy of both her and Milly's ever-growing fame in America, being left girlfriendless in Europe for the summer had its advantages. Not only was he free to screw his way from Les Caves to the Billionaires' Club without looking over his shoulder, but as a bit player in the Milly-Rachel feud, he also got to enjoy the novelty of being snapped by gossip-mag photographers wherever he went, which didn't do him any harm in the pulling stakes. But still, his new hedonistic lifestyle wasn't cheap. His current target, a stunning three-day eventer called Leonora with an aristocratic lineage that pissed all over the Delaneys and tits that could be seen from space, was maddeningly refusing to give it up without some token of commitment on his part. Last night she'd kissed him for two solid hours before buggering off home, leaving him with a hard-on the size of Brazil and a level of sexual frustration he couldn't remember experiencing since his early teens.

With today's cashish, he'd be able to get her a little something from Cartier and still have enough left over for the honeymoon suite at Claridge's. If that didn't charm the uptight bitch out of her knickers, nothing would.

All he had to do now was get out there and plow the race. Then he could focus on plowing Leonora.

Linda emerged onto the clubhouse balcony, pink gin in hand, and sat herself down next to Martha Tooley, a racing wife she knew slightly from Cambridgeshire. Against all the odds the clouds had lifted and a few hopeful rays of sunlight were filtering down onto the racetrack, making all the jockeys in their bright silks stand out like bejeweled jesters in the paddock below.

"Have you spotted Jasper yet?" asked Martha, handing Linda her binoculars.

"Not yet. Ooo, yes, look," she said excitedly. "There he is!"

Wearing the blue and green colors of the Dhaktoubs, Jasper turned and waved to her before guiding his horse, an enormous bay called Babylon that looked more like a shire horse than a racehorse, toward the starting stall. As always before a big race, he was nervous and could have done without his mother's eager, hopeful, overbearing presence in the stands. But in his current financial position, he couldn't afford to be churlish. Keeping his good standing at the Bank of Linda was more essential now than ever.

"Lovely looking horse," said Martha truthfully. "Is he the favorite?"

"I'm not sure," said Linda, who knew he was but felt bad putting the pressure of even more expectation on Jasper. His results this season had not been great, and she was worried that he might soon lose his place riding for Ali—although Jasper himself seemed remarkably unconcerned by his string of lackluster performances this summer.

Once the race got under way, Linda was embarrassed to discover that she was actually clasping Martha's hand with nerves.

"I'm so sorry," she said, blushing when she realized what she was doing.

"Don't worry," said Martha kindly. Linda wasn't a particular friend, but like all the Newmarket wives Martha felt sorry for her, being widowed so young and then having all that ghastly business with Milly to deal with. Cecil Lockwood Groves had been such a lovely man. He'd be turning in his grave if he could see the way his children were behaving, not to mention what had happened to the business he'd spent his whole life building. It was tragic. "I used to be exactly the same when my son was racing. Terrifying, isn't it?"

Linda nodded gratefully. "It is," she said. "And I so want him to do well. Recently . . . well, I feel a bit disloyal saying it. But his results haven't been as good as I'd have hoped."

Admittedly, she didn't understand much about the mechanics of racing. But even Linda couldn't fail to notice the way that Jasper continually seemed to lose momentum in the last crucial moments of his races, snatching defeat from the jaws of victory, as it were. She groaned with disappointment now, along with much of the crowd, as once again he did the same exact thing, mistiming his sprint finish and pushing

Babylon forward just two or three seconds too late. This time he was second by no more than a neck.

"Damn and blast!" she said, springing to her feet, maternal concern written all over her face. "I'd better get down to the paddock. He'll be awfully upset with that."

"Good luck," Martha called after her.

Down below, all was bright and wet, with the newly rediscovered sun bouncing off the glistening grass and dripping trees. The ground, however, was still treacherous, and Linda had to tread slowly and carefully as once again her heels sank like daggers into the ooze.

"Blast," she muttered to herself. "Where is he?" Craning her neck, she tried to make out the Dhaktoub colors through the crowds. Eventually, she spotted him on the far side of the paddock.

"Darling," she called, shrilly. "Yoo-hoo! Jasper!"

Still mounted, Jasper was chatting animatedly to Ali Dhaktoub and his trainer and obviously couldn't hear her. Oddly, as she drew closer, Linda could see that all three of them were smiling. Surely they ought to be looking miserable, after missing out on yet another supposedly surefire win?

Moments later, their smiles evaporated, however. For there, advancing purposefully toward them through the surrounding crowd, were a group of uniformed policemen. Seven of them, by Linda's count.

What on earth was going on?

Shocked silence fell across spectators and press alike as the senior officer, distinguishable by his multistriped cap, strode directly up to Jasper.

"Mr. Lockwood Groves? And Mr. . . . ." he glanced down at his notepad, "Ali Mishari Dhaktoub?"

"Yes?" said Ali.

Jasper, who'd turned a violent shade of green, said nothing.

"What seems to be the problem, officer?" Ali smiled thinly.

"I'm afraid I'm going to have to ask you to come with me, sir. You too, sir." The policeman nodded toward the trainer, who was trying surreptitiously to step back from the group, like St. Peter when the first cock crowed.

"May I ask why?" said Ali. Whatever he might be feeling inside, externally at least he remained calm and unperturbed.

"I'll explain everything at the station. Sir."

The policeman was in his fifties and, though Ali was no expert on ranking within the force, had enough white stripes on his shoulder to indicate that he was not a man to be trifled with. This, combined with his polite but extremely firm manner and the fact that he had evidently deemed it necessary to bring reinforcements, persuaded him that cooperation was, at this point, almost certainly the best option.

"Very well," he said curtly. To his amazement, handcuffs were produced. Before he had time to protest, he found himself being grabbed by two men, cuffed, and frog-marched toward the waiting squad cars.

Jasper, who'd remained still as a statue on Babylon up to this point, as though by not moving he could somehow make himself invisible, now whimpered audibly.

Up till now Linda had remained frozen, like everybody else, watching with horror as the drama unfolded. But as Jasper was forced reluctantly to dismount and the press, jolted out of their coma, surged forward to photograph him being handcuffed, flashbulbs erupting everywhere, she battled her way to the front.

"Jasper!" she yelled hysterically. "Let me through! I'm his mother. Jasper!"

He looked up briefly, but her voice was soon drowned out by hundreds of others as microphones and cameras were thrust unceremoniously into his face.

"Don't say anything," yelled Ali over his shoulder. Flanked by an officer at either side, he had finally lost his cool and could be heard loudly demanding to be allowed to call his solicitor.

It was unnecessary advice anyway. Jasper was far too scared to open his mouth.

His last view before he was bundled inside the squad car was of Linda, mouthing something at him that he couldn't make out, her face a study in panic.

"Wait, that's my mother," he said, struggling between his two burly escorts. "I need to speak to her."

"Right now, son," said the larger one, ignoring his protests and man-handling him firmly into the car, "I'd say your mum was the least of your worries. Wouldn't you?"

To Jasper's horror, he reached into his coat pocket and pulled out the cash-filled envelope with Ali's distinctive, looped handwriting on the outside.

"Recognize this?"

Jasper went from green to white.

"No," he said, his voice barely above a whisper. "I don't. But I'm not saying another word till I speak to my brief."

Outside the Santa Barbara County Courthouse, Bobby was having some legal problems of his own.

"It's not over yet." Jeff Buccola, the four-hundred-bucks-an-hour attorney he'd hired to fight his case against Comarco, made an effort to sound upbeat. "We can keep stalling on those soil samples for another few months at least. Every specimen they bring in, every piece of evidence they put forward, we can challenge."

"Oh yeah?" said Bobby caustically. He was tired of being given false hope by this bozo. "And what am I gonna pay you with, Jeff? Beans?"

His training tour had been a great success financially, and Thunderbird getting placed at the Belmont had been the icing on the cake of an exceptional season. Overnight, the horse's value had more than quintupled. But that wasn't much use to Bobby if he couldn't sell him, something that Barty, unsurprisingly, refused to countenance.

"Look, Bobby, I'm sorry about Highwood, really I am," he said, over celebratory beers on the night of the race. "But you can't seriously expect me to part with him now? This is just the beginning of his career. You know that. Besides, even if we sold him, your share'd get swallowed up in that case faster than you can say 'lost cause.' All you're doing is delaying the inevitable."

He was right, of course, on both counts. It made no sense to sell Thunderbird or to go on with the court case. But the latter wasn't a choice. It was a matter of honor, like a captain going down with his ship. While he had a penny to his name, Bobby must keep fighting for Highwood, no matter what. He didn't expect Barty to understand.

The judge today had been sympathetic, especially after Bobby's impassioned speech about his family having worked the land in the Santa Ynez Valley for generations, and the irreparable damage to the landscape, water table, and overall ecosystem at Highwood that Comarco's planned drilling would cause. But effectively, his hands were tied.

The law in this instance was clear: landownership rights and deeds of title applied only to the surface land, not the natural resources beneath it.

"Call me on Monday," said Jeff brusquely, clicking shut his briefcase. He felt sorry for Bobby, but at the end of the day the kid had only himself to blame for his problems, and he was tired of his client's arrogance and moodiness. What did he want him to do, change the frickin' law? "We'll discuss next steps then."

Hurrying down the courthouse steps Bobby almost crashed straight into Dylan, who was bounding back up them two at a time. Along with the rest of his family he'd come to lend Bobby moral support. But he'd had to sneak out of court twenty minutes early to make a prearranged call to Amy, so he'd missed the final verdict.

"What happened?" he asked breathlessly.

For reasons he couldn't quite articulate, Dylan had decided to keep his budding relationship with Jimmy Price's daughter a secret, so he couldn't explain his absence. Though he hadn't seen her since their chance meeting at the Gagosian, they'd become regular text-message buddies. Before he knew it, the little snippets of contact he shared with Amy had started to become the highlight of his days. Whenever things at the ranch got too bleak, or he needed to talk to someone about art and life—or anything other than Todd Cranborn, oil wells, and legal fees—he turned to Amy. Kind, encouraging, and funny, she seemed to have the knack of knowing exactly what to say to make him feel better. Talking to her was like taking a deep breath of oxygen after hours underwater. Like being brought back to life.

"They ruled in Todd's favor," said Tara.

"Again," added Summer bitterly. "And what are *you* grinnin' about?"

"Me? Oh, nothing. Nothing. That's awful." Guiltily, Dylan wiped the smile off his face. It wasn't right to be feeling any happiness, let alone showing it, while everyone else's world was in meltdown. "It's not over though, right?" he said, turning back to Bobby. "We can appeal again. Right?"

"You can. But I wouldn't advise it."

En masse, they spun around to see Todd, flanked by two lawyers that looked more like minders, standing smugly behind them. He hadn't been in court, so what he was doing here now was anybody's guess.

"No point pouring good money after bad, is there, Bobby?" He smiled. "How does that Kenny Rogers song go again? 'You got to know when to fold 'em.' Now, that's the sort of cowboy wisdom I can appreciate."

"Why don't you go on home, Mr. Cranborn," said Wyatt, stepping forward. "We're not looking for any trouble. Are we, Bobby?"

Bobby, who was grinding his teeth so hard he was in danger of shooting sparks out of his mouth, looked as if trouble would suit him just fine.

"Milly not here?" Todd feigned surprise. "When we split up she seemed quite passionate about how I'd wronged you. I'm surprised she couldn't be bothered to put in an appearance in your hour of need."

"We don't speak anymore," said Bobby. He wasn't sure why he was even dignifying Todd's taunting with a response, but the words seemed to fall out of his mouth. "As you well know."

Though strictly speaking, this was still true—Bobby and Milly had not, in fact, spoken—she was very much in the forefront of his mind. The first time she sent him a check for the legal fund—guilt money as he still thought of it—he'd sent it straight back without even reading the accompanying letter. But when she tried again, his resolve had deserted him. He hadn't accepted the money, of course—wild horses couldn't persuade him to do that—but against his better judgment, he had opened her note.

In some ways, it was vintage Milly: garbled, overemotional, full of childish spelling mistakes that for some reason made his eyes well up with tears. But in others it was different, more mature. He'd tried to read the changes in her character and her life between the lines.

I'll be at the All American in August, she wrote at the end, *assuming I haven't lost my job by then. And I know you will too. Sean told me you've been training Dash for Dixie for Marti Fox.*

Damned Sean and his big mouth. What else had he told her?

I'd like to think we could meet as friends, she went on. *But whatever you decide—whether you take the money or not—please know that I'm truly sorry, Bobby. For everything.*

He'd thought about it so many times, run every possible motive she could have had over and over in his mind till it ached with confusion. And he still didn't know what to think. All he did know, for sure, was that whether she was to blame or not, he missed her. He wished he didn't. But there it was.

Hearing Todd mention her name now only made him feel it more acutely.

"Why don't you fuck off, Cranborn," he snarled, "before you get hurt."

"Easy," whispered Dylan, laying a hand on Bobby's arm. He could feel his biceps twitching with longing to lay into the guy. Not that he blamed him. He wouldn't have minded taking a swing at Todd himself.

"Don't worry," said Todd. "I'm on my way." But he couldn't resist one passing shot before he left. "You know, I reckon you had a lucky escape with Milly, actually. She turned out to be more trouble than she was worth. Clingy. Needy. And as for the sex," he chuckled maliciously, "you'd have more fun screwing a skeleton."

That was it. Brushing Dylan aside, Bobby launched himself into the air with a roar of pent-up fury, wrestling Todd to the ground. The two lawyer minders scuttled back like terrified crabs, watching in awe as Bobby flipped their client over, grinding his face into the hard stone of the steps, before yanking his arm backward so painfully that Todd couldn't help but scream.

"Don't you ever, *ever,* speak about Milly like that again," he shouted. "You hear me, you fucking nasty, depraved little son of a bitch?" On the last word he twisted Todd's arm still further, till it looked in serious danger of dislocating. "You're not fit to know her."

"Bobby, let him go," said Wyatt calmly but firmly. Bobby wavered for a moment, holding his position, before finally doing as he said and dropping a spluttering, wincing Todd facedown onto the hard stone steps.

The two lawyers instantly rushed forward to help him to his feet, but Todd shrugged them off. His cheek was scraped and bleeding from where Bobby had ground it against the step, and his right arm hung limp at his side. He was evidently still in some pain.

"First degree assault," he hissed. "In front of witnesses. Smart move, Cameron. And here I was thinking you could barely afford the one lawsuit."

Turning away, he limped off to his car, leaving his threat hanging in the air behind him like a bad smell.

"What did you do that for?" Everyone else looked concerned for Bobby, but Summer was outright angry. Ever since that awful day when he'd found out the truth about Hank being her father, Bobby had had to watch her anger and resentment toward him grow. When he came back to find her, after Diana dropped the bomb, she'd been expecting him to make love to her. Instead he'd been colder and more distant than ever—and he couldn't tell her why.

No wonder she resented him. She must think he'd been trifling with her feelings on purpose, leading her on just to let her down and humiliate her for the second time. But what could he do? He'd promised never to tell her the truth, and it was a promise he intended to keep.

"I had to do something," he said, defending himself. "You heard what he said about Milly."

It was like gasoline on Summer's flames.

"Milly?" she shouted furiously. "You're worried about *Milly*? She's the one who got us into this mess in the first place."

"No," said Bobby sadly. "She's not, Sum. It was me. I'm the only one to blame."

But Summer had already stormed off, sobbing, down the street.

"Don't worry about her," said Wyatt, wrapping a reassuring arm around Bobby's shoulders. "She's just emotional. We all are. Today's been a tough day."

"Yeah," said Bobby. He felt like crying and running away himself. "Yeah. It has."

CHAPTER TWENTY-EIGHT

The All American Futurity is to two-year-old American quarter horses what the Kentucky Derby is to three-year-old Thoroughbreds: the race that really counts.

Every year at the end of August the normally peaceful village of Ruidoso, New Mexico, bursts into life as thousands of fans make their annual pilgrimage to the Ruidoso Downs racetrack and casino to watch the greatest quarter horses in the world compete in the Labor Day final.

Thanks in no small part to Milly, whose T-Mobile ads had helped bring the sport to a much wider audience, this year the buzz in the village was even higher voltage than usual. Unheard-of crowds of over twenty thousand were expected for today's final, many of them hoping to see the English cowgirl stage her much-vaunted return to form after a hugely disappointing second season.

Milly herself had done her best to stay isolated from all the gossip in the weeks leading up to the race. She'd barely set foot outside Palos Verdes and had been focusing as hard as she could on her training. She'd even taken her life into her own hands and turned down engagements that her sponsors had specifically requested she attend.

"You realize you're hardly in a position to start dicking us around," the new press liaison officer for T-Mobile had told her sharply the second time she cried off. "Your contract expires at the end of next month, and renewal is still very much an open question."

But for once Milly held her ground. "Make your mind up, would you?" she said. "Either you want me to win at Ruidoso or you don't."

"Of course we need a win," the press girl snapped.

"Then bugger off and let me train in peace," said Milly, hanging up. No one had called back, which she decided to interpret as a positive sign. If she'd been fired, she was pretty sure someone would have called to tell her so. And for the first time in months—since her win at the Humboldt County Fair, in fact, the day that she'd gotten home to find Todd hard at it with Candy—she felt both her own performance and Cally's were genuinely improving.

Gill thought so too.

"You see," she said, the day before they drove down to New Mexico, when Milly had pulled off a personal best time up at the gallops. "You two do have chemistry. All you need to do is trust him a little bit."

"I guess," Milly said doubtfully, although deep down she was delighted and flooded with relief. After so many disasters, she was starting to believe the hype that maybe she *was* a one-season wonder and had lost her touch.

"'I guess' nothing," said Gill firmly. "You never did a quarter mile that fast with Demon. Your only problem is confidence."

She was right, of course. The truth was that by dumping her for Candy, Todd had shattered Milly's already fragile confidence into a million pieces. It was hard to stick it back together on demand, especially with Rachel snapping hungrily at her heels like a piranha fish, and both her sponsors and Jimmy giving her a hard time about everything from her weight to her attitude.

She didn't know for sure whether Todd's affair with Candy was still ongoing, and she didn't want to know. But the dreamy, faraway look in Candy's usually ice-cold eyes was a pretty clear indication that it was. Milly hadn't told a soul about what had happened that day. Not, as Candy and Todd both assumed, out of loyalty to Jimmy but out of straightforward embarrassment and humiliation. Whatever she might feel about Todd—hatred, anger, righteous indignation—it was a blow to her pride to have to admit that he'd sexually rejected her for another woman. Not to mention blatantly used her to carry out some spiteful vendetta against Bobby. Whichever way you cut it, he had made her look weak and stupid. She wasn't in a rush to share that with the world.

It was that same feeling of weakness that stopped her challenging Jimmy directly about whether or not he was planning to drop her in favor of Rachel. If he was, she figured, she'd know about it soon enough. And as nothing she said would change his mind anyway, there wasn't much point in humiliating herself by asking the question. The best thing she could do was get her head down and keep working. Try to prove to him once and for all that *she* was the one with the talent.

Slumped over the toilet in her trailer on the morning of the big race, Milly threw up violently for the second time in an hour.

"Are you okay?" Gill rapped gently on the door. Pre-race nerves were to be expected, especially with the press hounding the poor girl to death every time she set foot outside and fans demanding to have their picture taken with her or their programs signed. But she really sounded unwell in there.

"I'm fine," Milly croaked halfheartedly. She was still on her knees, her clammy forehead pressed against the cool porcelain of the toilet bowl. "I'll be out in a minute."

Christ, she felt awful. She'd never known nerves like it.

If only Demon were here. Sure, Cally was coming on in leaps and bounds. But she still missed her darling Demon horribly.

"You look like death warmed up," said Gill, not unkindly, when she finally emerged. Handing her a hot, sweet tea she forced her to take a seat on the makeshift couch.

"Thanks," said Milly shakily. "Look, don't get mad." Sipping at her drink, she shivered like a shipwreck survivor. "But, do you happen to know if Bobby Cameron's here yet? I'd go out and look myself, but it's such a zoo out there, I can't face it."

Gill sighed. This, she suspected, was the real reason Milly's digestive system had decided to go into orbit. It wasn't Todd, or the rumors about Jimmy and Rachel, or even the pressure of the race that was terrifying her. It was the prospect of running into Bobby again.

After he'd returned her first letter and check, Milly had summoned up all her courage and decided to try again. Somehow, she needed him to know how sorry she was, how she hadn't meant for any of this to happen, how Todd had duped her too. But she never received a reply. Ever since then, she'd been haunted by the thought that, as far as Bobby was concerned, she had deliberately betrayed him and Highwood.

"I haven't seen him," said Gill patiently. "But there are twenty thousand people out there. It's pretty unlikely our paths would cross by chance."

"Yeah," said Milly absently. In her mind she was obviously miles away. "Yeah. I guess you're right."

"Here." Dylan handed Bobby a Dixie cup of warm beer and sat down beside him on one of the old canvas chairs outside Marti Fox's trailer. "Drink up and cheer up, wouldya? You're frightening the horses."

Today's race would mark the official end of Bobby's training tour, which ought to have been a cause for celebration. Even if Dash for Dixie hadn't a hope in hell of getting placed.

The beer was disgusting, but knowing how long Dyl must have stood in line for it at the overcrowded, overpriced bar, Bobby drank it anyway.

"Thanks," he said. "Oh, here, before I forget." Reaching into his jeans pocket he pulled out a fat roll of fifty-dollar bills bound with a grimy plastic band and pulled off five of them, which he thrust into Dylan's hand. "Your wages. For the last three days."

"My what?" Dyl frowned, swatting the money away. "Don't talk crazy. That money's for the fund and you know it. Besides, all I did was hold a couple o' lead ropes while you did your thang. I know it's sad, but coming out to Ruidoso is my idea of fun, not work."

This was only partly true. He'd actually flown down to New Mexico for two reasons: to act as moral support for Bobby, which these days was about as much fun as having root canal surgery without anesthetic—and to see Amy.

For the past three days he'd done the best job he could with the first part of his mission, listening patiently for hours on end while Bobby poured his heart out about losing Highwood.

And it was heartbreaking. The last of the quarter horses had been sold to a rival outfit in Los Olivos, and the new stables, that less than two years ago had been Bobby's pride and joy, were being used as temporary storage sheds for Comarco's equipment. Thunderbird was now the only horse he owned, even then only in part, and he was thousands of miles across the country in Kentucky. All that was left of the cowboy idyll he'd inherited were the few remaining untouched meadows and a hundred-odd head of cattle. Not forgetting, of course, legal debts the size of the Grand Canyon.

What Dylan didn't know was that it wasn't only the nuts and bolts of the ranch that Bobby was losing. Ever since Diana had told him about Hank's affair, he'd had to face up to the fact that his father was not the man he thought he was. He'd spent his entire life trying to live up to an ideal that didn't exist, that had probably never existed. In some ways, that was the heaviest blow of all.

He couldn't wait for Summer to go back to Berkeley. Having her around at home was indescribably painful. He couldn't stop himself looking for glimpses of Hank in her face, then thinking back to their kiss. True, it was only a kiss. But remembering how he'd felt then opened the door to a Pandora's box of awful, disturbing images. She was his sister. His *sister*. Some days he felt so guilty and revolted by it, he could hardly breathe.

"We should go on up to the stands, you know," said Dylan, grimacing. This wasn't beer, it was cat's piss. "The race starts in twenty minutes and there's already a crush out there you wouldn't believe."

In fact, it wasn't the race that made him anxious to get back to the action but the prospect of finally seeing Amy again in the flesh, for the first time since New York. Absence, in this case, had certainly made his heart grow fonder, although he was also nervous. They'd both built today up into such a big thing, but they hadn't even kissed yet. What if it was a disaster?

"You go," said Bobby, flinging his crumpled plastic cup into the trash. "I'm gonna stop by the paddock first, take a last look at our boy. I'll join you in a minute."

It was a five-minute walk from the trailer to the paddock, where this year's sixteen fastest, fittest two-year-old quarter horses and their riders had already begun to gather. For all of them this was the most important race of the year; for some, the most important of their lives.

Easing his way politely through the crowds, Bobby told himself it was only professional to show his face trackside. He really ought to bid a final good luck to Dixie and his jockey. It'd look churlish not to.

The truth, though, was that he couldn't keep away.

He had to see her.

He wouldn't go up to her or anything. Just hang back in the crowds and take a look. Then he could make a lightning dash over to Marti, make his excuses, and get out of there.

No problem.

Milly emerged from the weighing room looking greener than ever and walked straight into a sea of cameras.

"Over here!" they yelled. "Milly!"

"How're ya feelin'? Confident?"

"I'm fine, thanks," she said, forcing a smile as she tried unsuccessfully to jostle her way through.

"How's Cally doing?"

"Word is you shaved two seconds off your best time with Demon in training last week. Is that true?"

"Has Rachel Delaney called to wish you luck?"

It was hopeless. She obviously wasn't going to make it out to the paddock without help. Ducking back through the changing rooms where the press couldn't follow, she bolted for the ladies', locking herself in a cubicle and trying to get her breath back.

"Breathe," she murmured to herself, fighting down the nausea. "Just focus, all right?"

She heard the door open and two female stewards coming in to check their makeup. At first she was able to tune out their idle chatter. But then she heard a name that made her sit up and take notice.

"It's Delaney, not De Mornay," one of the women was saying. "You know. Rachel. The one who hates Milly, the one who's dating her brother."

"Yes, yes, I know, what*ever*," snapped her friend. "But how do you know she's signed. I mean, you haven't seen the contract, have you?"

414

Milly felt all the hairs on the back of her neck stand on end. What contract? Signed what?

"Of course not," said the first steward. "Jimmy Price is more secretive than the Kremlin, you know that. But I heard his wife telling her friend about it with my own ears. He's putting her on the payroll."

"D'you think that means he's dropping Milly?" asked the other. "But what if she wins today? He couldn't drop her then, surely?"

"I dunno. He might. I mean, let's face it, she doesn't look well, does she? I've seen starving Ethiopians with more meat on their bones than that one. If anyone needs to 'get more,' it's her. More potato chips!"

Milly heard them laughing as they left, slamming the door shut behind them.

Her mind was racing. She thought today was going to be a make-or-break. But was it already too late? Had Jimmy really signed that bitch behind her back?

Thankfully, there was no time to dwell on what she'd heard. She was already late. Pulling herself together with an effort, she slipped out of a side door with her head down and made it out to the paddock, where Cally was waiting.

Bless him. He looked as relaxed as a grandpa off for a Sunday stroll, quietly munching the grass as if he hadn't a care in the world.

"There you are," said Gill, looking relieved as Milly vaulted up into the saddle. "I was starting to panic you'd run off."

A few seconds later, Milly wished she had. She felt her heart drop down through her rib cage into her boots and blinked.

But no, she wasn't imagining things. There, standing right in front of her like Clint Eastwood in an old Western movie, was Bobby.

She hadn't laid eyes on him since that terrible night in Bel Air, the night she'd first slept with Todd. She was shocked by how different he looked.

Back then he'd been so strong. Furious, yes, and hurt but still physically powerful, like a dying bull shrugging off the matador's spears, roaring and charging even as the blood poured out of his side. But now? Now he looked resigned, tired, almost broken in an awful sort of way.

She knew she wasn't one to talk, but he'd lost a lot of weight. And he had a distinct slump to the shoulders she was sure had never been there before. Where was the Bobby she remembered, the Bobby of fire and fury, the arrogant, cocky, devil-may-care cowboy she'd first seen from the top of the stairs at Newells and fallen so totally and helplessly in love with?

And then it happened. He looked up and caught her staring.

In that split second the deafening cacophony of Ruidoso Downs faded into white noise, and the crowds seemed to melt away, till it was just the two of them standing there. If her heart was still beating, Milly couldn't feel it.

Bobby, on the other hand, was aware of nothing but the pounding of his heart, getting faster and faster and louder and louder till he was sure it must be audible to passersby.

He'd seen countless pictures of Milly on TV and in the papers since the last time they met. But seeing her in the flesh was different. She looked ill. Tiny, pale, underweight. Just terrible. The urge to run over, lift her down from her horse and carry her away, was so strong he felt himself being pulled physically forward. But every step he took became more faltering and uncertain, till in the end he simply stopped in his tracks and stared back at her.

"Hi." Her voice was so faint that at first he didn't hear her, just saw her lips shape the word. Clearing her throat she tried again. "I didn't know if I'd see you today."

"Yeah, well," he said gruffly. "Here I am."

Milly felt herself starting to get the shakes and gripped Cally's mane for support.

"You sent back my letter," she said. "I understand why. I mean, I think I do."

"No you don't," said Bobby caustically. "How could you? You don't understand anything."

He wanted her so much. Wanted to forgive her, to love her, to be everything to her. But in some inexplicable way, his desire seemed only to fuel his rage. It was like he was programmed to lash out, to keep on pushing and pushing until he'd pushed her away completely—like some twisted form of self-defense.

"All you ever cared about was your own success, no matter what the price. Well, now you've got it. I hope you're happy, that's all."

He started walking off. Desperately she called after him.

"I'm *not* happy! Bobby, please. I didn't know about Comarco. Todd never told me anything. You have to believe me. I didn't know!"

But he was already gone.

"Oh, shit. Shit, shit, shit. That doesn't look good."

Dylan was up in the stands watching the race. Standing beside him, in the place that should have been Bobby's, was Amy. She was holding his hand and—despite the nightmare playing out in front of them for poor Milly—grinning from ear to ear.

It hadn't happened the way she'd imagined it. But it was perfect just the same. Having spent a fruitless hour trying to track Dylan down when she'd first arrived—stupidly she'd been in such a rush this morning at the hotel, getting the boys dressed and ready, she'd forgotten her cell phone—she'd all but given up hope when, miraculously, he bumped into her at one of the ice cream stands.

"Hey!" His eyes lit up immediately, banishing all her worries about him having changed his mind and not being interested anymore. "Is one of those for me?"

Glancing down stupidly at her hands, she remembered she was holding two ice cream cones, peace offerings for the boys who she'd left alone with their dreadful mother for far too long. The ice cream was already beginning to melt, sending trickles of sticky, slow-running goo dribbling down her wrists.

"Actually, they're for the kids," she said, beaming up at him, unable to hide her delight at seeing him again.

"Hmm." Dylan grinned. She was even sweeter and prettier than he remembered. "Well, do they deserve them? Have they been good?"

"Good? Hell no!" Amy giggled. "They've been vile, as usual."

"In which case," said Dylan, prying them out of her sticky hands, "I reckon we should eat 'em ourselves."

But he didn't eat them. Instead, he dropped them both unceremoniously on the ground, pulled her to him, and kissed her so hard and for so long that people stopped to stare at them.

From then on Amy had been lost in a delirious fog of happiness. She allowed him to whisk her off to watch the race with him and Bobby, only Bobby never made it. She didn't even care anymore that her father would be apoplectic, left to cope with the boys on his own.

Dylan McDonald loved her. That was all that mattered.

But even in her cocoon of bliss, she felt sorry for Milly as the race unfolded, and she could tell Dylan did too.

"Something must have happened," she said, shaking her head. "She's been riding so well. Oh, poor Milly. It's just not fair."

"It's a lot of pressure." Dylan shrugged. "Maybe the crowds are throwing her off?"

"No," said Amy. "She's used to that. It's something else. It must be something else."

It was only a four hundred and forty yard race, but Milly made it look like four thousand, staggering out of the gate slumped forward onto Cally's neck like a drunk. For someone so light, she managed to act like a deadweight as the horse made a valiant effort on his own, dragging her toward the finish like an injured soldier. By post six they were already trailing the field. By the time they crossed the wire, there was clear daylight between Milly and the rider ahead of her.

The whole thing was over in under thirty seconds. But it was without doubt the worst race of her life.

"Do you think I should get down there?" asked Amy, her face clouded with concern.

Dylan nodded. "I think *we* should, yes."

How she loved the way he said "we"!

Watching her gaze up at him with those wide, palest-of-blue eyes, Dylan felt himself melt. Slowly, still slightly nervously, he bent his head to kiss her again, pressing his dry lips against her own, delighting in the feel of her soft, porcelain skin against his day-old stubble.

"I don't care what anybody thinks," Amy whispered, drunk with happiness. "Not Dad, not Candy, not Milly, not any of them. I don't want you to be a secret anymore."

"Me either," he said, hugging her so tightly she could barely breathe.

"Come on," she said, reluctantly wriggling free. "We have the rest of our lives to do this. Right now I think Milly needs me more than you do."

"I very much doubt that," said Dylan, biting his lip with frustration. "But okay. Let's go."

Unfortunately for Milly, Amy wasn't the first member of the Price family to make it to her trailer.

"What in the fuck was that?" Jimmy bellowed, his fat jowls shaking as he paced back and forth. "Are you fucking retarded or something?"

"Go easy on her," said Gill. She had no idea herself what had gone wrong. But tearing into the poor girl now wasn't going to help anyone.

"Go *easy* on her?" The concept was obviously a new one for Jimmy. "I've been going easy on her for the past six months, Gill. What am I, a fucking charity? You think T-Mobile is gonna go easy on her?" He gave a short, derisive laugh. "People invested a lot of time and money in you, Milly. *I* invested a lot of *my* time and *my* money." He jabbed out each word with an accusatory finger. "But you let me down. You let yourself down. Jesus."

Milly could hear his words but only as a faint, distant echo, as if her ears were stuffed with cotton or she was just emerging from a deep sleep. When Bobby had stormed off in the paddock, something fundamental had snapped inside her. Like all the myriad pressures of her life had finally reached boiling point, and her systems had simply stopped functioning.

She didn't even remember riding Cally down to the starting gates. Nor could she explain to Jimmy, Gill, or anyone else what had happened during the race. It was all a blur.

"There's no easy way to say this, Milly," said Jimmy, lighting a new cigar. "So I'm just going to tell you straight. You're fired."

"Hey, now hold on, hold on," said Gill, leaping to Milly's defense. Someone had to. She herself was just sitting there as mute and unmoving as a statue. "Let's not be too hasty."

Today had been heartbreaking for Gill, too: watching all her hard work of the last month being washed down the drain.

At the worst possible moment her cell phone let off a series of insistent, high-pitched beeps. Some reporter, no doubt, looking for the first quote from Cally's trainer on the shock result. She realized then that she'd been so caught up shielding Milly from the slavering bloodhounds outside, she didn't actually know who'd won.

While Gill was delving into her purse to retrieve the damn thing and turn it off, there was another brief knock on the trailer door and Amy walked in, hand in hand with Dylan.

"Where the hell have *you* been?" Jimmy immediately turned his fury on his daughter. "Poor Candy's been going outta her mind with the boys. And who is this clown?" He glared at Dylan, who glared back.

For once Amy ignored him, rushing straight over to Milly and hugging her.

"You poor thing," she said gently. "What on earth happened?"

For the first time since the race, Milly seemed jolted out of her stupor. Looking perplexedly from Amy to Dylan and back again, she finally broke her self-imposed silence.

"You? And Dylan?" She nodded toward their still-entwined fingers. Amy nodded, beaming like a lighthouse.

"But how? I mean, when did you? . . . I don't understand."

"We'll explain later," said Amy. "You're what's important right now. Tell us what went wrong, Mill."

The tears that had been welling in Milly's eyes for the last few minutes finally began to trickle down her face. It was like the floodgates opening.

"I ran into Bobby," she sobbed. "Right before the race. And he hates me, Amy. He really does. He hates me."

"Damn it," muttered Dylan under his breath. "I knew it. Stupid, stubborn son of a bitch . . ." Then, turning back to Milly, he said, "Look, sweetheart, he doesn't hate you. I know that for a fact."

"But you didn't see his face, Dyl. The way he looked at me." She shook her head miserably.

"Trust me." Dylan took her hand. The year and a half since they'd last seen each other seemed to melt into nothing in an instant. "He's just lookin' around for someone to blame, that's all. Losing the ranch has been so tough on him."

"He's lost it?" Milly looked horrified. "He's lost Highwood?"

"Well, no, not yet," Dylan corrected himself. "But the writing's on the wall. He can't afford to keep fighting the case."

For the second time in as many minutes, a cell phone went off. This time it was Milly's.

"Don't answer it!" said Gill. But it was too late. On autopilot, she'd already picked up.

"Hello?"

"Milly?" The voice on the other end of the line was so crackly and faint that at first she didn't recognize who it was.

"Yes? Who's this?"

"Milly, it's me. Mummy."

It took a couple of seconds to sink in.

"Mummy?"

"Yes, darling. Oh, Milly." Linda's voice started cracking into tears so violent that she was soon struggling to get her breath. "Something . . . something awful's happened."

No shit, thought Milly wryly. I've just been fired; my career's over; Rachel's about to steal what was my job, along with any other remaining shreds of my life that she hasn't already taken; Bobby hates me; I have half the world's press waiting to begin a feeding frenzy on my public humiliation—and you call to tell me you've got problems!

"Don't cry, Mummy" was all she actually said, drying her own tears. As always, Linda's extreme neediness brought out her own sensible, coping side. Someone had to hold it together. "What is it? I'm sure it can't be that bad."

"It is!" Linda wailed. "It is, it's terrible. Jasper's been charged with fraud! And they won't grant him bail or anything. He's in York prison, Milly. *Prison!* And he won't let me see him. He won't even let me call . . ."

She broke down at that point, the few words that made it through her subsequent heaving sobs not coherent enough to mean anything to Milly, or anyone else for that matter.

"Listen, Mummy, try not to panic," said Milly, when at last she was able to make herself heard, adding, with devastating understatement: "I'm a bit in the middle of something right now. Can I call you back in half an hour?"

"Half an *hour?*" Linda was on the verge of hysterics. "It's one in the morning here, Milly. I need to talk to you *now.*"

Milly sighed. "I'll ring as soon as I can, I promise." God knows what sort of a mess J. had got himself into this time. But there was obviously no way her mother could cope on her own. She'd have to go back to England, and the sooner the better.

Hanging up, she rolled her eyes at Amy, who had the good sense to giggle. Suddenly, nothing seemed quite so important anymore. In fact, Milly had an awful feeling she might be about to burst into laughter herself—hardly appropriate under the circumstances.

Jimmy, on the other hand, looked far from amused. He'd expected tears from Milly, and, if not begging, at the very least a groveling apology for today's fiasco. Instead she seemed more concerned about Bobby Cameron's problems and arranging trips to England than being given her marching orders.

"Amy," he barked. "Go back and take care of your brothers. Milly and I aren't finished yet. And you can apologize to Candy while you're at it for running off like that."

Amy took a deep breath.

"You know what, Dad?" she said. "Screw you."

"Excuse me?" Jimmy was too surprised at first even to yell at her. "What did you just say?"

"I said, 'screw you.'"

Milly felt her heart swelling with pride and grinned at Dylan, who was obviously feeling the same thing. It was about time Amy stood up to that fat, bullying bastard.

"I'm not your slave," she said calmly. "If Candy doesn't want to look after her own children, she shouldn't have had them."

"Don't you dare speak disrespectfully of Candy!" said Jimmy, finding his voice at last. "She's a wonderful mother."

"She's a *terrible* mother!" said Amy. "Honestly, Dad. I love you. But how can you be so blind?"

Getting to her feet, Milly pulled on a sweater and checked her reflection briefly in the mirror, blowing her nose and wiping away her remaining tearstreaks on her sleeve. Amy and Jimmy obviously had things to discuss. She may as well leave them to it and face the inevitable onslaught of reporters outside. She still had no idea what she was going to say or how she could explain what had happened. But the sooner she got out there and showed her face, the sooner it would all be over.

"Where do you think you're going?" fumed Jimmy, seeing her trying to sneak out the door with Gillian. "I haven't finished with you yet."

Maybe it was the hectoring tone of his voice that riled her. Or perhaps the fact that she no longer had anything to lose. But something made her spin around and give it to him with both barrels.

"You just fired me, Jimmy, remember? In case you're not familiar with that term, it means I don't work for you anymore."

"You get back here!" he shouted. "You owe me an apology, young lady, not to mention some goddamn respect."

"I owe you nothing," said Milly. "You made me money, I made you money, and now it's over. End of story. Besides, with me out of the picture you'll be free to finalize things with Rachel Delaney. Oh, sorry, my mistake." She smiled sarcastically. "You already have, haven't you?"

"Rachel has nothing to do with this. . . ." Jimmy stammered. It was the first time Milly had ever seen him on the back foot, even for a moment. She found it oddly gratifying.

"Even if I'd won today, you were still going to replace me, weren't you?"

"Not necessarily," he lied.

"Look, Jimmy. I'm grateful for the start you gave me," she said. "But this whole English cowgirl thing—it's not what I want anymore." It was only once she'd said the words out loud that she realized she actually meant them. "So you and Rachel, you go right ahead. Don't feel bad about replacing me."

"I don't," said Jimmy nastily. "Not for a second."

The door swung open to reveal a scowling Candy with a screaming child in each hand. Her beautiful cream Ralph Lauren jacket was covered with every sticky substance from chocolate cookie smearings to snot, her hair was so tangled it looked like she'd lost a fight with a wind propeller, and her usually immaculate makeup had been pawed and slobbered on by her children into a blotchy, hideous mask.

It would be fair to say she wasn't looking her best.

"Shit," whispered Dylan to Amy. "Who invited Cruella De Vil?"

"Jimmy!" Candy sounded furious, her baby-doll cadences replaced by a steely tone. "Ah've been lookin' for you everywhere. And *you!*" She pointed a bony finger at Amy, shaking with rage.

"This is ridiculous," said Gill, whose temper was finally starting to fray. "It's like Times Square in here."

"I'm sorry, baby," said Jimmy, relieving Candy of both the boys when Amy made no move to do so. "I came to tell Milly I'm letting her go."

"Good," said Candy, her ill temper making her more than usually vindictive. "I should think so too after that race. Disgraceful."

Milly had been on the point of leaving—if Jimmy wanted to rant and rave he could do it at someone else for a change. But Candy's taunt pushed her over the edge. There were some things she simply couldn't let go.

"You know, Jimmy," she said casually, "if you want something you *can* feel bad about, try this for size: Your wife's been screwing my boyfriend—sorry, my *ex*-boyfriend—behind your back."

Jimmy's mouth opened, then closed. He looked at Candy, searching her face for signs of denial. But Milly's ambush was too sudden. Candy had no time to hide the guilty rush of blood to her cheeks.

Every ounce of color drained from Jimmy's face. Amy looked pretty stunned too.

"That's right," said Milly. "It's been going on for . . . hmmm, how long must it be now, Candy? Three months? Four?"

"You liar!" shrieked Candy. But it was too late. Nobody believed her.

"I caught the two of them in bed together." Milly twisted the knife. "Back in June. That's why Todd and I broke up, in case you ever wondered."

And with that she walked out and slammed the door, leaving the atom bomb to explode behind her.

CHAPTER TWENTY-NINE

"All rise."

The judge hobbled back into the courtroom and everybody else got wearily to their feet. With his red ceremonial robes and white curly wig, Mr. Justice Carmichael reminded Milly of a slightly scrawny Father Christmas who'd had his beard shaved off and with it all his ho! ho! ho! jolliness. He looked even more somber and miserable than usual this afternoon, which she prayed was not a bad omen for Jasper.

"Oh, God," whispered Linda, surreptitiously grabbing her hand. "This is it."

"He'll be fine," said Milly, trying to sound more reassuring than she felt. "Whatever happens, Jasper will cope. We all will."

It was touch and go this morning whether her mother would even make it to court for the verdict, her nerves were so fraught. Ever since Milly had gotten home (if you could call Linda's ghastly town house with its ruffled curtains, shag carpeting, and heavy use of chandeliers "home") Linda had been a nervous wreck, suffering every conceivable symptom of stress from nausea and tension headaches to fever, panic attacks, and even occasional fainting spells. Sitting rigid backed beside Milly now, she was so highly strung you felt she could snap at any moment, like an overtuned guitar string.

She uncrossed her legs again—it was a devil to try and get comfortable on these bloody wooden seats—her mind wandering back over all the changes of the last six weeks. Being back in England felt desperately strange after so long away. Everything seemed unaccountably smaller: from the roads and the cars right down to the blueberry muffins in Starbucks that must have been half the size of the ones in California. But the strangest thing of all was not being at Newells.

Apparently, the agents had accepted an offer for the place—but from whom and for how much Milly was unable to discover, despite repeated phone attempts using pseudonyms and dodgy accents, pretending to be a foreign buyer. For now, though, it remained unoccupied, and a week after she got back Milly made the ten-minute drive from Newmarket to take a look, and see what changes had been made since her dad's funeral.

She knew it would look different, of course. But nothing had prepared her emotionally for the shock of seeing her beloved home empty and abandoned. The stables in particular made her want to cry. Cecil had always kept them gleaming and spotless, his pride and joy. But now doors hung loosely from their hinges, old pieces of bridles and stirrups lay rusting in the gutters, and giant drifts of dead leaves lay piled up against the walls of the stallion barn.

Fixing one of the stable doors back in place herself, Milly looked up to see a grimy wooden nameplate still nailed just beneath the roof. Wiping off the worst of the dirt with her sleeve, her eyes welled up with tears when she saw the name: Easy Victory.

Standing there, seeing Easy's name, brought back a flood of memories, both painful and happy. She remembered the day that Cecil first bought Easy. How gawky and unprepossessing a horse he was to look at, but how much she'd adored him even then. She remembered her last ride with him, before her accident ruined everything and kept her out of the saddle for two long years—years that at the time had felt like forever but now seemed like nothing more than a tiny blip. She remembered how poisonous Rachel was the day Easy covered her mare, when she'd first started flirting with Jasper. (Needless to say, his arrest had been the death knell for their sham of a relationship. Which was about the only good thing to have come out of the whole sorry affair, in Milly's view. Apart from it bringing her back home, of course.)

But most of all she remembered the night of Easy's death. She remembered the way Bobby had comforted her when she'd believed no comfort possible.

With all her heart, she wished he were here to comfort her now.

That night, she drove back to Newmarket with her resolve hardened.

She still intended to get Newells back somehow—she had to—but in the meantime she would set about undoing every strand of damage Rachel had caused piece by piece.

"You're terribly thin you know, darling," Linda insisted, spooning the most enormous heap of shepherd's pie onto her plate as Milly tried to outline her plan of action. She was about to protest, but the delicious medley of oniony, meaty smells assailing her nostrils got the better of her, and she realized she was, in fact, famished.

"Never mind that," she said, reaching straight for the ketchup, and proceeding to drown out the flavor of the home-cooked beef with a sticky river of red sauce, gobbling down the resulting slop greedily while she spoke, to Linda's silent horror. "I need you to look into livery stables for me. See if you can find us a decent rate from one of daddy's old mates."

Linda looked blank.

"I'd do it myself," said Milly, swallowing so fast she succeeded in burning the roof of her mouth. "But I'm going to have my hands full, what with Jasper's court case and tracking down Radar and Elijah and the others. Never mind transporting them all back here."

"I'm sorry," said Linda. "Transporting who? Back where?"

"Do *listen*, Mummy," said Milly, exasperated. Sometimes it was like trying to keep the attention of a three-year-old. "I may not have enough money to buy Newells back. Not yet anyway," she added defiantly. "But I do have some savings left out of my T-Mobile money. Enough to find out which knacker's yard that cow sold Daddy's stallions to and go and buy them back."

"But, Milly," Linda protested weakly. She'd never understood Milly's obsession with horses, never mind how she could be worrying about Cecil's old stallions, of all things, while her brother's future hung in the balance and her family faced social ruin. "They could be anywhere by now. And what if their new owners don't want to sell them?"

"Course they will," said Milly confidently. "Everyone wants to sell if the price is right."

In fact, finding the horses did prove to be a mission, and at times quite a harrowing one. Many of her dear old friends had been shipped abroad, to places where she knew she had next to no chance of tracking them down. She cried her eyes out the day she learned that Elijah had last been seen getting into a truck bound for Saudi Arabia—one of Jasper's connections had bought him for a song, apparently. As if the Dhaktoubs hadn't caused her family enough grief already.

But there were moments of joy too. Radar turned out to be less than twenty miles away. Old Anne Voss-Menzies, it seemed, had never lost her interest in him and had jumped at the chance to acquire him when Rachel started selling off Newells's stock.

"I'm really not sure I want to part with him," she said, sensing Milly's desperation when she turned up at Cedarbrook, checkbook in hand. "He's just coming into his own this season."

The price the old witch ultimately wrangled out of her was nothing short of extortionate. But Milly didn't care. Just seeing Radar prick up his ears and whinny in delighted recognition when she ran out across the field to greet him was worth all the money in the world, and then some.

She wished she could spend all her time with her beloved horses. But unfortunately, this wasn't to be. Someone had to take charge of Jasper's defense. Linda was far too much of a nervous ninny to deal with lawyers or make important decisions. And Jasper himself, despite having been transferred to a relatively cushy remand center outside Cambridge, remained so deeply mired in terror and self-pity about his upcoming trial that he was no use to anyone, least of all himself.

Which meant it was Milly who got to spend hour after hour holed up in solicitors' offices choosing counsel and agreeing on a strategy for the defense. Although quite how J. intended to defend himself, other than by pleading guilty and looking remorseful, she had no idea. Even by his standards the Dhaktoub scam had been a mind-blowingly stupid, risky thing to do.

The fact that Milly was kept so busy did at least mean she had mercifully little time to dwell on the mess she'd left behind in California. The six weeks since she'd left already felt like six years. A single long letter from Amy was the only contact she'd had with her old life.

Dad's filed for divorce, Amy wrote, *and Candy's moved into Todd's place, with the boys, if you can imagine that.*

Even Milly had to smile at the mental picture of Todd playing the doting stepdad to Chase and Chance. Not to mention Candy trying to cope without Amy. They wouldn't last a day, surely?

Turns out she never signed a prenup, so Dad's screwed basically, Amy continued, *although money seems to be the last thing on his mind right now. Honestly, you should see him, Mill. He's just so . . . sad. But he's also like a different person. He's been really sweet to me, and he even called Donny the other day. That's the first time in six years.*

What else can I tell you? You probably don't want to hear about Rachel, but I thought you should know that she's not *riding for Daddy after all. Randy Kravitz offered her a bunch of money to stay, and all this Candy business has totally distracted Dad from racing anyway. On a happier note, I saw this photo of her in last week's* Enquirer, *which I know you'll appreciate.*

Darling Amy, she'd ripped out a picture of Rachel at some charity do in Palm Beach looking distinctly triple chinned. It was probably a bad angle. But still, any shot of Rachel looking fat and ugly had to be worth keeping.

Dylan's fine. He brought me out to Highwood for the first time last week. Oh my God, it is so beautiful! I don't know how you could ever have wanted to leave.

Milly had had to stop reading at that point and take a couple of deep breaths. But after a few minutes she forced herself to go on.

And you'll never guess what. Dad's considering helping Bobby get the appeal going again. He's so mad at Todd, I think he wants to get back at him any way he can, including stopping him getting that oil. We'll see. At the moment Bobby's refusing even to talk to Dad. Dyl's been trying to talk him around.

Typical Bobby, thought Milly. Stubborn to a fault, even when he was being offered a lifeline. She could understand him not taking her money. But now that they had a common enemy in Todd, surely he could bury the hatchet with Jimmy?

We all miss you, especially me, Amy signed off, *and Dylan says hi! Good luck with your brother's trial—we're thinking of you—and make sure you take care of yourself. Xxx. Amy.*

The letter was bittersweet. Most of the news was good—but nowhere did Amy say that Bobby had had a change of heart toward Milly or that he no longer blamed her for everything.

Maybe she simply had to let it go? She might want Bobby's forgiveness and his friendship. But she had no right to expect either if he wasn't willing to give them.

In the meantime, she had her own fish to fry. Jasper and Linda might not be easy, but they were all the family she had. And right now they needed her more than ever.

Taking their lead from the judge, everyone sat back down in their torturously uncomfortable seats and waited for him to begin his summing up.

Glancing to her left, Milly saw Ali Dhaktoub's family and supporters. Sitting on the other side of the aisle, they were dressed to a man like urbane Westerners in Hugo Boss suits and silk ties from Liberty. As Cecil would have said, not a towel head in sight.

Ostensibly, they were here to "support" Jasper. But everyone knew that their real reason for being in court was to try to glean something from today's proceedings that might be helpful in the appeal they planned for their own son. Ali had been tried separately last week and received a four-year sentence, which had rocked his wealthy, powerful family to the core and made the front pages of the papers in England and across the Middle East.

It had also, needless to say, scared the shit out of Jasper. Although Zac Spiro, his young but brilliant barrister, had assured him he was very unlikely to be treated so harshly himself, especially since he'd pled guilty.

Milly liked Zac from the beginning. He was handsome, albeit not in a classic Brad Pitt sort of way. There was a diffident, vaguely academic look about him that, combined with his striking six foot five frame, lent him the air of a bookish, Jewish Clark Kent. But his wicked, wry sense of humor had been a godsend in the days leading up to the trial, and he and Milly had spent many long evenings burning the midnight oil at various Newmarket pubs, running over strategy and tactics.

It rapidly became obvious that there was a spark between them, or at least a latent attraction. They'd even talked about it. But they both agreed that now was not the time to pursue it.

Unfortunately, however, desire, once acknowledged, is a tough thing to put back in its box. Ever since Zac had admitted how he felt, the two of them had been circling around each other like a pair of wary dogs, unsure whether to mate, play, or rip one another's throats out.

"The seriousness of what you have done cannot be overestimated," the judge began inauspiciously, his booming voice bringing Milly back to the present with a nasty jolt. Jasper, openly quaking in his seat at the front of the court, looked white as a sheet.

"Furthermore, the fact that you not only carefully planned but repeated the offense on numerous occasions over a twelve-month period shows a forethought and awareness of what you were doing that, in my view, compounds the situation."

Fuck, thought Milly. This doesn't sound good.

The judge went on. "On the other hand, and in mitigation, I am convinced that the physical violence and reprisals that you suffered at the hands of Mr. Dhaktoub's associates, and your fear of further such reprisals, played a large part in your decision to carry on with a scheme which you might have otherwise wished to abandon."

On the other side of the court the Arab contingent shook their heads bitterly, but Milly was too busy watching J. to notice. Despite all the bad blood there'd been between them, she couldn't help but feel sorry for him today.

"Taking all this into consideration, as well as the fact that you sensibly decided to plead guilty to both charges, I have decided to impose a custodial sentence of six months, with parole eligibility at no less than three months."

The hammer came down with a very final thud and Zac spun around and grinned at Milly, who smiled back. Six months was a great result, better than any of them had realistically expected. If he made parole he might even be home in time for Christmas. Even Jasper looked visibly relieved, giving a tentative wave to Linda before he was led back down to the cells.

"Six months?" Linda turned an anguished face to Milly. "That seems an awfully long time for such a silly mistake. How's he going to survive in there for six whole months?"

"Oh, Mummy." Milly frowned. "He's been very, very lucky, thanks to Zac. He could have gotten far longer. Anyway, he'll probably only serve three. That's twelve weeks. That's nothing."

"Will they let us see him?" Linda asked Zac, who was unable to wipe the grin off his face as he came over to join them. He was happy with the result, of course, but happier still to see Milly looking foxier than ever in the sexy forties-style suit she'd worn for court.

"They should," he said kindly. He could see Linda was on the brink of tears. This whole thing had been a nightmare for her. "If you come with me now, they normally give them ten minutes or so with their barristers before they whisk them off."

Waving his pass at the duty officers, he ushered them through a back door leading to the interview rooms and cells. But at the last minute, Milly hung back.

"Aren't you coming?"

"No." She shook her head. "I think Mummy'd rather see him alone."

"Fair enough." Zac smiled. She wasn't just sexy, she was nice too—which was more than could be said for her brother. Jasper's unique combination of blind arrogance and craven cowardice had not endeared him as a client.

"Here," he said, scribbling something on a piece of paper and handing it to her.

"What's this?"

"It's a secret code to a Masonic lodge in Cambridge," he said, deadpan. Then, when she didn't laugh, "Of course it's not, you idiot. It's my number, isn't it?"

She opened her mouth to say something, but he cut her off.

"If you don't want to call, you don't have to," he said. "I won't be offended. But you look like you could do with some feeding up."

"Thanks a lot!" said Milly.

"So I thought I'd offer you some dinner. Think about it."

But before she had a chance to think about it, he was gone, pushing Linda ahead as the heavy oak courtroom door swung noisily shut behind them.

CHAPTER THIRTY

The run-up to Christmas was definitely not the season to be jolly as far as Todd Cranborn was concerned.

He'd thought Milly was high maintenance. But compared to Candy Price, he now realized, she was simplicity itself. Her daily tantrums, astronomical personal expenditure, and vanity on a scale that surely bordered on the megalomaniacal—all of these he could have stood if it weren't for the rest of her baggage. Namely, Chase and Chance, who clearly hated him almost as much as he loathed them, and Jimmy.

He'd expected some retribution from Price, of course. Everyone knew that Jimmy was not a man to be crossed lightly, and betrayals didn't come much deeper than waltzing off into the sunset with the guy's wife. But Todd thought, he really truly believed when he began the affair, that eventually it would all blow over. That Jimmy would come to terms with it, give Candy her lousy divorce, and move on to the next model.

What he hadn't understood, of course, was that Jimmy's love for Candy was not only real, it was total, all-encompassing, and deeply, deeply obsessive. The fact that the girl had made her choice meant nothing to him. If he couldn't have her, he intended to make damn sure that no one else could either. He wanted Todd not only punished but eviscerated and, if at all possible, torn limb from limb for having stolen her away from him in the first place.

His first move had been to pull out of their Orlando real estate projects. So far, so predictable. But then he'd begun a systematic and frighteningly effective attack on all Todd's other businesses. Not only had he reignited the court case at Highwood, hiring some hotshot lawyer to get a string of delaying injunctions against Comarco long enough to keep them from drilling for three long, expensive months. But he started calling in favors elsewhere too. Soon deal after deal started collapsing around Todd's ears in places as far apart as New York, Chicago, Pittsburgh, and San Francisco, as former partners and colleagues deserted him like rats on a sinking ship. Clearly, Todd had underestimated the clout a man like Jimmy wielded in the most surprising and disparate of circles.

Before long he found himself vulnerable and overextended on a whole raft of ventures. Just when he'd landed himself the most demanding woman on the planet to support (Candy, apparently, expected first-class service in everything, from material comforts to sexual performance. If he didn't fuck her at least twice a day, *and* improve her orgasm each time, she became unbearably moody. How on earth Jimmy had managed to run a multimillion-dollar company and keep up his racing interests while married to her was a complete fucking mystery), he was, for the first time since his early twenties, financially stretched.

Despite everything, though, Todd still found himself attracted to Candy in a way he'd never been with any other woman. The thought that she might up and leave him once her divorce money came through kept him awake at night even more than Jimmy's escalating personal vendetta. So when she'd demanded he take her and the kids away to Telluride for two weeks' skiing at Christmas, he'd given in.

But as the vacation drew nearer, he realized there was no way in hell he could afford to take fourteen days off. Sooner or later he was gonna have to bite the bullet and tell her majesty that a long weekend was the most he could swing.

He was pondering just how he might do this one Sunday afternoon in early December, when he was interrupted by a tentative knock at the door.

"If it isn't world war three," he said, as Sally, the latest exhausted drudge employed as the boys' nanny, stuck her head around the door, "I don't want to know about it."

Candy was out—shopping, as usual—and the kids, mercy of mercies, were asleep, no doubt recharging for another six hours of solid screeching before bed. Todd ought to be working. But after the marathon Candy had put him through in bed this morning (Three erections in an hour, for God's sake. What was he, nineteen?) he was way too shattered even to think about it.

"I'm reeeeally sorry," said the girl nervously, "but I do think you ought to come. It's the police."

"The police?" Frowning, he got to his feet and pushed past her into the hallway. "LAPD you mean? What the hell do those guys want?"

But the three black-suited men huddled just inside the front door were not LAPD. If anything they looked more like FBI.

"Are you Todd Cranborn?" asked the man in front, pulling out a nondescript badge from his inside jacket pocket and flashing it at him so quickly it could have been anything.

"You know I am," snapped Todd. "You're standing in my house, Columbo. The question is, who are you?"

The confrontational approach was a mistake. At a nod from their boss, the other two suits glided forward, each taking one of Todd's arms and pinning them quite painfully behind his back before snapping on a pair of cuffs.

"What the hell . . ." he spluttered. "This is outrageous."

"I'm arresting you on suspicion of fraud," said the first man. "Tax fraud, to be more precise. You have the right to remain silent—"

"Screw you," said Todd. "You better believe I'm not remaining silent! This is bullshit. I don't know anything about any fraud. I pay my goddamn taxes."

"It appears the IRS disagrees with you about that," said his tormentor, nonchalantly examining his cuticles while Todd's blood pressure shot past high toward lethal. "They have information, which has been passed along to us, about what I can only describe as repeated and systematic attempts to defraud the State of California of rightful property and other taxes."

Fucking Jimmy. He'd gone too far this time. Sure, Todd sailed pretty close to the wind on some of his real estate deals. But he was nothing if not meticulous when it came to his legal position. His accountants might be creative, but they weren't criminal. At least, he didn't think they were.

"You are *so far* out of your depth with this," he hissed, as they bundled him out of the house and into their waiting, unmarked SUV, just as Candy's pink Porsche swung back through the gates. "I'm gonna have your ass on a plate, you just see if I don't."

"Todd?" Sashaying across the cobbles in sky-high Jimmy Choo crocodile boots and a black leather miniskirt that left nothing whatsoever to the imagination, Candy cut such an arresting figure that for a moment the FBI men were thrown off stride. "What's going on?"

"Nothing for you to worry about, baby," he assured her. "Just get on the phone to Jack Green, would you, my lawyer. His name's in the brown address book on my desk. Tell him I need him right away."

He did his best to sound confident, but inside his mind was racing.

What did Jimmy have on him? What the hell had the son of a bitch managed to dig up now?

Rather to her surprise, Milly thoroughly enjoyed the run-up to Christmas. And Zac Spiro had a lot to do with it.

It began with him dropping by the town house with spurious excuses: like claiming to have some information on Jasper's parole date (that he could perfectly easily have delivered by phone or e-mail) or that he thought he might have accidentally overcharged Linda on the VAT for his fees (he hadn't). But the real reason for his visits was so obvious that eventually he was forced to declare it, asking Milly out for a dinner date in Ely one weekend.

Her first instinct had been to say no. To shut him down before things got out of hand and she started—heaven forbid—reciprocating his feelings. Amazingly, it was Linda who talked her out of it.

"Oh, darling," she said, glancing up from the vast saucepan of blackberry jam she was making. "It's only dinner, for goodness' sake. Do give the poor boy a chance. It'll do you good to get out, meet some new chaps."

She was right, too. It did do Milly good.

Zac was utterly hilarious throughout dinner, making her laugh in a totally abandoned, carefree way she'd almost forgotten she was capable of. When he dropped her home, happily drunk, a few hours later, he walked her up to the front door and she let him kiss her.

It was a nice kiss. Not earth-shattering. Not a knee-weakening harbinger of lust. But a pleasant, gentle, satisfying sensation. She liked it.

That first kiss had set the tone for the relationship that followed. After the emotional roller-coaster ride of the last year, Milly was quite happy to take contentment over ecstasy, and that was exactly what Zac provided. It wasn't that she wasn't attracted to him—he was handsome enough and, although she only had Todd to compare him to, seemed to be a perfectly skillful and adept lover—it was just that sex was the smallest part of what drew her to him. His friendship, his humor, his intelligence and good advice, were all more-important parts of the package. And if that meant sacrificing passion—the same passion that had caused her such heartache and misery over Bobby and had blinded her to reality with Todd for so long—well, she reckoned that was a price worth paying.

For his part, Zac was smart and instinctive enough to sense her reticence. He was very careful not to push her farther than she wanted to go or ask for more commitment than she felt ready to give. He had enough good sense to take things slow, easing his way into her life and her family almost by osmosis.

But Zac wasn't the only change for the better on the home front. With the stress of the trial over, Linda began to get back to her old self. Or rather, to a slightly softer, less-overbearing version of it. Gone were the worst excesses of her crippling social insecurity. Even she had to face the fact that with one child in *Playboy* and the other in prison, she was no longer in much of a position to cast aspersions on other people's propriety. But her inner snob, though subdued, certainly wasn't dead.

"What were you thinking of wearing, darling?" she'd asked Milly a few weeks ago, when she'd arrived home after a long day at the stables with Radar and Stanley, another of Cecil's old guard she'd managed to track down and rescue.

"Wearing?" Helping herself to a mug of mulled wine from the steaming saucepan on the Aga, Milly eased herself down into the kitchen armchair, a much-loved reminder of Newells. "To what?"

"The Delaneys' Christmas Eve drinks party, of course," said Linda. "We'll have to get you something new."

"You are kidding," Milly said, choking on her drink. "After everything Rachel's put us through? You still want to go?"

"It's not a question of wanting to go," said Linda with all the solemn earnestness of someone who clearly did, desperately, want to go. "It's about being polite."

True, Rachel had behaved disgracefully. The way she'd abandoned poor Jasper in his hour of need was what had finally brought Linda around to Milly's way of thinking: The girl was a nasty piece of work. But it would take more than that to keep Linda Lockwood Groves away from Mittlingsford's answer to Elton John's White Tie and Tiaras Ball. After all, it wasn't poor Michael and Julia's fault that their daughter had turned out to be a faithless slut, was it? Whatever Rachel may have done, her parents remained linchpins of Newmarket society. The Delaneys were not a family to be scratched out of one's leather-bound Smythson's address book lightly.

At first Milly had refused point-blank to even consider it. But Zac made her change her mind.

"Oh, come on, it'll be fun," he said. He was helping her muck out Stanley's filthy straw a few days after Linda received the invitation.

They'd been going out for over a month by then, so he was used to spending time around her horses. But somehow he still managed to look as out of place in a stable as a black man at a Ku Klux Klan meeting.

"You can laugh at how fat Rachel's gotten," he said, turning over the fresh hay with a pitchfork, "and I can enjoy all the other blokes staring at me and wishing their birds were Playmates."

"I was *not* a bloody Playmate!" said Milly, flinging a lump of dung-encrusted straw in his general direction. "I was a quarter horse jockey, okay?"

"A quarter horse jockey who got her kit off," Zac teased her.

Milly pretended to look cross, but secretly she loved the way he was so cool about her pictures and all those awful, cringe-making cowgirl ads she'd done in the States. After her mother's pained hand-wringing, it was lovely to be able to laugh about it with someone.

"Please let's go," he insisted. "The Delaneys' house is supposed to

439

be stunning. Besides, your mother's outfit alone is bound to make it worth the trip. You know it, really."

Needless to say, Linda was overjoyed by Milly's change of heart and thrilled with Zac for persuading her, showing her appreciation in the time-honored manner of baking him an enormous batch of homemade biscuits.

"Are you quite sure you're not Jewish, Mrs. LG?" he asked, as she stood over him proudly, watching him eat until he thought his stomach might explode, Mr. Creosote–like, all over the table.

"Shush, dear," she said indulgently. "Eat your biscuits."

Given the fact he had never been to Eton, hadn't a landed estate to his name, and had actually grown up in Golders Green, it was odd that Linda should have such a soft spot for Zac. But for whatever reason, she did. She was forever pushing Milly to "take things to the next stage" with him. Whatever *that* meant.

Unfortunately, when Christmas Eve finally dawned, everyone at the town house woke up with the sort of hangover that could stop a train.

Two days ago they'd gotten word that Jasper was to be released early for good behavior. He would therefore be home in time for Christmas—and the Delaney party, if he chose to go to it. After much hysterical crying and hand flapping from Linda, it was decided that Zac and Milly would go and collect him from the prison gates, thus sparing her the humiliation of being photographed in such insalubrious surroundings by local reporters. Linda would stay home preparing Jasper's welcome-home meal and putting the finishing touches to her Christmas decorations.

After the initial awkwardness of seeing one another again—an awkwardness intensified by the fact that Jasper appeared to have "found God" in prison and would insist on banging on about the peace of Christ to anyone who would listen—the four of them took the sensible option of getting incoherently drunk as soon as possible.

Hence the green, sheepish faces around the breakfast table in the morning.

"I know I said I'd go, Mummy," rasped Milly, her voice like sand-paper. "But I really can't face it. Can't you tell Sir Michael I'm ill?"

Grabbing a Tesco's Finest mince pie from the open packet on the table, she booted the cat off the armchair and sat down, demolishing half the pie with one giant bite.

"Absolutely not." Linda was resolute, though the truth was, she felt none too chipper herself. "He'd see through it in an instant. Everyone would think you hadn't come because you don't like Rachel."

"Well, I don't like her," said Milly reasonably.

"All the more reason to make the effort," said Jasper, who'd just shuffled in in one of Cecil's old dressing gowns, which totally swamped him. He'd lost a shocking amount of weight in prison. "Rachel may have wronged us. But this is our chance to forgive, to turn the other cheek. Love and mercy are the great levelers, you know."

"Exactly," said Linda, who had no idea what he was talking about.

Milly caught Zac's eye across the table and tried not to giggle. St. Jasper of Her Majesty's Prisons was going to take a little getting used to.

Pulling into the drive at Mittlingsford that evening was a surreal expe-rience. The manor was lit up with candles, just as it had been the night of the summer party when Cecil had had his first stroke, and Rachel had hijacked her way into the drama at the hospital. If anything, the house looked even more beautiful tonight. A light dusting of afternoon snow lent it a magical, Hansel and Gretel feel, and the faint snow-muffled boom of church bells in the village added to the general air of Christmas spirit.

"I'm really glad you're here," said Milly, squeezing Zac's hand for moral support as they walked up to the porch.

He squeezed back. "Me too."

It was odd, given the very public, vocal nature of the battle between them in the press, that Milly hadn't actually seen Rachel in America at all. Everything she knew about her career and life—her early success in the Belmont, her high-profile romance with TV heartthrob Mickey Malone after the breakup with Jasper, and her much-photographed weight gain when that relationship collapsed—she'd gleaned from the gossip mags. The same rags in which Milly herself had, until recently, been such a regular fixture.

The only reason Rachel was back in England now, apparently, was to try to shed the excess pounds out of the glare of the media spotlight. Clearly, she still had hopes of returning to the States and recapturing her early success there, although she'd be doing it with another owner. Randy Kravitz had fired her the moment her weight shot up, a turn of events that had pleased Milly enormously when she heard about it, notwithstanding Jasper's wise words on mercy and forgiveness.

The thought of seeing her archrival in the flesh tonight probably ought to have made her nervous. A few months ago, it would have. But a combination of Zac, being out of the spotlight herself, and the joy of being reunited with Radar and the others had restored a lot of Milly's natural confidence. Now what she mostly felt was curiosity. Try as she might, she couldn't help but hope that Rachel really did look as awful as she had in last month's *Star*.

She wasn't disappointed.

"Fucking hell," whistled Zac under his breath when he saw her. "Rosie O'Donnell's gone blond and been eaten by a marshmallow!"

Rachel, advancing toward them in a billowing pink-taffeta dress, did indeed look frightful, not to mention the size of a barge. Her hair was still thick and lustrous, and her breasts, now even more mammoth than before, were very much front and center, wobbling above her basque bodice like two enormous blancmanges on a plate. The kindest word one could use to describe the overall effect was "matronly." But Milly wasn't feeling kind.

"Rachel." She smiled thinly. "My goodness. You *have* changed."

"I might have gone up a couple of dress sizes," Rachel shot back defensively. "But at least my family aren't the laughingstock of the county." The jibe was specifically intended for Linda, who was standing only a few feet away, making conversation with a gaggle of racing wives, and who duly blushed scarlet when she overheard it.

"Quite frankly, I'm surprised you decided to show your faces this year, what with Jasper in prison and your—what should one call it—

fall from grace? I'm sure Mummy only invited you out of pity. But I suppose you had nowhere else to go?"

"Allow me to introduce myself," said Zac, stepping forward before Milly could jump on her and rip her throat out. "Zac Spiro. Absolutely charmed to meet you. I've heard so much about you."

His delivery was so deadpan that for a minute Rachel didn't know how to react. She was even more thrown when, moments later, Jasper appeared at his side.

"J.?" she stammered. "What are you . . . ? I mean, shouldn't you be . . ."

"Hullo, Rachel." Leaning forward with a strange grimace on his face (he'd actually spent long hours in front of the mirror in his cell perfecting what he thought of as his "serene and beatific" look, which in fact made him look like he was having trouble passing wind), he kissed her on both cheeks.

"They gave me early parole for good behavior," he explained. "But how are *you*, Rachel? Are you happy?"

It was very disconcerting. The way he took both her hands in his and looked deep into her eyes when he spoke. Not like a lover. More like a psychiatrist. As if she were the one whose life needed sorting out.

"I'm perfectly happy, thank you, Jasper," she said primly.

"I hope so," he said, giving her the trapped-wind look again. "Because I'd hate for you to think you weren't forgiven. We all forgive you for what happened." He turned to Milly. "Don't we?"

Milly was about to reply in no uncertain terms that she most certainly did not forgive her, and never would as long as she had breath in her body. But Rachel was too quick for her, exploding with righteous indignation.

"*You?*" she spluttered. "You forgive *me?*"

"I do," said Jasper. Self-absorbed as ever, he seemed utterly oblivious to her outrage and actually tried to pull her into a hug before she wrenched herself free. "I've learned to let go of my anger, Rachel. You should try it sometime. Maybe then you wouldn't have to turn to food for comfort. You could turn to the Lord."

Milly didn't think she'd ever loved her brother till that moment. The look on Rachel's face was almost worth losing Newells for.

"Before you turn to the Lord, though, Rachel," she said gleefully, "do fill us in on the latest with Mickey. I hear he's dating that Czech gymnast now, Paulina whatever her name is. Are you two still in touch?"

"No," said Rachel icily. "We're not. And contrary to what you may have read, it was me who dumped Mickey, not the other way around."

"Ah, there you are." Rachel's father, all smiles as usual, swooped down on his daughter like a genial hawk. "And Milly!" He beamed, including her in his bonhomie. "How are you, my dear? It's so nice to see the two of you burying the hatchet at last."

"Hello, Michael," Milly said, kissing him with a warmth that she knew would infuriate Rachel still further. "Merry Christmas."

"I think your ma wants a word," he said. They all turned to look at Linda, who was indeed gesturing frantically in a sort of strange beckoning motion to Milly and Zac. Jasper had already wandered off, no doubt to spread the Good News to the rest of the Delaneys' godless guests.

"What were you doing?" Linda hissed theatrically, when Milly finally went over. "You promised me you wouldn't cause a scene with Rachel."

"I didn't!" said Milly indignantly, turning to Zac to back her up. "I hardly said anything. Jasper was the one who got her started."

"Well." Linda sounded far from mollified. "In any case, there's something else." Reaching into her gold Escada evening bag, she pulled out a stiff white envelope. "It came for you yesterday and I quite forgot to give it to you. I think"—her voice dropped to a whisper—"I think it might be from Bobby."

Milly felt her earlier sangfroid melting like spring snow and an unpleasant prickling sensation spreading all over her skin like measles. The postmark was indeed from Solvang.

"You know, it's easier to find out who it's from if you actually open it," said Zac gently, watching her turning the envelope over and over in her shaking hands.

Tearing back the flap, Milly did just that, pulling out a formal printed invitation.

"It's from Amy," she said, after a long pause. "She and Dylan are getting married. The wedding's at Highwood, on New Year's Eve."

"Well, that's good news. Isn't it?" said Zac. "I mean, you like Dylan, right?"

"Oh yes, yes of course. He's lovely," Milly said absently. Her mind was obviously already somewhere else, and if she was happy, she didn't look it.

"You'll need to get your skates on and book a flight, though," said Linda. "Lots of people'll be heading off to the sun for New Year. I expect it could be pretty booked up already."

"Oh, I'm not going," said Milly, attempting a nonchalant laugh. "I couldn't possibly."

Zac gave her a look. It was one of his infuriating lawyer looks, an I'm-a-barrister-and-I-see-right-through-you stare that left you with no option but to crack and admit whatever it was he had known all along. Sometimes it bothered Milly how easily he could read her.

"What?" she said, pouting. "It's too much of a hassle. And it's too short notice."

He looked at her again.

"Stop looking at me like that!"

But Zac didn't stop. And she knew he was right. It was Amy and Dylan's wedding, for heaven's sake. She had to go.

It was only Bobby that held her back. Milly couldn't justify it or explain it even to herself, let alone to Zac. The combination of fear and hope that the thought of seeing him again stirred inside her—it was beyond words.

Part of her wanted to run away. To hide in Zac's arms, to cloak herself forever in the blanket of peace and calm that he provided. But another part knew that she would only be delaying the inevitable. And that was the part that scared her.

"Sooner or later you're gonna have to see him," said Zac. "Face your demons. This is as good a time as any."

"I know," said Milly, leaning into him like a baby bird nestling under its mother's wing. "I know."

CHAPTER THIRTY-ONE

Summer looked at her reflection in the mirror and sighed. The burgundy wool jacket was beautiful, a real work of art, but something about the rest of her wedding outfit wasn't quite jelling. Maybe it was the spiky three-inch heels that felt so foreign to her? Or the long, flowing burgundy skirt that matched the jacket and brought out the rich bronze of her skin but was still strangely, stiffly formal to the girl who spent 99 percent of her waking hours in blue jeans?

Whatever it was, she wished she felt more comfortable, and confident, today of all days.

Dylan, her darling, darling brother, was getting married. That in itself might have been a bittersweet event had it not been for the fact that he was quite clearly marrying the nicest, sweetest, kindest woman in the world. All the McDonalds adored Amy. Within hours of meeting her for the first time, any doubts they'd harbored about Dyl bringing home a spoiled heiress from the city vanished into thin air.

Of course, Dylan had already told them in glowing terms how wonderful and down-to-earth his future bride was. But he was clearly blind drunk with love and not a reliable witness. It was Amy herself who won them over. As soon as she came out to stay at Highwood, her gentle, loving nature and touching devotion to Dylan were so apparent, the family were instantly sold. Then, a few weeks later, she'd gone on to do the impossible and brokered a peace between her father and Bobby, clearing the way for Jimmy to pour money into the fight against Comarco.

Only ten days ago, her efforts had at last borne fruit: The oil company had decided to cut their losses and withdraw their claim on the ranch. After a year of hell, with an ax hanging over all their heads, the

McDonalds could finally start getting back to normal. And they had Amy to thank.

Fiddling with the strap on her new shoes, Summer tried to lift herself out of her funk. She had so much to be grateful for. Her beloved home was safe. Dylan was happier than he'd ever been, both with Amy and with his art taking off at last. And to cap it all, Jimmy Price had called excitedly two weeks ago to tell Amy that Todd Cranborn had been charged with fraud and money laundering. Though he hadn't yet been found guilty, it looked certain that he faced, at the very least, a hefty fine and perhaps even prison time. Wyatt and Maggie were far too Christian and forgiving to rejoice in such news. But Summer, Tara, Dylan, and Amy had gone out and bought the biggest bottle of champagne they could get their hands on in Solvang and celebrated into the small hours.

Only Bobby was notably absent from the celebrations. Whether it was a delayed reaction to all the stress, or that the relief was too much for him, none of them knew. But for someone whose ass had just been so comprehensively saved, he seemed unaccountably down.

Summer would have liked to help him. But her own heart was still too fragile, and in any case she had no idea what to say. Being at Berkeley had taken the edge off her misery somewhat. She'd dated a couple of different guys and thrown herself into campus social life, at least in part to take her mind off the pain of Bobby's rejection. But a broken heart doesn't heal in a day, or even a semester.

Watching Bobby's reaction when Dyl told him Milly would be flying out for the wedding—the way his face had drained of color and his hands had started to shake—still made her feel like her heart was being ripped out and pushed through a paper shredder. She wished it didn't. But it did.

"Can I come in?" It was Dylan, knocking tentatively on the door before opening it and sticking his head into the room. "I need some help."

Smiling, Summer beckoned him over and sat him down on the bed while she undid the mess he'd made of his bow tie.

"You're such a baby," she teased him. "I can't believe that at your age you still don't know how to do this."

"We weren't all on the debate team, you know," he said, holding up his hands, "or Future Lawyers of America."

"There," she said, finishing the knot perfectly and in record speed. "Perfect. So, how're you feeling? Not having second thoughts, I hope?"

It was a joke, but Dylan looked horrified.

"Not on your life," he said. "All I'm frettin' about is sealing the deal before Amy has a chance to realize what a mistake she's making and how much better she could've done than me."

"Baloney," said Summer loyally. "You're the catch of the century. Have you seen her this morning?"

Dylan shook his head. "It's bad luck. But we spoke on the phone and she seems good. A little nervous, you know, but Milly's with her. She seems to be doing a good job of calming her down."

"Really?" said Summer. "Funny, but I don't remember Milly ever being much of a calming influence on anyone. I'd have thought she'd be about as much use to a nervous bride as a deaf-mute interpreter. But maybe that's just me."

"Sum," Dylan said, frowning. "Come on now. You promised to make nice. Why do you still have such an issue with Milly, anyway?"

"Is that a serious question?"

"She's made her mistakes," he admitted. "But deep down she's a good person, she really is. You'd like her if you gave her half a chance."

"Ha! I doubt that *very* much," said Summer. But seeing his face fall she relented. "Don't worry. I'll be civil, I promise. I won't pour nitroglycerin onto troubled waters. I'd like to. But I'll restrain myself."

"Good," said Dylan. "Because I know she's nervous coming back here, seeing Bobby and everything. And this is supposed to be a happy day. For all of us."

"Oh!" said Amy. "You look lovely!"

She was beaming at Milly, who'd appeared in her bedroom doorway in a bottle-green halter-neck dress and matching emerald earrings. She'd picked out the dress in a Newmarket boutique as sexy but suitably understated for the wedding. Knowing from experience how impossible it was to please Bobby with an outfit, she was happy to settle for Amy's seal of approval.

"Thanks. But, my goodness, if anyone looks lovely, it's you," she said truthfully. "Dylan's going to die of pride."

It was hard to believe that the gorgeous, voluptuous woman in front of her, poured into a simple, bias-cut, Vera Wang gown, was the same fat, unhappy girl she'd first met at Palos Verdes less than two years ago. It wasn't just the weight. Everything about Amy looked different. Her hair was longer and had been cut into choppy layers, which some clever stylist had shot through with subtle honey low lights, taking the edge off her white blond, Nordic look and adding instant warmth to her glowing skin. Her face was still as playful as ever, its every expression suffused with the kindness and goodness of her character. But now that they were no longer shrouded by fat, her perfect, doll-like features looked even more striking.

If it's true that inside every fat girl is a thin girl waiting to get out, then this was Amy's thin girl. Everything about her seemed to vibrate with the happiness and elation of her triumphant escape.

Milly was staying at the Ballard Inn. To her somewhat embarrassed surprise, she discovered when she got in last night that she was to be included as one of the Price family party, staying in an adjoining room to Amy and even traveling in the second bridal car over to Highwood.

"I'm not so sure that's a great idea," she said, more than slightly panicked, when Amy told her the plan. "The last time I saw your father, I was telling him his wife had been having it off with Todd, and, if I remember correctly, suggesting that he could stick his job where the sun don't shine. I expect I'm the last person he wants muscling in on his daughter's wedding."

But Amy was adamant.

"Trust me," she said. "He's changed."

She wasn't kidding. At supper last night Milly had sat next to Jimmy, and if she hadn't known better, could have sworn he'd been abducted by aliens and replaced by a humble, charming imposter. Outwardly he was the same cigar-smoking, bouffant-haired Trump-alike he'd always been. But divorce had obviously changed him.

He greeted her with genuine warmth: "I'm *so* glad you could make it," and proceeded not only to forgive her for her outburst at Ruidoso but to thank her for her plain speaking.

"It's funny how sometimes we don't see the most important things, even when they're going on right in front of us," he said. "And I don't just mean Candy. I've realized I've been a crappy father to Amy too. She's a wonderful, wonderful girl."

After that there was no stopping him. He bent Milly's ear all night about how fantastic it was rediscovering both his elder children. He'd finally done what he should have done years ago: reached out to Donny and admitted his share of responsibility for the death of his and Amy's mother. The two of them were now back on speaking terms. And he was also fighting Candy for custody of the twins.

"She took them with her when she left, but she only wants them as a tool to screw more money out of me," he said. "But you know what?" He shrugged. "I don't care anymore. All I want is my kids and the pleasure of knowing I've fucked that son of a bitch Cranborn over. You know Candy left him the day he got indicted?"

Milly hadn't known it, and honestly wasn't sure she cared any longer. But she certainly found herself warming to the new Jimmy Price.

"What can I do?" she said, closing Amy's bedroom door behind her now and joining her friend on the bed. "Does anything need pinning? Or perhaps you'd like something from downstairs? Water? Fruit juice?"

"I'm fine," said Amy. "Relax. Tell me more about Zac."

They'd begun swapping gossip last night after supper and ended up talking into the small hours. Amy filled Milly in on developments at Highwood, as well as giving her all the racing gossip from Palos Verdes and a long, detailed description of Dylan's courtship. In return Milly told her about her new life in England, rehabilitating the horses, and made her scream with laughter doing impressions of Jasper's saintliness. She'd also made the odd passing reference to Zac.

"There's really not much to tell," she said. "He's lovely. He's really funny and kind. He's very clever. My mother adores him."

"But?" said Amy.

"But what?" Milly frowned. "There is no 'but.' He's a good man. I'm lucky to have him."

"But do you love him?" asked Amy. "I know he's tall, dark, and handsome and all of that. But how does he make you feel?"

Milly thought for a minute.

"Safe," she said eventually, deftly answering Amy's second question but not her first. "He makes me feel safe."

"Well, I think he sounds lovely," said Amy firmly. "And very romantic, the way he pursued you and everything. You must miss him, being away."

"I do," said Milly. And she meant it too. Whenever her anxiety about seeing Bobby again threatened to overwhelm her, which was roughly every minute and a half since her plane landed in California, she felt herself longing to call Zac.

"It will be all right, won't it?" she said, breaking her self-imposed rule not to wobble in front of Amy. "What if Bobby still hates me? And what about Wyatt and Maggie? How can I face them again after all the trouble I caused?"

Amy took her hand and squeezed it.

"It'll be fine," she said soothingly. "The McDonalds aren't the type to hold grudges, you know that. And everything turned out all right in the end, anyway. As for Bobby"—she paused for a moment, as if wondering how best to phrase it—"he's mellowed too. Trust me. No one's going to give you a hard time. I wouldn't have brought you here if they were, now would I?"

"I guess not," said Milly, hugging her. "Thanks."

But inside she still felt a gnawing sense of apprehension that no words of comfort from Amy, or anyone else, could banish.

By the time the bridal party pulled into the long driveway at Highwood, the sun was already high in the sky over the ranch and a beautiful winter's day was in full bloom.

The adobe barn, which had been transformed for the occasion into a makeshift chapel, looked stunning, as peaceful and spiritual a setting for a wedding as any church. Once all the hay bales and farm machinery had been cleared out, the floor swept clean, and the wooden walls painted bright, gleaming white, it was already almost unrecognizable. But the addition of some old Victorian benches from the big house, four huge bouquets of white lilies and red roses, trailing loops of ivy festooned from the rafters, and hundreds of tiny cyclamen-scented candles in clear glass jars lining the central aisle completed the picture.

"It looks incredible," said Bobby to Tara, who was handing out orders of service to the late arrivals at the barn door, kissing her on the cheek. With only a little help from Summer and her mother, Tara had been responsible for the whole thing. "You realize you could make millions as a fancy wedding planner in the city?"

"And leave all this?" She grinned, waving at the backdrop of green pastures, newly cleared of drilling equipment, behind her. "Never!"

Shifting awkwardly in his rented tux, Bobby looked about as comfortable as a penguin in the Sahara. Being best man was nerve-racking enough—he must have checked his pocket for the rings at least ten times in the last hour—but waiting for the bride (and, of course, Milly) made it even worse.

He was well aware that they were all worried about him. Wyatt, Dylan, all of them—they'd all expected him to be swinging from the rafters with joy when Comarco dropped the suit. But the fact that it was Jimmy Price who'd rescued Highwood and not him stuck in his craw, however much Price might have changed. It was like the final blow to his already badly battered pride, and he didn't know how to deal with it.

Even today, when Dylan was the center of attention, he couldn't shake the feeling that people were looking at him: whispering about his lucky escape and how foolish he'd been to play fast and loose with Highwood and his inheritance in the first place.

Not that any of them could possibly judge him more harshly than he judged himself.

At long last a vintage 1950s Ford pickup truck, decked out in white ribbons and followed by another, identically decorated, pulled into the yard.

Amy emerged first, stunning in bias-cut organza. Jimmy, beaming with pride, helped her out of the car, waiting patiently while she re-arranged her veil. Moments later, the door to the second car opened and Milly stepped out.

Surreptitiously checking out her regained curves in her figure-hugging green dress, Bobby felt almost angry. Why did she have to turn up here looking so infuriatingly, distractingly beautiful? As if he didn't have enough to worry about today.

Though it might be obvious to Summer and anyone else with a shred of sensitivity, Bobby himself was still resisting the idea that he had any lingering feelings for Milly. For Dylan's sake, he'd agreed to be polite to her today, but that was as far as it went. If she really expected him to just forget what she'd done—forget Todd, forget those tacky ads, forget the way she'd betrayed him . . .

He stopped himself mid–internal rant when he noticed her taking the arm of a handsome, chestnut-haired boy.

"Who the hell is that bozo?" he asked Tara, an irrational stab of jeal-ousy making him drop his guard.

"Why, Bobby?" she teased him. "Is he standing in your spot?"

"No," he mumbled, instantly regretting his show of weakness. "Of course not." But he was blushing so cutely, Tara had to laugh.

"Relax," she said. "That's Donny, Amy's brother. He's gay."

Bobby's shoulders loosened visibly.

"Now, go get back in there and tell Dyl they've arrived."

He did as he was told, hurrying through the doors and back up the aisle, cursing himself for being such a sentimental fool. What was it to him who Milly was with?

The congregation all turned and looked over their shoulders as the organ struck up some introductory chords of Handel. Sean O'Flanna-gan, sitting in the third row from the front, gave Bobby an encouraging wink, which he just had time to return. And then it started.

Clinging onto Donny's arm for dear life, Milly felt every bit as awk-ward as Bobby, whose eyes she was studiously avoiding. Amy had spent most of yesterday trying to convince her that the McDonalds weren't the sort of people to hold grudges. But that didn't stop her feeling mortified. She knew how deeply everyone at Highwood cared about their cowboy culture. Even if they didn't blame her for Comarco, they must surely despise her for the whole, tacky "English cowgirl" thing, and for dragging their heritage through the mud.

Luckily, she was distracted by a collective, romantic sigh from all the women in the room as Amy appeared in the doorway and began her stately progress toward the altar on Jimmy's arm, her eyes locked lovingly with Dylan's all the while.

Grow up, Milly told herself firmly. This is their day. It's not about you.

Unfortunately, at that moment Bobby also turned around, and for a second the two of them were face-to-face. Despite all the stern talkings-to she'd given herself about having moved on and being with Zac now, Milly instantly felt her organs liquefy.

She should never have let Zac talk her into coming.

She'd told herself she wanted Bobby's forgiveness, his and the McDonalds'. But seeing him now, she knew for sure it was more than forgiveness she wanted.

Much more.

Which was a shame. Because if his haughty scowl was anything to go by, he didn't intend to give her even that.

If the barn-cum-chapel was impressive, Tara had really excelled herself decorating the big house for the reception. The musty, down-at-heel grandeur that Milly remembered had been replaced by bright, airy rooms filled with color and light. The formal dining room, once the loneliest space in the house, had been transformed into a culinary Aladdin's cave, its vast table covered with a bright red cloth, on top of which dishes of all shapes, sizes, and colors bore the spectacular wedding buffet. Red and white silk cushions had been strewn everywhere, as people found themselves spots around the living room and parlor to sit down, eat, and talk; and six enormous heaters enabled them to spill out onto the veranda too, amid the bright strings of Christmas lights. An enormous Christmas tree dominated the entrance hall, and a local barber shop quartet were singing a mixture of carols and cowboy favorites as the guests streamed in from the cold and helped themselves from the huge, industrial-sized vat of hot mulled wine bubbling away in welcome in the corner.

"Cheer the fuck up, would you?" said Sean, accosting Bobby as he stared up the staircase after Milly, who'd gone to use the bathroom. "Your face during the ceremony could have curdled milk."

"Sorry." Tearing his eyes away from the stairs, he forced a smile.

"Don't apologize to me," said Sean. "You're not my best man."

Bobby looked anxious suddenly. "Was I that bad? D'you think Dylan noticed?"

"Naah," said Sean. "You're all right. The way the dopey git was staring at Amy I doubt he'd have noticed if you ran a bulldozer over his balls. But, for God's sake, if you've something to say to the girl, say it. Then you can both start enjoying yourselves. Or at least pretending to."

Bobby took his advice, heading upstairs with the grim look of a man preparing for battle. Meanwhile Sean turned back to the party. The first person he saw, as luck would have it, was Summer standing miserably in the corner.

"You look like you've lost a shilling and found sixpence," he said, immediately cursing himself for coming out with something so inane.

Smooth, Sean. Real smooth.

"Like I've *what?*" She frowned.

"An old Irish expression," he explained, handing her a cup brimming with mulled wine. "It means you look disappointed. And fed up."

"Oh, no, not really. I'm fine," she said, not very convincingly. It was funny. When they e-mailed she felt she could tell him anything. But here, in the flesh, he was almost like a stranger again. She'd seen the way he kept looking across at her during the service. It was flattering, of course—he was an attractive guy—but she simply didn't think of him in that way. Didn't think of anybody that way really, except Bobby.

She smiled nervously.

"Feel free to tell me to go fuck myself," said Sean. "But I'd say you're still in love with him." He looked up at Bobby's retreating back. "Am I right?"

Summer's smile was instantly replaced with a frown. Since when did she owe Sean an explanation of her feelings?

Unfortunately for her, Sean found her anger even more sexy. She already looked a knockout in that burgundy suit. But there was nothing like a woman on the brink of losing her temper to bring out the fire within.

"No," she said coolly. "You're not right, as it happens. In fact, you're way off. I'm just worried about him, that's all."

She turned to go, but Sean was too quick for her. Reminding himself that faint heart never won fair lady, he grabbed her by the elbow before she could get away.

"He's not right for you, you know. He's too bloody moody."

"I thought you were supposed to be his friend?" said Summer indignantly.

"I am," said Sean. "That's why I'm telling you this. You're not right for each other. Bobby doesn't know what he wants. You need a man who can take the lead."

"Oh, do I?" she said. He was so cocky, it was almost funny. "And who might that be? You, I suppose?"

"Yes," said Sean matter-of-factly. "Me. I think we should get married."

She laughed. He was so ridiculous, it was impossible to keep her anger going. "You've got a screw loose, O'Flannagan. You do realize that?"

"Maybe," he said, with unnerving confidence. He still hadn't let go of her arm, and she suddenly felt acutely conscious of the warmth of his grip. It was a not altogether unpleasant sensation. "Or maybe not."

He looked deep into her eyes, and she saw that all the jocularity and bravado were gone. He was deadly serious. "I can make you happy, sweetheart. I know I can. Just give me a chance."

"I'll think about it," Summer said. And pulling herself free at last, she disappeared back into the crowd.

Upstairs, Milly ignored the GUEST RESTROOMS THIS WAY signs that Tara had carefully positioned along the corridor and made straight for what had once been her room, locking herself in the bathroom. She wondered if that would have changed too, but the copper tub was still there, and apart from a few fresh towels and the vase of short-stemmed roses on the windowsill, everything was much as she remembered it.

Heading straight for the mirror, she wailed in horror at her flushed

456

cheeks and mascara-smudged eyes. Bloody weddings always made her cry, but Amy saying her vows had been a real tearjerker.

Getting to work on a makeshift repair job with the concealer and blusher she'd brought with her, she patched up her face as best she could, washed her hands, and opened the door, only to find herself running headfirst into Bobby.

She was so shocked, she actually screamed.

"Whoa!" he said, laying one hand on her shoulder, like he would a jumpy mare. "I didn't mean to scare you. I just thought, you know . . . we should talk."

Milly swallowed hard. He was without doubt the one person in the world to whom she had the most to say. Yet now that she was here in his presence, she was barely able to articulate a single coherent word.

"I feel like a straitjacketed monkey in this son of a bitch suit," he said, filling the silence.

Inside, he was kicking himself. Was that really the best he could do? Had he taken the plunge and followed her all the way up here just to make small talk?

"I know what you mean," she mumbled. "I'm itching like crazy in this dress. And my poor feet have blisters in places I didn't know it was possible to rub."

Sinking down onto the bed, *her* old bed, she pulled off her shoe and held up one stockinged foot for his inspection.

How did she always manage to do this to him? To turn things around? He'd intended to have it out with her about Todd, to really say his piece. But instead he found himself cupping her calf tenderly in his hand, trying to stop himself from shaking.

He hadn't intended it to be a flirtatious gesture. It just sort of happened. But there was no denying the intimacy of the position, and it wasn't long before their eyes locked.

"Where does it hurt?" he asked, horrified to hear his own voice sounding hoarse with desire.

Milly's reply was barely a whisper.

"Everywhere."

And that was it. Like magnets hurtling through space, they flew at each other, lips, hands, and bodies grinding and grappling in a frenzy that was part lovemaking, part fighting.

"I hate you," said Bobby, between kisses so violent he almost flayed her skin off with his stubble.

"No, you don't," she replied, drinking in his desire like a humming-bird gorging on nectar. God knew she'd waited long enough for him to show it. So long, in fact, that she'd convinced herself her own feelings for him had died.

As it turned out, all they needed was a little mouth to mouth.

"Don't fucking interrupt me when I'm talking to you." He grinned.

Pushing her back onto the bed, he propped himself up on his fore-arms on top of her, pinning her down with the weight of his body while he kissed her again, starting at the mouth, then moving down her neck till she could feel his stubble brushing against the tops of her breasts.

"Wait," she said breathlessly. So much was running through her mind. She needed to explain to him. About Todd, and how she'd gone with him in the first place only because *he'd* rejected her. How after her fa-ther died, and Rachel brainwashed her mother and took Newells, she'd so much needed him to understand, but he'd been too wrapped up in Highwood and his horse training to care. And then later, how she'd clung on to Todd and her newfound fame through fear, more than any-thing, terrified that if she didn't she'd never make enough to get Newells back and that she'd end up broke and alone.

"Please. We should talk," she said. "There's so much I need to tell you. To explain."

"Talk? What for?" said Bobby, reaching beneath her to try to un-hook her bra. His own thought processes at that moment were rather simpler and more focused: He was about to have sex with the one girl he'd always wanted. Talking could most definitely wait.

"Bobb*eeee!*" Wriggling free, Milly got up and walked over to the window. The bedroom was right above the veranda, and she could see the tops of the heads of various members of the wedding party huddled in conversation below. But her eyes were drawn to the hills beyond. The afternoon light was already fading, but she could make out the craggy northern slopes where Bobby had taken her on her first cattle drive the day she'd arrived.

"Beautiful," said Bobby, walking up behind her and wrapping his arms around her waist.

"Highwood?" said Milly dreamily. "Yes. Yes, it is."

"I didn't mean Highwood," he said, pressing himself against her so she could feel his hard-on in the small of her back.

"Look, I'm sorry," she said, turning to face him. "I'm sorry about Comarco, I'm sorry about Todd, I'm sorry about the whole *Playboy* thing."

"Oh, God," Bobby groaned, putting his hand over her mouth to shut her up. "Can we please not talk about that? Ever?"

They were interrupted by a knock at the door. Tara walked in and, seeing them together, grinned broadly.

"Reeeeally sorry to interrupt," she said, "but Dyl wants to start the speeches. We need you."

She looked apologetically at Bobby, who turned back to Milly. Stroking her face with a tenderness she'd thought she'd never feel from him, he said gently, "We've waited this long. I guess another half hour won't kill us."

A few minutes later, Milly floated downstairs in a delirium of happiness. For a moment she thought she actually was delirious—because wasn't that Sean O'Flannagan, locked in a passionate clinch with Summer McDonald?

Opening one eye, Sean saw her and gave her a triumphant thumbs-up behind Summer's back. Milly returned it with a grin. Evidently it was to be a day of hatchet burying all around.

Bobby, meanwhile, was alone in the pantry, trying to calm his breathing and willing his blood supply to make the trip back from his penis to his brain so he had a chance of making it through his best man's speech.

"There you are!" Dylan walked in looking harassed. "I've been looking for you everywhere. It's almost time for the speeches, dude. You can't disappear on me now."

"Sorry," said Bobby. "I just, er . . . I just ran into Milly."

Dylan frowned. "You didn't have another fight with her, did you?" he said anxiously. "I told Amy there wouldn't be any trouble."

"No, no," said Bobby. "Nothing like that. I was, er . . . I was very polite."

He didn't know why, but he didn't want to tell Dylan, or anyone, about their reunion just yet. Having waited so long to win her heart, he wanted to keep Milly all for himself, at least for a little while longer. Besides, he still wasn't sure how things would play out between them. She was, he assumed, booked on a flight back to London tomorrow. Would she take it? Would *he* take it? Would she stay for a while?

These were all things they needed to talk about, alone. Just as soon as he'd gotten her into bed. And finished his speech, of course.

"Good," said Dylan brightly. "I'm glad you worked it out. Amy was talking to her last night. Says she seems *so* much happier back in England. Especially with this new boyfriend. The lawyer guy."

Bobby felt his fists clenching and his breathing quicken.

"She has a boyfriend?"

"Yeah," said Dylan, unaware of his distress. "Sounds like it's quite serious too. I'm pleased for her though, you know? After all that shit with Todd, she deserves some security and some happiness."

"Yes." Bobby nodded like a zombie. "Yes, she does."

Somehow he got through the speech. Afterward, he couldn't remember a word of what he'd said, but people seemed to laugh and applaud politely at all the right places.

How could she do this to him? Is that why she'd come here, as some sort of sick joke? To get him to make a fool of himself over her, then throw it in his face that she was hooked up with some guy back home?

It was cruel. It wasn't the Milly he remembered. But then maybe he was right the first time. Maybe the Milly he remembered, the sweet horse-mad girl of old, had gone for good. Maybe Todd Cranborn had destroyed her, the way he destroyed everything else he touched?

Once or twice he looked up during the speech to see her smiling at him from the audience. But he managed to look away, holding it together just long enough to make it to the toast before bolting out the door and into the night.

Milly watched him go, perplexed. Why had he shot off like that without coming to get her first? She tried not to let her imagination run away with her. Maybe he just wanted to sneak away with as little fuss as possible and expected her to meet him outside? Yes, that was probably it.

She set off after him but was waylaid by an ecstatic-looking Amy.

"Hey." Milly smiled, trying not to look impatient. "Are you having fun? It must be a relief in a way, now that the ceremony's over."

"It is," said Amy. "I can't quite believe I'm Mrs. Dylan McDonald though. Can you?"

"It's what you were born to be," said Milly proudly. "I'm so happy for you, honey. For both of you. Dylan looks like the cat that got the cream."

"He does, doesn't he?" Amy beamed. "And we're happy for you, too. About Zac, I mean. Dyl's just been telling Bobby all about it. We all think it's about time your love life turned around."

Milly's head started to spin.

"What?" She trembled. "Dylan said something to Bobby? About Zac?"

"Sure," said Amy, looking troubled. She hoped she hadn't put her foot in it. "Why? Is something wrong?"

Blindly, Milly stumbled through the throng of guests out into the hallway. Opening the front door, she ran down the steps.

"Bobby!" Desperately, she tried to make out his form, any form, in the gathering darkness. "Bobby, where are you?"

Just then she saw a figure on horseback about twenty feet away. He turned at the sound of her voice and for a moment just stared at her standing there. Then, without warning, he gave the horse a violent kick in the ribs, sending it off at a gallop through the yard gates and into the open country beyond.

"Bobby!" She wanted to cry but the sob caught in her throat as she ran hopelessly after him into the blackness. "Come back! Please. It's not what you think."

But it was too late. He was gone.

CHAPTER THIRTY-TWO

Jasper watched Milly as she rode Radar back and forth along the gallops at Dewhurst and blew on his gloved fingertips against the cold.

The local livery stables, run by an old mate of Cecil's, was now home to four of the old Newells stallions and the place where Milly spent the bulk of her days. It was, she continued to insist, only a temporary home, although the prospect of buying back Newells was looking as distant as ever. It was hard to see how she was going to do it in her own lifetime, never mind Radar's. But she had to keep her hope alive.

Today was Valentine's Day, and it came slap bang in the middle of the bleakest, most bitter February that anyone in Cambridgeshire could remember. An icy Siberian wind had been blowing in off the fens all day, whipping her face till it was red and raw with cold. She looked frozen, tired, and altogether miserable.

Seeing Jasper waving, she cantered over toward him.

"Fucking hell," she moaned, executing a perfect flying dismount and rubbing her gloved hands together feverishly. "It's like the motherfucking Arctic out there. The ground's sheet ice. One slip and this poor boy's leg'll shatter like a jigsaw puzzle."

Jasper winced at her bad language and gave her a po-faced look. Part of his "new spiritual outlook" involved a total ban on swearing, which always struck Milly as a trifle unfair; especially given that another part of it seemed to involve wearing a series of ghastly grandpa sweaters that positively begged for an expletive from anyone who laid eyes on them. He was wearing one of the horrors now, a shaggy green monstrosity with Mr. Rogers buttons and patches on the elbows. It was almost enough to make her wish for the old, vain Jasper back.

"Zac called," he said. "Asked me to remind you about dinner at

Chez Pierre tonight. I take it that means things are all rosy again with you two?"

"Course they are," said Milly, not 100 percent convincingly. It was already six o'clock. She should be in the shower by now, washing her hair for their date, not running around up here like an Eskimo with a death wish. But subconsciously she kept putting it off.

The fact that even Jasper had noticed something amiss with her and Zac was some indication of how obvious their problems had become. Ever since she came back from California, something indefinable had begun happening in their relationship, and it wasn't good.

She hadn't told Zac about Bobby. At the end of the day there was nothing really to tell, except a kiss that would never be repeated and would only hurt him if he knew about it. There'd been no big fight, no angry confrontation. Nothing.

But as much as she still cared for Zac, and as much as she desperately wanted the comfortable peace of their relationship back, the peace that had so calmed and sustained her before Amy's wedding—it was gone. Something had changed. And she couldn't change it back.

"Do you have any Valentine's plans?" she asked, deftly changing the subject as she led Radar back down the hill for a rubdown. Even the new Jasper was unable to resist any turn in conversation that brought the subject around to himself.

"Me?" he said, pouting. "No. My Valentine's date is a baked potato and watching the rugby on Sky," he added, so plaintively she actually felt sorry for him.

"You're welcome to join Zac and me if you'd like," she heard herself saying.

"On Valentine's Day?" Jasper laughed tactlessly. "No offense, Mill. But I'm not that desperate."

Back home in her room, after a long, hot shower to soothe her aching muscles and chase the deep-seated chill out of her bones, Milly appraised her naked self in the mirror. Critically, she cupped and lifted each breast in turn. Despite the return of her healthier figure they were still smaller than she would have liked.

Zac was always telling her she was beautiful. That he loved her body just the way it was. She wished, wished more than anything, that she could turn the clock back and take comfort from his love and devotion like she used to. Like she had before Amy's wedding. Before Bobby. Before the kiss.

But when Bobby rode away from her that night, it was as though someone had slowly sawed through her heartstrings one by one.

He had every right to be angry with her. She should have told him about Zac, straightaway. But in the heat of the moment, abandoning herself into his arms at last, it hadn't seemed important. That was the God's honest truth. In comparison to her love for Bobby, to their history together, Zac felt like little more than a footnote.

It was awful, but it was true. Zac hadn't crossed her mind. Which only made her feel more guilty now.

She'd hung around at Highwood till after three A.M., waiting for Bobby to come back. But he didn't, and in the end she'd gone back to Ballard to collect her things and try to snatch a few fitful hours of sleep before her flight at noon. All her calls to Bobby's cell the next day had gone unanswered. In the end she left a brief message of apology, asking him to call her back so she could explain, and got on the plane, more miserable than she could ever remember being in her life.

He never called, not then, nor when she got back to England. And, heartbroken as she was, Milly was too proud to beg. There was nothing for it but to try to throw herself back into her old routine. Put the whole thing behind her.

Of course, she should have come clean with Zac right away and ended it between them the moment she got home. In her heart, she knew that. But a combination of not wanting to hurt him, her own loneliness, and a dread of any more confrontation and pain held her back. Somehow it was never quite the right time to tell him.

Instead, she tried to carry on as though nothing had happened. As though by willing things to get back to normal, they would. But it was no use. Every time Zac touched her, she thought of Bobby.

It was horrible, unforgivable, the worst sort of betrayal. But she couldn't help herself.

* * *

"Come on." Zac looked anxiously at his watch. "Where the blazes are you, woman?"

It had cost him a small bloody fortune to secure the prestigious corner table at Chez Pierre on Valentine's night and they had it only till nine thirty. He'd wanted to pick up Milly at home and make a real date of it. But she'd insisted on meeting him at the restaurant.

Perhaps she wanted to make an entrance? Christ, he hoped that was it, and she didn't have some other, more sinister reason for arriving under her own steam. It wasn't in his nature to be paranoid. But she'd been so off with him recently, it was hard not to take it just a little bit personally.

Ever the lawyer, Zac had tried to probe her several times about the wedding and what exactly had happened at Highwood. But Milly was a slippery witness, and none of her answers were remotely satisfactory. On the surface she sounded reassuring: Nothing had happened. He was imagining things.

It was the sort of response that drove him crazy because it was completely un–cross-examinable and yet, at the same time, utterly emotionally unconvincing. He had no choice but to take her word for it. And yet he knew, he just knew, that he wasn't being told the whole truth.

He tried to silence the nagging, doubting voice in his head when, at last, she walked into the restaurant and, smiling, walked over to join him.

"Sorry I'm late," she said, kissing him perfunctorily on the cheek. She wasn't dressed up—in fact, in jeans and a tight navy sweater, she was easily the most casually dressed woman there. But in his eyes, she'd never looked sexier.

"You're forgiven. But only because you're so beautiful," he said, taking her hand in his. "And because I've already had a glass of wine which was almost as good as it should have been for the extortionate price they charged me. Happy Valentine's Day."

"Thanks," she said nervously. "And to you."

And to you? Jesus. She hated hearing herself sounding so cold and formal. He deserved better than that. But she really did not know how to begin.

In the end, as usual, Zac did the hard part and broke the ice for her.

"What's wrong?" he said, shooing away the hovering waiter.

"Nothing," Milly said, cursing herself for her cowardice. "I'm fine."

"Are you?" Wearily, he pushed his chair back and closed his eyes. "Because I'm not."

She had the good sense to stay silent, waiting for him to continue.

"When you walked in just now," he sighed, "every head turned. No matter who they were with, or how beautiful their wives or girlfriends were, every man in here turned around to look at you."

"I'm sure they didn't," Milly mumbled awkwardly.

"Trust me," said Zac. "They did."

"Well . . . is that such a bad thing?" she said, after a pause so long that one of them had to fill it. "I mean, you're the one I'm with, not them."

"Ah, but *are* you with me though, Milly? Are you really?"

He picked up his wineglass and stared at the purple-red claret as he swirled it around and around. He hadn't intended to confront her tonight. He hadn't wanted to. But there was only so much anxiety and fear that one man could repress.

"What do you mean?" Milly was surprised to find herself trembling as she spoke. Part of her longed for this to be over. But another part wished she could burrow against his chest and hide there, safely, forever and ever.

"Are you in love with Bobby Cameron?"

She looked down at her lap but said nothing.

"Are you?"

"Bobby's not a part of my life anymore," she said, picking her words carefully. "You know he's not."

"That's not what I asked," said Zac. "Please look at me."

Reluctantly, she dragged her eyes up to meet his.

"Do I have your heart, Milly? That's really what I'm asking. I don't care about Bobby. But I need to know. I think, after all we've meant to each other, you owe me that much at least. Don't you?"

Slowly, one solitary, fat tear began rolling down Milly's cheek.

"Oh, lovely one," he said, reaching out for her hand across the table.

He never could bear to see her cry. "It's all right. You can't help the way you feel. No one can."

"I wish I could," she said, sobbing. "I tried. I really tried." She shook her head miserably. "But I can't change it. I can't *make* the love go away."

"I know," he said, entwining his fingers with hers. "Believe me, I wish I could change the way I feel about you. But it doesn't work like that."

"He doesn't love me back, if that makes you feel any better," Milly blurted out.

"It doesn't," said Zac truthfully. "And he's a bloody idiot."

He signaled to the waiter, mumbling something about being happy to pay a cover charge for the table, and paid the bill, which appeared mercifully swiftly.

They agreed they would talk again, tomorrow probably and in the coming weeks. They were too good friends just to walk away from one another forever. But right now they both needed to be alone and the sooner the better.

"Are you sure you'll be all right driving?" Zac asked, helping Milly into her coat at the front desk and then across the car park to her little red Mazda.

"I'm fine," she said, sniffing bravely. "I'm so sorry, Zac. I really am."

"Shhh," he said, pulling her to him in an all-enveloping bear hug. "Stop apologizing. It sucks, it does, but I'll live. We both will."

If he was honest, despite the sadness, he already felt the tiniest flicker of relief. Few things in life are more agonizing than clinging on to vain hope, and part of him was glad to be put out of his misery at last.

Pulling away, Milly got into her car.

"I'll call you in the morning," he said, waiting for her to buckle up and turn on the ignition before closing the driver's door behind her.

"Not if I call you first."

She kept the smile glued to her face as she pulled out of the car park and all the way to the A145. It wasn't until she reached the drizzly outskirts of Newmarket that she allowed her mask to slip. Pulling over to the side of the road, she turned off the engine, undid her seat belt, put her head in her hands, and started to cry.

467

* * *

It was almost eleven thirty by the time she finally parked her mud-splattered car in front of Linda's town house.

She grabbed a dirty old sweater from the passenger seat and pulled it over her head. It was covered with horsehair from her earlier ride, but she didn't care. She was suddenly freezing cold, despite having had the car's heat fan on full strength all the way home. Besides, no one was going to see her.

Fumbling in her purse for her house keys—her eyes were so red raw and puffy from crying she could hardly see in the lamplight—she swore under her breath as she struggled to get them into the lock with her cold, useless fingers.

"Jesus!" Leaping out of her skin as the front door suddenly sprung open, she found herself looking at a shadowy male figure, standing in her mother's hallway like the grim reaper.

"If you're looking for money you can fuck off!" she shouted, adrenaline turning her fear into fury. "My brother's upstairs and he's built like a brick shithouse. One scream and he'll be down here to sort you out."

"I doubt it," said the figure.

The familiar cowboy drawl froze Milly to the spot.

"He was the one that let me in."

Turning on the light, she saw Bobby, leaning back against the wall with his long legs crossed, like he owned the place.

"Nice dinner?"

"No," she said, cursing her mother for opting for such glaring overhead lighting. It must be making her mascara-streaked cheeks and throbbing red nose look even worse than they had in the car. "It was awful, if you must know. Bloody awful."

"Good." Stepping forward, Bobby pulled her to him. "Because that's the last time you'll be having dinner with that guy. Or any other guy for that matter."

Milly wasn't about to argue. Nor was she going to make the same mistake twice and interrupt him while he kissed her. Which he did now, so passionately and for so long that she started to wonder if they'd still be standing in the hallway at daybreak, glued to each other like clams.

"Come with me," he said, leading her outside when he finally did come up for air. Dragging her down the street to his parked rental car, he opened the passenger door and ushered her inside. She still hadn't uttered a single word. There were so many questions flying around her head—what was he doing here, how did he know where she lived, was he staying, had he forgiven her—she didn't know which one to start with.

In the end she opted for the most obvious.

"Where are we going?"

Starting the engine, he looked across at her and smiled.

"Home."

By the time they pulled into the drive at Newells, the drizzle had turned into a full-blown storm. At night the empty house looked even more desolate than it did by day. Particularly tonight, with the wind whistling through the pine trees, bending their spindly trunks this way and that like tortured souls in hell, and the driving rain battering down on the iron roof of the old stallion barn like clattering arrows in some hopeless, endless battle.

"Look, I appreciate what you're trying to do," said Milly, as Bobby turned the engine off and sheets of water began flowing over the windscreen, making her feel like they were trapped in a submerging submarine. "It was a nice thought. But we shouldn't be here. It makes me feel . . ." She shivered. "Weird. Sad, in a way. And anyway, the place has been sold now, so we're officially trespassing."

"No we're not," said Bobby.

As overjoyed as she was to be with him, and as happy as she was to follow his lead, his arrogant pronouncements from on high were starting to get a bit annoying.

"It's all very well saying we're not," she said. "But we are. This isn't my home anymore, Bobby. I wish it were but—"

"Come on." Jumping out into the downpour, he ran around to her side and pulled her out with him. It was so cold, and she was so instantly drenched from head to foot, that for a moment all she could do was gasp with shock.

"This way."

469

Running across the yard, they headed for the shelter of the stallion barn, where the faint glow of an electric light was dimly visible through the cold, black wetness. When they got there, Milly expected it to be locked. But in fact the door wasn't bolted, and after a swift yank from Bobby it opened and she found herself being shoved unceremoniously inside.

"Sit down," he said excitedly, leading her, dripping and shivering, to an old wooden bench in the corner. "And shut your eyes."

Too cold and shell-shocked to resist, Milly did as he asked.

"Wait there."

After what felt like hours to Milly but couldn't in fact have been more than a minute, he was back.

"Okay," he said, no longer able to keep the excitement out of his voice. "You can open them. Happy Valentine's Day."

Standing not three feet in front of her, wrapped ridiculously in the most enormous red ribbon that went all the way around his barrel chest, swinging his tail and rolling his eyes like a dopey donkey, was Elijah.

"Oh, my God!" Milly screamed, flinging her arms around his neck and breathing in the scent of him that was like a magic carpet back to her childhood. "But where did you . . . ? How did you find him?"

"With difficulty," said Bobby, overjoyed to see the look of pure ecstasy written all over her face. It was even better than he'd imagined.

"I thought he was in Saudi Arabia," she said, stroking his mane in wonder. "I thought he was dead."

"Saudi, yes. Dead, happily not," said Bobby. "It wouldn't have felt right to restart the stud without him."

"Hmmm?" said Milly. She was so blissful to see her dear old friend again—Radar was going to go ballistic with happiness tomorrow when he saw him—she was only half listening. "What stud?"

"This one," said Bobby. "Here's part two of your valentine."

He handed her two identical sets of keys.

"*You?*" she said, openmouthed. "You're the one who bought Newells?"

"Strictly speaking I was the second buyer," he said. "A very nice Texan bought it from Rachel, but he ran into some cash-flow problems before he could complete. Right around the time my own cash-flow problems were resolved, as luck would have it."

"But three million, Bobby! You don't have that kind of money."

"Noooo," he admitted. "No, I don't. But Jimmy Price helped guarantee me a pretty spectacular mortgage."

"He did?" Milly looked suitably amazed. "Why?"

"I'm a nice guy." Bobby gave her that naughty, Cameron smile, and she felt herself melting like chocolate in a sunbed. "And . . . I sold him my stake in Thunderbird."

"But you can't do that." Milly looked aghast. "You love that horse. He's all you've got left now, with all the quarter horses gone."

"No he isn't," said Bobby, stepping forward and pinning her between his body and Elijah's. "I have you. And this place. We can build it back up together. Make your father proud."

He leaned forward to kiss her again, but this time she did hold him back.

"No, Bobby," she said. She was grateful, more grateful that he would ever know. But she'd lost him once through her selfishness, through blindly following her own dream at the expense of his. She wasn't about to do it again. "I can't let you do that. Highwood is your life. And what about making *your* father proud?"

"Turns out," he said, kissing her softly despite her protests, "my father wasn't much to live up to, after all."

She looked at him quizzically, but he didn't explain. Instead he took her hands and looked searchingly into her eyes.

"Highwood is a big part of my life. It always will be. But so are you. Besides, this whole nightmare with Todd and Comarco made me realize one thing: Highwood is a cattle ranch. That's all she's ever been and all she ever should be. And running a cattle ranch . . . well, it just isn't for me."

"But if you're not there, who is going to run it?" asked Milly. "Wyatt can't go on forever. And Dylan has a whole new life now."

"That's where Tara comes in," said Bobby with a smile. "Turns out the most natural rancher and cowboy of all of us is actually a girl. She told Wyatt a few weeks ago that she wanted to take on more responsibility at Highwood. He was a bit skeptical at first—you know how unreconstructed he is—but he'll come around."

"Yes, but, Bobby—"

"Listen," he interrupted her, placing a finger softly against her lips. "Training horses is what I do. It's all I can do, and all I've ever wanted to do. And all you've ever wanted to do was ride them. Here, we can do both. Together."

She opened her mouth to protest again. But then she realized he really meant it. And there were only so many times she could say "but" to someone who was offering to make every one of her dreams come true.

So she kissed him instead. And she would've kept on kissing him if Elijah hadn't decided he'd had more than enough of all this schmaltzy nonsense, not to mention the damn stupid bow he was wrapped up in like a Christmas cracker, and wandered off in search of a bucket of oats, sending both of them tumbling to the floor in a wet, giggling, surprised heap.

"Of course," said Bobby, peeling back Milly's wet sweater and running one hand hideously slowly over her smooth stomach, "we'll still spend a lot of time at Highwood. I want our kids to get to know their heritage. And I don't mean the T-Mobile version."

"Kids?" said Milly.

"Of course." He smiled. "Why not?"

And for once, she couldn't think of an answer.